Montana
Sky

Starry Montana Sky

DEBRA HOLLAND

Montlake
Romance

Text copyright ©2012 by Debra Holland
All rights reserved.
Printed in the United States of America.

Published by Montlake Romance
P.O. Box 400818
Las Vegas, NV 89140

ISBN-13: 9781612184678
ISBN-10: 1612184677

Dedication

This book is dedicated to my father, Robert
Holland, who encouraged my love for horses.
I know you're still with me, Dad.

Acknowledgments

I have many people to thank for supporting me through the process of writing this book:

Leeanne Banks for brainstorming the plot.

Louella Nelson, writing teacher extraordinaire.

My first critique group: Alexis Montgomery, Diane Dallape, Erika Burkhalter, Janis Thereault, Kelly Vander Kay, and Judy Lewis.

Kathleen Givens

Jill Marie Landis

Kelly Mortimer

Romance Writers of America, especially my local chapter of Orange County, California

Historical Disclaimer

Modern miniature horse breeders and owners would be dismayed to have these delightful little horses called "midgets," yet that fits the historical context of the 1890s. Also, while the Falabella breed of miniature horses was present in the 1890s in Argentina, it did not become a recognized breed until the mid-twentieth century. I've taken the liberty of calling the miniature horses in this series "Falabellas," even though that name might not have been used in the 1890s.

CHAPTER ONE

Argentina, 1894

Samantha Sawyer Rodriguez read the letter from her uncle's banker, the words first blurring into illegible chicken tracks. Then the meaning trickled through the haze of her disbelief.

Freedom.

Not only could she escape the restrictions and unhappiness of her current situation, but also fulfill her long-held dream of raising orphaned children—just like her favorite heroine in *Little Men* and *Jo's Boys*. Her son, Daniel, would finally have the brothers he'd always wanted.

She pushed her well-worn Louisa May Alcott novel off a brocade-covered chair, collapsed into it, and reread the letter, barely able to concentrate over the excited beating of her heart.

Finishing, Samantha clasped the telegram to her chest, staring out a glass window framed by red velvet curtains. She barely registered the familiar vista of the miniature Falabella horses grazing in the grassland around the estancia.

She offered up a prayer of thanksgiving, her heart too full of gratitude to even utter any words. But she knew the Lord understood.

Nine-year-old Daniel came into view, frisking with his favorite horse. Little black Chita, only thirty-six inches high, trotted next to the boy. The two kicked around a brown leather ball stuffed with rags. Samantha smiled at the sight. The playfulness of the tiny horses never failed to amuse her.

Eager to share her excitement, Samantha bounced off the chair and rushed through the door of the ladies' parlor into the marble-tiled entryway. Then, realizing her haste might be witnessed and chastised by her father-in-law, Don Ricardo Rodriguez, she smoothed her black silk skirt and schooled herself to a more ladylike walk. Her outward appearance might exhibit the feminine compliance demanded of her, but her heartbeat danced with an elation she didn't dare let her feet show.

Throwing open the carved wooden doors, Samantha blinked from the strong sunshine. She crossed the brick courtyard and hastened around the corner of the estancia to the grassland where the Falabellas grazed.

As she neared her son, the late-afternoon sun caught the auburn highlights in Daniel's dark hair and burnished his golden skin. His blue eyes sparkled with laughter, and he leaned over and hugged the little black horse around her neck.

"Daniel!" She waved the letter. "I have news," she called in the English she always used with him.

Her son straightened up from the horse. "What, Mama?"

Eager expectancy glowed in his blue eyes, and for a moment he looked so much like his father that a familiar pain pierced her heart and tempered her excitement. From long practice, she shoved her sadness aside. "I've inherited Uncle Ezra's ranch in Montana."

A puzzled look crossed his face.

Samantha laughed and hugged him. "My uncle Ezra moved west when I was a child. I vaguely remember him as having a long beard and carrying me around on his shoulders. We exchanged letters every Christmas. He died and left his ranch to us."

Daniel's blue eyes clouded over. "Died? Like Papa?" He tilted his head, studying her. "Are you going to cry?"

Samantha swallowed the lump in her throat. She leaned over, pulling her son into her arms and resting her cheek against his silky hair. "Not like Papa. Uncle Ezra was very old. And he wasn't very happy the last few years of his life. Now he's at peace with God in heaven."

"With Papa?"

"And with Papa. And with your grandmother and grandfather." She hugged him. "Now we're going to live on his ranch, except it will belong to us."

"Will *Abuelo* come too?"

She saw the wariness in his eyes. "No, your grandfather will stay here."

Relief washed over his features, only to be replaced by fear. He twisted in her hold. "Will *Abuelo* let us go?" His voice quavered.

Sudden anger knotted her stomach. "It's not for your grandfather to say. We're going."

Once again, she'd be butting heads with that domineering old man. He'd never forgiven his youngest son's choice of a Protestant American for a wife, so he continued to treat her with disdain. Samantha hated every minute of her cloistered life. Now she had the key to her gilded cage. And no matter what, she was *not* going to let Don Ricardo stop her and her son from flying free.

❋ ❋ ❋

For three days Samantha had plotted, planned, and worried so all the details of their escape would be in place before she faced her formidable father-in-law. She paused outside the carved wooden door leading to Don Ricardo's study, mentally girding herself, then tentatively raised her hand to knock. Over the last two years she'd learned to use her imagination defensively, keeping her true self protected from the bitter barbs the arrogant old man hurled at her.

Today, instead of entering Don Ricardo's male bastion with sinking spirits, she felt buoyed up by the letter in her hand, knowing she'd be able to face the coming encounter with a stronger heart than she'd shown in the past. But she still dreaded the interview. Her father-in-law wouldn't easily relinquish control over her and Daniel.

Soon, she promised herself. *Soon these scenes will be only bad memories.*

With resolution goading her, she knocked on a smooth circle edged by carved rosettes.

"*Pase,*" he called.

She pushed open the door and stepped into the room. Don Ricardo sat at his large mahogany desk perusing some papers, the inevitable gourd-shaped silver *maté* of his favorite yerba maté tea resting near his elbow.

Samantha had never acquired a taste for the bitter Argentinean beverage, especially when passed around in a communal *maté* and sipped through a tube-like *bombilla*. With her father-in-law, she knew she'd be spared the ritual. He had never favored her with the social privilege of sharing his yerba maté.

She waited for him to notice her—not that anything escaped him. Don Ricardo often made her wait like a servant until he saw fit to acknowledge her.

It's the last time. That thought kept at bay the anger she always felt in his presence. Sometimes the effort of containing her feelings would cause her to fidget, bringing a rebuke to his lips and putting her at a disadvantage. *But not today.*

Samantha studied him. The same aristocratic features—high cheekbones, thin nose, and winged eyebrows that she had so loved in her husband's face, and now her son's—had withered in the older man's features to skin over bone. A true reflection of the unforgiving spirit dwelling within. Her Juan Carlos would never have aged in the same manner. Even as an elderly man, he would have had laugh lines around his eyes.

Don Ricardo looked up, a frown crossing his face. "I'm extremely busy."

"This won't take more than a few minutes."

He nodded permission.

"I've received a telegram from Montana informing me that my uncle Ezra has died and willed his ranch to me."

The frown lines between Don Ricardo's eyebrows smoothed. His face eased into the first hint of approval she'd seen directed at her in a long time. "This is good news indeed. Give me the information, and I'll make arrangements to have the property sold. I'm pleased Daniel will receive an inheritance."

That's because you don't want to provide one for him. Only for your other grandsons.

"Actually, I plan to take Daniel and move to Montana."

The eyebrows snapped together, and he shot her a look of outrage. "Absolutely not!"

"I know you'll be glad to be relieved of your responsibilities toward us."

He stood up. "I forbid it."

Familiar fear leaped into Samantha's throat, but she stood her ground. "I've made arrangements. There's a ship sailing next week. Daniel and I will be on it."

"No."

She pretended she hadn't heard him. "We will be packed and ready in time."

"You are not taking my grandson away from me." He waved his hand. "From his heritage."

Sharp anger lanced through her fear. The man never paid any attention to Daniel except to criticize him. Now he was trying to claim him. "You've never been interested in Daniel—never approved of my son."

"He is the son of my son."

"You have other…more favored grandsons," she said, fighting to control the resentment that had been amassing for the past nine years. "You've done nothing but ignore him. Now he will learn of his other heritage. *My* heritage."

A sneer marred his handsome features. "Yankee."

She lifted her chin. "Yes."

He slapped the desk with his palm. "I say no!"

Anger warmed her cheeks. In spite of herself, her voice sharpened. "You have no right to stop us."

"I will not provide any money for this outrageous idea."

"I don't expect you to. My savings should be enough."

"A woman and a child traveling alone. It is not seemly."

"We won't be alone. Manuel and Maria are coming as well."

"Servants." His tone dismissed them.

She lifted her chin. "They've been with Juan Carlos and me since before Daniel was born." She took a deep breath. "Besides, I'll need Manuel's help with my Falabellas."

His face reddened. "The Falabellas. You are *not* to take even *one* of the Falabellas." He ground out the words.

"I have a right. They are mine."

"The Rodriguez family bred those horses. The Falabellas will stay here where they belong."

Out of his sight behind her skirt, she balled her hands into fists, squeezing until her nails gouged into her palms. "Juan Carlos and I raised six of those Falabellas. They belong to me. I'm taking them."

"Pah." He strode over to a sideboard where several crystal decanters rested on an engraved silver platter. Don Ricardo's doctor had forbidden him to have alcohol, and for a moment, Samantha thought she might have driven him to drink. How would she explain that to her brothers-in-law? She could just imagine the guilt-inducing wails of their wives.

But instead, he grabbed for the decanter holding water, hefting it with one hand. He poured water over his other hand, disregarding the puddle forming on the Aubusson carpet. "I wash my hands of you."

Samantha swallowed. She hadn't meant to sever ties with her husband's family. For a moment, she wavered.

"If you leave, you are no longer family. Daniel is no longer my grandson. Expect nothing from me."

"Then we will receive what you have always given us." Her anger exploded into hot words. "Acceptance is all I've ever wanted. And for you to love Daniel as you do your other grandchildren. But instead, you've denied us your approval." She turned to leave. "You don't know what you've lost. Now you never will." With her head held high, she stalked out of the room.

CHAPTER TWO

Sweetwater Springs, Montana

After being stuffed with good food and wine, and regaled with conversation and flirtatious glances from the young widow now playing the piano, Wyatt Thompson attempted to feign relaxation in the Livingston parlor. If he were home, he'd be making a final check on that lame horse he'd moved into the barn and spending some time with his daughter before tucking her into bed. But having partaken of the fine spread laid out by his hostess, it would hardly be good manners to race off to his own ranch. So he forced himself to listen to the music played by Edith Livingston Grayson.

He set his teacup and saucer on a mahogany side table, glowing with inlaid mother-of-pearl, and shifted his weight on the uncomfortable blue velvet settee. To his right, Caleb Livingston sat stiffly upright in a carved oak chair, concentrating on his sister's playing. Why didn't Livingston have comfortable chairs in his own parlor? Something a man could spread out in. The banker could certainly afford them. He hoped Edith hadn't chosen the furniture.

Wyatt shifted again. His boots slipped forward on the thick Persian carpet. After spending a day in the saddle, his long legs ached to sprawl in the familiar posture he'd use when lounging in his leather chair at home. He dragged his wandering feet back and leaned an elbow on the wooden arm of the settee.

The hearth fire popped and crackled in front of him. The lingering aroma of Edith's perfume laced the smoke-scented air. He traced the fragrance to its source, admiring the picture Edith made seated at the piano. Clad in a lavender gown, sable hair curling in tendrils around her oval face, she seemed absorbed in her playing, her brown eyes intent on the sheets of music in front of her. From time to time, she glanced up at Wyatt or her brother, measuring their reaction to the music.

Livingston tapped one finger on the arm of his chair. He reached over and picked up his tea from the table, sipped it, then waved the cup toward his sister. "Edith has studied with some of the finest teachers in Boston." Unmistakable pride gleamed in the brown eyes so similar to his sister's.

Wyatt nodded agreement. "She plays beautifully."

One of Edith's dark eyebrows raised in a coquettish acknowledgment. She tinkled a light arpeggio on the keys, which flowed into a Chopin étude—one of Alicia's favorites.

The change of music spiked painful memories through Wyatt, and he wanted to charge from the room like a calf avoiding a branding iron. He steeled himself against the familiar sadness.

He'd selected a piano for Alicia as a gift to celebrate the birth of their baby. But instead of a celebration, there'd been death and years of grief. He'd canceled the piano order, and since that day, the sound of music had been absent from his home. He hadn't realized how much he'd missed it.

Since Alicia's death, Edith had been the first woman to engage his interest. He opened his eyes to take in the vision of her.

She had lowered her gaze, dark lashes fanning out on her cheeks. Her lush lips, slightly pursed, made a kissable invitation, teasing his attention. While he'd resolved never to love again the way he'd loved Alicia, a relationship based on attraction and mutual respect might be satisfying.

Wyatt's gaze slid to Livingston, tapping his finger on his knee in time to the music. Just as adequate a chaperone as Alicia's mother. But Wyatt had learned plenty of ways to escape a chaperone. And with Edith being a widow, and therefore not held to the strict standards of an unmarried woman, some evasions were even quite respectable. They could spend time alone without causing a scandal or Livingston forcing them to the altar.

He closed his eyes again, sliding his feet forward a few inches. Yes, maybe the time had come to bring music back into his home.

※ ※ ※

The next day, still mulling over his options with Edith, Wyatt rode his quarter horse, Bill, into the town of Sweetwater Springs. He passed the open-fronted blacksmith shed, and a whiff of smoke and the metallic smell of red-hot iron evoked bitter memories. Memories that made his stomach tighten, and his hand unconsciously covered his scarred side.

The blacksmith, Red Charlie, paused in the act of shoeing a piebald gelding. Hammer on the upswing, the broad-shouldered man looked over. A slight smile broke the usual impassivity of his high-cheekboned face.

Wyatt touched his hat in greeting.

The big man nodded, then swung his hammer.

Wyatt and two other ranchers, John Carter and Nick Sanders, had been the only men to support the idea of an Indian owning his own blacksmith shop. Although it pleased him to see Red Charlie's new business prospering, every time Wyatt rode by, the scars on his right side pulled a little in remembered pain.

He'd been fourteen and homeless when he'd apprenticed to a blacksmith. Wyatt had run away after the drunken man had attacked him with a heated poker, pressing it against his ribs, permanently scarring the flesh. But his experiences with the adolescent gang of boys he'd run to had branded his soul far worse than that poker had seared his side...

"Get up there, Bill," he said, and nudged the big gelding into a trot, heading toward the school.

Wyatt reined in before the narrow porch of the white clapboard schoolhouse where his daughter took lessons. He'd arrived early to escort eight-year-old Christine back to the ranch. He welcomed having the extra minutes to relax in the warm sunshine of the spring day and sort through his thoughts about Edith. The singsong chant of multiplication tables drifted through the partially open front window. He grinned. He and Christine had spent their ride into town rehearsing those tables. She had them down pat.

From the corner of his eye, he caught sight of Reverend Norton hastening toward him, rusty black frock coat flapping behind him like the wings of an elderly crow. The reverend teetered to a stop, obviously trying to gather his ministerial dignity around him, and then waved a letter he held.

"Good day, Reverend." Wyatt dismounted. Might as well let the man talk in comfort instead of having to stiffen his neck.

"Wyatt. I've just received a letter from Mrs. Samantha Sawyer Rodriguez. She's Ezra's niece and has inherited his ranch."

Wyatt's interest quickened. In the drought years, he and Ezra had clashed over boundaries and the use of a river that split their two properties. He'd tried several times to buy Ezra's small, dilapidated ranch, but could never pin down the wily old man. Despite the lack of a firm commitment, Wyatt had come to think of that ranch as his own—the last parcel necessary to round out his spread in the valley west of town. With Ezra's death, he'd planned to buy the land from the heir.

Relief relaxed his shoulders. A woman. *Good.* The ranch would be his in no time. He played the reins through his fingers and said, "Rodriguez? Sounds Mexican." He pictured an older black-haired woman with withered brown skin.

"She lives in Argentina."

She's far away. Even better. "What about her husband?"

Reverend Norton glanced down at the sheet of paper. "She's a widow with one son."

"If you'll give me her address, Reverend, I'll write and make an offer for Ezra's property. A widow woman should appreciate the extra money."

Reverend Norton shook his head. "She's moving out here."

"Movin' here?"

The minister's blue eyes lit with what Wyatt recognized as his preaching zeal. "Going to breed horses and take in orphan boys to raise up as God-fearing citizens. Just the solution for those Cassidy twins. An answer to our prayers, she is."

Not to mine. Frustration stabbed through him. Bad enough to have to wait to buy the ranch, but to have those Cassidy hellions living nearby—near his daughter—was too much. His jaw tightened.

Before Alicia had died, he'd sworn to her he'd take care of their baby. Guiding his feisty daughter through the hazards of life in Montana already challenged him, what with shielding her from the dangers of ranch life while trying to foster her strong spirit and see to her manners.

Like her mother, she adopted any stray or hurting animal. One time she'd even brought home an orphaned wolf cub. He didn't even want to think about adding the Cassidy twins to the picture. Who knew what Christine would do with wounded children? And those twins had certainly known the heavy hand of their drunken father. But his innocent daughter had no idea how hurting boys could injure others.

He clenched his fists with the frustration of it all, then released them, hiding his feelings from the minister.

"Mrs. Rodriguez and her son will be arriving next week," the reverend said. "And just in time too. Mrs. Murphy told me she couldn't take much more of those Cassidy boys. A week ago Thursday, they chased a goat through her garden. Tore right through her clothesline. Dragged her sheets through the mud and ripped a hole in her best apron. Livid, she was. Apoplectic."

"I can imagine," Wyatt murmured, wondering how his plump housekeeper would have responded to the situation. Probably tan their backsides. If she could catch them.

"It took some appealing to her sense of Christian charity, but I persuaded her to keep them until Mrs. Rodriguez gets here."

Ignoring the issue of the twins for the moment, Wyatt switched the topic back to the widow. In spite of his misgivings, he felt a twinge of interest about the horses. "You say this Rodriguez woman is goin' to raise horses?"

"Yes, that's what I wanted to talk to you about. They arrive on Tuesday. All the way from Argentina."

"Horses from Argentina?"

Reverend Norton glanced down at the letter. "A stallion and five mares. Falabellas. Must be some South American breed."

"Never heard of it. What—"

"They'll be traveling with a groom, but he doesn't really speak English. Mrs. Rodriguez has requested help in transporting the horses from town to the ranch." Reverend Norton cast him an approving smile. "Since you'll be neighbors, I knew you'd be glad to help with the horses and settling her in."

Wyatt could feel angry words fighting to escape past his teeth. He clamped down on the phrases he wanted to spit out. One didn't speak that way to the minister. But the effort to contain his feelings almost choked him.

A reprieve arrived in the clatter of children's boots on the wooden schoolhouse stairs. A chorus of voices greeted them.

"Pa!" Christine called as if she'd been separated from him for days instead of hours, rushing into his arms.

From long habit he swung her up, her blue skirts fanning out around her gray stockings and black-buttoned boots. By the time he set her down, he'd regained his composure.

She grinned up at him, her mother's sweet smile laced with Christine's own hint of mischief.

Wyatt's heart turned over, and he patted his golden-haired daughter on the head. "Run and saddle up your pony. Chores awaitin'."

"Yes, Pa." She shoved the satchel containing her books and slate into his hands, then headed for the livery stable.

Reverend Norton cleared his throat. "Then I can count on you to welcome Mrs. Rodriguez to Sweetwater Springs?"

Wyatt nodded.

"Good. I'll see you at Sunday service." The minister turned and flapped off toward the church.

Wyatt hoisted himself back into the saddle, his mind busy formulating new plans. He wasn't about to give up on that ranch. It wasn't right for a woman alone to undertake the backbreaking work of running a decrepit spread. She deserved the easier life she'd have if she sold to him. He'd just have to convince her of that.

CHAPTER THREE

"Sweetwater Springs." The conductor moved down the aisle of the swaying train, his voice preceding him as he announced the next stop. "Sweetwater Springs."

Beside Samantha, Daniel bounced up and down on the leather seat. "We're here, Mama. We're here."

Samantha closed her book, tucking it into the floral tapestry carpetbag at her feet. "And none too soon," she said, feeling as if the grime of traveling had ground into her skin.

"Can I go to the horse car?"

"No, dear, wait until the train stops." Samantha smoothed back the hair from his eager young face, straightened the thin black tie at his throat, and brushed at the dust on his black suit. "Then you can help Manuel unload the horses."

With a hiss of steam, the train slowed to a stop.

Samantha glimpsed what looked to be two-story wooden buildings lining a wide dirt street. From what she'd seen of other western towns, these buildings probably had false fronts to make them appear more imposing.

Beside her, Daniel bounded out of his seat and sprinted up the aisle for the door.

"Daniel, come back here and take this." She held up the shabby black carryall once belonging to her father and reached down for her own carpetbag.

Daniel snatched the carryall and scooted back down the aisle, carpetbag bumping against the high-backed seats. She sighed and hurried after him, sending apologetic smiles to the passengers disturbed by her son's passage. It hadn't been easy keeping a high-spirited boy amused during the long train ride.

Thank goodness he'd spent most of his time with the horses, in the company of Manuel Sanchez and his wife, Maria, who'd insisted on traveling in the stock car. Samantha had known they'd keep Daniel safe.

Stepping from the train to the depot platform, Samantha inhaled the spring air. Crisp and cool. Not like the humid heat of Argentina. The ground still rocked under her feet, the rhythm of the train wheels echoing in her memory. She stiffened her weak knees, hoping the numbness in her posterior would soon wear off. She shook out the wrinkled folds of her black skirt and straightened her bonnet, running her fingers over the crown, checking to see that the dyed black *nandu* feathers hadn't bent.

Beside her, Daniel danced with impatience. "The horses?"

A short, stocky young man dressed in faded tan work clothes trotted up the steps to the platform. With his round brown face, dark hair and eyes, he could have fit right in on her father-in-law's estancia. He stopped a few yards from her, brown eyes downcast. "Señora Rodriguez?"

She nodded. "*Sí*, yes."

"I'm Pepe from the livery stable, ma'am." He spoke with a Spanish accent. "Señor Thompson wanted me to help you with your baggage and bring the horses to the stable, until he could be here."

"Mr. Thompson?"

"*Sí*, señora." The dark eyes glanced up before lowering. "He said to leave your things here at the depot." He jerked his head to indicate the only brick building in sight. "He thought you might like to buy supplies."

"Does Mr. Thompson own the livery stable?"

"No, the ranch next to Señor Sawyer's."

A glow of warmth suffused Samantha. Her neighbor. How kind of him to help. A good beginning to their new life.

She glanced down at her son. "Daniel, leave your bag here and take Pepe to the baggage car and point out our trunks, then go to the stock car and introduce him to Manuel and Maria." She pointed to the brick building. "After you've settled the horses at the stable, meet me there, please."

"Yes, Mama." He dropped the carpetbag at his feet and scampered off.

Pepe picked up the bag and placed it next to a bench. "I'll get your trunks." Then, with a quick upward glance and a shy smile, he followed Daniel.

Supplies. Samantha set her carpetbag next to Daniel's and walked down the steps, mentally ticking off a list of what they'd need for the next few days. Flour, beans, rice. She had it all written down, but didn't want to forget anything.

She held up her black coat and skirt to avoid the spongy ground, picking her way around mud puddles. She took her time, enjoying walking on terra firma after so many weeks traveling by sea and train, even if terra firma still didn't feel very firm.

She gazed around her new town with interest, noting several saloons, a bank, and other businesses. The white-framed church with a cross on its steeple caught her attention. In order to marry Juan Carlos, she'd had to convert to Catholicism. For so long she'd worshiped in an ornate stone cathedral, reciting Mass in Latin, and hearing the sermon in Spanish. One of the pleasures of her new life would be attending a simple Protestant service, and she looked forward to Sunday.

A faded sign next to the door of a rickety wooden building advertised hot baths and clean laundry. She sighed at the thought.

A chance to bathe would be heavenly. Tonight, she promised herself. Surely Ezra's ranch house would have a tub.

She paused at the wooden steps to the brick store. Black letters on the glass window announced Cobbs' Mercantile. Peeking in, she noticed a jumble of goods. A dress form wore a pink flower-sprigged shirtwaist, a pair of high-buttoned black boots sat side by side with three sets of cowboy boots, a gray hat with a four-cornered crown lay near a basket with several jars of jam, and a rake and shovel stood propped in the corner.

Her eyes lingered on the pink shirtwaist. *Color.* Her father-in-law had forced her to wear black for the last several years, and she could hardly wait to discard her widow's garb.

With a deep breath, Samantha summoned up her courage and strode up the stairs. She would be making new acquaintances, people she'd associate with for the rest of her life. The unknown Mr. Thompson and Pepe seemed kind. She hoped the others she'd meet would be the same.

❋ ❋ ❋

On Tuesday afternoon, Wyatt reined in by the front of the livery stable, mentally consigning Reverend Norton and his good causes to the devil. Not that he had any fear the minister would actually be facing Old Nick. It was just that Wyatt had better things to do with his time than play cowboy to a bunch of fancy Spanish horses belonging to the woman who'd taken over Ezra's ranch—like dealing with the horses and cattle on his *own* ranch. But he'd given the preacher his word.

He slid off Bill, looping the reins over the rail. He pushed open the barn doors, then stalked inside, peering through the gloom. Although he wouldn't admit it to a soul, the idea of these

South American horses had tantalized him. Maybe they'd be of high enough quality to add to his breeding stock.

A kitten skittered across the dirt floor, and he did a dance step to avoid tramping on it. "Hey, little fella. Watch where you're goin'." He reached down, scooped the kitten up, and cradled the furry body against his chest. Running a finger over the tiny gray head, he remembered his daughter chattering about the litter of kittens she played with whenever she stabled her pony before school. Maybe he should talk to Mack about taking this one home to her.

Still holding the kitten, he looked up. A quick scan showed familiar horses: Cobb's bay, Banker Livingston's team, Doc Cameron's roan, the Appaloosa Nick Sanders rode to town, and a few of the horses Mack Taylor, the livery stable owner, rented out. No South American horses hung their sleek heads over the doors of the stalls.

With a grunt of annoyance, Wyatt set the kitten on the nearest bale of hay, turned on his heel and strode outside, rounding the corner toward the stable office. "Mack!" he bellowed, charging through the door.

Mack Taylor half rose from behind a table, where the remains of a meal rested, and wiped his gray-bearded mouth with his stained brown sleeve. Pepe, lounging against a wall, straightened.

Wyatt didn't give him a chance to speak. "Where are those Falabellas? Did they arrive?"

Mack and Pepe exchanged glances. Mack straightened, amusement wrinkling his narrow broken-nosed face. He ran a hand through his grizzled shoulder-length hair. "Arrived right on time. No problem et all."

"Then where are they?"

"In the stable where they belong."

"No, they're not. I've just come from there." He took two strides into the room. "If you've gone and lost that widow-woman's horses, the ones I took responsibility for—"

Mack raised a placating hand. "Now, Thompson. I ain't never lost me a horse in my life. Never even had one stolen. Let's just mosey out to the stable and have us another look. Perhaps you didn't see 'em."

"You sayin' I'm blind? Those Falabellas aren't there. I recognized every horse in the place."

"Let's us go look-see." Mack stepped out from behind the table, yellowed green eyes squinting in amusement.

Pepe followed. Although the young man kept his eyes downcast, Wyatt could tell by the set of his shoulders, he, too, found the situation humorous.

Wyatt let them pass, then fell in behind, puzzlement creeping into his anger. Were they playing a joke on him? The top of his ears burned at the thought. While Mack enjoyed a laugh as much as any man, he wasn't known for being a prankster.

He followed the two men through the doors of the barn. Sunlight filtered through the entrance and an open window above the hayloft—more than enough to illuminate the dim interior. He glanced down the row of stalls, again assessing and dismissing each curious occupant.

Just as he thought, no South American horses. With one part of his mind, he took stubborn satisfaction in being right. With another, he started worrying—a gut-churning feeling of concern. Regardless of what he'd felt about the Spanish widow's acquisition of Ezra's ranch, he'd taken responsibility for her horses, and Wyatt Thompson took his responsibilities seriously.

He couldn't even report them stolen. Nobody to take the report. With the retirement of Rand Mather six months before,

Sweetwater Springs no longer had a sheriff. Wyatt would have to track the thieves down himself. And how could he explain this to Reverend Norton, much less to the widow?

Mack leaned over the nearest empty stall. "There ya are, little fella. Thompson here worried ya done gone and disappeared on us."

What the...? Wyatt stepped beside him. It must be a foal, he thought, assessing the tiny brown animal with the black mane and tail. But his experienced eye dismissed that thought almost as soon as it came. This compact miniature horse didn't possess the unfinished, stick-legged look of a foal.

Mack glanced at Wyatt's stunned face and cackled. Pepe's soft laughter joined his.

"Midgets?"

"Yep, midget horses. Damned strangest thing I ever did see. Cute little critters, though. Look at the rest."

Wyatt strode down the aisle, peering over the top of the stalls. Black, chestnut, brown, dappled gray, and a cream-colored one with black legs, mane, and tail—none of them stood higher than his hips.

The burning sensation spread from his ears, across his forehead, and into his cheeks. Why hadn't that widow woman mentioned midget horses? He ground his teeth. Not a good way to begin relations with his new neighbor.

❋ ❋ ❋

Samantha stepped into the crowded interior of the mercantile and closed the door behind her. A sharp scent of vinegar and dill from a ceramic crock of pickles next to the door caught her attention. She loved pickles, especially the kind she'd eaten as a child in Germany.

From the crock, her gaze roved the loaded shelves and aisles, disregarding farm implements and ready-made men's wear, and settled on bolts of fabric stacked on a nearby counter. She pulled off one of her black kidskin gloves, reached over, and ran a reverent finger over the plush pile of a bolt of green velvet. She could envision herself in a dress made from this material. Maybe after she learned the exact state of her finances, she'd indulge herself.

From behind a heavy oak counter to her left, a stout woman wearing a crisp blue cotton dress bustled forward. Samantha resisted brushing at the folds of her coat. She hadn't felt crisp, much less completely clean, in a month. The woman's close-set brown eyes seemed to scrutinize the rich quality of Samantha's black coat and hat. Her fleshy face scrunched into a smile, showing pointed eyeteeth. The smile didn't quite reach her eyes. "May I help you?" she asked, voice strident.

"I'm Mrs. Rodriguez."

"Raw-dree-gez?" The smile faded from the woman's face. "I'm Mrs. Cobb. My husband and I own this store."

"Mrs. Cobb." Samantha nodded. Her stomach tightened. She hoped the woman wasn't reacting to her Spanish surname. "I've inherited my uncle Ezra Sawyer's ranch. I thought I'd stock up on supplies for the next few days. At least until I find what's needed."

Mrs. Cobb huffed. "Probably everything. Ezra let that place run to rack and ruin. Of course, there wasn't anyone to help him. No family."

"No, there are no other living family members, except for my son and myself. And we've been living in Argentina." Why bother explaining herself to this woman?

"Argentina?" Another huff. "Place full of them Mexicans... Catholics."

I'm Catholic. She wanted to snap out the words. *Be polite, Sam.* "I believe Mexicans live in *Mexico*, Mrs. Cobb. Argentina is in South America."

"Same as," Mrs. Cobb snorted in disgust. "Makes no difference."

Ignorant woman. Samantha clamped her mouth shut on the stinging words she wanted to say. She pulled a folded sheet of paper from her pocket. "I have a short list of staples, which should hold us for now." *Then I'll place a large order so I don't have to visit this store very often.*

"That will be cash," Mrs. Cobb said. "American. No heathen money." She waited, apparently for Samantha to agree.

Biting back her temper, Samantha nodded.

Mrs. Cobb plucked the list from her hand. "There'll be no need for milk or eggs. Wyatt Thompson's been keeping Ezra's livestock, what's left of them, at his ranch. He'll probably get them back to you tomorra."

Mr. Thompson again. She'd have to be sure to thank him for all his efforts. Maybe bake him and his family her special cake like she used to make for Juan Carlos. She'd have to purchase extra flour and sugar.

Mrs. Cobb hurried to the counter. Samantha followed. A whiff of coffee from the bags of beans stacked next to the grinder lightened her grim mood. The idea of fresh coffee after years of yerba maté was just the pick-me-up she needed right now.

Mrs. Cobb began setting sacks on the countertop. Samantha turned to see Daniel clattering toward her, a smudge on his face, and his tie askew. He skidded to a stop, eyeing the glass jars of penny candy.

She ruffled his hair. "Slow down, son. And you don't need to ask. Yes, I'll buy some candy, but you have to wait until after we've eaten before you can have a piece."

"May I choose which?"

"How about one of each? But first, I want you to meet Mrs. Cobb." She turned his shoulder until he faced the woman.

Daniel swept her a formal bow. "*Buenos días*, Mrs. Cobb."

Mrs. Cobb stiffened. "We *only* speak English here."

Before the woman could say anything more, with a sharp movement, Samantha lifted the lid from the nearest candy jar and pulled out a peppermint stick. "Here, Daniel. You may eat this outside. I'll join you in a few minutes."

Samantha's anger boiled, and she struggled to contain it. She didn't want to start her first day here by slapping the haughty look off the face of the shopkeeper. In silence, she paid for her purchases. Then she made arrangements with Mrs. Cobb to have them delivered to the livery stable, grabbed the lighter paper-and-string-wrapped packages off the counter, and sailed out of the store.

Once outside she forced herself to slow to a leisurely pace. Daniel mustn't see how upset she was. In Argentina, they'd both suffered from her father-in-law's prejudice against her being a Yankee. Now it seemed they faced similar preconceived notions—in reverse. She glanced down at her son's happy face, blue eyes bright against his golden skin, his lips sticky with candy, and vowed to protect him from all the Mrs. Cobbs of Sweetwater Springs.

CHAPTER FOUR

From Mack's continuous cackling as the man exited the barn, probably for the nearest saloon, Wyatt knew the story would be all over town in a matter of hours. The heat in his face singed the outside of his skin like a fresh sunburn. He had a reputation in these parts as a calm, logical man of substance. People respected him. He'd built a prosperous life, erasing the disasters and shame of his younger years. Now, in just a few minutes, some Spanish widow had managed to overset his hard-earned serenity. And he hadn't even met the woman! Wyatt turned and stalked down the aisle, keeping a wary eye out for the kitten.

From outside the door, a boy's voice called, "In here, Mama."

Before Wyatt had time to step out of the way, a young boy careened into him. Something jabbed into his side. He grabbed the boy's shoulders before he could hit the ground and set him on his feet.

"Pardon, *Señor.*"

Wyatt surveyed his captive. A little overdressed for a weekday. He didn't recognize the child, but he was familiar with the sticky red-and-white candy clutched in the boy's hand. His daughter's favorite. Wyatt glanced down at himself. Just as he surmised, a red stain blotched his once-clean white shirt.

The boy's gaze followed Wyatt's. A chagrined look crossed his face. "*Lo siento...*I mean, I'm sorry, sir."

"Slow down, son, and watch where you're going."

"Yes, sir. Sorry, sir."

A melodic woman's voice asked, "Is there a problem?"

Wyatt looked up. The Spanish widow no doubt. Clad in black from head to toe, she clutched an armload of parcels and sacks. The shadows near the door obscured her features. He gave a gentle push to the boy, heading him back outside. "Perhaps you should wash up. Use the pump by the horse trough."

Pepe rushed over. "Señora Rodriguez, let me take those for you." He lifted the bundles out of her arms and disappeared outside. Popping back in the barn, he said, "Is there anything else I may do for you, Señora?"

"*No, gracias*, Pepe."

"*De nada,* Señora." Pepe hurried back out.

I should have helped her. Wyatt buried the quick spurt of shame under rising anger. She was the cause of his current predicament. "I take it you're the owner of these *midgets*?"

She stepped into the light, and her beauty caught him in the gut—like a kick from one of her midget horses. Under her black straw hat, he caught a glimpse of flame-colored hair. Auburn brows and lashes framed wide blue eyes. A flush of peach crept into her cheeks and a determined chin, now lifted several inches higher than before, gave her a spirited demeanor. Not the withered, dark-skinned widow he'd been expecting.

"Falabellas," she corrected.

"I don't care what highfalutin name you give them. Those horses are midgets."

"No, they're not."

"What good are *Falabellas* anyway? Can't even ride them."

He caught the flash of her cornflower blue eyes and watched with appreciation as her bosom swelled with anger. She tightened her jaw and visibly forced herself to give him a civil reply. "They can pull a special buggy. And they're very playful."

"Playful?" His words dripped with derision. Shame brushed across his conscience, but not enough to stop him.

"Yes."

"Who needs a playful horse? A good horse is a hardworkin' horse." Didn't she know anything? She would never make a go of her ranch with her kind of horses.

"They're very good with children. Although you might not approve of that either."

He heard the civility slip from her voice and secretly smiled. There was a way to reach past her cool exterior. "If you're implying that I don't approve of children, I must inform you I have a daughter. Christine will be out of school in a few minutes, and you can meet her. Perhaps we can get these…these…"

"They're Falabellas."

"I get the name. Falabellas. Do you herd them like sheep or lead them like donkeys?"

"Chico and Mariposa will pull the buggy," she said, crisping each word. "The rest only need lead ropes. I'll hire a horse for Manuel, my groom. If we keep the bigger horses to a slow walk, these will be fine. Although I don't know what business it is of yours, Mister…?"

Beneath the chill in the widow's icy blue eyes and cool voice burned a passion as fiery as her hair. He could sense it. Like the fires of hell, a man could be consumed by such a blaze. Might even heat up the cold emptiness inside him. He shoved that thought aside. *Best focus on the matter at hand.* "I'm the help you requested in your letter to Reverend Norton."

He swept her a mocking bow. "Wyatt Thompson, at your service."

She stepped back a pace, stiffening her shoulders. "I'm sure we can manage on our own, Mr. Thompson. I'd not want to put you to the trouble."

"Trouble?" Somehow arguing with her drained away his anger. He grinned. "We'll just have to see about that."

"Mr. Thompson—"

"Just call me Wyatt."

Footsteps clattered behind them.

"Pa!"

He turned, knowing his daughter would throw herself into his arms, and he'd better be ready for her. With Christine's growth spurt this year, gone were the days he could swing her up to his shoulder.

Christine ran into the stable, blonde braids bouncing on her shoulders, pink calico skirt flying behind her, blue coat tucked under one arm. She dropped her schoolbag and launched into a hug that landed around his waist. He leaned over and gave her a squeeze.

"Pa, you weren't waiting outside the school."

"I know. I'm sorry." He took her hand, turning her to face the widow. "This is Mrs. Rodriguez, our new neighbor."

Christine dipped a wobbly curtsy. "Pleased to meet ya, ma'am."

He watched the woman's face soften and caught his breath at her beauty. Something stirred deep within him.

She lightly touched Christine's shoulder. "Thank you, Christine. How old are you?"

"Eight, ma'am."

"Eight. That's wonderful. My son Daniel is nine. I hope you two will be friends."

"Christine makes friends wherever she goes. Like her mother that way," Wyatt said, feeling his forehead crease at the thought.

It was enough to give a man gray hairs wondering whom she'd befriend next.

The child smiled up at him.

"Remember I told you about Mrs. Rodriguez and her Falabella horses from Argentina?"

Christine looked around. "Where are they?"

"Go look in the empty stalls." He touched a cautionary finger to her cheek. "And no squealing when you see them."

He wasn't a bettin' man, but he knew no one would be able to resist his daughter when she wanted something, and she'd want to be around those little horses. Samantha Rodriguez would have to accept his assistance and be done with it.

Satisfaction settled the kicked place in his stomach. But he didn't stop to wonder why it had suddenly become important for him to help the attractive widow.

❋ ❋ ❋

Thompson. Her neighbor. The man she'd thought so kind. This man! Samantha would *not* accept *his* service. Although watching the interplay between him and his daughter gentled some of her annoyance.

He stepped forward into the square of light thrown by the open stable door. Sunbeams bronzed his brown hair and tanned skin, highlighting his high cheekbones and slightly aquiline nose. Amusement glinted in his gray eyes. He seemed to have recovered from his previous irritation.

When she tipped her head to look up at him, a shaft of warmth tingled through her. She could feel her cheeks flush. What was wrong with her? She'd seen handsome men before. Her husband's family was full of them. But none of them had caused this reaction in her. She flushed deeper. In dismay she noted the candy stain on his shirt. *Daniel's work.* She'd apologize to him and offer to wash his shirt, but she wouldn't accept his help.

Trying to ignore Wyatt Thompson's unsettling presence, Samantha turned away to watch his daughter. She loved to see children's reactions when they first discovered her little horses.

Christine stood on tiptoe, peering over the stall door. "Pa, oh, Pa." Her words slurred in an excited whisper. "What are they?"

Samantha smiled at the girl, some of her anger draining away. The beautiful, fair-haired child must take after her mother. Samantha buried a strange pang of disappointment at the thought of his having a wife. "They're miniature horses. That's as big as they get."

"Please, ma'am, please, may I touch one?"

She warmed to the child. "Of course you may."

Footsteps sounded outside the barn. Daniel ran into the stable, his face scrubbed free of candy. When he saw Christine, he slid to a stop, panting. A dazed expression crossed his normally animated face. Until their trip west, Daniel hadn't seen many blond, blue-eyed children, and Samantha could tell her son was smitten to speechlessness.

She hid a smile, nudging him forward. "This is Daniel." She waved toward a stall. "Introduce Christine to Chita."

Stepping forward to lean over the stall door next to Christine, Daniel said, "Chita is my very own horse. Mama gave her to me on my last birthday. She's my best friend."

Wyatt slanted a humorous look at Samantha, then looked at his daughter. "Christy, I'm going to help Mrs. Rodriguez and Daniel herd the little horses to ol' Ezra's ranch."

"Little" instead of "midgets." Samantha heard the word and wanted to smile.

"Please," said the child, "may we come with you? Pa's good with horses."

Wyatt quirked an eyebrow at Samantha as if daring her to refuse. The creases around his eyes deepened, and the sensual threat in his smile shot straight to her heart. His stare challenged her. "That is if she'll have us."

CHAPTER FIVE

Rounding the bend of a tree-shaded hill, Samantha slackened the reins of the harness. Her brown Falabella, Chico, tossed his head, his black mane flying. At the little stallion's side, gray Mariposa slowed. Tucked between Samantha and Maria on the buggy seat, Daniel bounced up and down. "Look, Mama, I can see the house."

They'd arrived. Samantha's arm muscles burned with strain. Driving the buggy on the hilly Montana terrain took a greater toll on them than the flat grassland near the hacienda. Not that Don Ricardo had ever allowed her to go very far—another way of keeping her in his control.

She glanced over at Wyatt Thompson. The big man on the brown gelding towered over the two little horses he led. He'd stayed away from her on their ride to the ranch, which suited her just fine. Her annoyance still simmered beneath the surface. She had no desire to have it flare up again. Perhaps he felt the same. His black hat shadowed his features, and the few times he'd looked over at her, his face had remained expressionless. At least now he showed no trace of his earlier disdain.

Christine rode her pony beside the buggy. Underneath her blue wool coat, her kilted-up pink calico skirt exposed mended gray woolen stockings and high-button boots. As the pony trotted, Christine's blonde braids, tied with matching pink ribbons, bounced against her shoulders. Over the course of their journey, excitement sparkled in the child's big blue eyes. She'd asked a thousand eager questions, which Daniel answered, and the children were fast becoming friends.

If it weren't for Wyatt's presence, Samantha would have relaxed and enjoyed herself. She tried to focus on the scenery around her: skeleton trees budding with feathery spring leaves, velvety tips of grass poking through the mud, the arching blue sky, but her awareness kept returning to the man.

He was a magnificent male specimen, so much larger than most South American men. On his powerful gelding, Wyatt topped Manuel, riding on a rented Appaloosa, by a foot. Manuel led the other two miniature horses, and, from time to time, the two men exchanged a few words of broken English or Spanish. Thankfully, Wyatt didn't seem to feel the same prejudice shown by Mrs. Cobb. His bad opinion of her precious Falabellas was enough.

She tore her gaze away from Wyatt, taking stock of her ranch. On the other side of a rushing river, several small outbuildings clustered around a large barn with peeling brown paint. A large corral and a small one circled between the barn and the house.

Samantha knew Ezra had originally built the house for an Eastern bride, but she'd died before their marriage. Samantha had always thought the story of Uncle Ezra's lost love was so sad. But after Juan Carlos's death, she had a greater empathy for him. Now Samantha prepared herself to find a bachelor's neglected house, reflecting the emptiness of his life.

They crossed a rickety wooden bridge. The hooves of the horses and the buggy wheels clattered over each loose board. She held her breath during the short passage. One of her first tasks would be to have the bridge strengthened before it collapsed. Once safely on the other side, she sighed with relief.

Up close, she could see the once-white house had weathered to a dingy gray. The late afternoon sun glinted off two dormer windows. The porch roof sagged across the front. The house looked like the face of an aging giant who winked and smiled in welcome. In spite of its dilapidated appearance, Samantha's spirits lifted.

❊ ❊ ❊

Wyatt tried to see Ezra's ranch through Samantha's eyes. He knew about its run-down state and for several years had pondered how he'd fix it up. When she caught sight of the house, he hoped she'd turn around that ridiculous excuse for a buggy and head back into town.

Samantha had slackened the reins, allowing her arms to rest on her lap, stopping the buggy. A beatific smile lit up her face, softening the blue eyes that had earlier sparked with anger.

Heat flooded his body. His groin tightened, and he shifted in the saddle. Oh no, he told himself. *Not* her. He had another woman all picked out. He hadn't started courting Edith yet, but he wasn't going to allow a temporary attraction to change his plans—especially not for a woman who wanted to take in the Cassidy twins. Yet, despite what he told himself, he couldn't take his gaze off Samantha.

A tug on the lead ropes nearly unbalanced him. The midget horses, straining to get closer to their mistress, showed an unexpected strength. He settled back in the saddle, firmly gripping their leads. He needed to keep his mind and body where they belonged.

Just then, in response to something her son said, the widow's eyes lit up with laughter, and a mischievous smile danced across her face.

He'd just set himself one heck of a task.

❊ ❊ ❊

As soon as Samantha drew the buggy up before the house, Daniel jumped out. "Come on, Christine."

The girl slid off her pony and looped the reins over the porch rail.

Wyatt reached in the pocket of his coat. "Wait, Daniel." He pulled a key out of his coat pocket. With a quirk of his brows he asked Samantha's permission to give her son the key. When she nodded, he tossed the key to Daniel, who deftly caught it.

The two children hustled up the wooden stairs. Daniel unlocked the door, pushed it open, and they disappeared inside.

Samantha shook her head in amusement. Daniel had found a kindred spirit. Her gaze met Wyatt's, and, in his eyes, she saw humorous bemusement. For a few seconds, they shared the silent communication possible between parents about their children, and she warmed to him. Then he seemed to catch himself, and his eyes frosted over, dampening the brief connection.

She hoped he wouldn't discourage the children's friendship. On the estancia, Daniel's numerous older cousins hadn't been inclined to pay attention to a child not favored by Don Ricardo. So he'd turned to the companionship of the miniature horses. She glanced over at Chita, frisking at the end of Manuel's lead. Samantha could tell the little black horse wanted to follow Daniel inside.

"Perhaps you can take the horses and buggy to the barn," she told Manuel in Spanish. "I'll check out the house." She climbed down from the buggy, handing the reins to Manuel. "Thank you for your help, Mr. Thompson."

He nodded and touched his hat. "I'll just collect my daughter, and we'll be on our way."

Good riddance, she thought, suppressing an unexpected pang of disappointment. "Your wife must be wondering where you are."

An old sorrow shadowed his gray eyes. "Christine's mother died giving birth to her."

Her heart wrenched in a familiar grief. "I'm sorry. I know what it's like to lose the one you love."

"You learn to live with it."

"I know." The brief moment of shared sympathy lingered between them.

Then Wyatt cleared his throat. "I'll be by tomorrow with your livestock."

"Thank you," she said, heading over to the house. "I'll go find the children." When she stepped onto the porch, the wood dipped under her feet. Rotten boards, she thought. She trod gingerly, hoping the floors of the house wouldn't be in a similar condition.

The heavy wooden door pushed open with a squeak of protesting hinges. *Oil can.* She started a mental list of things she'd need. Hopefully there'd be one around somewhere. Then the wave of excitement building up in her for weeks crested, washing her over the threshold and into the house.

A hallway with a door on either side led to a flight of steps. To her relief, the dusty, wide-plank floorboards appeared solid. Overhead, the sounds of boots pounding against the floor and excited voices indicated the location of the children.

She stopped to examine the unconventional hall tree, standing against the right wall. Instead of the usual wooden or metal hooks for holding coats, hats, and umbrellas, the antlers of some animal, perhaps a deer, held a motley collection.

A ragged fur coat hung on one side, with a battered leather hat next to it. A jacket made of wool blanket material, originally bright with reds and greens, had faded into rust and dead-leaf colors. A glance at the dim mirror in the center of the hall tree showed Samantha her own face, skin pale, blue eyes shadowed with fatigue from weeks of travel.

Careful footsteps sounded on the porch, telling her Wyatt tread lightly. An image of the wood splintering beneath him made her wince. But if the porch held his weight, maybe she wouldn't have to rush on the repairs.

Almost hidden behind the fur coat hung a blue scarf, the tight-knit yarn holed in places from moths. Nostalgia rose in her. She reached out and fingered the scarf. Samantha could remember her mother knitting it in the parlor of their house in Spain. A Christmas present for Uncle Ezra.

Sudden tears blurred her vision. She lifted down the scarf. Somewhere near the bottom should be some uneven stitches. Hers. In her memory, she could feel her mother's arm around her—the slow click of the needles as Samantha struggled to repeat her mother's smooth motions. She heard again the gentle tone of instruction, felt the soft hands guiding hers.

Even as a part of her mind heard the squeak of the front door, she lingered in a dream state. Samantha's searching fingers found the place, just south of a small moth hole. A smile played about her lips, while the tears gathered in her eyes and slipped down her cheek.

Behind her, Wyatt spoke, his voice gentle. "Ezra wore that scarf every winter. Refused to get a new one."

Embarrassed to be caught crying, Samantha dabbed at her eyes with the scarf. The dust in the wool tickled her nose, and she sneezed. She fished around in her sleeve for a handkerchief, only to realize that she'd given it to Daniel.

"Here." Wyatt reached into his pocket and pulled out a large white square.

"Thank you. It's the dust." She wiped her eyes, then blew her nose. Staring down at the handkerchief, she realized she couldn't hand it back to him in a used condition. It wasn't the same as borrowing her husband's personal linen. She could feel heat creeping into her cheeks.

"I'll wash it and return it at the first opportunity. And if you bring me back your shirt…" She nodded in the direction of the stain.

He grinned. "It's no problem. I have plenty more."

She replaced the scarf, then removed her bonnet and hung it on the rack.

Wyatt waved at a doorway. "Do you want to check the rest of the house to see if there are any major problems you'll need help with?"

She chose the left-hand door, opened it, and stepped into the parlor. Her nose crinkled at the musty smell, and she fought another sneeze. She crossed to the window and pulled open the dusty curtains, velvet by the feel of them. In the dim light from the dirty window, she could see the tatters in the green material. "A good cleaning would probably cause them to disintegrate," she murmured to herself.

Looking around, she shook her head. The faded beauty of the room pulled at her heart. The marble-topped mahogany tables and sideboard looked like a good polishing would put them to rights, but mice had made homes in the green velvet sofa and matching chairs. In several places, the William Morris wallpaper dangled in shreds. No pictures hung on the walls, nor were the usual kind of knickknacks scattered on the tables. Ezra must have planned for his fiancée to lend the finishing touches and, after she'd died, had never changed anything.

Wyatt spoke from behind her. "Never saw Ezra use this room. He lived in the kitchen. Lately, he even slept there."

Samantha's throat constricted. She should have written to Ezra about her circumstances. Guilt squeezed her chest. If only she'd swallowed her pride...Ezra might have sent for her and Daniel. Then his last years wouldn't have been lived in loneliness and squalor.

Wyatt seemed to sense her emotions. He touched her shoulder. "He was a cantankerous old man. A real loner. He wouldn't accept help. I sent my housekeeper over, but he wouldn't let her in the door."

She risked a look up at him and saw only sympathy in his eyes. "But I'm his niece. It would have been different."

"I doubt it. He could have sent for you. He just wanted to be left alone."

Samantha brushed a finger over the marble top of a side table, leaving a dust trail like the wake of a boat. "If I tell myself he's at peace in heaven, reunited with the woman he loved, I don't feel so guilty."

Why was she confiding in this stranger, a man she'd almost quarreled with earlier? But somehow she knew he understood what she felt at that moment. Too bad he hadn't been as understanding about her horses. Not willing to reveal anything else, she turned away. "I should check the kitchen."

She crossed through the hallway and entered the right-hand door. Ezra's kitchen had the lived-in look lacking in the parlor. A pine table, scratched and gouged from long use, dominated the middle of the room. On one side of a black cast-iron stove sat a worn leather armchair. On the other side, a narrow bed piled with quilts testified to where Ezra had slept. A shelf above the stove held some pots, pans, several blue splatterware plates and mugs, and an old coffee can. A battered coffeepot perched on the stove, ready for a morning cup of coffee.

Wyatt walked over to the sink and pushed the handle of the pump. "The water here's good to drink." Rusty water poured through. "Although you wouldn't know it by lookin'." He continued pumping until the water ran clear. "That's better."

"Thank you."

Samantha continued her inspection. Cobwebby strands of dirty lace curtains hung on the windows. She circled the table, crossing to the grimy side window, and glanced out.

A peeling whitewashed fence surrounded what must be the vegetable garden. She'd have to get busy with the planting. Her fingers curled in anticipation. At the home she'd shared with Juan Carlos, she always had a garden, but at the estancia only the servants worked the land.

The sound of the children's footsteps clattered down the stairs and out the door. She concentrated on the room again.

In contrast to the rough surroundings, a china cabinet next to the window held blue dishes. She picked up a plate, rubbing her gloved hand over the dust-gray surface. Blue Willow. Ezra probably had never used them. Samantha carefully set the plate back in place.

Samantha inhaled, and exhaled a deep promise. She'd take this house, clean it, restore it, and make it into a home. She'd use the china and everything else. Then she'd fill this house, haunted with Ezra's final lonely years, with boys who'd only known lonely lives. There'd be no more loneliness. For any of them.

CHAPTER SIX

At the sound of a carriage, Samantha hurried across the kitchen to the window overlooking the front. *Who could possibly have come to call?* Through the dust-smeared glass, she could see an older white-haired man in a black coat climbing down from a rickety old buggy. He turned and ordered the two ragtag boys in the buggy to step down.

Wyatt joined her at the window. "Reverend Norton. And those two Cassidy hellions he's been trying to find a home. Told him to hold off 'til you're settled. Place won't be safe with them about. Probably burn the barn down before the week is over. You'd best send them away."

Samantha stifled a gasp. Her initial dismay at having unexpected callers fled. *How dare he tell her what to do. She'd had enough of that from her father-in-law. Especially about children.* "I'll do no such thing."

"Wait, Samantha." He touched her arm. "Those boys are nothing but trouble. They've fought, stole, set fire to Widow Murphy's haystack, and that's only what we know for sure. No one's willing to adopt them." His voice softened. "I think you have enough to handle right here without takin' on anything else."

"Every child deserves a home and a loving family. I prayed that the Lord would give me the opportunity to raise some orphans. Now that God has answered my prayers, I'm not going to turn my back on those boys just because you disapprove, Mr. Thompson." Samantha whirled out of the room, down the hall, and out onto the porch.

The minister towed the two reluctant boys up the steps. He flashed the boys a reproving look before smiling at Samantha. "Ah, Mrs. Rodriguez. I'm Reverend Norton."

"Reverend Norton, how nice to meet you."

The minister nodded. "I see Wyatt's been helping you. No problem with those Faleebelles?" His blue eyes twinkled at Wyatt, who'd followed her onto the porch.

Wyatt's jaw clenched, and he ground out, "No problem at all, Reverend."

"Good, good. Well"—he smiled at Samantha—"I know you aren't quite settled in yet, but your letter said you'd a mind to start taking in orphaned boys."

The boy Norton gripped in his right hand tried to twist away. The minister's body swayed, prompting the second boy to start a struggle.

"That's right, Reverend," she said.

Wyatt stepped forward, grasping a shoulder of each boy. "That's enough." He used a firm tone that lacked the hostility Samantha would have expected given his words in the kitchen. "Stand up and mind your manners."

The boys stood acquiescent under his hands. Samantha took a moment to study them. Identical twins, maybe about eleven years old. Dull brown hair worn too long, thin faces and bodies, as if they'd never had enough to eat; clothes threadbare and far too small. Identical surly looks.

Samantha's heart beat faster. Could she do it? Take these boys and heal their misery? Before she'd even settled into her new life? She remembered *Little Men*, and Jo March's struggle with Dan. Samantha would have *two*. And she didn't have a husband like Fritz Bhaer to help her. Wyatt stepped back, releasing the boys. She caught a flash of fear in one pair of green eyes, a glimpse of sadness on the face of the other twin. Then, like a hand brushing over a pattern in the sand, the fleeting expressions vanished, replaced by sullenness. But that proved enough for Samantha.

"Hello, boys."

Their gazes dropped to the tips of their muddy, scuffed boots, sliced open to accommodate their cramped toes.

The minister touched the boy on his right. "This is Tim Cassidy." He nodded at the other. "Jack Cassidy." Their father died last month. They've no relatives, and if you won't take them, I'll have to send them to the orphanage."

An orphanage. In a flash Samantha shrunk to six years old, peering through a rain-smeared windowpane, as a woman in a black coat dragged her newly orphaned friend, Günter, down the steps of the house across the street. She'd never forgotten the look of despair on his face.

"Of course I'll take them." Since the boys didn't look up from their boots, Samantha made her voice as warm as possible. "I'm afraid we've just arrived, and the house is a mess. We'll have makeshift conditions for a while."

No response. Samantha studied the twins, trying to find a way to tell them apart. Both wore patched tan denim pants several inches too short and coats awkwardly made from an old green blanket. Tim's worn cotton shirt had once been blue, while Jack wore a faded brown one. How to tell them apart? If the boys were in the habit of switching shirts to fool people, she'd have problems. The faint scattering of freckles across their faces gave her a clue. Jack had a patch of freckles on his right cheek similar to the stars that formed the constellation of Pleiades.

She smiled in satisfaction. "Why don't we go out to the barn so you can meet the other members of the family?"

Reverend Norton nodded. "Good idea. I'd like to see those Faleebelle horses everyone's talking about. But I have to make another call."

Out of the corner of her eye, Samantha saw Wyatt grimace.

The minister nodded, "I'll be back in a few days to check on everything. I'll see the toy horses, then."

Samantha stepped forward to grasp his hand. "Good-bye, Reverend Norton. We'll see you on Sunday."

A pleased smile crossed his austere face. "I was wondering about that. We'll be glad to have you worship with us." He waved at the twins. "Bye, Jack, Tim. You two mind Mrs. Rodriguez now."

Neither boy replied. Samantha put an arm around each boy's shoulders. "Let's go to the barn and see the Falabellas."

Wyatt's gaze met Samantha's. "I'll collect my daughter. We have chores waiting for us." He fell into step beside Tim, continuing to look at her. "Ezra has a team of horses and a saddle horse. The team's broke to ride. I've been running his cattle with my own. He never had a big herd. His two men have been working for me. I'll send them back tomorrow with the cattle."

"Thank you." Samantha said, overwhelmed by the responsibilities piling up around her.

He pointed to a small building, weathered gray like the others. "The bunkhouse. The men bed down there. There's also a cabin behind the barn a ways. It could be fixed up nice for Maria and Manuel. In better days, the foreman used to live there."

Maria would be thrilled to have her own little house instead of sharing the servants' quarters of the hacienda.

"And the chickens and goats."

"Goats?" Under her hand, Jack's shoulder twitched, and she caught a fleeting glance of interest. She asked him, "Did you boys ever raise goats?"

Jack flicked a brief look upward. "Yep. Nanny and her two kids. Good milk."

"Thank goodness," she murmured. At least Jack would talk.

Wyatt nodded. "Ezra also kept goats for the milk." He pointed to a small corral made of barbed wire with sticks threaded through and anchored in the ground to form a flimsy fence. "The goat pen."

"Oh." Samantha was familiar with goat milk and cheese from her childhood when her family had lived in Germany. Daniel would probably like having goats. How did one make goat cheese? She'd have to learn. She added the task to her ever-growing list. Fatigue dropped onto her like a heavy cloak. She sighed. What she wouldn't give to throw herself down on a soft clean bed and sleep for days.

Wyatt stopped. Something glimmered in his eyes, gone too soon for her to identify. He echoed her sigh, pulling off his hat and rubbing his head. "Look. You've just arrived and are exhausted. Why don't you all come home with me? Get a good night's sleep and start fresh in the morning."

"Why...thank you." The heightened awareness of his presence, which she'd been trying to ignore, sprang to life. Spend the evening with him, sleep under the same roof? Her heartbeat quickened at the thought. "But we couldn't possibly intrude."

The corner of his mouth lifted in a half smile. "My house-keeper will be there. It'll be proper, and you'll be quite safe. Mrs. Toffels will welcome you with open arms and a warm meal."

Samantha opened her mouth, intending a firm refusal, but to her surprise and chagrin, a yes slipped out.

His grin widened, showing straight teeth. "It's settled, then. Let's go round up the children."

Samantha sent up a little prayer of gratitude that Don Ricardo wasn't here to see the decisions she'd made in the last few minutes. Her father-in-law might have made good his often-uttered threat to permanently lock her in her room. She slanted a glance up at Wyatt.

Freedom.

Right or wrong, she had made a choice. Excitement threaded up her spine. She could even choose this man. *Not,* she hastily reined in her thoughts, that she would pick *him.* Or he, her for that matter. But still, no one would ever again tell her what to do. She resisted flinging wide her arms. *Montana. My own ranch. A whole new life.*

❋ ❋ ❋

Passing the empty goat pen, with its long shadows stretching across bare dirt, Jack Cassidy couldn't help feeling a twinge of interest as he imagined goats running around the empty enclosure. But caution kept him from allowing his feelings to show. He'd learned all too well how a flicker of expression could earn him a blow. And with the woman's hand on his shoulder, unless he twisted away quick-like, he'd be an easy target.

Behind his impassivity, his thoughts jumped around like fleas on a mangy dog. Maybe he could find a way to steal his nanny goat back. Maybe the lady'd let him keep it here. She was new in town and all. She wouldn't know Widda Murphy had kept his goat, claiming the animal was payment for the twins' keep.

The woman's hand rested on Jack's shoulder, gentle-like. His father or other men tended to grip his muscles in a squeeze, reminding him who was boss. Her touch tweren't that different from his ma's. His shoulder twitched at the memory. The pain of Ma's death two years ago still burned like a boil on his heart.

He didn't much care that his pa had passed on. He missed his nanny goat more than he missed the old drunk. 'Cept now they were stuck in the care of do-gooders, and that was worse. Widda Murphy had complained all the time, words spilling out of her pinched mouth like water from a pump. All them words wore on a boy.

His foot scuffed against a clod of soil, sending dirt and a pebble through the slashed-open leather in the toes of his boot, and reminding him of his cold feet. He winced, but refused to stop. His gaze slid to the man, dressed in a pressed white shirt and denim pants, complete with almost new lookin' boots. Better to limp along rather than shame himself by drawing attention to the outgrown footwear.

The lady glanced down. "You all right?"

Jack nodded, tearing his gaze away from the concern in her soft blue eyes. He sensed her look away, and he dared a quick upward glance trying to take in her beauty. Never did see hair like that before. Alive, like a crackling fire, not like his ma's limp browny-gray. But he'd overheard people say that marrying his pa had sure taken away his ma's looks—aged her and all.

Feelings more bitter than willow bark tea clogged his throat. Tweren't fair that Ma had it so hard. Tweren't fair that this lady with her soft eyes and skin had the raisin' of them now.

He tried to catch his brother's eye, but Tim plodded along like their old mule, his gaze on the dirt ahead of him. Tim had always been the quiet one, keeping his thoughts to himself. Too often, Jack had to stand up for his brother. But Jack could tell by the set of his twin's shoulders that he too had his guts churnin' to butter.

As the four of them continued toward the barn, worries gnawed on Jack's mind like a beaver on a tree. Would the lady be like Widda Murphy, always talking bad at them? She didn't look like she'd lash out with a fist like Pa had. But Widda Murphy had gotten in a few stingin' slaps until the twins had learned to dodge. The hand resting so soft on his shoulder could as quick slap across his face. Well, if necessary, he could move faster than a calf twisting to avoid a lasso.

He tensed his body. As long as she remained this close, he'd better be ready.

❋ ❋ ❋

As the afternoon faded, the warmth of the spring sunshine slipped away. Samantha shivered. When they approached the barn, she could see it looked as run-down as the house. Her spirits sank. Paint had flaked off, exposing weather-beaten gray boards. The remains of last autumn's leaves banked in piles against the walls, no doubt rotting the boards. Cobwebs dangled from the eaves. Samantha gave a wide berth to a brown spider scurrying up a web.

Wyatt pushed the half-closed barn door all the way open, and then with a flourish of his hand, waved her through. Samantha stepped inside. As she waited for her eyes to adjust to the gloom, she inhaled the familiar barn scents: horses, fresh hay—

Fresh hay?

She hadn't ordered any. She'd planned for their sacks of grain to last until she could get into town and order more feed. And the interior of the barn looked suspiciously clean. She glanced up, checking for spiderwebs, but couldn't see any. She looked over at Wyatt. "Are you responsible for the hay?"

He nodded. "Sent some men to clean and stock the place." A teasing glint lit his gray eyes. "Course, I didn't expect a bunch of midget horses. Would have sent over half the amount."

"Falabellas," she corrected automatically, feeling a glow kindle in the vicinity of her heart. "I appreciate all your help."

"You're welcome."

"Come on, boys, let's meet the horses." She ushered them closer to the stalls.

From the other side of the barn, Daniel pelted down the aisle, followed by Christine. "Mama." At the sight of the twins he skipped to a stop, his eyes widening in curiosity. "Hello."

"Daniel, this is Jack Cassidy"—she patted Jack's shoulder—"and his twin brother, Tim. Remember how we've talked? They've come to live with us."

Daniel eyed the boys and then met her gaze. "They'll be my brothers?"

She smiled at him. "That's right, son."

"Good." He seized Jack's wrist. "Come on. Meet Chita." Daniel turned, preparing to drag the boy down the aisle.

With a growl, Jack jerked away. Fisting his hand, he punched Daniel in the shoulder.

"Ow." Daniel was no stranger to being picked on. Before Samantha could react, he'd hit Jack in the stomach.

With a wuff of expelled air, Jack doubled up, but quickly recovered, clenching both hands in front of him. Ready to fight, Tim sprang forward next to his brother.

Wyatt stepped in between the boys, grabbing one of Jack's fists and blocking Tim with his hip. "That's enough." He stared down at Jack. An unspoken communication seemed to pass between them, and Jack dropped his hands. Tim relaxed his arms.

Wyatt glanced over at her, a sardonic look in his eyes. *See*, he seemed to say.

Samantha avoided his gaze, instead focusing on Daniel. Her heart squeezed at the tense way he'd drawn his brows up—the hurt look in his eyes. She'd seen that look many times when Daniel's cousins wouldn't play with him. In her fantasy, she'd imagined having to win her orphan boys' trust, but it had never occurred to her that Daniel would have to go through a similar process. She hadn't intended for her son to suffer from adopting wayward boys. Had she made a mistake in taking in the twins?

She suppressed a sigh at the thought of all the work awaiting her. The excitement and freedom that had buoyed her up for the last few hours seeped away with each new obstacle, until now she felt as flat as an empty pillow casing. Not wanting to communicate her exhaustion to anyone, she struggled to keep her step light, and prayed for some extra energy. They all needed her to be strong—to be in control.

Wyatt looked at Jack and gently nudged his shoulder. "I think you should go with Daniel and Christine." A hint of steel slid under the suggestion in his words. He softened his command by grinning. "I think you'll like what you find."

Christine slipped her hand inside her father's and leaned against him. She studied each twin. "Please come see the little horses," she coaxed. "You'll like them."

Jack glanced away, then back again, his gaze caught by Christine's blue-eyed appeal. Samantha watched the resistance fade from his face. He stiffly nodded his head.

Christine's answering smile would have been hard for anyone to resist. She dropped her father's hand, waving for the twins to follow.

Samantha suppressed a smile. In a few years, Christine's suitors would be cluttering up the porch of Wyatt's house—unless he was the type to stand guard with a gun. She noted the harsh set of his face as he watched the children and had her answer. Definitely the protective father-with-a-gun.

Turning to him, she cocked an eyebrow. "Let's see if the Falabellas can work their magic."

"Midget magic. That'll be somethin'," he said, his tone wry.

In spite of her tiredness, Samantha refused to have Wyatt's poor opinion of the twins bog her down. With time she'd be able to help them. Then he'd see...She fell into step behind the children.

Daniel unlatched the first stall door, holding it open for everyone. "This is my mare, Chita." The little black horse nuzzled Daniel's hand.

Tim stepped forward, gently touching Chita's back, then ran his palm across her side, dislodging the dust of the journey. "I'll be damned."

Daniel's eyes widened, and he looked at Samantha in inquiry.

She bit her lip, shaking her head at him in silent communication. *Don't say anything.* Now that Tim had finally spoken, she didn't want to reprimand the first words he'd uttered. She was sure there'd be plenty of other opportunities to teach the boys proper language.

Jack remained mute, but the eager look in his eyes went straight to her heart. She leaned over and touched his shoulder. "There are more." She smiled at both boys. "Chita is Daniel's mare. Chico's my favorite. You each can pick out a horse to be your own friend."

Wary disbelief froze their faces, as if they were afraid to trust her.

She held up an admonitory finger. "But they will be your responsibility to care for. Including the mucking out."

That seemed to reassure them. Silently they went from stall to stall, running their hands over each small body, and making soft clucking noises. Without a word, Tim ended up on his knees in Bonita's stall, his arms wrapped around the little chestnut mare. Jack crouched next to Mariposa, stroking the dusty gray coat and murmuring low words into a twitching ear.

The scene tugged at her emotions, and Samantha blinked back tears, already feeling a mother's connection with the boys. Relief pushed away some of her weariness. Watching the gentle way the twins interacted with the horses, she relaxed. *My new sons. There's good in them. I know it. I'll just have to bring it out.*

CHAPTER SEVEN

Wyatt rode next to Samantha's small buggy, his mind whirling. Behind him on the horse's rump rode Jack Cassidy, loosely clutching Wyatt around his waist. On the other side of the buggy, Christine chattered away to Daniel. Trailing behind them, Tim doubled up with Manuel.

He shook his head, still amazed at his impulse to invite his new, unwanted neighbors to stay the night. How could he keep the Cassidy twins at a distance from Christine, when he'd gone and welcomed them into his home? He'd have to worry about that later. In good conscience, a man couldn't let them sleep in Ezra's dusty, dilapidated house.

The sun descended behind Copper Mountain, fading the blue sky to purple and coating their surroundings with gray shadows. An aspen grove sheltered a small fenced cemetery plot, the shivering of the new leaves in the breeze providing an accompaniment to any spirits who might linger to chat. He never rode past without thinking about Alicia. When time permitted, he liked to stop, sit on the wooden bench next to her grave, and talk to her about the ranch, her garden, and especially their daughter. A little girl growing up without her mother. He wondered what Alicia would say about his day...about Samantha.

Wyatt tried to sort through his feelings. He'd started the morning frustrated that the widow had taken Ezra's ranch. He'd been annoyed by her midget horses, had almost quarreled with her, and then had felt an unexpected attraction. He'd ended up guilty about the thought of riding away and leaving her on that run-down ranch with those rapscallion Cassidy boys. Now he hauled those very boys to his home. He didn't want to think about what the evening might bring...

A vision of Samantha in his bed, firelight playing over her naked white skin and burnishing a tendril of auburn hair curling over her breast, rose to his mind. He imagined brushing aside the hair, touching the softness of her breast with his fingers, his mouth—

"Mr. Thompson? Mr. Thompson!"

He snapped to attention, the heat in his groin leaping up to flush his face. What was he thinking? To invite a lady over for the night, offer his hospitality and the protection of his home, then think lewd thoughts about her...He was a gentleman, not a cad. He only hoped his imaginings weren't written on his face for Samantha to read. Or for Alicia's spirit to see. "Sorry, my mind wandered."

Her upturned face reflected only curiosity. His relief washed away the embarrassment.

"I was wondering how much longer before we reach your ranch?"

"We've been on my land for a while. I should have told you when we crossed the boundary." He pointed. "Round that clump of trees we'll see the house and barns. Then it's only a few more minutes."

"Thank goodness."

Although fatigue shaded her eyes, she sat erect on the buggy seat, shoulders straight. A shaft of admiration pierced him. She'd traveled a long way and put up with who knows what kind of inconveniences and hardships. When she'd arrived, she received an unfriendly welcome from her nearest neighbor, found her new home to be too run down to spend the first night there, and was now on the way to a strange house. He had no doubt that tomorrow she'd be up to her elbows in soapsuds, scrubbing her home from floor to ceiling. She didn't seem like the kind of woman to leave all that work to Maria.

Wyatt admired that quality. He leaned closer. "You must be tired and hungry."

"Very."

"I'm sure you'd like to get cleaned up."

She sighed. "Yes. And the boys could certainly use a bath."

He cleared his throat. "Won't be a problem. Had a bathing room installed in the house last year. You can enjoy a bath"—he pushed aside a vision of her soaking in his tub—"while the boys bathe at the bunkhouse. I'll see to them."

"The twins might make it difficult for you."

"I'll handle them."

"Thank you." Appreciation lightened the weary look on her face. "Just being able to sleep in a bed that doesn't move will be a treat. Are you sure you have enough room for all of us?"

He grinned. They rounded the last cluster of trees. "Just look."

"Oh, my," Samantha said.

As always, the sight of his ranch settled satisfaction deep in his belly. So different from the hovel where he'd spent his youth… He never took the view for granted. His gaze swept around, making sure all was well. The big white house gleamed golden in the final rays of the setting sun. The lilac bushes planted by Alicia in the corner of the picketed yard were budding. In a month any slight breeze would waft the sweet scent this way. He inhaled in anticipation, smiling when he noticed Samantha straightening in her seat, interest in her blue eyes.

Except for some horses in one of the corrals, the yards around the two red barns looked quiet, the porch of the white bunkhouse on the far side of the house empty of lounging men. The ranch hands hadn't come in from moving the cattle to the north pasture. But it was near suppertime, and they'd be riding in soon. Best get this strange assortment of guests settled in first.

But he stilled the reins for a moment, and Bill paused. For the last ten years, step by step, he'd been planning his life. Acquiring Ezra's ranch had been his next move. Then he planned to court Edith Grayson. Having a wealthy banker as a brother-in-law had its appeal. Although now he wasn't so sure. The solid ground he'd been striding over could turn to quicksand. If a man wasn't careful, he could be pulled in over his head.

❋ ❋ ❋

Wyatt led them to the nearest barn. Samantha slackened the reins of the buggy, relieved to allow her aching arms some rest.

A young man of about fifteen strode out of the barn. Tall and whipcord thin, with a shock of orange hair and splatters of freckles covering his face, he walked with a clumsy gait, as if he'd not grown into his legs. His plaid work shirt was too short, displaying bony wrists and hands. Catching sight of the Falabellas, he stopped with a tripping motion, his hazel eyes widening. Behind the faded blue bandana he'd tied around his neck, his Adam's apple bobbed up and down.

He reminded Samantha of a scarecrow who'd suddenly learned to walk, and she hid a smile of amusement. Boys his age were very concerned about their dignity; she didn't want to embarrass him.

Wyatt motioned him over. "Harry, I'd like you to meet Mrs. Rodriguez, her son Daniel, Manuel and Maria, and I believe you know the Cassidy boys. Harry is our stable hand."

Harry barely glanced at them, his eyes flicking back to the horses. "What, what?" he stammered.

Wyatt threw Samantha an amused look. "Falabellas." He rolled his eyes. "I can see I'm going to be repeating that a lot in the next few days. I'll get them settled in and get myself away from the barns before the hands come in. If we're lucky, they won't notice them." He nodded at Harry. "Unless someone recovers his powers of speech and tattles."

Samantha laughed. She was glad to see he'd developed a sense of humor about her miniature horses.

"Christine," he said to his daughter. "Take the ladies in to meet Mrs. Toffels." He turned to Samantha. "Our housekeeper."

"But, the boys."

"I'll keep an eye on them."

Samantha relinquished her responsibilities into his capable hands. How good it felt to be taken care of. Of course, it was only temporary. By tomorrow, she'd be rested enough to resume charge of her household and menagerie.

She handed the reins over to Harry. He looked bemused, as if uncertain what to do with them.

Wyatt dismounted and strode to her side. He extended his hand. She placed her fingers in his palm, feeling the strength in his hand, and stepped down from the buggy.

Christine ran to her side. "Mrs. Toffels makes the best cinnamon cookies."

Samantha smiled at her. "I can hardly wait to try them."

Christine pushed open the picket gate, reaching out to grasp Samantha's hand. Together, they walked up the brick pathway, Maria trailing behind.

In long beds parallel to the porch, red tulips bloomed, as beautiful as any she'd seen in Europe.

Christine noticed her appreciation. "Pa orders those every year from Holland. I help him plant them. Before she died, my mama planted them. Pa says the flowers help us remember her."

Touched by Wyatt's gesture toward his deceased wife, Samantha blinked back the sudden moisture in her eyes. She'd tried to find her own rituals to help Daniel remember Juan Carlos. How much more difficult to give a child memories of a mother she never knew. She wondered if Wyatt was still in love with his wife. Was that why he'd never remarried? She pushed away a sudden feeling of disappointment by blaming it on tiredness. Her new neighbor's life was none of her business.

As Samantha followed Christine into the kitchen, the sweet aroma of fresh-baked apple pie greeted her. She inhaled an appreciative breath, immediately taken back to the memories of the apple strudel she had loved as a child.

She used to help the cook roll out the dough. Together, they'd stretch it by running their knuckles underneath until it was almost paper thin. Then they'd scatter the apple slices and spices over the dough and, starting with one edge, fold it into a roll. She'd made apple strudel for Juan Carlos and Daniel on several occasions. But at the estancia, Don Ricardo wouldn't allow his daughters-in-law near the kitchen. She'd missed being able to bake.

The Thompson kitchen looked like a perfect place to spend an afternoon baking. The immaculate room looked as different from Ezra's dirty, dilapidated kitchen as could be. The ample workspace held similar furnishings: stove, table, china cabinet, but instead of a bed and worn leather chair, this kitchen had a pie safe and a rocking chair, with a black-and-tan dog curled up on a small braided rag rug next to it.

The dog thumped its tail on the floor in greeting, but didn't rise to meet them. A shelf under the window held clay pots of green sprouts, probably herbs. A red-and-white checked cloth covering the table matched the crisp curtains at the window.

At a six-hole cast-iron stove, a woman dressed in blue gingham looked up from the pot she'd been stirring. With an exclamation of surprise, she set the wooden spoon across the top of the pot and smoothed her white apron.

Samantha's first impression of Mrs. Toffels was of cozy plumpness. She was short and stout, with her bosom overflowing her apron. Her round face crinkled into little smile wrinkles at the sight of them. Tucking a straying strand of gray hair back into her bun, she bustled forward.

"No, don't tell me. You must be our new neighbor, Mrs. Rodriguez." She pulled out the rocking chair. "You just sit right down here and rest. You must be exhausted, poor dear."

Samantha touched Maria on the shoulder before moving to the rocker. "This is Maria Sanchez. She's been with me since my son, Daniel, was born."

Mrs. Toffels scooted a wooden chair away from the table, motioning Maria to take a seat.

Maria smiled shyly and ducked her head before sitting down.

A woof drew Samantha's attention to the dog, its muzzle grizzled gray. Christine skipped over and crouched down by the dog, patting it on the head. The dog thumped its tail.

Mrs. Toffels waved to the dog. "Don't you mind Matilda here. She's an old, old lady and doesn't stir herself too much anymore."

"Thank you." Samantha sank into the rocking chair and rested her hands on the arms to support her aching muscles. "It will feel good to rest a moment." She felt relieved that on first acquaintance, the cook didn't appear to have the bigoted opinions held by Mrs. Cobb. She could relax.

The housekeeper reached over and pressed Christine to her ample bosom. "Hello, darlin'."

Christine, eager to communicate her news, danced out of the embrace. "You should see their little horses, Mrs. Toffels." She bounced up and down. "Small like foals, except they're full grown. They're called Falabellas."

"Well now, that sounds mighty interesting, and I want to hear all about them. But first I'm sure Mrs. Rodriguez and Maria will need a pick-me-up. They've come a long way. Why don't you get the cookie jar? I'll put on a kettle for tea." She looked at Samantha. "Or would you prefer coffee?"

Samantha smiled at the housekeeper. "Tea would be welcome. Christine's been describing your wonderful cinnamon cookies."

Mrs. Toffels beamed. "They sure are her favorite."

Standing on tiptoe, Christine lifted a blue salt-glazed jar off one of the shelves. She pulled off the top and brought it to Samantha. "Here, Mrs. Rodriguez, try one."

"Thank you, my dear."

Christine offered the jar to Maria, who took one with a shy duck of her head.

Mrs. Toffels handed a plate to Samantha. "I sure was hopeful when Wyatt told me a widow was taking over Ezra's ranch."

"Hopeful?"

"That you'd be young and pretty." Her face crinkled into a smile. "And you are. I'm always partial to red hair. Stir up some interest in the neighborhood, that's what I say. Some people around here need to pull their heart out of a grave."

Samantha gulped, her relaxed feelings flying out the window. *Surely Mrs. Toffels wasn't matchmaking between her and Wyatt.*

"I understand about burying your heart with your spouse."

The woman sent a shrewd look. "I'm sure you do. But life's for the livin'. That's what I say. And I should know. I've buried two husbands, myself."

Christine hovered near the housekeeper, oblivious to the undercurrent of their conversation. "May I please have some cookies too?"

"Just one or you'll spoil your supper."

Supper. With a start, Samantha realized Mrs. Toffels needed to know there were more unexpected guests. Feeling a little embarrassed for having descended on the unsuspecting woman with her rapidly growing band of dependents, she hesitantly spoke up. "Mrs. Toffels, I should warn you that I've brought two other adults and three growing boys with me."

The housekeeper looked surprised. "I thought Wyatt mentioned you had one child."

"I do. However, I've just acquired two more."

Christine piped up. "Reverend Norton brought Jack and Tim Cassidy. They're going to live with her."

Mrs. Toffels picked up her spoon and resumed stirring. "You're a saint to take them on, Mrs. Rodriguez. A saint, indeed. I've been worried about them. Those boys need a proper home."

A proper home. A proper home. The words echoed in her thoughts. The image of her run-down ranch sprang to mind, seeding momentary doubts. Would she be able to provide a proper home for all of them?

CHAPTER EIGHT

Jack Cassidy watched the womenfolk head up the brick pathway to the big white house. Instead of following them, the man Thompson turned toward the bunkhouse and motioned for the boys to come with him.

Jack slowed his steps, lagging behind. He took quick sideways glances, studying the house and barn. Neat outfit. Fresh paint, no weeds, or horse droppings, or discarded rusty bits and pieces of metal scattered around. The orderliness made him uncomfortable—like he didn't fit inside his skin. He looked down, trying to avoid the shame. But seeing his open-toed boots only made it worse.

So he studied Thompson's broad back, not trusting him. Jack wasn't sure where the man was taking them, and he wanted to be able to run if necessary.

Flowers. Jack caught sight of the little green buds on the lilac bushes and flinched, trying to escape a memory. But the remembrance plumb sunk its teeth into him, worse than a dog's bite. He couldn't shake it off. His ma had always loved lilacs, but in a drunken rage, his pa had torn out the bushes she'd planted. She never tried again. But every spring, Jack had cut blooming branches from other people's yards and brought them to her. Since her death, the fragrant flowers always twisted an ache inside him.

Thompson walked them around the corner of the long white bunkhouse past the porch. On the side, set away from the big house and the barn, and facing the mountains, a high fence screened a horse trough with a pump set at one end. Jack tried to puzzle out why there was a horse trough here, when Thompson already had one in front of the barn.

Thompson waved to the pump. "You"—he pointed at Tim— "how about filling it up?"

Tim flicked a look at Jack. The man's request seemed harmless enough, and he nodded at his brother. Tim stepped over and pumped the water. Jack watched, wishing his ma had had one of these. Hauling water from the crik had sure been a heap a trouble.

"This is where the men wash up," Thompson said. "I've sent Harry in to heat up some pails of water. In the meantime, you boys strip down."

Strip down. Bathe. No way! He'd wait until summer and swim in the crik. That usually got him clean enough. Even Widow Murphy hadn't been able to force the twins to take a bath. "I ain't takin' no bath."

The Thompson man glanced at him, gray eyes sharp as a shard from a broken mirror. "Yes you will, my boy."

Jack didn't like how the man's calm voice ran against the look in his eyes. *He's a big 'un. Might not be a good idea to go up against him,* a small whisper said in his mind. He batted it away. *Give in now, who knows what would happen next.* "I ain't takin' no bath!"

Thompson ignored him, turning away. "Daniel, you go first."

The boy nodded and fingered his tie.

Coward, Jack thought.

Thompson touched one of the metal hooks set into the fence. "Hang your clothes here."

"*Sí*, I mean, yes, sir."

Jack cleared his throat. "I told ya, I ain't takin' no bath."

"You want to eat?"

"Rather starve."

"Too bad. You'll miss Mrs. Toffels's chicken and dumplings. And I'll bet she's made apple pie for dessert."

Jack wavered. Apple pie didn't cross his path too often, but he sure did remember those times it had. Birthdays mostly. His ma had always tried to make a pie for the twins' birthday. Been a long while since he'd had himself a piece of one. "I'll wash my hands and face," he conceded. After all, his ma had always made him wash up before dinner. He might as well do it here too.

The big man dropped his hand onto Jack's shoulder and squeezed. Not hard or painful like his pa would have done. But Jack caught the warning. "Look at it this way. You have a choice. Either you strip off your clothes and wash all over, or I'll do it for you. And I have a heavy hand with the soap and scrub brush."

Footfalls on the porch of the bunkhouse, a jangle of spurs, announced the arrival of several wranglers. A short, stocky man with buckteeth stepped next to Thompson. "Well, what have we here?"

Thompson eyed Jack, sending him a silent message. "Company. About to have a bath."

Jack took in the three other men flanking Thompson and knew he was outnumbered. He could maybe escape Thompson, but not all the rest of the hands. The idea of being wrestled down, stripped, and thrown in that trough burned his neck like a noose. He'd go along with this bath thing for today—have himself some of that apple pie. But too much soap and water might make him grab hold of Tim and light out for the hills.

❉ ❉ ❉

A feeling of peace began in Samantha's stomach, like the glow of a coal uncovered from the ashes, sending relaxation through her. With a contented sigh, she leaned against the back of the rose velvet wing chair in Wyatt's parlor, relishing the warmth from the blaze in the fireplace. Tomorrow would bring its challenges. But now, clean and well fed, with the children tucked into bed, she could savor these few minutes before she retired to sleep.

Across from her, the matching wing chair held a needlepoint pillow with cabbage roses worked in pinks and reds. Roses also decorated the vases perched on the enormous mahogany mantle. But it was the portrait above the mantle that caught her attention.

Christine's mother. It was evident by the curling blonde hair and big blue eyes. The pink full-bustled dress she wore matched the roses she carried in her hands. Did Wyatt still miss her? Samantha envied his having a portrait of his wife. Juan Carlos had never sat for a portrait, nor had a photograph taken. They'd always meant to—

The sound of measured footsteps interrupted her contemplation.

Wyatt. She already knew the sound of his tread. He entered the room, balancing a cup and saucer in each hand. Before the meal, he'd helped the boys take baths and had bathed himself. With his dark hair slicked back behind his ears, and wearing a clean gray shirt that silvered his eyes, he brought a masculine presence into the feminine room.

Samantha looked away, uncomfortable with her heightened awareness of him.

"I thought we should celebrate your first night with a cup of hot chocolate."

"Hot chocolate." She sat up. "Oh, I haven't had that in so long."

"Good." He handed her the cup and saucer before stretching out in the wing chair opposite her. A mischievous smile brightened his face. "Don't tell the children. Christine would never forgive me for leaving her out of the treat."

Samantha laughed. "Nor would Daniel." She lifted the cup to her lips and sipped. The rich cocoa taste trickled around her tongue, evoking sweet memories from the past. "The last time I had hot chocolate was the Christmas before my husband died."

"I hope I haven't brought back sad memories."

"On the contrary. We seldom had hot cocoa in Argentina. But as a child in Germany, I drank it quite often." She smiled at him. "Germans make the best chocolate. Unbelievably delicious. At the time, I took it for granted. I didn't realize how spoiled I was."

"Germany, Argentina. You've been quite a traveler."

"My father was in the diplomatic corps. I've only spent a few years in the United States."

"Life on a ranch in Montana will be quite different for you."

Something about his tone made her cock her head. But his friendly expression didn't change. "I'm looking forward to it. It shouldn't be too different from what I'm used to. I've spent the last two years on my father-in-law's ranch."

Silence fell while they drank their hot chocolate.

Samantha savored the last few sips before she set her cup and saucer down on the marble-topped side table. "That was wonderful. So different from the yerba maté Argentineans drink all the time."

"Yerba maté?"

"Yes, it's a dried herb. It's made as an infusion in a gourd and sipped through a silver *bombilla*—something like a straw with a mesh on the end." She wrinkled her nose. "It's often shared. A person will drink and pass it on to someone else. I never acquired a taste for it."

"Perhaps if we were to make hot chocolate in a gourd…"

"Actually, only the workers used a *maté* gourd. We used silver ones."

"I like the idea of sharing."

"Not with my father-in-law, you wouldn't."

A half smile played across his face. "I meant sharing a *bombilla* with you…sipping chocolate…"

At the intimacy of his suggestion, the peaceful coal in her stomach blazed into a flame. She could feel her cheeks redden and hoped, in the fire-shadowed room, he wouldn't notice. "Thank you for the chocolate." She stood up. "It's been a very long day. I should retire."

He slowly unfolded his long body from the chair.

She scooted sideways to the door, trying not to appear as if she were fleeing. After all, from what could she possibly be fleeing? *Or whom?*

Amusement glinted in his eyes, then seeped into his smile. "I hope you find the bed comfortable."

"I'll sleep well on anything that's not rocking."

His smile widened.

Flustered, she nodded. "Good night." She hurried through the doorway. Once in the hall, she pressed her hands to her cheeks but didn't slow down. All she'd been through in the last few days had certainly unsettled her. Hard work should bring her back to normal. And she certainly had enough of that before her. No time for her handsome neighbor to distract her.

❋ ❋ ❋

The next day, Samantha dropped the scrub brush into the tin pail of dirty water and wrinkled her nose at the sight of her red, water-pruned hands. Living on the estancia had softened her skin. The last few hours, while she'd worked, she'd ignored the sting of the lye soap, but now the irritation increased.

She straightened and pressed her fists into the small of her back. Finally, she'd cleaned the kitchen to her satisfaction. Tiredly, she surveyed her new home. Everything was as neat as soap and water and two pairs of women's hands could make it. How much more gratifying to work on her own house rather than relax in the luxurious prison of her father-in-law's estancia.

Across the room, Maria's shy gaze met hers, and the two women exchanged silent acknowledgment. "It's fit to live in again," she told Maria in Spanish. "We can begin in the parlor after we eat."

Samantha assessed the space. It looked bigger now that Wyatt and Manuel had moved Ezra's bed and chair to one of the bedrooms upstairs. Coffee in a pot of Wedgwood blue enamel-ware simmered on the newly blackened stove, inviting them to sit and have a cup. Sunlight sparkled through clean windows, lighting up the whole room. A white linen tablecloth covered the scarred pine table, now set with the Blue Willow dishes.

Early that morning, Christine had gathered an armful of red tulips for Samantha. The bouquet filled her mother's cut-glass vase in the center of the table, brightening the kitchen with color. Samantha had kept the vase packed away during her years on the estancia. Now, at last, it had a place to shine.

She swallowed a sudden lump in her throat, remembering her mother arranging flowers in that vase. A familiar sadness misted her eyes, and she wished her mother were here with her. She'd have loved Montana.

Samantha lifted her chin, inhaling the soap and ammonia-smelling air. She comforted herself with the thought that perhaps her mother still watched over her and Daniel. Sometimes, she fancied she could even sense her mother's presence.

A flurry of hammering drove her to the window to peek out at Wyatt. This morning he'd offered to fix the bridge. When she'd demurred, insisting that he'd already done enough for them, he'd pointed out that he didn't want Christine to be riding across an unsafe bridge or hurting herself running across the rotting wood of the porch. Of course, Samantha had to give in to his reasoning.

Bending on one knee, Wyatt pounded down the new planks. Even from this distance she could see his back and arm muscles move with every stroke of the hammer. Her heartbeat thudded to his rhythmic movement. As if he sensed her scrutiny, he stopped, flashing her a smile before resuming his work.

Flustered, she turned away from the window. "Pour the coffee, please," Samantha said to Maria. "The men and boys will be hungry. I'll call them in, and we can open Mrs. Toffels's basket of food."

She walked out to the front porch, stepping gingerly. Cupping her hands around her mouth, she called out, "Time to eat."

Around the corner of the house, the boys beat the dust from the rugs. She heard Daniel's whoop and yell. "Come on. Let's go eat."

At the bridge, Wyatt nodded at her. "Be right there," he called.

Samantha smiled and walked back inside. In a few minutes, she'd have a hungry horde descending on her. But Mrs. Toffels had packed enough food—fried chicken, baked beans, sourdough biscuits, tiny new carrots, a jug of lemonade, and two apple pies—to feed an army.

She held her breath as she heard the clatter on the porch. Only a few more hours and she wouldn't have to worry about someone falling through that rotting wood and breaking a leg. Wyatt's help was an unexpected blessing. Somehow she'd have to repay his kindness.

The three boys appeared in the kitchen. She smiled and released her breath. "Wash up, please."

Daniel piped up. "We washed in the horse trough."

"Well, you can just do it again. Properly. With soap and clean water. And a towel."

Both twins looked rebellious.

"Mrs. Toffels made apple pies for us. Sure would be a sin to waste them because you boys hadn't cleaned up."

Wyatt's voice boomed out, "Wouldn't go to waste. Manuel and I can eat the boys' share." He exchanged an amused glance with her.

Daniel slid past her, heading toward the sink. "I'll wash right up."

Samantha put her hands on her hips, eyeing the twins. "Well, boys?"

Jack nodded, walking around her to follow Daniel. Tim lined up behind him.

There. Firm persuasion and a hint of bribery. Works every time.

Samantha set out the chicken and the rest of the fixings, while Maria poured coffee and lemonade. The boys hurried through their washing up and scrambled for chairs. Manuel and Maria settled down between Tim and Jack.

Wyatt pulled out a seat for Samantha, and she smiled at him. "Thank you."

Jack reached out to help himself to chicken.

Samantha touched his hand. "Grace first." She looked over at Wyatt. "Mr. Thompson, will you do the honors?"

He nodded, clasping his hands and closing his eyes.

As his sonorous voice recited a simple prayer, Samantha's heart filled. She had a good neighbor, plentiful food on the table, and her son and the first two of her boys around her. Her dream was coming true.

From underneath her lowered lids, she glanced across the table at Wyatt, warmth swelling in her breast. *If only it could always be this way.* She didn't dare let herself continue the thought.

As if they hadn't eaten for years, instead of earlier gorging on Mrs. Toffels's abundant breakfast, the twins dug into the chicken and beans. In a few days, she planned to work on their atrocious table manners, but for now, it was more important to put some meat on their skinny bones, and let them know they'd never again go without sustenance.

Except for requests for refills, they ate the meal in silence, everyone too hungry to talk. Then, with the edge off his hunger, Daniel began to rattle on about the boys' doings and asking plenty of questions of Wyatt.

Samantha felt pleased to see how patiently the man responded. Her father-in-law had always brushed Daniel's questions aside or ordered him to be quiet—a cruel thing to do. Silence had never come naturally to her son.

Samantha waited until the boys were well into their apple pie. "School tomorrow for you three."

Resigned to the inevitable, Daniel shrugged his shoulders.

Jack kept his eyes on his plate. "Ain't goin' to no school."

Tim mumbled around a mouthful of pie. "Me either."

Samantha strove for a light tone. "Of course you are. School's important."

Ducking his head, Jack answered, "Our pa had no use for book-learnin'. Said would just make us 'uns lazy cusses."

Across the table, Wyatt's gaze met hers. She looked away, wishing he wasn't witnessing her first power struggle with the twins. She didn't want him to think he'd been right about her taking the boys in. Nor did she want him to intercede. She had to handle this herself. "Have you two ever been to school?"

"When us 'uns was little, when Ma was alive," Tim said.

"Sounds like getting an education was important to your ma. Don't you think she'd want you to attend school, now that you have a chance?"

Jack shook his head. "Ain't goin' to no school."

"Me either," Tim agreed.

She remembered her earlier attempts to get them to wash up. She needed a bribe. Though she didn't like to resort to that kind of mothering, sometimes it was necessary. "Before I take you to school," she said to Jack, "we're going to stop at the mercantile and get you some new clothes and school supplies."

"Don't need no new clothes. Ain't goin' to school."

"But wouldn't you *like* new clothes? New shoes?"

Across the table, Tim swallowed, obviously wavering.

As if sensing that his brother was weakening, Jack pressed his lips into an obstinate line. "Us 'uns ain't goin' to no damn school!" He shoved his empty plate across the table, knocking it against the vase of tulips. Several spilled out.

Samantha gasped.

As the vase teetered, Wyatt's arm snaked out, his hand clutching the glass before it tipped over.

With slow precision, Wyatt righted the vase. Then he threw down his napkin, scraping back his chair. He strode over to Jack, placing his hand on the boy's shoulder, and swiveling him around in his seat. "That's enough of that language and behavior. There are ladies present."

Maria jumped up and leaned over the table to pick up the scattered blooms.

Wyatt dragged the chair away from the table so Maria could have more room. "You two are going to school if I have to ride over, hogtie you, and drag you to town. Is that clear?"

Jack nodded, the previous day's sullenness returning to his face.

Wyatt looked over at Tim for his agreement.

Tim nodded, misery on his face.

As soon as Wyatt had gotten up, Samantha's stomach had started churning. Although relieved at the twins' acquiescence, she felt annoyed with Wyatt for interfering. With more persuasion, surely the boys would have agreed to go to school.

But what if they hadn't?

Samantha pushed the thought away. She needed to have a firm talk with Wyatt.

❋ ❋ ❋

Wyatt sank the last nail into the porch. With a weary sigh, he wiped his face with his sleeve and sat back against the reinforced railing. In a few minutes he'd need to leave to fetch Christine from school, but for now he savored the peacefulness, although life on a ranch was never entirely quiet.

He could hear the rush of the river as it sped away from the nearby mountainside. At the goat corral, bleating testified to the presence of the animals herded over that morning. In the house, the women conversed in Spanish, the soft words rolling around each other.

He wondered how things were faring on his ranch. He had plenty to do there, yet here he was fixin' up someone else's property. Your future property, he reminded himself.

Through the open door, he heard footsteps. *Samantha.* He climbed to his feet.

She came outside. "Mr. Thompson, would you like some lemonade?"

He turned to face her.

She held out a glass. Their hands touched as he took the glass, and she blushed.

He nodded his thanks and drank, grateful for the bite of the tart liquid. After he'd drained the glass halfway, he paused, surveying Samantha. The stained and dirty apron she wore over her black dress a testament to her hard work. Dust feathered the line of her jaw just below her cheek.

Before he could stop himself, he reached over. With one finger, he brushed her face, tracing the smudge. An unexpected shock of energy raced up his fingers. He cupped her chin, wishing he could coax her forward and kiss her.

As if Samantha felt it also, her eyes widened and her soft pink lips parted. Then she stepped back, distancing herself.

"You have dust on your face. I was just wiping it off."

"Oh." She picked up the edge of her apron and scrubbed her skin. Was she trying to wipe away his touch?

Red cheeked, she let her apron fall. "Better?"

"Yes." Better that he not let a smudge of dirt entice him.

Samantha took a deep breath.

He watched her bosom rise and fall. She would look lovely in a low-cut dress. Pale-blue silk. Like Alicia's favorite. But the memory of his wife cooled his thoughts. He lifted his glass, gulped down the remainder of the lemonade, then handed the glass back to her. "Thank you. I'd best be goin'. Need to fetch Christine."

"Mr. Thompson." Samantha clasped both hands in front of her.

"Call me Wyatt."

"Wyatt. I want to thank you for all you've done for us. You've been a good neighbor, and I don't know how I can repay you."

"Out here we all look out for each other."

"Still, I'm very grateful."

He looked around, seeing all the work to be done. "You might have bit off more than you can chew."

She stiffened. A flash of annoyance replaced the gratitude he'd seen in her eyes. "I have iron teeth." She bared them at him.

He couldn't help the laugh rising from his belly. She had a temper, this one. "It isn't your ability to bite that I'm doubtin'."

She lifted her chin.

"Those twins are a handful. It's only goin' to get worse since you don't have a man around to keep them in line."

"You've made your opinion known."

Her tone froze his laughter. "But you haven't listened."

"I don't need your advice, nor your interference with the twins."

"Interference?" Anger coiled around his chest. Didn't the woman realize she'd taken on too much? She'd never be able to handle those boys.

"I would have gotten them to change their minds about school. I just needed a little more time. Then *you* stepped in."

"Good thing too. 'I ain't goin' to no school'," Wyatt mimicked Jack. "He'd dug his heels in like a stubborn calf. When that happens you just have to rope 'em in."

"The boys aren't animals."

"Sometimes they act like it."

"They can be taught civilized manners."

"I'm not sayin' they can't be tamed a bit." In the midst of his annoyance with her, he still admired how anger flared Samantha's prettiness into beauty. Her blue eyes sparked, peach animated her pale skin, and her fiery hair almost crackled around her head in a corona. Her bosom heaved with indignation. It was almost worth arguing with her just to see her response. "Just that you've taken on a lot of responsibilities."

"I can handle them."

Stubborn woman.

"The boys must learn to mind *me*," she said. "And they won't do that if you keep stepping in."

He raised both hands in surrender. "Fine. You deal with them. Just don't come to me when they're runnin' wild, and they've taken your boy with them."

"You need not worry about that."

He swiped his hat off the rail and set it on his head. "Good day, Mrs. Rodriguez." He turned and strode away without a backward glance.

Fine. Let her stand or fall on her own. If she falls, I'll buy her ranch.

Yet for some reason that thought no longer gave him the same sense of satisfaction it once might have.

CHAPTER NINE

Daniel's fidgeting increased the closer they came to town. When his elbow stabbed into her side, Samantha released an impatient breath. Transferring the reins of the buggy into one hand, she patted his knee. "Daniel, why are you so wiggly?"

He shrugged, but his eyebrows winged upward, a sure sign of distress.

Trying to reassure him, she said, "I remember every time I had to attend a new school in a new country, I was nervous. It's not easy...not knowing the routine, not having friends. At least you know the language."

He glanced up at her, his blue eyes vulnerable. Her heart twisted. When they'd lived in town in Argentina, Daniel had enjoyed school. He'd had plenty of friends and a kind teacher. But on the estancia the tutor favored the other grandchildren. His cousins had been cruel or indifferent, and over the last two years, she'd watched her son's cheerful cockiness steadily erode.

She squeezed his knee. "It will be different here. You've already made friends with Christine."

"Aw, she's a girl."

Samantha's lips twitched in an attempt to hold back her smile. "What about Jack and Tim?"

"They don't like me."

"They will. Just give them time."

"What if they don't?"

She understood his unspoken words. His cousins never had.

She looked over at the twins, each riding one of Ezra's horses. Both rode with easy competence, slightly slumping in the saddle, bony wrists and hands protruding from too-short sleeves, split-open boots resting in the stirrups.

She leaned close. "Jack and Tim haven't had much love in their lives. They haven't attended school too often either. This is almost as new for them as for you."

Sudden hope brightened his face.

"In fact"—her voice dropped to a confidential whisper—"I think they might be scared too. I'm sure the other children have made fun of them before...with a drunken father, outgrown clothes. They'll probably need friends just as much as you do."

"Think so?"

"I do."

Daniel inhaled a slow, deep breath, settling back in the buggy seat. He didn't say anything, but Samantha could see she'd given him something new to think about.

If only it were so easy for her to set aside her concerns. What if the other children made fun of him? Or of the twins? What if the teacher was prejudiced? The worrying occupied her mind until they reached the outskirts of town.

Several people going about their business stopped to stare at the Falabellas. Some children playing under the big oak next to the schoolhouse laughed and ran over to them. Samantha reined the horses in to a slow walk. By the time they'd reached the mercantile, a murmuring crowd surrounded them.

Chico, ever the showman, arched his neck and tossed his black mane. Gray Mariposa trotted more sedately at his side. Samantha pulled up before the store. "It's all right," she called out to the children. "You can pet them."

She placed a hand on her son's shoulder. "This is Daniel. He'll tell you all about them." She stepped out of the buggy and handed the reins to the boy. "You stay here with the horses, please, son. The twins need to come inside with me."

Daniel nodded. The other children immediately engulfed him in a storm of rapid questions. Daniel perked up, looking happy and pleased. Chico and Mariposa would smooth out her son's path. But what about her other boys?

Looking up into Jack's green eyes, she could see his reluctance to dismount. A quick glance at Tim's face showed his emotions shuttered away from the world. She didn't blame them for wanting to escape the curious stares and whispers. Nor for not wanting to brave Mrs. Cobb. *She* didn't want to face the woman either. Stiffening her spine, Samantha nodded toward the mercantile, willing the boys to obey her. "Come along, boys."

Slowly, both of them slid off their horses, looping the reins over the hitching rail. They fell into step behind her.

Now for Mrs. Cobb.

The interior of the store hadn't changed over the past two days—jumbled goods, vinegary scent. This time Samantha felt different, wary instead of hopeful. She doubted Mrs. Cobb would welcome the twins' presence. She braced herself in the same way she'd prepared to face her father-in-law—girded in mental protective armor. If only she could shield the twins.

Mrs. Cobb bustled out from a backroom, the false smile pasted on her face melting away when she saw the twins. "Get those hooligans out of here." As if shooing a stray dog out the door, she flapped her hands.

Samantha dropped a hand on each boy's shoulder. Their muscles tensed under her fingers. *How dare the woman treat them like animals.* Next the old witch might grab a broom and start whacking away. Samantha iced her words. "These *customers* require a *complete* set of new clothes, right down to their shoes."

Her words brought the woman to an abrupt halt. "Stay right there, you two." The shopkeeper pointed at the boys. "Don't touch anything. I'll fetch Mr. Cobb."

Samantha raised her eyebrows in the same gesture Don Ricardo had used with those he wanted to intimidate.

It seemed to work. Mrs. Cobb rushed to explain, "He always helps the menfolk."

Samantha's eyebrows stayed lifted. "Very well."

As soon as Mrs. Cobb left the room, Samantha ushered the boys toward the shelves stocked with men's clothes. They needed so much, but because she was unsure about the state of her finances, she'd better just purchase one of everything. After she met with the banker, she could always come back for more. Her gaze strayed to the bolt of green velvet fabric. Maybe she would buy something new for herself.

She picked up a blue denim pair of pants and held it to Jack's waist. Too big. Setting it aside, she chose another pair. Still too big.

From the doorway to the other room, Mrs. Cobb's voice shrilled, "Oh, Mrs. Rodriguez, here is my husband to help you." She walked toward them.

A tall, thin man trailed in her wake. His bulbous, red nose twitched, and he threw a contemptuous glance at the twins.

Samantha's protective hackles rose. She lifted her chin and raised her eyebrows. "The twins need a complete outfitting— from head to toe." She watched disdain war with greed on their faces.

Greed won.

He pointed to a set of wooden shelves tucked in a corner. "Boys' pants over there. The middle pile should fit them."

"Thank you." Samantha kept her tone cool, but lowered her chin a notch. She pulled the top pair of blue denim pants off the shelf and held it up to Jack. It seemed like the correct size. She handed it to him and picked up another pair, measuring it against Tim. The right length and width.

Turning to a rack of shirts, she said, "You two need to have shirts in different colors so your teacher can tell you apart. Blue or tan, which do you want?" She glanced at each of them. Jack shrugged, not meeting her gaze.

Looking like a puppy afraid of punishment for accepting a treat, Tim pointed at a tan shirt.

Samantha smiled, pulling the shirt off the rack and holding it against him. "Very nice." She handed it to him.

A shy smile glimmered in Tim's green eyes, almost making it to his mouth. His expression tugged at her heart, and she had to resist hugging him. Someday she'd like to see him let loose a genuine carefree grin.

She turned to Jack. "Blue for you." She handed him the shirt.

Behind her, Mr. Cobb cleared his throat. "I'll see to the underclothes."

"Thank you, Mr. Cobb. And we'll need boots for each of them." She remembered the hats she'd seen the men wearing. "And hats."

He walked over to a wicker basket overflowing with boots. He sorted through and selected several pairs, then motioned the boys over. He set a boot next to Jack's cut-open boot. "New fashion in footwear, boy?"

Samantha wanted to throttle the man. She balled her hands to restrain herself. "There's no need to ridicule the boy."

Mr. Cobb's gaze slid away from hers. He shook his head. "Wrong size." He tried another boot. "That should work. Your brother will probably take the same size."

Not much time left. Samantha needed to get the children to the schoolhouse. She wanted to talk to the teacher before classes started. "Mr. Cobb, the twins need to change so they can get to school."

He gave such a sharp shake of his head Samantha wondered if he'd cricked his neck.

"Please, Mr. Cobb. They can't go to school looking like that."

He shook his head again.

Samantha lost her attempts to be conciliatory. "Mr. Cobb, I hardly think you're displaying a Christian attitude," she said sharply. "These boys are orphans, and Reverend Norton consigned them to my care. I don't think he'd approve of you not letting them change into decent clothing."

An uncertain look crossed his face, and he ran his hand over his balding head before glancing back at his wife. She shook her head.

Samantha could feel spots of angry color burst out on her cheeks. In a swift movement, she pulled the clothes from the boys' hands, tossing them at the storekeeper. "Keep them. We'll order from the catalog. The boys can wait a few weeks before starting school." She grabbed for both boys' hands. "Come along. We're leaving."

Alarm flared in Mr. Cobb's eyes, and he stepped out of her path. "Now, Mrs. Rodriguez, there's no need to be rash." The words came out in a choked garble. He tossed a fearful glance at his wife.

In response, Mrs. Cobb bustled over, a placating hand raised to stop Samantha. "Mrs. Rodriguez. We spoke overhasty. There's no need to take on so."

Samantha ground her teeth together to keep from responding to the false lilt in the woman's voice. "Then you'll allow them to change?" She nodded at the doorway. "There."

"Of course." Mrs. Cobb shot a stern glance at her husband. "Frank, go with the boys."

Samantha resisted the impulse to dust off her hands. Turning her back to Mrs. Cobb, she pretended to survey the store while she fought to control her temper.

Moments later, the click of several pairs of boots on the wood floor caused her to turn around. The twins, now dressed in their new clothes, shied away from Mr. Cobb's hurried attempts to propel them toward her.

"Thank you, Mr. Cobb. You can leave the boys to me now." She smiled with pride. Although obviously uncomfortable in the stiff new clothes, their sullen looks had vanished. "Very handsome, both of you. Please take your horses, and have Daniel drive the buggy to the livery. I'll meet you there."

Taking a deep breath, she turned toward the Cobbs to finish her shopping list. She'd won the first battle. Now for the schoolteacher.

❋　❋　❋

With her arms laden with school supplies, Samantha hurried out of the mercantile and headed toward the livery stable. Crossing the dirt street, she picked her way around muddy potholes. Today of all days, she needed to keep her clothes immaculate.

She could see the three boys waiting for her outside the wide-open barn door. "Here, boys," she called out, holding up the straps of three brown leather satchels. "One for you." She handed it to Jack. "This one's for you, Tim. And here's yours, Daniel."

Daniel peeked inside. "Candy!" He pulled out a peppermint stick.

"That's for lunch. You each have one. A treat for your first day of school."

"Thanks, Mama."

"There's also a slate, some chalk, paper, and a pencil. And here's your lunch buckets." She handed each one a shiny new tin.

Jack held up his own peppermint stick as if he'd never seen one. His gaze slid to her, then back to the candy. She could see him swallow and wondered what he was thinking.

"Thankee." The words squeezed out in a choked whisper.

The word burrowed into Samantha's heart. She wanted to reach out and pull him into her embrace, but sensed it was too soon. She contented herself with a smile and a light brush of his hair. "You're very welcome."

Tim shuffled his feet. "Thankee," he echoed.

"You're welcome, Tim. Now, all of you go get your lunches out of the buggy and put them inside your buckets."

Samantha draped an arm across Daniel's shoulders and another around Tim's. Regretting the lack of a third arm, she made do with an encouraging smile for Jack. She indicated the school with a lift of her chin. Already she could see other children angling toward the white frame building. "Come along, boys. Your teacher is waiting."

Wearing a green calico dress with a circle brooch pinned to the high neck, the schoolteacher stood on the narrow steps of the schoolhouse talking to a few children, holding the bell in one hand. She looked young and friendly, but that could change in an instant.

Samantha approached the school with tense shoulders, her chin up, and her stomach knotted. *Dear God, please may she be kind to my boys.*

Up close, Samantha confirmed her impression of the teacher's youth. Pretty and petite, she wore her light-brown hair pulled into a braided bun. The teacher's soft gray gaze welcomed the boys. She shot a quick smile at Samantha, then a longer one at the twins. "Jack and Tim Cassidy, I've been hoping you'd come to school."

Samantha's tight shoulders eased a fraction.

The teacher held out her hand. "I'm Miss Stanton."

Samantha lifted her arm from Tim's shoulders and took Miss Stanton's hand. "Mrs. Rodriguez." Like a cat studying a mouse, Samantha watched the teacher's eyes, looking for any reaction to the Spanish surname. When the welcome look didn't change, she relaxed still further. She nudged Daniel forward. "And this is my son, Daniel."

"I'm pleased to meet you, Daniel. I've heard you're from Argentina?"

Daniel nodded.

"Well then, you'll have much to teach us about your country. Perhaps you can give a report on the kinds of animals they have there?"

Animation brightened Daniel's face. "Like the emu and the guanaco and the armadillo? Mama says those animals don't live in Montana."

Miss Stanton laughed. "Yes. And your little horses too."

Warmth kindled in Samantha's heart toward the woman. *Everything's going to be all right.*

Miss Stanton looked over Samantha's shoulder, and a wistful look slid across her face then vanished so quickly Samantha wondered if she'd imagined it. "Nick, I see you've brought the Carter children into town today."

"Mornin', Miss Stanton," a voice said behind Samantha. "Had to pick up some more lumber."

Samantha turned, catching the eye of a green-eyed man whose brown hair waved to his shoulders. In his hands he held a black hat, which, judging by the hatband crease in his locks, he'd just removed. He nodded at her.

Miss Stanton gestured to Samantha. "Mrs. Rodriguez has just moved here from Argentina. Mrs. Rodriguez, this is Mr. Nick Sanders."

"Pleased to meet you, ma'am."

Samantha nodded. "Mr. Sanders."

"I saw your little fellas just now when I stabled my horse. Had a hard time pullin' the children away from them." He waved at a group of children with animated faces clustered near the steps and talking together.

Samantha laughed. "They do have that effect on people." She tapped Daniel's shoulder. "This is my son, Daniel. And I'm sure you know Jack and Tim."

Nick nodded. "Hello, boys." He raised his voice. "Mark, Sara."

Two children broke away from the group and ran to him. "This here's Mark Carter, and this is his sister Sara. The Carters have the ranch next to mine. Children, meet Mrs. Rodriguez and Daniel."

Mark, who looked about Daniel's age, spoke up first. "Pleased to meet you, Mrs. Rodriguez." His blue eyes sparkled, and he smiled hello at Daniel. "Now we'll have more boys than girls in school."

Sara stuck her tongue out at her brother, then turned her back on him, flipping a long brown braid over her shoulder.

A wary look flickered across Mark's face when he looked at the twins. "Hello, Jack, Tim."

The twins both nodded.

Sara bounced on her toes. "Mrs. Rodriguez, my mama is looking forward to meeting you in church on Sunday. Reverend Norton told us you'd be there."

The gossip flies as swiftly in Montana as it does in Argentina. "I look forward to making her acquaintance." Samantha studied the children, trying to size up what kind of friends they'd be to her boys. They seemed pleasant. But it was hard to tell with children. As she'd seen with Daniel's cousins, the most angelic looking could be little fiends.

Sara's face lit up. "There's Christine." She skipped down the stairs, already chattering to her friend before she reached her.

Christine, her blue coat slipping off her shoulders, tucked her hand into Sara's. She tilted a welcoming smile toward Samantha. "Good morning, Mrs. Rodriguez."

"Good morning, my dear."

Miss Stanton touched Daniel's arm. "Come on. I'll show you all where to put your things." The boys trailed after her. Daniel turned for one last look at his mother. Samantha blew him a kiss, and he scrunched a face at her.

Out of the corner of her eye, she saw Wyatt Thompson approach and turned to meet him. As she met Wyatt's gaze, her shoulders stiffened again, and the blood slid faster through her veins. What was it about this man that so affected her?

"Good morning, Mr. Thompson."

He touched the brim of his hat, placing one booted foot on the first stair of the schoolhouse. "Morning, Mrs. Rodriguez." His gaze followed the twins. "Already achieved that touch of polish, I see."

Uncomfortable with his closeness, Samantha shifted her weight back a half step. "Yes, indeed."

He glanced at Nick Sanders. "Sanders. I'll bet you're in town for more lumber."

Nick laughed, his eyes glinting emerald. "Not much of a guess. Although my wife"—he hesitated on the word—"wants some things from Cobb."

Wyatt clapped him on the shoulder. "Still in newly wedded bliss, I see. I remember it well."

Red seeped into Nick's face. "Elizabeth and I were married two weeks ago," he explained to Samantha.

Laughter crinkled the skin around Wyatt's eyes. "Nick built her a house before the wedding. Never saw one go up so fast in my life."

Nick's flush deepened. "It's not completely finished yet. Elizabeth just refused to wait any longer." There was a touch of wonder in his tone.

Emotion welled into Samantha's throat, and she swallowed. She remembered how Juan Carlos had acted those first weeks they were married. Proud, happy, as if not quite believing his own good fortune. What a special time that had been—how she missed him. "I wish you happiness in your marriage, Mr. Sanders."

"Call me Nick, ma'am." The red receded from his cheeks, leaving behind a glow. "Thank you. I'll pass your good wishes to Elizabeth."

"Will I meet her on Sunday?"

"Yes, ma'am."

"I'll look forward to it then."

He sent her a shy grin. "I think you'll become friends."

"Of course."

Nick replaced his hat. "I'd best be goin' after the mail."

Wyatt smiled, although sorrow lingered in his eyes. Was he having similar memories? "See you, Sanders. Don't want to keep your bride waiting."

With a grin and a shake of his head, Nick left.

Samantha watched him walk away, envying him his happiness. Although the pain over her husband's death had lessened over the last two years, true joy eluded her. She glanced at Wyatt's profile. Would those feelings ever return?

❋ ❋ ❋

One foot still perched on the schoolhouse step, Wyatt stared after Nick Sanders's retreating back. Although he wished the man happiness in his new marriage, Nick's obvious joy had jangled the aching, empty place inside Wyatt that still remembered Alicia. Time had scabbed over the wound of her death. But every once in a while something would bump against his heart, reminding him that he hadn't entirely healed. Perhaps he never would.

Next to him, Samantha sighed. "His wife must be very happy."

Wyatt remembered what a glowing bride Elizabeth Hamilton had been. "She sure looked it on her wedding day."

"Don't most brides? I certainly felt that way."

"Most I've seen." He remembered his own wedding—Alicia's radiant countenance, the joy evident through her lace veil. He knew a similar happiness had emanated from his face. He'd been misty-eyed, yet he'd sported a grin that wouldn't quit.

"I'll look forward to meeting Nick's wife."

"I'm sure you'll like her. She came out from Boston last year to stay with the Carters—wealthiest ranchers hereabouts.

For a time the gossips seemed convinced that our banker, Caleb Livingston, would be the lucky man, but Sanders, the dark horse, came from behind and won the fair lady's affection."

"How romantic."

"Speaking of Livingston, here he comes now. That's his nephew, Ben, who's with him—newly come from Boston."

Samantha turned, surveying the banker. "Oh good, I planned on going to the bank next."

"Well, looks like the bank is coming to you."

She smiled, playfully wrinkling her nose at him, then turned to face the new arrivals.

Livingston, dressed in a navy broadcloth business suit, stopped in front of them, Ben by his side. Next to them, Wyatt felt grubby in his denims and tan shirt.

Livingston nodded at him. "Thompson." He directed a look of admiration at Samantha.

For some reason that irritated Wyatt.

"Don't tell me," said the fellow. "You must be Ezra's niece, Mrs. Rodriguez. I've heard of your…" He glanced over at Wyatt, the right side of his mouth crooking upward. "Falabellas."

Samantha cocked an eyebrow at Wyatt. "Everyone seems to have heard of my little horses."

"To be expected." Livingston drew her attention back to him. "I'm Caleb Cabot Livingston, and this is my nephew, Benjamin Cabot Grayson."

Ben bowed, a miniature of his uncle, in his own navy suit. "I'm pleased to meet you, Mrs. Rodriguez." His words were clipped in Boston precision, but Wyatt knew his fancy manners and innocent brown gaze melted all the ladies, including his own daughter. Somebody needed to show that boy what it took to be a man in the West.

Wyatt could see Samantha's thoughts flit across her face: *What a handsome boy. So well mannered. So different from the twins.* He knew she'd say something about those twins, and she didn't disappoint him.

"You might have heard, Ben, that I've taken in the Cassidy twins. I hope you'll be friends with them."

"Of course, ma'am." Sincerity radiated from his face. "I'd better get inside." He bowed again, then turned and trotted up the stairs into the building.

For a moment Livingston couldn't disguise his annoyance. "I thought Reverend Norton planned on shipping those two incorrigibles off to an orphanage."

Samantha bristled like a provoked porcupine. "No child deserves to live in an orphanage."

Wyatt choked off a laugh. *Not a good move, Livingston, disparaging her precious twins.*

The banker made a quick recovery. He smiled, showing his straight teeth. "A loving home will be good for them. If anyone can tame those boys, Mrs. Rodriguez, I'm sure it will be you. I wish you the best."

The militant look in Samantha's eyes calmed. "Thank you, Mr. Livingston," she said, her voice still crisp. "I know it won't be easy."

"You're showing true Christian compassion, Mrs. Rodriguez. I admire you for it."

Wyatt didn't like the blush spreading over Samantha's porcelain skin. *Hypocrite. He dislikes the idea of those boys being around as much as I do.* He'd never realized how the handsome banker oozed charm like a swamp seeping mud. He'd always seemed a businesslike man, even if he had a mite too many upper-class

Boston notions for Wyatt's taste. A little bud of jealousy unfolded in his chest.

Livingston crooked his arm to her. "There's some business I need to discuss with you, Mrs. Rodriguez. May I escort you to the bank, so we can go over your accounts? I'll make sure you are well taken care of."

"Thank you, Mr. Livingston." Samantha slid her arm through the banker's, slanting an almost flirtatious smile up at him.

The jealous bud hardened inside Wyatt. She'd never smiled at him like that. *What am I thinking? I don't need Samantha Rodriguez to flirt with me.*

Samantha flicked a little wave at him. "Good day, Mr. Thompson."

Livingston nodded. "Thompson."

Rather than watch them stroll together to the bank, Wyatt headed toward the mercantile, deliberately shifting his focus to the list of supplies Mrs. Toffels had given him. Yet he couldn't stop the niggling thread of awareness that followed Samantha and Livingston.

CHAPTER TEN

Samantha enjoyed the sensation of walking down the street with her hand tucked into a gentleman's arm. Under her feet, the dirt road still held its springtime sponginess. The banker guided her around the remaining mud holes with the air of a Sir Walter Raleigh.

It had been so long since she'd been the recipient of a chivalrous gentleman's attention. And while she wasn't sure she liked him, he certainly was handsome...

She glanced up at his profile, admiring the perfect line of his nose, the high angle of his cheekbone. A picture of Wyatt rose in comparison—skin more tanned, a Roman nose that fit his broader face, gray eyes glowing silver when he teased her. She nudged the thought aside. Why was she even thinking about that annoying man?

Mr. Livingston cleared his throat. "I hope your journey wasn't difficult."

Samantha pursed her lips in a rueful grimace. "From South America to Montana? Challenging. I relaxed when Daniel was sleeping, and I didn't have to worry about the little monkey climbing the rigging, falling overboard, or absorbing the, the... less than gentlemanly language of the sailors. But the ocean was beautiful. I could stare at it for hours, watching the light change against the waves. So hypnotic."

A kindred look flashed in his brown eyes. "One of the things I miss is the ocean. I spent some of my life in Boston. My grandparents had a pleasure yacht, and as a boy, I finagled time aboard whenever I could."

"The West has its own beauty," Samantha said. "I love the grandeur of the mountains. There's a wildness about the land-scape that is so different from the mountains of Europe. The Alps, for example, appear more civilized. All those quaint little villages perched on the mountainside."

"You sound like you've traveled widely."

"My father worked in the diplomatic corps, and we lived in Germany, Spain, and then in South America."

He came to a stop in front of a whitewashed brick building. "Perhaps we can further discuss your European adventures. I'd like to invite you to dine with my sister and me. She's been miss-ing elevated female society."

"Thank you for your invitation. Perhaps when I'm more set-tled." Was there really a dearth of educated females in Sweetwater Springs? The image of Mrs. Cobb sprang to her mind. That would be a pity. Not that a female needed to be educated to be a good friend. Her dear Maria was an uneducated Indian peasant, yet had always been one of Samantha's staunchest supporters. But Elizabeth Sanders sounded interesting. And she'd come from Boston. Samantha wondered why Mr. Livingston's sister didn't like her.

He guided her up the two wooden stairs, across the small porch to the door, upon which letters in black paint spelled out Livingston's Boston Bank. "Welcome to my bank, Mrs. Rodriguez. Not very imposing compared to what you're used to, I'm sure."

"Nonsense, Mr. Livingston. This building is perfectly appro-priate to Sweetwater Springs."

"I'm only sorry a lady such as yourself has to enter it."

"Whatever do you mean?"

"I mean that you, as a woman, shouldn't have to trouble yourself about business affairs. I hope you will allow me to advise you."

Shades of my father-in-law, only said with much more charm. "So kind of you to offer. Of course, I'll listen to your advice. It would be foolish of me to do otherwise." *Just don't expect me to follow it.*

He bowed slightly, then opened the door, stepped back, and allowed her to walk inside.

Behind a high wooden counter, an elderly man jerked his head up from the ledger he'd been studying. Underneath the green visor he wore on his balding head, his faded blue eyes surveyed Samantha. "Good morning, Mr. Livingston. Ma'am."

"Horace. I'd like you to meet Ezra's niece, Mrs. Rodriguez. Mrs. Rodriguez, this is my clerk, Horace Hatter."

"Pleased to meet you, ma'am. Ezra and I were good friends when we were young. Death of his fiancée changed him something fierce. Never was the same after that."

"Yes, I know."

Mr. Livingston placed his hand on the small of her back. With the other, he waved toward a closed door. "This way, please."

Once inside the room, she let her gaze rove over the office, past the large mahogany desk to a gilded birdcage in the corner. At their entrance, three finches fluttered as if welcoming them. "Oh, you have birds. My husband had the most dreadful parrot. The nasty thing would bite anyone but Juan Carlos. And the things it said! I almost wrung its neck many a time. These little ones look much more peaceful."

"They are." He waved toward a straight-back wooden chair in front of his desk. "Won't you please sit down?" He looked over at a silver tea service resting on a small table. "Would you like me to have Horace make you some tea?"

"No, thank you. I'm fine. I'm eager to get started."

He reached for a sheaf of papers. "I anticipated that you would be paying me a visit and prepared Ezra's paperwork for you to see."

"Thank you."

He sighed, concern shadowing his brown eyes. He ran the tips of his fingers over the edge of the papers. "I must be blunt, Mrs. Rodriguez. These last years, Ezra allowed things at the ranch to slip. He seemed to just stop caring. There's still some money left in his account, but it won't last long."

"How long?"

"With careful husbandry, you'll be able to outfit the ranch with what it needs—repairs, new stock, wages for the hands. But if you don't start turning a profit, you'll be wiped out by winter."

Six months. "I see."

He raised his hand as if to stop her from saying more. "There's more bad news. The property taxes haven't been paid for the past two years."

"Would the bank be willing to extend me a loan to pay the taxes?"

"Frankly, Mrs. Rodriguez, I don't feel comfortable with that idea. Ezra's property is in poor condition—not good collateral. And I think turning it around will be beyond your capabilities—beyond any woman's. Ranching is a hard life."

Samantha strove to keep her tone even. "I'm aware of that, Mr. Livingston. For the last two years, I've been living on a ranch in Argentina."

"Not the same as running a place, I'm afraid. I'd advise you to sell and move to town."

"To town?"

"Wyatt Thompson has been wanting to buy the property. I'm sure he'll make you a fair offer."

Wyatt wants to buy my ranch.

A feeling of betrayal slithered into her heart. Despite her rejection of his advice, she'd thought he'd been concerned for her, when all the time he'd just wanted to get his hands on her land.

Not sure if she felt more annoyed with Mr. Livingston or with Wyatt, Samantha's anger flared. "I'm not interested in selling." *Especially not to Wyatt Thompson.*

"I can understand your emotional attachment to the property. Perhaps when you've had a chance to think more rationally on the subject…"

Biting back an acerbic reply, she said, "I've already given it much thought. But thank you for your concern."

She retained her calm facade while they closed the conversation, and Mr. Livingston ushered her out of the office.

Out in the street, she expelled her breath in a huff, then started making a mental list of all she needed to do. She'd show these men that a woman could work a ranch!

✻ ✻ ✻

Sunday morning, Jack, dressed in the crisply ironed clothes Samantha had laid out for him, crossed his arms across his chest and rocked back on his heels, as if digging his new boots into the wooden floor. The early sunlight shining through the kitchen windows played across his freckled face. "I ain't goin' to no church," he said, his mouth set in the stubborn look now familiar to Samantha.

She paused in the act of pouring milk into the glasses on the table. Behind her at the stove, Maria continued swirling batter around the bottom of a frying pan to make the crepe-like German pancakes. Samantha couldn't wait to introduce the twins to her favorite Sunday morning breakfast.

In the last few days, the twins had been quiet and obedient. Yesterday the three boys had groomed the horses, mucked out their stalls, cleaned the wagon they'd use to drive to church today, and taken baths without a fuss. Samantha had begun to think they were settling in. Jack's words of rebellion caught her off guard. She glanced over at Tim, already sitting at the table next to Daniel, catching the distressed looked he aimed at his brother.

She set down the pitcher. "Why not?"

Jack tightened his arms across his chest. "I just ain't."

Samantha inhaled a deep breath of the bacon-and-pancake scented air. "Church is a special place where we worship the Lord."

"There ain't no God."

As she read the painful meaning behind the boy's words, Samantha's stomach tightened. She motioned for Jack to join the other boys.

Without uncrossing his arms, he thumped himself down next to his brother.

Smoothing the blue-striped cotton apron she'd tied over her black cashmere dress, she took her seat. She looked at Tim for confirmation. "Do you really believe there is no God?"

He looked down at his plate. "Not for me," he mumbled.

"Why do you think that?"

Jack interjected, "We prayed when Ma was sick. She died."

Daniel's blue eyes lit up in understanding, and he bounced in his chair, eager to share. "When my papa was hurt in the accident, I prayed for him to get better. I sure was mad at God when my papa died."

Samantha nodded in agreement. "I was too. I also lost my mother and father in the same accident." She reached over to touch Tim's shoulder. "I still miss them very much, just as I know you two must miss your mother. I tell myself that we all have to die at some time. It's hard to lose the people we love. We can't always know why bad things happen. But I do know, most times, I see good things coming out of bad."

Jack's mouth firmed. "Our ma dyin' weren't no good."

"No, it wasn't."

"Our pa was a mean cuss."

"But you're here now with Daniel and me. I hope you think that's good." She held Jack's gaze, until he ducked his head. "I know it's a tough change. With time, it will get better."

In silence, Maria glided over to the table with a platter of the wide, thin pancakes and handed them to Samantha. She took one and set the platter on the table. "Sunday breakfast before church is always special. I used to eat these as a child." She spread butter over the pancake, then reached for a jar of Mrs. Toffels's strawberry jam. "First butter it, then add the jam. After that, roll it up." She demonstrated.

Daniel's winged black eyebrows rose, and he wiggled, reaching for the platter. "I remember how, Mama."

"Even after two years," she teased.

"Yep."

"Well then, go ahead." She passed him the plate.

"Thanks, Mama."

Samantha smiled at Jack. "I've been looking forward to today. Daniel and I haven't had a chance to attend church for quite a while. Having you two attend with us will make me very happy."

Jack's set mouth relaxed, but his arms remained crossed.

Samantha handed the platter to Tim. "Help yourself."

Jack sat in silence for another few minutes.

Samantha cut up her pancake and proceeded to eat a few bites. "Could you just go for me?"

"No, ma'am, I cain't do it."

"You're sure?"

"Ain't goin' to no church."

"What about you, Tim?" She held her breath waiting for his answer.

Tim avoided Jack's gaze. "I'll go," he mumbled staring down at his plate.

Jack looked like he'd been struck. He opened his mouth to say something.

Although pleased with Tim's acquiescence, Samantha shook her head at Jack, warning him to remain silent.

Jack slumped in his chair.

"You'll stay here and help Manuel."

"How come they don't have to go?"

She fixed him with a stern gaze. "Maria and Manuel are Catholic. They have to wait for the traveling priest to arrive before they can attend a service. Although they are welcome to worship with us, they aren't comfortable with the idea. That's why they aren't going to church."

With a furtive sideways glance at her, Jack picked up his fork and began to eat. In a few minutes the militant look on his face faded to normal boy-with-an-appetite, and he dug into his breakfast.

Samantha wished she could feel as calm as she tried to portray. The boys' revelation of their lack of religious convictions disturbed her. Her faith had been the one thing she could cling to when life seemed too painful to go on—a solace the twins had never found. Somehow she'd have to help them find faith, in her, in themselves, and most importantly, in the Almighty.

CHAPTER ELEVEN

Wyatt glanced one more time into the looking glass in his bedroom, making sure his black tie sat straight. A darned nuisance, but a necessary part of Sunday attendance. Besides he was going courtin' today. A man needed to dress the part.

The navy broadcloth suit fit snug across his shoulders, and he knew his gray shirt matched his eyes. Alicia had certainly told him so. She'd bought him his first gray shirt. Ever since, he'd worn them in her memory. Humming a snatch of tune, he flicked a speck of lint off the lapel.

Ready.

In the hall, he could hear the clatter of Christine's boot heels as she skipped down the steps. Mrs. Toffels had made her a new blue dress, and she'd chattered away all through breakfast about how excited she was to wear it to church today.

With a smile, he strode out of the room to follow his daughter. It pleased him to spoil her—giving her everything he'd lacked as a child. She would never have to do without, never be abused, never be hurt. He'd see to that. His daughter would never need anything.

Except a mother, a little voice whispered in his head.

Well, he'd been planning to remedy that ever since he'd met Edith Grayson, the banker's sister. He'd been attracted to her cool dark looks, calm ladylike demeanor, and how well she'd raised her son. She'd be the perfect new mother for Christine. It was time to implement his plan and begin courting her.

An image of Samantha Rodriguez rose in his mind. Opinionated and temperamental, what with her ridiculous toy horses, determination to collect wayward boys, and a fiery beauty so different from Edith's, she'd been a difficult woman to banish from his thoughts. His body started to respond to his picture of Samantha, how it would feel to kiss her, to…

It's Sunday—not a day to think of physical pleasures.

Wyatt ran his hand across his face, as if trying to erase his fantasy. Although the good Lord who'd created Eve for Adam would surely understand, for his own peace of mind, he needed to put Samantha from his thoughts. It had been too long since he'd seen Edith. Once he was in her presence, things would be back to normal.

He strode into the kitchen, sniffing in appreciation at the scent of the apple pie resting on the stovetop. "Ready?" he asked Mrs. Toffels.

"Just let me finish packing the food for the Nortons." Wearing her best black silk dress, a froth of lace pinned to the collar with a pearl bar pin, the housekeeper leaned over a woven basket set on the table. "I know Mrs. Norton has been ill this week and probably hasn't been up to cooking. Let's see…" She touched her finger to the side of her cheek. "Cold chicken, cold potatoes, a jar of my pickles"—her finger tapped with each word—"and the apple pie." She turned toward the partially opened window and let out a cry. "My pie!"

Bustling over to the window, she threw up the sash and leaned out, apparently searching the ground. "It's gone."

Wyatt pointed to the stove. A pie rested on the top. "There it is."

"No, that's the one I made for Sunday dinner. I set the Nortons' pie on the windowsill to cool before I put it in the basket."

As he surveyed the kitchen, looking for the missing dessert, Wyatt felt his brows pull together. If they lived in town, he'd have assumed some of the boys had stolen it. Certainly that had been the only way he'd ever tasted sweets. But here, the hands had already left for the south pasture.

"We don't have time to look for it, or we'll be late for church."

Mrs. Toffels's mouth rounded, crinkling her face in distress.

"Just give them the other one. We can do without for one Sunday." He opened the door and stalked outside and over to the window. He looked around, checking for footprints that would account for the missing pie. Everything looked fine. If a human or animal had stood by the window, there was no sign of prints among the tulip bed. He shrugged his shoulders and headed for the barn.

Pushing open the barn door, he blinked in the dimmer light. "Harry," he called.

The boy poked his head up from the nearest stall, placing the currycomb he'd been using on the top of the wall. "Yes, Mr. Thompson?"

"You know anything about Mrs. Toffels's apple pie?"

Harry squinted his hazel eyes. He ran a hand through his hair, making it stand on end like an orange feather duster. "Her pie?"

"It's missing from the kitchen windowsill."

His Adam's apple bobbed up and down. "I didn't take it."

Wyatt studied the boy's face, but saw only honest bewilderment. "You see anything unusual?'

"No, sir."

"Well then, it seems we have us a mystery. Go get your gun belt. Keep your Colt with you. Keep an eye out, hear?"

"Yes, Mr. Thompson."

"Now go get the team and help me hitch up the buggy, will you?"

The boy turned and with his gangly gait loped down the aisle.

Wyatt stepped back to the open barn door, staring at the house, disturbed by the implications of the stolen pie. An honest wanderer would have knocked at the door and asked to be fed.

Varmint.

Human or animal? Most likely human. An animal would have left the remains of the pie. And Wyatt Thompson didn't cotton to varmints on his property—around his daughter. He'd take whatever steps needed to protect what was his.

※ ※ ※

Samantha approached the white frame church, trepidation tightening her stomach. What would these people be like? Would they accept her Catholic son?

She resisted reaching for Daniel's hand as he half walked, half bounced along next to her. Her son had passed the age where he wanted to hold hands with his mother. On her other side, Tim radiated reluctance with every heavy step. She wondered how he'd fare without his twin by his side.

She could see people clustered around the outside of the building, a white clapboard with a bell tower, a cross spiking the sun-drenched blue sky. It was clear the congregation enjoyed mingling in the balmy spring weather before the service. She tried not to allow herself to scan for Wyatt; nevertheless, her gaze searched for a tall, dark man.

When she reached the first group, she recognized Nick Sanders, standing with another man and two women. Dressed in a black suit, he had a protective hand placed on the back of a blonde woman whose blue lace shirtwaist and skirt aroused Samantha's immediate envy. She smoothed down her hated black dress. That must be his wife, she thought.

Nick looked up and noticed her. He leaned over and said something to his wife, and she turned toward Samantha, a welcoming smile on her face.

Nick stepped over to greet her. "Good morning, Mrs. Rodriguez. I'd like you to meet my wife, Elizabeth." He ushered Samantha over to stand with their group. The quiet pride in his voice reminded her of Juan Carlos when he'd introduced her to new acquaintances, and she had a quick stab of missing him.

"Mrs. Sanders." Samantha held out her hand for a brief clasp. "Your husband assured me we'd become friends."

Elizabeth Sanders gave her husband a radiant gaze, a slight flush brushing her glowing skin. Her blue eyes matched the color of the azure sky arching overhead. "Then it must be true. Please call me Elizabeth." She touched Samantha's elbow. "Mrs. Rodriguez, as my newest friend, I'd like you to meet my oldest friend, Pamela Carter, and her husband John. Pamela and I grew up together in Boston." She extended an arm to indicate her friend.

The forest-green silk of Pamela's dress swished as she stepped forward to take Samantha's hand. Unlike the beautiful Elizabeth, Mrs. Carter's plump-cheeked, hooked-nose face could only be considered plain, until one saw the warmth shining from her brown eyes. "Elizabeth and I know what it's like to move to the West, Mrs. Rodriguez," she said, letting go of Samantha's hand. "It can be a bit of an adjustment. Let us know how we can help."

Samantha felt an affinity with both women, and her nervousness subsided. "Just having new friends is wonderful. I envy you your long relationship. My parents were in the diplomatic corps, and we moved around so much I never had friends for more than a few years."

John Carter, a narrow-faced older man with thinning sandy hair, nodded in understanding. His kind blue eyes held their own welcome for her. "Nick and I are Westerners, born and bred." He cupped his wife's elbow. "But we certainly have welcomed the beautiful women who've made Sweetwater Springs their home." He shot a teasing glance at Nick.

Nick's cheeks reddened, but he grinned and nodded.

Three children rushed up. Samantha recognized Mark and Sara Carter, who boisterously greeted Daniel and Tim. But she hadn't met the little girl trailing after them. The delicate-looking child sidled close to Pamela Carter. Long brown curls framed her dainty face; dark-lashed blue eyes peeked at Samantha before she ducked behind her mother. Sara and the little angel wore forest-green dresses, miniatures of their mother's gown.

Elizabeth laughed. "That's exactly the same reaction Lizzy had to me when we first met." She reached behind Pamela and picked up the child. Lizzy buried her head in Elizabeth's shoulder "Now, my dear, I know you aren't as shy as you're pretending to be."

John Carter reached over and gently tugged one of Lizzy's long curls. "Mrs. Rodriguez, this is our youngest, Lizzy."

Elizabeth chimed in, "And my goddaughter." She bent to her and said softly, "Remember the horses I told you about?"

The child lifted her head enough to glance at Samantha. "Baby horses?"

What a sweet child. "Yes, I have the little horses. But even though they're small, they're not babies."

Raising her eyebrows, Lizzy looked around.

Samantha interpreted her unspoken question. "They're back at the ranch. We used the big horses today."

Lizzy's pink lips puffed in a pout.

Samantha couldn't resist. "You'll have to visit so you can see them for yourself."

The child nodded gravely.

Nick laughed. "Mrs. Rodriguez, you've become the newest captive of our little bird. No one can refuse her anything." He reached over to take the child from his wife. "We'd better get inside."

Elizabeth squeezed Samantha's hand. "Mrs. Norton is ill. I'm playing the organ for her. We'll talk after church."

They walked away, still carrying Lizzy. Pamela waved toward her daughter. "You'll think we all spoil her."

John's grin crinkled the sun lines around his eyes. "And you'd be right." His smile faded. "She's always been frail. We've almost lost her several times."

Pamela nodded. "Every day is a gift."

Samantha's heart squeezed into her throat, and she thanked God for Daniel's robust health. He'd missed most of the childhood illnesses, instead being inclined to sprained ankles and broken arms. Those had been bad enough. She looked over at her son, chattering away to the Carter children, and couldn't bear the thought of losing him. He was all she had.

Over to one side, Tim stood by himself, arms hanging at his sides, a drooping, solitary figure in the midst of all the people. *No, not all I have,* she corrected herself. *My family is growing. And so is my circle of friends.*

She gestured to Tim. "Too bad more parents don't consider their children to be blessings."

"Some people don't deserve to be parents." John growled the worlds out.

"I can't help but agree."

John narrowed his eyes. Samantha could tell he was looking at the Cobbs. "Some folks will say you've gone and shot yourself in the foot, taking on those boys. But I admire you for it."

In the steeple, the bell tolled. Her heart beat in turn with the bell. The previous nervousness that had dissipated during her conversation with the Sanderses and the Carters poured back into her stomach. She hoped she wouldn't make a mistake in following the service. Everyone would notice.

Pamela nodded toward the church. "Usually Elizabeth and Nick sit with us. But today they'll be near the organ. Why don't you and the boys sit in our pew?"

"Thank you." Samantha dropped her voice to a whisper. "It's been so long since I've attended a Protestant church, I've been afraid of doing something wrong."

Samantha's confession didn't seem to bother Pamela. "Sit next to me. I'll nudge you when necessary."

Samantha collected Daniel and Tim. With a hand on each boy's shoulder, she followed the Carter family into the church, all of them trooping down the aisle. Inside, light flooded through the clear glass windows.

Curious glances fell on her from left and right. It was impossible to ignore them. Her cheeks warmed, and she lifted her chin, fighting the tension that locked her stomach tighter than her corset. For the last two years, any attention directed at her had always been critical. *It's normal for the congregation to be interested in new people,* she reminded herself.

Pamela stopped beside one of the wooden front pews. "You children can sit together provided you are well behaved."

Pamela didn't know her Daniel. Maybe the novelty of a new church would keep him quiet. To insure his cooperation, she held on to his shoulder, letting the other children file in first. She seated herself next to Daniel, Pamela on her other side.

Samantha looked around, liking the simplicity of the room. No dimly lit ornate interior, no scent of incense. No niches with saints, rows of candles burning before them. The only candles were white tapers set into heavy brass candlesticks on a linen-draped altar.

A wooden cross hung above, without, she felt thankful to see, the tortured figure of Christ drooping from it. A green glass vase set between the candlesticks held red tulips like those she'd seen growing in Wyatt's yard. She wondered if he'd brought them.

As if prompted by her thoughts, she saw Wyatt, holding Christine by the hand, striding down the aisle. Dressed in a navy suit with a gray shirt, he seemed to fill the room with his presence. Mrs. Toffels followed at a more sedate pace.

Samantha's heartbeat sped up. Annoyed by her response to him, she froze her gaze ahead of her.

Elizabeth began to play the organ. Samantha recognized the music of Johann Sebastian Bach, although she couldn't pinpoint the exact piece. Her parents had loved Bach's music. In Germany, they'd had plenty of opportunities to hear his work in church and by going to concerts. It had been a long time though, and she let herself be caught up in a wave of nostalgia.

The memories carried her through the rest of the service, and she followed Pamela's lead, rising and sitting, singing, and being still. It wasn't too different from what she'd remembered. Occasionally she did have to place a restraining hand on Daniel's leg when he wiggled too much.

Elizabeth chose another piece by Bach for a recessional. As they rose to leave, Samantha stepped out into the aisle at the same time Wyatt emerged from his pew.

Underneath her stiff corset, her stomach tightened. Why did this man so unnerve her?

"Morning, Samantha."

"Good morning, Wyatt."

Christine rounded Wyatt's side, tucked her arm through Sara's, and the two started whispering.

As Wyatt watched his daughter, his gray eyes silvered in amusement. He shrugged. "Little girls. At least they didn't squeal when they met up. Not bein' able to chatter for a whole hour is difficult."

"Or sit still." She glanced over her shoulder to see Daniel half skip, half walk down the side aisle, then slither through the crowd by the door, Tim behind him. She shook her head. She'd catch up with them later.

From the corner of her eye, she could see several women stop to observe them. Her cheeks warmed. She pretended not to notice, instead falling into line with the congregation.

Wyatt walked beside her. "Settlin' in all right?"

"Just fine, thank you." She remembered that he wanted to buy her ranch. Soon, they'd need to have a little discussion about that topic. He needed to know her ranch *wasn't* for sale. She tried to ignore him standing next to her, but it was difficult when her awareness of him jangled her nerves. Annoyance, she tried to tell herself. But she knew better.

Outside, Reverend Norton stood shaking each person's hand, his white hair ruffled by the breeze. "Mrs. Rodriguez, how nice to see you again. I'm only sorry I haven't had a chance to introduce you to my dear wife. I'm afraid she's home in bed."

"I'm sorry to not meet—"

"She'll be sorry too. I'm sure she'll be well by next Sunday." He looked past her shoulder. "Ah, our banker and his sister, Mrs. Grayson. Have you been introduced to them?"

"Mr. Livingston and I have met. However, I haven't had a chance to meet Mrs. Grayson," Samantha said.

"Well, let me remedy that." He performed the introductions.

Edith Grayson's lavender silk shirtwaist and skirt with its darker velvet trim made Samantha feel dowdy. Diamond drops glittered in her ears. Like her brother, Edith Grayson had striking chocolate-brown eyes and dark hair. They shared the same straight nose, although her mouth was wider, the full lips so lush and pink Samantha wondered if she painted them.

Those lips parted in a smile. "Mrs. Rodriguez, ever since my brother told me about you, I've been looking forward to making your acquaintance."

Caleb Livingston, tall and handsome in a different brown suit than the one he'd worn the day of their meeting, looked on with approval.

Samantha hoped she'd like the sister better than she liked the banker. "And I you."

"I understand you, too, are a widow?"

"Yes."

"We have much in common, then. Widows trying to raise our only sons in the Wild West. Is your loss recent?" She glanced at Samantha's black dress.

"Over two years. But in Argentina, a widow always wears black. I'm looking forward to escaping the color."

Mrs. Grayson smiled in understanding, and Samantha warmed to her.

"I'm afraid your choices in Sweetwater Springs will be very limited. But one manages." Edith shrugged her shoulders and ruefully pursed her full lips; a dimple lingered in the corner of her mouth.

Samantha thought of her limited bank balance. "I don't know that it will matter. I'll need to concentrate my spending on the ranch and the boys. You know how fast they outgrow their clothes." She smiled with pride. "I'm no longer just the mother of one."

Edith gestured at Tim, lingering on the edge of the crowd. "He must be one of those twins I've heard about."

"Yes, Tim Cassidy."

"Where's the other?"

"At home helping with chores."

"Are you going to trade them back and forth? One every other week?"

"I hope not." The wry tone puckered Samantha's mouth.

Edith laughed. "Sometimes just one boy can be difficult. I don't envy you three. Best of luck."

Wyatt joined them. "Good day, Mrs. Grayson."

Her lips widened into a sensual smile. "Mr. Thompson."

"I see you've met my neighbor."

"We were just getting acquainted. Tell me, Mr. Thompson..." Mrs. Grayson lowered her voice.

Mr. Livingston chose that moment to slide his hand under Samantha's elbow. "Perhaps I could escort you to your buggy."

"It's just a wagon."

"A practical vehicle." He ushered her away.

She cast one final glance at Wyatt, absorbed in his conversation with Mrs. Grayson. She swallowed the frisson of jealousy rising in her throat when they didn't seem to notice her leaving.

They deserve each other.

But why didn't that thought make her feel better?

＊ ＊ ＊

Wyatt focused his eyes on Edith Grayson's mouth. He'd wanted to kiss her ever since he'd set eyes on those lushly contoured lips, one of the reasons he'd put her on the top of his prospective wife list. Yet today, stare as he might, Edith's sensual lips failed to rouse his former responsiveness, and the words that issued from them buzzed in his ears. His attention wandered, following Samantha and Livingston.

"Mr. Thompson," Mrs. Grayson said. "Wyatt." Her voice softened to a velvet purr. She placed her hand on his arm.

Like a hooked fish, his attention reeled back to her.

"My brother wanted me to invite you to dine with us next Sunday after the service."

He paused before responding. If he accepted, everyone at church would know. *Samantha would know.* Somehow he didn't like that thought. Besides, he'd have to make special arrangements for Christine and Mrs. Toffels to get home. It felt like a larger commitment than he wanted to make. "Sounds like a mighty fine invitation, Mrs. Grayson—"

"Call me Edith."

"Edith. It's just that I'll have my daughter and Mrs. Toffels with me."

Her brows arched in a question.

"Your housekeeper? Couldn't she stay home with Christine next Sunday?"

He laughed. "Not Mrs. Toffels. To her it's a sacrilege when there's too much snow to get to church. She insists we hold prayers anyway. She wouldn't cotton to missing Sunday service."

"Oh."

"And I don't want Christine to miss. Her mother wouldn't be pleased with me."

"Her mother?"

"I'm sure she still watches out for her daughter. Don't you ever have that feeling with your husband?"

"No." She said the word with a flat intonation. "My husband…" Her lashes lowered.

Wyatt shifted in discomfort. He wasn't sure if she thought he was being ridiculous, or perhaps he'd stirred up old grief. That thought brought remorse. He knew only too well how unexpectedly a memory could strike, causing old pain. He'd have to make amends.

"If you and your brother wouldn't mind company some evening, I'd be glad to drop by."

Her lips curved into a sultry smile. "How about Wednesday? Come for dinner."

"This week, I'm busy with ranch work. How 'bout the end of the month? The moon should be full. Make the ride home easy."

"That would be delightful."

"It will indeed." He bowed slightly. "If you'll excuse me, I need to find my daughter and get her home."

"I'll see you next Wednesday." She turned, gliding away.

He watched her go, following the slow swish of her small bustle, and wondered why he didn't feel more excitement about next Wednesday.

CHAPTER TWELVE

Two weeks later, her dress kilted up to the tops of her boots to allow freedom of movement, Samantha stomped her foot on the top edge of the shovel, feeling satisfaction when the blade slid deep into the earth. The afternoon sun beat down on her back.

A long brownish-pink worm slithered back into the uncovered dirt, a sign of the richness of the soil. After several hours of digging, she'd almost managed to turn the dirt in the area of the garden she'd marked for potatoes. In another corner, Maria planted beans, while Manuel worked on the rows of corn.

In the next few days they'd plant squash, pumpkins, tomatoes, carrots, peas, cucumbers, and beets. Samantha eventually intended to set out an herb garden and expand the small orchard.

Propping the shovel against her leg, she rolled her shoulders trying to relax the cramp in her shoulder blades. Her body longed to stop and rest, but stubbornness kept her going. She had a goal to reach and a family to feed.

Working within the confines of Ezra's garden patch had been relatively easy, the ground soft from many years of tilling. But Samantha had visions of a much larger plot—one big enough to feed them throughout the year, and maybe bring in some much needed cash. But breaking the unworked soil was a much harder job. She needed to enlist the help of the boys when they came home from school.

With a sigh, she straightened, rubbing her back. Underneath her leather work gloves, the skin of her palms burned; she could feel blisters forming. On the estancia, Don Ricardo wouldn't allow her to work, and she'd lost the calluses she'd happily acquired during her marriage from hours of digging in her garden. The skin of her hands had become soft. So had her muscles. Or was it that she was getting older…?

No. Thirty-one wasn't old. She pushed a tendril of hair out of her eyes, tucking it under the straw hat she wore, hoping she hadn't left a muddy streak on her face. Sometimes she still felt like a young woman, although not now when her whole body ached from hard labor.

The overturned earth lay dark and rich beneath her feet. She inhaled the loamy scent rising from the ground and looked toward the mountain, where purple rocky ridges gave way to green tree-shaded sides. The mountain marked the edge of her property, and she wondered if she'd ever find time to explore its wonders.

The month of April was flying by, and she'd been so busy getting the house, barn, and garden in order, not to mention dealing with the chickens, goats, horses, and boys, she hadn't even ridden the entire boundaries of the ranch.

She'd entrusted the two hands, Mike and Ernie, with handling the small herd of cattle. As soon as calving season had begun, they'd camped out with the cows. Every few days, one of them would ride in for supplies and report their progress to her. So far they hadn't lost one single calf. She felt confident in their abilities. Still, once she completed the garden, she intended to explore her land.

She glanced over at the large corral where the Falabellas frisked. Mariposa had slowed down over the last week. Her foaling time drew near. Bonita also looked like she'd foal soon, although it would be a while before Pampita's or Bella's babies arrived. Young Chita was the only mare that hadn't been bred in Argentina. Next year, she'd be put to Chico, Samantha's only stallion.

In Argentina, Samantha had varied the studs, having planned on expanding the herd, before she knew she'd be coming to America. She was glad she had. There were no other Falabellas here to breed to.

She leaned on the handle of the shovel. Now that she'd stopped working, the dream she'd had last night—the one she'd tried to avoid all day—caught up with her. It had been a sensual dream, unlike anything she'd ever experienced.

Wyatt kissing her—no, not just kissing her, ravaging her mouth, trailing kisses down her neck and shoulders, making her body weak with need for him. She'd so wanted to give in to him, feeling her resistance melt with every touch of his lips, yet something inside had held her back. She wasn't quite ready to surrender herself to him. Oh, but how she had wanted to.

Something had awoken her, and she'd almost cried out from frustration and disappointment. She'd tried to return to sleep, find her way back into the dream, but slumber had eluded her. When full consciousness had returned, she'd felt ashamed of the cravings of her body—longings she'd thought dead and buried with Juan Carlos. Yet, they'd sprung forth, perhaps stronger from having been dormant, and for a man she wasn't sure she even liked.

A man who seemed interested in Edith Grayson.

She changed her grip on the shovel and sent it deeply into the ground. Work was the answer. Labor until she'd rendered her mind and body too tired to think, much less dream.

❋ ❋ ❋

The late April day had warmed enough for Wyatt to remove his jacket. He leaned against Bill's hindquarters, examining the underside of the hoof he supported in his hand to see if it needed cleaning. Harry had mucked out the stall, and while Wyatt worked, he inhaled the fresh scent of the straw blanketing the floor.

"Wyatt. Wyatt," Mrs. Toffels called from outside the barn.

He heard the anger lacing her tone; his thoughts flew to the whereabouts and safety of his daughter. It took a lot to rile his placid housekeeper—usually when something brought out her mother bear instincts regarding Christine.

"In here." He slid his hand out from under the horse's leg and stood up so his stout housekeeper could see him over the top of the stall.

Mrs. Toffels tottered into the barn, carrying a wicker laundry basket almost as wide as she was, overflowing with folded clothes. Seeing the basket, relief washed over him, and he relaxed. She wouldn't be lugging laundry around if anything were seriously wrong.

Spotting him over the top of the clothes, she changed her direction, making a beeline toward him. She plopped down the basket and straightened, arms akimbo. Under a green gingham dress covered by a spotless white cotton apron, her ample bosom heaved. "Wyatt, someone's stolen your shirt."

"My shirt?"

"Your favorite blue-and-gray-striped flannel one. I didn't notice until I had taken down most of the wash. I had hung that shirt on the end."

"Sure it didn't just blow away?"

As if he'd offended her, Mrs. Toffels drew herself up. "I peg *every* piece of laundry I hang out. That shirt had *three* pins on it."

"Of course." He stopped to think. The men had been out at the south pasture for the entire day, and he'd been about to join them. He'd seen Mrs. Toffels hanging out the wash after they'd left. None of them would have borrowed his shirt. But someone did. Three weeks ago, somebody absconded with the pie. Last week a loaf of bread, cooling on the kitchen windowsill, had vanished. Now his shirt…his *favorite* shirt.

He changed his mind about riding after the men. The varmint would probably head for the mountains, and Wyatt intended to be right behind him. "I'll take care of it, Mrs. Toffels. You go into the house. I'm goin' to ride on out and take a look. I might be late for supper."

"I'll pack something up quick that you can take with you."

"Send Harry into town for Christine, will you? I don't want her going to the Rodriguez ranch to play with those midget horses today. Until I catch the thief, I don't want her riding home alone."

Wyatt busied himself bridling and saddling Bill. Picking up his gun belt from a peg near the stall, he hefted it thoughtfully before strapping it around his hips. He led the horse outside and tied the reins to the fence. He'd fetch his Winchester from the house. In addition to catching a varmint, he might do some hunting.

Hoisting himself into the saddle, he set out for the river, marking the boundary between his ranch and Samantha's. He had a hunch the culprit might be one of the Cassidy twins. He hoped so. An outlaw would probably have stolen a horse. Dealing with the boys would be easier than confronting a renegade. Although facing Samantha about those twins might be worse than cornering a dangerous man.

Wyatt rode with all his senses alert. Although aware of the beauty of the early spring afternoon, he ignored the budding trees and bushes, instead looking through them for signs of life. He studied a hawk, flying overhead to see if its flight seemed relaxed or startled and scrutinized the new green grass for signs of human passage.

Passing near the ford of the river, he caught a glimpse of movement across the water on Samantha's property. A flash of blue and gray disappeared behind a tree.

Ha. He'd been right about those Cassidy twins. He'd bet it was Jack.

"Got ya." He urged Bill into the water, and the horse splashed across the stream. As a precaution, Wyatt pulled out his Colt. Not that he'd hurt the boy—just frighten him. But when he caught up with him and brought Jack home, Samantha would have to admit she'd been wrong about taking in those twins.

He rounded the last tree; the youngster took off running. Wyatt urged Bill after him, but even from one hundred feet away, he could see he wasn't chasing Jack Cassidy. Flying black hair, blue-and-gray-striped shirt, buckskin leggings. An Indian boy.

It only took a few minutes for Bill to overtake him. Wyatt turned the horse, cutting the boy off. He reined in, pointing his gun at the young Indian. "Hold it right there."

The youth looked to be about thirteen. His long black hair floated loose down his back. His scrawny body swam inside the oversized striped shirt, the tail of which hung down to the boy's buckskin-clad knees. His black eyes sparked with defiance, but in their angry depths, Wyatt could also detect a hint of fear.

He'd caught the thief all right. Now what in the hell was he going to do with him?

✳ ✳ ✳

Samantha stood at the window of her bedroom, looking past her newly planted garden to the broad range beyond. *Now I can get to know my ranch.* Her feet wiggled in anticipation. Finally, with the press of immediate chores lessened—the garden planted, the house clean and livable, the barn, outbuildings, and corrals serviceable—she could take time for herself. She still had a long list of fix-up changes she wanted to make, but they'd have to wait until the ranch started making a profit.

Today, while the boys were still in school, she'd start exploring. Excitement welled up from her toes to her stomach. Over the last weeks, she hadn't noticed how heavily the burdens of the ranch weighed on her shoulders; all at once she felt lighter. Turning from the window, she glanced around her room. On the big four-poster bed, a double wedding ring quilt pieced by her mother provided splashes of color—each square a window to the past.

Samantha stepped over to the bed and brushed her fingertips over an emerald velvet square taken from an evening gown of her mother's. Her beautiful mother had looked like a queen in this dress, with her glorious auburn hair elaborately arranged, emerald drops in her ears. Since her parents' death, Samantha kept the earrings tucked away, never worn. She remembered the bolt of velvet fabric at the mercantile...maybe someday.

Enough time spent in the past. Samantha walked over to the trunk she used for storage, lifted the lid, and shifted aside some blankets and clean linen. At the bottom lay Juan Carlos's possessions, saved for Daniel. She fingered a tooled leather belt adorned with silver medallions before pushing it aside and pulling out blue denim pants and a white cotton shirt she'd made for him.

They'd be too big, but she could roll up the pant legs and sleeves and use suspenders. She debated about wearing a blue-and-white gaucho poncho, but decided to wear a jacket instead.

Samantha changed clothes, pulled the pins from her hair, shook it out, then plaited the tresses into a long braid. She wished she had a full-length looking glass to see herself in men's clothing. The small mirror over the table only showed her face. Not that it mattered. There'd be no one around to see her anyway.

She skipped down the stairs like a child, grabbed Ezra's old coat and leather hat from the stand, and hurried out the door. She slowed at the corral, tempted to stop and play with her Falabellas. Her babies hadn't gotten too much attention from her lately, and she missed spending time with them. But as much as she longed to play with the Falabellas, she wanted to explore the ranch even more. She forced herself to continue walking toward the barn.

Once inside the barn, she squinted in the darker interior and strode down the center isle to the last stall. The only horse left in the barn suitable for riding was a Pinto gelding named Windy. When Samantha had first met him, she'd been fascinated by his markings, brown with big white patches. The hands, Mike and Ernie, had both assured her she wouldn't have any trouble with him.

"Hey, boy." Samantha rubbed the horse's velvet nose. "Sorry, no treats. You'll have to wait until we have a store of carrots and apples."

She put a bridle on the horse, draped a blanket over Windy's back, then dragged a heavy saddle from the top of the stall, and hoisted it onto the blanket. She cinched the girth and led the horse outside.

Flipping the reins back, Samantha hesitated a moment. At least with this saddle she wouldn't need a mounting block or a leg up. And riding astride was easier and safer.

Here goes.

She slid her left foot into the stirrup, pulled herself up by the horn, and swung her right leg over, tipping her boot into the other stirrup. Once settled, she expelled the breath she didn't even know she'd been holding.

Samantha headed Windy upstream. About eight feet wide, maybe two or three feet deep, the water splashed and gurgled over mossy rocks. Willows and aspens shivered sprouty new leaves amid the darker pines. The color of the sky fascinated her. She played with shades of blue: azure, aqua, and turquoise, trying to identify the precise color.

A rustle in the bushes and a flash of brown feathers, gone too quickly to identify, intrigued her. She'd have to learn all about the fellow creatures that shared her land.

To the rhythm of the horse's gait, a daydream played into her mind—she and Wyatt riding together while he shared with her his knowledge of the plants and animals. They'd talk about the ranches, their children…She jerked her thoughts back. She could only imagine what he'd have to say about her boys.

She forced herself to concentrate on studying the flora and fauna around her, become familiar with her surroundings. Rounding a strand of pines, she came upon a sight that abruptly ended her daydream, twisting her stomach, and stirring her to immediate action.

Wyatt. About to shoot a child.

❋ ❋ ❋

"No. No. Stop, Wyatt!" A screaming titian-haired banshee astride a Pinto horse galloped between him and the Indian.

With a muffled oath, Wyatt holstered his Colt. "I wasn't going to shoot him, Samantha. Although by startlin' me that way *you* could have gotten shot." His heart constricted at the thought.

"You were pointing a gun right at him."

In her eyes, he saw fear warring with anger, and her milky-pale face.

"I wouldn't have shot him."

Behind her, the boy sidled away. "You hold it right there," Wyatt yelled, hoping the Indian understood English. He didn't think his limited knowledge of the Blackfoot language would do much good.

The boy paused, body still tilting forward, ready for flight.

"Leave him alone," Samantha shouted, backing the Pinto to stand next to the boy. Her ivory complexion stayed pale, but no longer with fear. Instead, she looked spitting mad. Good thing he held the gun.

"Damn it, Samantha, he stole my favorite shirt and one of Mrs. Toffels's apple pies." Even as the words left his mouth, he realized how silly they sounded.

"You're going to shoot a *child* because of a *shirt*?"

He winced, regarding the battle light in her blue eyes. How could he make her understand? "No. But other men might have shot the little thief on sight."

"I never would have believed it of you, Wyatt, never."

"Believed what?" He could hear his voice rising.

She continued as if he hadn't spoken. "Although I should have known from your attitude toward my twins." Pink trickled back into her cheeks.

His ears started to burn, and he had to resist the temptation to yank her from the saddle and shake her so she'd listen, or seeing how anger sparked her eyes and animated her skin, he'd kiss her until her fury exploded into passion.

The boy started to edge away.

"I said stay still," Wyatt barked, realizing he was taking out his ire on the boy.

"You leave him alone." Samantha stopped to take a long look at the Indian. "He looks like he's starving."

Wyatt could hear the distress in her voice. "He probably is."

"Then you should feed him, not shoot him."

He opened his mouth to tell her that the boy would have received food and clothes if he'd asked, and furthermore, in a few minutes, he'd have shared the food Mrs. Toffels had stashed in his saddlebag. But Samantha had stopped paying attention to him. Instead she concentrated on the youth.

"Come back to my house," she coaxed. "I'll make sure you have plenty to eat and some warm clothes."

The Blackfoot boy looked down, his black hair veiling his face. He curled the toes of his worn moccasins into the ground.

"I have fried chicken and bread and strawberry jam. You can come stay at my house if you want." She shot Wyatt a withering look, then smiled at the boy.

That glance sent the burning from Wyatt's ears all the way down to his toes, making him lose his temper. "Oh, no you don't. You're not adopting this little thief."

"Oh, yes I am. You can't stop me."

"I can turn him in to the sheriff." He hoped she believed him.

"I heard we don't have a sheriff in this town."

So much for that bluff.

She turned back to the boy. "Don't worry. No one's going to hurt you."

The Blackfoot didn't look up. He probably wanted to escape them.

Wyatt leaned over, loosened the strap on the saddlebag, and pulled out the paper-wrapped sandwiches. He kneed Bill forward, holding the packet in front of the boy. "Take this. It's food."

The Indian jerked his head up, black eyes wary, but he accepted the offering.

"And keep the shirt."

"That's better." Samantha's icy tone thawed a few degrees.

She reached out a hand to the boy. He skittered away from her.

"I'm not going to hurt you. I want you to come home with me."

"He's an Indian, Samantha. Let him go back to his people."

She ignored Wyatt. "Do you have family? Someone to take care of you?"

A brief negative shake of the head was all the answer he gave.

"Then come home with me. You'll have your own horse."

The boy tossed his hair out of his eyes and stared at her, obviously not daring to believe her words.

She smiled.

Wyatt knew the power of that smile. He'd lost.

Samantha beckoned to the boy. "Your own horses. A little one to play with and a big one for you to ride."

She's doing it again. Pressure built in his chest. *Who knew what this Indian was capable of? Samantha might not be safe around him. Or Christine.* His concern increased as he thought of his daughter. He had to protect her. "You are not taking in another—"

"Don't you say another word, Wyatt Thompson. This is my ranch. My land."

"I'm well aware of that fact, Samantha," he said sarcastically.

"And I'm well aware that you want this ranch for your own."

He narrowed his eyes; his jaw tightened. "Yes, I do." He forced the words to sound cool.

Fire blazed in her eyes. "You won't get it."

"Samantha—"

"You're trespassing. I want you off my land." Her eyes narrowed. "Now."

"Fine." His anger churned hot, but he chilled his tone to match hers. "Don't expect to see me or my daughter on your land ever again."

CHAPTER THIRTEEN

Breathing hard, Samantha watched Wyatt's retreat. *Abominable man.* She still couldn't believe he'd pointed a gun at a child. But, slowly, regret seeped through her anger. She hadn't meant to go so far—order him off her ranch. Her temper had gotten the best of her. She should have given Wyatt a chance to explain. She bit her lip. But he'd already ridden Bill across the stream. Should she go after him?

Pride wouldn't allow her to.

Put him from your mind, she told herself. The refrain had become familiar. Maybe this time it would work.

Samantha turned toward the boy, who stood wolfing down the food as if he hadn't eaten in days. Studying his bone-thin frame, stark cheekbones etched in a dark face, she decided he probably hadn't. Sympathy panged her heart. "Slow down. If you eat too fast, you'll make yourself sick."

The boy paused, then took another large bite, but this time his jaw worked slower.

"That's better." She waited until he'd swallowed. "What's your name?"

"Little Feather."

His words were soft and rusty around the edges, as if he hadn't used his voice in a while. Poor boy. How long had he been alone? Even now he stood with his weight shifted away from her, prepared to bolt.

Samantha summoned the same calming energy from within her that she'd use to pacify a skittish horse. "Come." She leaned down and touched him on the shoulder.

Although he stood acquiescent under her hand, muscles rigid, she could feel the silent debate in his body. When his shoulders slumped, she knew he'd come with her. A rush of joy caught her by surprise. Already she felt a fierce attachment to him, born, perhaps, by her rescue of him. "Finish up that last bite."

He complied, chewing with a ferociousness that tangled maternal feelings within her.

She waited, resisting the temptation to brush the long hair back from his forehead. That kind of gesture might be enough to make him run. This was a wild one. She looked into his dark eyes. A wounded animal not unlike her twins. He'd require even more patience than they had. And freedom. But she would not allow doubt to shake her resolution. Still buoyed up by the answer to her prayer, she knew she'd find the resources within her to give each one of her boys the love he needed.

❀ ❀ ❀

The woman drove him crazy. *Stubborn. Irrational. Beautiful.* If they'd been alone, Wyatt might have swept her off her horse, kissing her until she was too breathless to argue.

If she'd only listened to him, he would have taken care of everything. How, he didn't know. But he'd have come up with his own solution to the Indian youth. He just needed some thinking time. Samantha hadn't given him any.

What would you have done? His conscience whispered.

Something, he snarled at it, annoyed by the question.

What?

The words niggled at him. It was enough to be arguing with a redheaded witch, but when a man started debating with himself, something was definitely wrong.

All right. He checked off his possibilities. He would have brought the boy home. Kept an eye on him, while Mrs. Toffels fed him and clothed him.

Then what?

Couldn't keep him, not around Christine.

Ah! Would have taken him to his people on the reservation. Surely there was an orphanage there, or a school or something. Hadn't he heard that? But he'd also heard stories about the Indian agent who ran the place. Didn't like what he'd heard.

Couldn't take him to Reverend Norton. The boy would have ended up with Samantha anyway.

He cast his thoughts around for other ideas.

Red Charlie. That was the answer. He'd have taken him to Red Charlie. The blacksmith didn't have an apprentice yet. Wyatt's scars burned in remembrance of the abuse he'd suffered at the hands of a cruel master, and he rubbed his side. But he knew Red Charlie would be fair to the boy. If necessary, Wyatt would have paid something for his room and board.

See. Triumph rose in him. He'd have figured out the perfect solution. He almost turned Bill around, heading back for another round of arguments with Samantha.

This time he'd win.

Then he remembered their last exchange, his banishment from her ranch, and the triumphant feeling drained away, leaving him tired. He couldn't go. He'd sworn not to.

Wyatt winced, thinking about Christine. She wasn't going to be happy about being exiled from the midget horses and from Daniel. She'd probably put up quite a fuss. All along, he hadn't been comfortable with her around the twins. He'd acquiesced, as always, for he found it difficult to deny his daughter what she wanted. Now, at least, he didn't have to worry about her being led into trouble by those twins.

He clenched his hands around the reins. He hoped she wouldn't cry. Christine was a resilient child who seldom shed tears. But when she did, it twisted his heart tighter than Mrs. Toffels's wrung out her laundry. Usually tears welling up in those big blue eyes rendered him powerless, and he'd do anything he could to make them stop. But now he'd need to stand firm. This time his daughter would obey him.

❅ ❅ ❅

Samantha stopped on her way to the barn. Her stomach tightened. She smelled smoke. *That's odd.* With one hand, she shaded her eyes from the late May sunshine, turning, trying to sight or sniff the source. Her gaze swept the corral, the outside of the barn, and the nearby haystacks piled to its left. Her eyes narrowed, searching; no sign of wispy gray trails.

Usually this time in the late afternoon, the boys played with the Falabellas. The little horses continued to work their magic, gentling the roughness of the twins and tethering Little Feather to the ranch. The Indian had arrived a week ago, and he still vanished much of the time, returning only to eat and sleep. Samantha let him be. You couldn't cage an eagle, but she still had hopes of taming this one.

Voices coming from behind the farthest haystack pulled her in that direction. Rounding the last pile, she saw her four boys seated, backs against the barn wall. Little Feather, his black hair neatly braided into two tails, wore Wyatt's shirt, which he'd refused to part with. Raising a pipe to his mouth, he inhaled. He tried not to cough and passed it to Jack.

Immediately angry, Samantha opened her mouth to yell at them, but abruptly closed it again, remembering her own childhood try with that pipe. *Her father's.* She'd always loved the smell when he smoked it and had memorized his ritual for lighting up.

One morning she and her friend Günter had stolen the pipe from her father's study and snuck outside. Lighting up and smoking had not been what she'd expected. Both of them had gotten nauseated from the nasty taste, and they'd never tried again.

She'd bank her anger, wait until her boys received the same lesson.

Tim inhaled, his cheeks puffing out. His eyes rolled, and he choked. Samantha clapped her hand over her mouth to avoid laughing.

Her amusement faded when her son took the pipe. She bit her lip to keep from calling out. He needed to experience his own consequences, but later they'd have to have a talk about his not following the older boys into trouble. She sighed. She doubted it would do much good.

Little Feather leaned over, correcting the angle of the pipe. Daniel sucked on the pipe, his mouth puckering with the effort. He held his breath. Samantha restrained herself from running to him. Then he released the pent-up air in a fit of coughing.

Samantha let out the breath she'd been holding. While she waited for Jack's turn, she thought through her next moves. Somewhere along the line, she'd lost her anger, realizing that the boys were finally becoming friends—something she'd been wishing for. And their mischief would have its own punishment. The nausea would hit soon. She'd send them all straight to bed without supper—not that they'd want anything to eat. And they'd hate to be in bed while it was still light out.

Actually, it might be good to have the boys in bed early. Tomorrow Elizabeth Sanders and Pamela Carter and her children would come to tea after church. Samantha had a lot of preparing to do before then. She wanted everything to be perfect.

Jack finished, covering his mouth with one hand to quiet his coughing. By now they should all be a little green about the gills. Time for discovery.

Samantha advanced on them. Jack saw her first and jumped up, with one hand behind his back. The other boys followed, trying to look innocent, but not quite succeeding.

Without a word, she stopped in front of Jack and held out her hand, palm up. His green eyes shifted away from her. She waited. Slowly he brought his arm around, placing the pipe in her palm.

"Whose idea was this?"

Jack looked down at his feet. "Mine, ma'am. Little Feather was tellin' us about how the braves in his tribe pass around the pipe."

"I see." She raised an eyebrow at Little Feather.

The Blackfoot boy nodded in agreement.

"So you thought you'd emulate the braves?"

Jack crinkled his brow. "Immulate?"

"Do like they do—copy their behavior."

"Yes, ma'am."

Little Feather uncurled his clenched fingers until his wrist cocked his hand upward.

Samantha tried to understand his silent communication. Supplication? Stop the questioning?

His hand raised a few inches. "Peace pipe. Tradition of my people."

Two sentences. A lengthy conversation for Little Feather.

At least they had a good reason for committing mischief. "Sharing peace sounds like a good idea, boys. However, smoking near a haystack is dangerous. You could have started a fire."

Jack screwed up his face, discomfort crinkling his eyes.

"How are you feeling now?"

Jack placed a hand on his stomach. "Not too well."

"I believe you boys will be needing to lie down. I suggest you all go take your baths and go straight to bed."

Daniel jerked up his head in protest, but the look she sent him froze anything he wanted to say.

Silently, the four started toward the barn. She watched them go, hiding a smile in case one of them looked back. A successful lesson. Would that all of them could be handled so easily.

Who knew what mischief those children would get into next?

CHAPTER FOURTEEN

Perched on the edge of the worn green velvet wingchair in her parlor, Samantha lifted the white teapot decorated with violets off the engraved silver tray. She poured a tiny stream of fragrant Earl Grey tea into a matching violet-dotted teacup. She assumed Pamela Carter and Elizabeth Sanders, sitting on the sofa to her right, would be watching her performance.

While her hands busied themselves with the tea ritual, Samantha tried to calm her nervousness. Every detail of the afternoon must be perfect. Her mother's tea service, the plates of cookies and small sandwiches looked enticing enough. And in her black cashmere dress, Samantha presented a respectable appearance.

She so wanted Pamela and Elizabeth to like her. Would they make unfavorable judgments based on the dilapidation of her home? She knew they both came from wealthy Boston backgrounds and were comfortably situated in their marriages.

Surely they would notice how the sunshine streaming through the bare windows revealed peels in the sage-green patterned William Morris wallpaper. Although Samantha attempted to paste back the loose strips, some of the edges had crumbled, leaving crooked, pine-exposed gaps.

At least they couldn't see the mouse holes in the furniture. Crocheted doilies made by her mother covered the hollow spots in the sofa and chairs, and lent a feminine touch to the table in front of them. When she'd arrived, she'd given one of the friendlier barn cats the run of the house, and her mice infestation had ended.

"Sugar?" Samantha inquired.

"No, thank you." Pamela shook her head. A wispy tendril of hair, escaping the neatly coiled brown knot covering her neck, brushed across her cheek. She absently tucked it behind her ear, before accepting the cup and saucer Samantha handed her.

The small gesture evoked a quick nostalgic memory. Samantha's mother had had the same fine hair, which always slipped from its pins.

Pamela's kind smile lightened her plain, hook-nosed face. She took a sip before setting the cup and saucer on the table, then settled back on the sofa, fingering the garnet brooch pinned to her coffee-colored velvet shirtwaist.

Samantha glanced up at her guests. "It's been so long since I've done this."

Pamela's brown eyes warmed with interest. "Do they not serve tea in Argentina?"

Samantha shook her head. "Not quite." She poured tea for Elizabeth Sanders, sitting to the other side of Pamela. "Sugar, Mrs. Sanders?"

"Please, and remember, I've asked that you call me Elizabeth." A dimple appeared in her smile. "Although the novelty of being called Mrs. Sanders has not yet worn off."

Pamela chuckled. "I'm glad I don't have to call you Mrs. Sanders. After knowing you all my life as Elizabeth Hamilton, I'm glad I can just call you Beth." She glanced over to Samantha. "Please call me Pamela."

"Certainly, if you'll call me Samantha."

Elizabeth leaned forward. Her blue lace dress matched the color of her eyes. Pearl drops hanging from her ears bobbed with each turn of her head. "Tell us about your country?"

"Oh, Argentina's not my country, really. I'm American. My father worked for the diplomatic corps. I've lived in Germany, Spain, and Argentina. I met my late husband while he was attending school in Buenos Aires. We married after he finished his studies."

"Did you continue to live in Buenos Aires?"

"In a little town on the outskirts of the city. My husband wanted enough land for his Falabellas."

"Ah, the famous little horses."

They all laughed, settling into conversation and sharing stories of their backgrounds. As they spoke, Samantha could feel the friendship bonds weaving between them—delicate as a spiderweb, but strengthening as they chatted. Pamela's caring personality grew more evident, while to Samantha's surprise, elegant Elizabeth had a quick sense of humor. Samantha relaxed, feeling confident that all was going well.

Her guests had been kind enough to bring welcoming gifts. Elizabeth Sanders had brought a framed watercolor of a mountain stream, translucent green water rushing over stones, pine trees shadowing the surface. Samantha planned to hang the beautiful picture over the worst cracks in the wallpaper. Pamela Carter's flower-embroidered pillow already graced the sofa next to her. Touched by the thoughtfulness of the two women, Samantha hoped by the time the visit was over they'd truly be friends.

Then a slight movement out of the corner of her eye caught Samantha's attention. She stiffened. Oh please, *no*. A quick sideways flick of her gaze verified her suspicion.

A mouse.

Peeking out from a hole in the arm of the sofa to the left of Pamela, the lace edge of a doily capped its head like a veil. That wretched barn cat had obviously let one get away.

Please go back, she willed the creature. She didn't dare look at it. The other women might follow her gaze and see it.

The mouse ignored her mental plea, creeping out of the hole and down the leg of the sofa. Samantha strove to look interested in the conversation, but the mouse skittering under the sofa held her attention. The vermin resurfaced, trailing around the hem of Pamela's dress, which had pooled at her feet. It peered into a fold. Samantha held her breath.

The heat of mortification crept into her cheeks. *Go away.*

She held herself rigid, as if the stiffness of her body were a conductor's baton by which she could direct the mouse. But it was no use, the tiny body wiggled deeper into the fold.

❋ ❋ ❋

Jack Cassidy lounged against the wooden fence of the corral watching Daniel, Tim, and the Carter children play with the Falabellas. At the first sign of guests, Little Feather had taken off. Jack figured the Blackfoot boy probably wouldn't be back 'til supper.

At the far side of the corral, Daniel, Mark, and black Chita kicked the gunnysack ball Miz Samantha had made. Nearby, Tim showed Bonita, his chestnut mare, to Sara.

On impulse, Jack had given little Lizzy his own Mariposa to play with. A fool thing to do, and no tellin' why he had. He'd never seen anyone like the child. Tiny, with long curly hair, wearing a lacy white dress, that weren't much different than other gals'. But she'd looked up at him with her wise blue eyes and skin as thin and fine as a raindrop…like a fairy or a princess from the stories Miz Samantha had been telling them…and something deep and lost inside him had just opened up to her.

She must have whupped a spell on him, because he'd guided Mariposa over to her, introduced them, and had handed over the lead rope. Lizzy's hand, resting in his rough one, was the size of a new maple leaf and softer than the feel of Miz Samantha's Sunday dress.

Uncomfortable, he'd backed away, but continued to watch the little 'un. She didn't say anything. Not like her sister, who was talkin' away to Pampita like she'd never use up all her words. Just silence and fingertip touches to the little mare's dappled gray hide. But Jack could tell girl and horse were havin' their own conversation…like they already knew each other. He itched inside like he needed to scratch, but didn't know how to reach in there.

He needed to get away, find somethin' else ta do. He glanced around. Seeing the haystacks near the barn gave him an idea. He whistled for his brother. Tim left Bonita and started over to him. Daniel also knew the signal, and he motioned for Mark to come along and bring Chita with him.

Jack waved toward the barn. "Let's go jump in the haystacks."

Mark rubbed Chita's ears, plainly reluctant to leave her.

"See who can jump the farthest," Jack challenged.

Interest quickened on Mark's face. "All right. But afterwards, I want to get back to this little one."

Jack waved. "Come on." Not bothering to open the gate, he scrambled over the fence. The rest of the boys followed.

Sara, an annoyed look on her face, lifted up the hem of her white dress and followed them. "I'm coming too."

"We ain't gunna play with no girl." Jack pointed his chin in Lizzy's direction. "You stay with her."

Sara got a stubborn look on her face, like Pa's old mule when it refused to budge another step. "No. She can come with us. She won't get in the way, she'll just watch."

Jack knew the futility of arguing with a mule. He shrugged, watching her climb the fence. When she reached the top, the bottom of her dress caught on the splintered wood. She yanked her skirt loose, tearing the lace away from the hem. She looked unconcerned, but he hoped her ma wouldn't hit her for it, the way their pa would whale on them whenever they'd added a new hole to the collection in their clothes. Or even worse, her ma could blame him. It wasn't his fault. He'd tried to stop her.

Putting the thought from his mind, he raced around the barn, the other children pelting after him. Two hills of hay piled double-high to the height of a boy beckoned him to jump and slide. Several dents marred the side on the nearest heap where a pitchfork had pulled out enough for the horses. Massed to the left, a mounded muck load, so covered with straw and hay that it resembled a haystack, hadn't yet been carted away.

Jack ran to the nearest haystack, scrambling up its slippery side. There was a trick to the climb, involving shoving the toes and hands deep into the hay. The blades scratched and tickled his hands, and he breathed in the dusty-sweet scent. Ever since he'd arrived here, he'd been wantin' to jump on these stacks, but he'd always been too busy with school and chores. But they'd been there, beckoning.

The other boys scampered right behind him to the top, then juggled next to him, trying to stay in a bunch. Sara struggled with the climb, hampered by her dress. As she leaned forward, her long brown hair trailed, picking up wispy spikes. He snickered.

Soon she'd look like a yeller porcupine. Lizzy settled herself on a hay bale near the barn, seemingly content to watch.

Which first? Leap to the next mound, or skim down like an otter on a mudslide and climb back up again?

Daniel solved the problem for him. Flinging his arms behind, then forward, he dove to the next haystack. Popping to his feet, he balanced on the top, flailing his arms, and laughing.

Jack ground his teeth. *I'm first.* Not waiting, he bounded across, pushing Daniel aside when he landed. "Out of my way."

Losing his grin, Daniel flopped onto his back. Before he had time to get up, Tim sailed through the air. Jack caught a glimpse of the mischievous look on his brother's face. Then Tim shoved him, and Jack fell across Daniel's stomach. With a wuff of expelled air, Daniel's chest caved.

"Hey." Daniel punched Jack in the side. "Get off me."

With a grin, Jack rolled off.

Tim thrust his arms in the air. "I'm king of the hill."

Jack reached over, hooked Tim's ankle, and flipped him down. "Ain't no more."

From the other stack, Mark called, "Make room, or I'm landing on you."

Jack bounced to his feet. Ignoring Daniel, he grasped his brother's hand, pulling him up. "See if ya can," he called to Mark.

Mark jumped, lunging into Jack. They grappled for position. Daniel's feet slid over the side, dragging Tim down, but by clinging to Tim's leg, Daniel managed not to slip off.

In his fall, Tim jerked at Jack's arm. At the same time, on his other side, Mark pushed at Jack. As he fell, Jack stubbornly clung to Mark's shoulders, taking him down with him.

Laughing, they all lay sprawled over each other like a litter of puppies. Jack felt funny inside, like a lantern had been lit in his chest, and he couldn't wipe the stupid grin off his face.

He glanced over at the other stack. Sara stood with her hands on her hips. That mule look settled on her face. "My turn."

Jack jostled the other boys aside to get to his feet. "No, ya ain't. Ain't no room for girls over here."

With a few pushes, the other boys shuffled to their feet.

"No girls. No girls." Daniel chanted.

"No girls. No girls." As all the boys joined in, the chorus swelled.

Sara's face turned as red as his old winter long johns. She shook her fist at them.

A gang. He and Tim and Daniel and Mark. All together. For the first time ever, Jack felt the power of belonging, of not being on the outside. In a heady rush, he raised his voice even louder. "No girls."

Sara stuck her nose in the air and turned away from them.

Jack laughed, feeling triumphant.

With a swift movement, she gathered up her skirt with one hand, flung her other arm back and forth and hurdled toward the other mound.

Oh, Lordy. Jack opened his mouth to yell a warning, but it was too late. Sara landed feet first on top of the straw-covered manure pile. She twisted to face them and swiftly sank. Her eyes bulged in horror.

Jack couldn't help the snicker that burst from him. Sara sure looked funny up to her knees in manure, her formerly clean white dress bunching up in the top of the muck.

"Don't laugh at me!" she screamed.

Jack chortled. He'd never seen anything so hilarious in his life. She was goin' to stink to high heaven.

"I'm sinking."

She was. Up to her hips. Jack's amusement sizzled up faster than water sprinkled on a hot skillet, replaced by a bolt of terror. That manure pile was a lot higher than Sara. In a minute, she'd be over her head. She'd drown in shit, and it would be all his fault.

His heart thumping fit to burst, he plummeted down the haystack.

Apparently realizing her danger, Sara screamed—piercing shrieks that normally would have made him clamp his hands over his ears. But instead, he frantically dug his way into the smelly muck.

She sank, already mired to her shoulders. He knew he had only seconds to reach her. As he worked, her body lowered more, her neck covering up. Her eyes bulged with fear, and the screaming changed to whimpers that tore at him with the sharpness of a bear's claws. On either side of him, the other boys joined him, each burrowing like a dog after a bone.

Sara plunged down farther. She tilted her chin back, straining to keep her face free. The whimpering cut off. Jack knew she didn't dare move her mouth.

His tunneling hands struck something. Sara's arm. "I've got her!" he yelled. He pulled. The mound refused to release her. He thrust his arm in deeper, his face pressing into her shoulder.

Breathing in the stench, he wiggled his fingers across her back until they curled around her side. Like a draft horse, he pulled. Her body shifted a few inches toward him. His ear pressed to her chest, and he could hear her heart fluttering like a bird caught in a trap. At least she wouldn't sink any deeper. "I'll hold her. You guys dig her out."

Mark scooped dung from around her front; Tim and Daniel tackled her backside. As she loosened, Jack pulled her out a few inches more. Looking up at her face, he saw tears streaking down her sludge-splattered cheeks. "Got you," he whispered to her. "Won't let ya go."

She swallowed and gave a slight nod, as if she were afraid to move.

"Be all right." He spoke to her gentle-like as if she was Mariposa. "Have ya out in a hog's breath."

The terror in her blue eyes changed to trust, and it stabbed into his gut deeper than a knife. No one had ever looked at him like that. And he didn't deserve it now. His teasing had gotten her into this, but he wouldn't let her down.

By now the boys, covered in muck themselves, had freed Sara to her waist. Jack wrapped his other arm around her shivering body, squeezing her in his embrace.

Bracing his feet, he yanked her out. With a sucking sound, she shot free, the unexpected momentum carrying them backward and down to the ground. With a thud that knocked the wind out of him, Jack fell flat on his back, Sara jarring on top of him. For a moment, he lay there, hearing his own harsh breaths and feeling her safe in his arms.

She drooped her head onto his chest, her back shuddering with her sobs. Protectiveness rose in him. Awkwardly, he tightened one arm around her and patted her shoulder with the other hand. "Got ya safe, now. No need for that there cryin'."

Mark dropped to his knees beside them, his freckled face pale. "Sara, Sara." He added his pats to Jack's. "I'm sorry, Sara. I'm so sorry."

Lizzy crouched down by Sara's head, fluttering finger touches on her sister's head and crooning. The concern on the tiny girl's face made Jack feel lower than a snake's belly.

Sara rolled her head to look Jack in the eyes. The drenched blue of her gaze melted the walls he held around his heart. "You saved my life."

Uncomfortable, he loosened his arms. "I ain't no hero."

"Yes, you are," she insisted, laying her head back on his chest.

With an old kind of wisdom, he knew that in a minute he'd set her aside, go back to being a boy. But for a few more seconds he cradled her, vowing to himself that he'd change. Someday, he was gunna grow up, marry Sara Carter, and spend the rest of his life making this afternoon up to her.

✳ ✳ ✳

"Oh, dear." Samantha relaxed her shoulders, giving in to the inevitability of vermin trouble. "Be brave, ladies, and raise your feet. There's a mouse coming your way."

Gasps and the chink-rattle of teacups hastily lowered onto the table greeted her announcement. Both women lifted their feet, bunching the fabric of their skirts in their hands.

Rising, Samantha waved the mouse in the direction of the door. "Shoo." She herded it through the doorway by stamping her feet.

In the hall, Maria stepped out from the kitchen, a damp dishcloth in her hand.

Samantha pointed to the mouse.

Maria nodded her understanding, flapping her hand to urge Samantha back into the parlor.

Would the women leave? Dreading what she'd find, Samantha returned to her guests. To her surprise, calm faces and relaxed bodies greeted her.

Elizabeth's laughing eyes telegraphed her feelings. "Dreadful little creatures, aren't they?" She exchanged a reminiscing look with Pamela. "Remember when your brother"—she glanced at Samantha—"the youngest, Bobby"—and back to Pamela—"released those mice during your mother's dinner party?"

Pamela laughed. "Mrs. Millicot fainted dead away, and Miss Florence climbed up on her chair and emitted those shrill shrieks."

"We both fell to giggling like schoolgirls."

Pamela reached over and touched Samantha's hand. "At least this time one of our boys didn't do it."

Samantha managed a smile, hiding relief at their reactions. "Yes, we know they're behaving themselves. I'm sure the Falabellas have all their attention."

"The children have been eager to play with those little horses. It's all they've been talking about for days." Pamela leaned over to choose one of the *alfajores* baked by Maria. Her plump fingers fluttered above the cookies and settled on one.

Screams pierced the calm of the afternoon. Pamela dropped the pastry. "Sara." In a flurry of skirts, she was off the couch and out the door of the room.

Now what? Samantha flew after Pamela, Elizabeth right behind her. On the porch, she scanned the area: river, goat pen, Falabella corral, hen house, barn.

No children.

All three women hitched up their dresses, heading in the direction of the shrieks. The screams stopped, the silence feeling even more ominous.

Please, Lord, let them be all right.

Samantha panted, her breaths sharp and shallow from the constriction of her corset. Not for the first time, she cursed the fashions that so restricted freedom of movement.

The women reached the barn. No children in sight.

Pamela halted. She glanced around, her eyes wild and her brown hair falling out from its pins. "Where are they? Sara!"

"Mama." The call sounded faint.

Samantha pointed. "Behind the haystacks." She picked up her skirts and ran over. She rounded the refuse heap and slammed to a halt.

As if expecting condemnation, the children stood in a row, all of them covered from head to toe with manure and straw. Stench clung to them like a miasma. Only Lizzy, in her white lace dress, which had originally matched her sister's, appeared unscathed.

Pamela stepped in front of Sara. "What's happened here?" Her hand hovered, not quite touching her daughter's shoulder. "Sara, are you all right?"

Sara nodded.

"Mercy sakes, child. Why are you all covered with...?" Pamela couldn't seem to bring herself to say the words.

Now that she knew the children weren't hurt, Samantha's ire rose. What did they mean by playing in the refuse pile? How could they ruin her first tea party? She glanced sideways at Pamela and Elizabeth. Had their budding friendships just been severed?

Jack shuffled forward. "'Twere my fault. Us 'uns was jumping on the haystacks. I wouldn't let Sara on ours." He pointed to the nearest stack, now noticeably smaller, hay scattered around it. "We teased her. So she jumped on that there one. Didn't know what were under the straw." He looked down, scuffed his boot in the dirt, then glanced up at Pamela. "I deserve a whippin'. But please don't punish the rest of 'em."

With a march step, Tim joined his brother, resolution gleaming in his green eyes, a stubborn tilt to his chin. "I'll take the whippin,' too."

Although still annoyed with them, pride for the twins' acceptance of responsibility and protection of the other children spiked through Samantha's anger.

Sara gazed up at her mother in entreaty. Her white lace dress, no longer recognizable beneath the wet brown stains, clung to her sturdy body. Her lip quivered. "Jack saved my life. I almost got buried in there. I thought I was going to die."

Pamela ran a hand across Sara's head. "Thank the Good Lord you're safe."

Yes, Samantha echoed in her mind. *Thank you, God.*

Pamela patted her daughter's head. "You nearly scared me to death with your screams. I don't know whether to hug you," she sniffed comically, "or back away ten paces." She looked over at Samantha. "What do you suggest we do now?"

Samantha studied the muck-covered children. The amount of hot water she'd have to heat to give them all proper baths boggled her mind. She glanced at the creek and shivered. The children would be blue with cold if they bathed there. "If the children do a quick rinse, soap, rinse in the river, we dry them immediately, wrap them in blankets, and sit them in front of the fire, they should be all right."

Pamela patted Sara's head. "That sounds like the best plan."

Samantha pointed to the barn. "Boys, go find Manuel. He'll have to help you. Sara, run to the house and have Maria bring soap and towels."

The children scattered, following her directions. Lizzy scooted over to her mother and clutched her skirt.

Elizabeth covered her mouth with her hand, but a giggle leaked out anyway. "I've never seen such a funny sight. What a relief to know they're unharmed. You realize this is a story we're going to tease the children about for years to come."

As Elizabeth's mirth-filled blue gaze met hers, Samantha's own laughter bubbled up inside. Everything was going to be fine. Maybe not today, but in the future, this would become a special story. Come to think about it, Louisa May Alcott had nothing this bad in her books. Maybe someday, she'd have to write her own tales about her wild boys. She tapped her chin. *Sam's Boys.* She liked the way that sounded.

In the meantime, she'd have to survive raising them.

CHAPTER FIFTEEN

Wyatt headed down the narrow road leading from town to his ranch. Overhead, the plump June moon silvered the night into gray shades—enough light to trace the familiar route. But even the light of the moon couldn't dim the familiar patterns of the stars. A bright one with a reddish cast seemed to wink at him. Bill flicked his ears at the distant hoot of an owl. Then silence, broken only by the clop of Bill's hooves, settled around him.

The last time he had ridden away from dinner at the Livingston mansion, he'd been replete with food and feminine company, his thoughts lingering on Edith Grayson. Tonight, while physically satisfied, his emotions proved anything but. Edith's presence had been as beautiful as ever, her lips still as sensuous. Only somehow, he'd lost the desire to kiss her.

Flame-colored hair danced across his mind. Samantha's hair. That woman had proven difficult to banish from his thoughts. Elusive memories kept sliding through at odd moments. He'd gone over his last argument with her at least twenty times, often arriving at different, but equally satisfying, conclusions. The best involved them ending up without a stitch of clothing, no children anywhere in sight.

His fingers curled around the reins as though grasping a lock of her hair. Realizing what he was doing, he unclenched his hand around the leather. He needed to put that aggravating woman out of his mind. Easier said than done. Somehow she'd embedded herself under his skin like a burr under a saddle blanket.

Lost in thought, Wyatt allowed Bill to pick his way home without much guidance. Maybe, if he talked to the annoying woman, explained himself, then he'd feel better. She wouldn't continue to unjustly label him a potential child killer, his reputation would be restored, and he'd have some sense of resolution. Maybe then she'd stop haunting his thoughts and let him get back to normal. He doubted it, but it was worth a try.

Only he'd have to catch her in town. He wasn't about to go back on his word and set one foot on her land. In addition, they'd need some privacy in case she lost that redheaded temper and started yelling at him for the whole town to hear. That was the last thing he needed.

Still pondering ways and means, he neared the ranch. The sound of galloping hooves, coming from the direction of the ranch, startled him from his musings. The hairs on his neck bristled; he sensed trouble.

No one should be out and about at this time of night. He pulled Bill to the side of the road, straining through the shadows to see the rider. He recognized Harry's lanky form and shouted for the young man to stop. Even in the darkness, Wyatt could see Harry's eyes, wide with apprehension.

Wyatt slowed Bill. "What's goin' on?"

"It's Christine, Mr. Thompson. Mrs. Toffels sent me to find you. Christine ain't come home."

Fear grabbed Wyatt in a choke hold. He kicked Bill into a gallop, heading toward the house. He could hear Harry following behind.

Reaching the gate, he swung off the horse, tossing the reins at Harry.

Mrs. Toffels threw open the door, and gathering her skirts, rushed down the brick path. Panting, she drew herself up in front of him. "Christine didn't come home for dinner."

As if hoping his daughter would magically appear, Wyatt frantically looked around, seeing a thousand shadows that could hide a hurt child. "The men?"

"They're out searching."

"What about Samantha's ranch?"

The housekeeper twisted her hands in her apron. "You forbade her to go there."

"Maybe she didn't listen." As he spoke the words, certainty grew in him. He should have known Christine wouldn't stay away from those Falabellas. "Harry, stay here. Search the barn and outbuildings again. Don't miss an inch. If Christine's found, come get me at Ezra's."

Harry bobbed his head. Dismounting, he handed over Bill's reins.

Wyatt swung into the saddle and turned the horse toward the river. *Please, God, please let me find my little girl safe at Samantha's.*

❋ ❋ ❋

Pulling her black knitted shawl around her shoulders, Samantha stepped onto the porch. She couldn't shake a feeling of uneasiness. She sniffed the night air as if trying to find a source for her feelings. It wasn't the boys. She looked over her shoulder through the lighted kitchen window. All four boys, homework finished, sat at the kitchen table playing a quiet game of checkers. Or at least right now it was quiet. Any minute, they'd start squabbling over a move.

Shrugging her shoulders as if to rid herself of her feelings, Samantha returned to the warmth of the kitchen. She chose a chair by the stove and picked up her basket of darning. The boys burrowed through their socks quicker than a gopher after the tulip bulbs.

Pounding on the front door startled her. The boys jerked to their feet. Before she could leave her seat, she heard the sound of the door being thrust open. "Samantha!" *Wyatt's voice.*

His boots clicked on the wood floor of the hallway, then Wyatt appeared in the kitchen doorway. He was dressed in a black suit, his wet pants plastered to his long legs, shedding slow water drops onto the plank flooring. His anxious gray gaze slid past her to the boys, before returning to rest on her face. "Is Christine here?"

"Christine? No." Recognizing the fear in his eyes, her hand flew to her throat. "Is she missing?"

"Christine never came home tonight. I was hoping she was here."

"No, I haven't seen her since...since our..."

His shoulders sagged. He turned to leave.

"Wyatt, wait." She grabbed up a blue blanket draped over a chair. "You're wet."

"The river's risen. Must be a storm in the mountains. Didn't take the time to ride to the ford."

She handed it to him. "Dry off and tell me what you've done so far."

"I wasn't home. I was in town." He passed a hand over his eyes.

Samantha could hear the remorse in his voice.

"When Christine didn't come home in time for supper, Mrs. Toffels sent the hands out looking for her. When I got home, I was sure she'd snuck over here. I'd hoped..."

Samantha touched his shoulder. "I'm so sorry, Wyatt. Let me get my coat. We'll all help look for her."

Jack cleared his throat.

Samantha looked over at the boys and saw identical guilty expressions on all four faces. "Boys," she said, her tone ominous.

Jack lifted his chin. "She was here. Tweren't the first time either. She likes playin' with the little ones."

Samantha fisted her hands on her hips. "Why didn't I see her?"

"She stayed out of sight in back of the barn."

Daniel piped up. "But she left when the supper bell rang."

"The supper bell. That was hours ago."

Samantha met Wyatt's eyes; they didn't have to speak. Each knew.

"We'll talk about this later. Go get your coats. Then, Daniel, you get Manuel and tell Maria to come to the house in case Christine comes back here. Tim, run to the bunkhouse and get Ernie and Fred. Jack, gather all the lanterns, light them, and then help saddle the horses."

Some of the bleakness had left Wyatt's eyes. "There are enough of us that we can spread out within lantern distance and cover enough ground riding from here to my ranch."

"Finish drying off. I'll go change and get some extra blankets." She touched his shoulder. "We'll find her, Wyatt."

He placed his hand over hers, curling his fingers around her palm. "Thank you."

Samantha squeezed his hand in response, praying that her supportive words would come true. Feeling his chilled, callused hand, she had to quell a sudden urge to cry. This wasn't the time to give way to her emotions. They had to find Christine.

❀ ❀ ❀

Wyatt held up his lantern, willing the darkness to part and reveal his daughter. The hilly ground trapped pockets of blackness that even the moon's glow couldn't illuminate. About twenty yards to his right, Samantha's light bobbed with each step of her horse. He knew two of the boys rode on her other side, with the hand, Ernie, being the farthest away, only a pinprick of yellow betraying his presence. To his left, Little Feather, riding without a saddle, dipped his lantern, studying the ground.

Every few minutes one of them shouted her name. Each time, Wyatt held his breath, listening for an answer. Still no response. He cleared his throat. "Christine!" He heard his call echo down the line of other riders.

The heaviness of the night pressed against him, and, knowing he needed to keep all his senses alert, Wyatt tried to contain the fear boiling in his guts. But terror kept spiking through him. He knew all too well how fragile life was. A hundred horrific things could have befallen his precious little girl, and he couldn't help worrying at the list. His mind kept mumbling prayers, just like the night Alicia died.

If something happened to Christine, he didn't think he'd be able to go on. Having a motherless baby to care for had been all that had kept him from giving up when his wife had died, taking with her the only love he'd allowed into his heart since he was a small child.

He heard the rapid thudding of hoofbeats, riding hard from the direction of his ranch. His heart thudded in time to the sound. He squinted, trying to make out the rider, but figuring it must be Harry.

They must have found her. Home safe. His shoulders relaxed in relief, only to be jerked back upright as his thoughts took an alarming turn. *She could be injured. Or worse.*

Impatient, he kicked Bill into a canter. Drawing closer, he could discern Harry's lanky form. "Did you find her?" he called.

Harry reined in. "Her pony come home without her," he panted, "wet to his neck."

CHAPTER SIXTEEN

Samantha rode closer to Wyatt, just in time to hear Harry's words. Although dressed warmly in Juan Carlos's clothes, she shivered. "Oh, dear Lord."

Drowned.

At the fearful thought, her heart leapt into her throat. *No. Oh no.* She looked into Wyatt's face. The anguish in his eyes forced her to stay strong. He needed her.

She shoved aside her dreadful fantasy, refusing to believe Christine had been swept off her pony and drowned. When they found her, the child would need a calm woman to minister to her. She looked over at the boys and the hands who'd ridden over to hear the news. They all needed her strength too.

Daniel's blue eyes looked huge in the glow of his lantern, his face strained with fear. She tried to give her son a reassuring smile, wishing she could hug him and shield him from this experience. He adored Christine. If something had happened to her...

"Keep your faith, son," she murmured.

Daniel swallowed, nodding.

Samantha urged her horse closer to Wyatt. Reaching over, she squeezed his arm. "She could have fallen off before the river, and the pony continued home. Or even after she'd crossed the river. We'll keep searching until we find her." Even through his jacket, she could feel the tension in his muscles. She ran her palm across his forearm in silent comfort, then pulled her hand back.

Wyatt nodded to her, then glanced around at the others. "Harry, ride back to the ranch. Round up the hands. Have them search between the house and the river. If you don't find her, split up. Some ride upstream, some down. We'll take this side." He looked at Samantha.

"That sounds sensible," she said.

He flung out his arm. "Everyone back to your places." He nudged Bill forward.

As she rode, Samantha strained to hear any sound, while searching out the shadows. Her arm ached from holding the lantern high enough to see. Every few minutes, she had to rest the lantern on her leg. Fears tangled in her mind like the fabled Gordian knot—fears for Christine's safety, concern for her boys' emotions, her awareness of Wyatt.

Wyatt.

The shame of how she'd treated him prickled at her. Her dreaded temper. She seldom lost it, but when she did, it was like an explosion, sometimes harming those around her.

Juan Carlos had been calm to her storm, helping her weather her feelings. Because of him, she had mastered her more quick-tempered nature—or so she'd thought. But she'd also taken her husband's support and understanding for granted. He'd known her, trusted that she didn't always mean the things she said or did when she lost her temper. He had known she'd subside and be more reasonable, and he'd wait to approach her until his practiced eye caught signs that her tempest had passed.

But Wyatt didn't know her. Until this moment, Samantha hadn't realized that deep down inside herself, she'd waited for him to come to her. Somehow she'd thought he'd magically know she wasn't still angry—that she regretted ordering him off her land. Her own blindness to her character appalled her. Remorse intertwined with her fear and shame. She should have gone to Wyatt—apologized. Invited him and Christine to visit. Then the child wouldn't have had to sneak away.

Samantha's own weakness of character had led to this situation, and she vowed to do everything she could to prevent her temper from ever again getting the best of her.

* * *

Wyatt rubbed a hand across his weary eyes, then resumed his strained staring into the darkness, trying to see any clue that would help him find his daughter. To his right, the river roared over boulders, higher by a foot than when he'd crossed several hours ago. If Christine had been caught in the raging water...

He'd been through bad times in his life, times that had almost broken him, but nothing compared to the agony of not knowing whether his child lived or whether she...He swallowed the feeling, despair dropping to his stomach where it rested like a rock. Emotions wouldn't help, they'd only get in the way—make him miss something. He needed to focus.

Up ahead, Little Feather halted his horse. Wyatt rode closer. In the glow of the lantern, he could see the boy squinting toward a brushy island in the middle of the water, his nostrils flared, body still, as if listening with his skin.

Wyatt followed his gaze but couldn't see what caught the Blackfoot's attention. He tried to mimic the boy's stillness, but the rush of the river masked any sounds, sending the scent of dampness whirling around his nose. A memory tugged at him— of how Christine's little-girl skin smelled when he hugged her before tucking her into bed. A lump clogged his throat. What if he never had a chance to hold his daughter again?

Little Feather lifted a hand, pointed across the swirling black water to the island. "Christine there."

A rush of hope shook him. "Christine." Her name lodged in the constriction of his throat, emerging as a barely heard croak. Impatience tearing at him, he again forced the sound out, "Christine, Christine!"

Samantha cantered toward him, followed by the boys. "Did you find her?"

Little Feather pointed to the island. "She there."

Samantha held up her lantern. "Where? I don't see her."

Neither did Wyatt, but he clung to the hope that the Indian boy knew. "I'm going after her."

Samantha leaned over and grabbed his arm. "Wyatt, the water's too high. What will we do if you get swept away?"

Damn. He wanted to shake off her restraint, but she was right. He looked around the silent circle, lantern light illuminating worried faces. It wouldn't help his daughter for him to be foolhardy.

Wyatt wedged his own lantern between his body and the saddle horn. Pointing to a coil of rope lashed to Tim's saddle, he said, "Give me your lariat."

The boy leaned over, fumbling with the ties.

Wyatt resisted the urge to bark at him to hurry.

Tim untied the rope, tossing it over.

Wyatt squinted into the night, while his hands worked to open the lasso at the end of the rope. In the dim light, his target would be guesswork. What looked like a solid rock could really be a rotting stump. His life, and that of Christine, might depend on his choice.

He chose the large bump nearest the island's edge. Circling the noose overhead, he let it fly, watching it settle around the hump. He pulled, backing Bill, feeling the tether tighten. Yanking it a few times, he decided it would hold. He looped the rest around the saddle horn.

Samantha leaned over, untying a coil from her saddle. "That won't help you if you get swept off. Tie this one around your waist."

Jack nudged his horse closer, holding out a hand. "I'll take the end. Brownie here'll stand firm."

Wyatt hesitated, cursing that he'd sent the hands upriver. Dared he entrust his life to a rapscallion boy? But he didn't have a choice. The river rose higher every moment; he had to reach Christine. And the boy was right. Brownie was a good cow horse. He handed over the rope.

Jack tightened his hand around it. In the glow of the lantern, Wyatt could see the determination in the boy's eyes. Somehow he knew Jack wouldn't let him down.

While Jack secured the rope to his saddle horn, Wyatt glanced at Samantha. "Be ready with those blankets."

"I will. Be careful." Her voice cracked.

He leaned over and squeezed her hand, resisting a quick impulse to kiss her—draw in some of her fire. He'd need it in the icy water. "Pray." He released her and urged Bill forward to the bank of the writhing, frothing course.

The horse hesitated at the edge. Wyatt kicked him again. Bill snorted and splashed into the river. He trusted the animal to pick the best footing through the treacherous current. After two steps the water swirled around Wyatt's knees, spilling into his boots. The icy deluge bit, then numbed his feet and legs.

Bill's hooves slipped, and the gelding plunged sideways into a hole, scrambling to keep upright. As the water tore at him, Wyatt held his right arm high to keep the lantern aloft and gripped his legs around his mount. For a frantic moment, Wyatt thought the horse might be swept over onto its side, taking him along. But with a heave of his forelegs, Bill recovered his footing.

Wyatt righted himself in the saddle, soaked from his left shoulder down, but at least he hadn't lost his light.

His breath squeezed through a chest constricted by cold. Shivering, he panted out words of encouragement, urging Bill forward.

As Bill fought his way through the current, the next few minutes stretched longer than pulled taffy. Finally, the horse lunged up onto firm ground, took a few steps onto the island, and stood, sides heaving.

Where was she? Wyatt's gaze darted around, trying to spook out any shadow.

Was the Indian wrong?

Fresh fear knocked him like a blow, rendering him dizzy. He blinked his eyes to clear them and, in his panic, almost missed the child lying sodden half under a bush.

"Christine." He slid off his horse, his legs rubbery.

God. Please.

He dropped to his knees next to her, swinging the lantern to see her face. Eyes closed, hair in wet braids, skin paler than moonlight. He dropped the lantern, and reached out a shaking hand to touch her face. For a second, the chilled skin beneath his fingers made him think the worst, then under his fingertips, he felt the faintest pulse in her neck.

Alive.

"Christine, baby." He ran his hands along her limbs, then her ribs. Not feeling any obvious damage, he scooped her up, cradling her limp body to his chest, and dropping kisses across her forehead. Praying he wasn't making any of her injuries worse, he lifted her to rest against his shoulder like he'd carried her when she was an infant. Moving as little as possible, with one hand he eased himself awkwardly into the saddle, grateful that Bill stood solid as stone.

He shifted Christine across his lap, hugging her close.

She whimpered. "Pa." Her eyes half opened.

He bent close. "I'm here, sunshine."

"I knew you'd come, Pa." Her eyelids drifted down, and her head rolled back.

Another wave of fear clutched him. He had to get her warm, see to her injuries. He reined Bill toward the water. But first they'd have to brave the river.

❋ ❋ ❋

Jack pressed his knees against Brownie's sides, urging the horse forward a few steps, to slacken the rope stretching from the pommel of his saddle across the water to Thompson. Between them, the river flowed by, slick and black, the current splashing over rocks. The fat moon overhead whitened the frothy bubbles, like lace on obsidian.

The lantern Thompson carried cast only a fuzzy illumination around the island, but it was enough for Jack to see the man take two strides and drop to his knees.

Christine.

Was the young 'un dead? He swallowed. The guilt wrapping around his spine ever since Thompson said she had disappeared tightened until he thought his bones might snap. He'd refused to have much to do with her. He weren't that interested in little gals. She were Dan's friend. Yet, from time to time, something about her spunkiness had caught his attention, and he'd joshed Tim when his brother had mentioned she were a pretty 'un.

They'd done wrong in keeping her visits secret. He knew that now. Never gave it no mind before—weren't none of his business what Christine did. He preferred to let others go their own way, like he wished people would leave him alone. None of their damn business what he and Tim did. Too many do-gooders poking their noses in where they didn't belong. He'd ignored the opportunity to be a do-gooder hisself with Christine, and now look where that had got 'em.

"She's alive." The man's voice echoed across the water, hollow somehow, as though his daughter might be hurt bad or somethin'.

Remorse squeezed Jack's ribs against his lungs.

Thompson straightened with Christine bundled in his arms. The big man mounted his horse and headed toward the water.

As the rope slackened, Jack backed Brownie, keeping the line taunt. He squinted through the moon-splashed darkness. Thompson had left his lantern on the island, and Jack had to strain to watch their progress while continuing to slowly back Brownie.

Frowning in concentration, he gritted his teeth, determined to maintain a steady watch. If Thompson's horse went down, it was up to Jack to keep the man and Christine from being swept away.

In the river, Bill slipped.

"Back, Brownie, gal." Dread sharpened Jack's words; he softened his tone. "Back, now."

Time slowed worse than when he had a bellyache from eating green apples, and his insides pushed and pulled with the movement of the horse fighting the powerful current.

Bill scrambled for purchase, then slipped again.

Jack's heart thumped like a carpenter driving home nails.

The horse recovered its footing, and finally Thompson reached land. Jack released his breath in several deep pants. They'd made it.

Miz Samantha nudged her horse to meet them. Lifting her lantern high, she leaned over and touched Christine's cheek. "She's as cold as ice." She handed over a blanket. "Wrap her in this."

Thompson folded the blanket around the girl.

Miz Samantha draped a second around Thompson. "Let's get her to my house. It's closer."

In the lantern light, he caught a glimpse of Christine's face. Shock and fear cut into him. Usually the gal had pink bloomin' in her cheeks like the roses in Widda Murphy's garden. But now she was paler than the ghosts he'd heard about in stories.

Is that how people look right before they died off? How his mother had looked? His pa had done chased the twins off when she was a dyin', so he didn't know.

Thompson looked over at Jack. "Go for Doc Cameron. Have him come to the Rodriguez place."

Jack nodded, the responsibility jerking him upright in his saddle. "The rope?"

"Untie me."

Jack reached over. Under the blanket, he ran his hand over the rope around Thompson's waist until he reached the knot. As he fumbled with the stiff twine, he sensed the man's impatience. The bellyache feeling cramped his guts. "Loosen, damn you." He muttered a half curse, part plea. As if in response to his words, the line slithered free. His stomach unknotted.

Jack coiled the rope, lashing it to the saddle. Then he aimed Brownie in the direction of town. He wanted to gallop like a gang of outlaws with the sheriff after them, but settled for a steady lope, knowing he couldn't flounder his horse. The doc might not even be home, and then he'd have to ride on and find him.

Could the doc help Christine? People sure did say powerful good things about the man. Happen if his pa had let the doctor tonic his ma, she'd still be alive. Bitter sadness panged, and he had to brush away the moisture in his eyes with his coat sleeve. *Can't be a sissy boy now.* But even so, the memory of Christine's ghost-like features haunted him.

Doc Cameron would help her. Had to. And the sooner he fetched him the better.

Please, God, let Doc be home.

The words slipped out of his heart before he knew he'd thought them.

A prayer!

He hadn't prayed since his ma had died—not even when they was searching for Christine. Wished a lot, but not prayed. But now...maybe 'cause of the duty Thompson had entrusted him with...it weighed on a boy...made him think different somehow. What if the do-gooders were right and there really was a God? One who might help the little gal. If so, he might as well jump into the whole damn pond instead of just sticking a toe in.

Please God up there. Make the gal be well. Make her... He remembered her playing with little Bella earlier in the day. Sunshine had sparked off her golden hair, and happiness had fair danced across her grinning face—and those little gal squeals... He winced at the memory. Why gals made those damn shrill hollers when they was havin' fun were beyond him.

Make her be able to squeal again, God. Just like before.

Something inside him warmed, like a torn place in his chest seaming together, mending some of the tatters of his soul and bringing a soft kind of comfort. He relaxed in the saddle, but didn't slacken his pace.

Caught up in his musings, he soon reached the outskirts of town. When they'd stayed at Widda Murphy's, he and Tim had slipped out often enough to know how the night shrouded the buildings. They knew how to flit from one end to the other without even making a dog bark.

Luckily Doc Cameron's house stood near the edge of town, and Jack slowed Brownie as they drew nearer. He had always secretly admired the two-story white frame building with its generous porch and twinkly clean windows above flowers and ivy spilling out of green-painted boxes. The garden had been an envy of his ma's. More than a few times she had commented on Mrs. Cameron's way with growing things.

Jack had vowed that he would get her a house like that when he grew up, complete with roses growing on a picket fence. The familiar bitterness circled his heart, dimming the God-warmth there.

He'd just wait and see if the doc were home before he'd give a nod to the Almighty.

Arriving at the white fence surrounding the doc's house, he slid off Brownie and wrapped the reins around the top rail that held the fence together. He trotted up the brick path, rushing the stairs in one bound. In three steps, he'd crossed the porch. Raising his fist, he pounded on the green door, waited a few seconds, then knocked again.

After a minute, the door flew open. Doc Cameron stood outlined in the doorway holding up a glassed candleholder. The doc must have jumped out of bed to answer the door. He'd shoved his nightshirt into his trousers, because the cloth bunched up on one side, and his hair, rusty in the candlelight, spiked out wilder than usual.

He didn't wait for the man to speak. "Christine Thompson done fell in the river. She's in a awful bad way. Come quick, will ya, Doc?"

"Run to the livery stable and get my buggy. You know my horse, right?"

"Yes, sir."

"Good, laddie. Go, then. Hitch it up, drive the buggy here, and I'll be ready."

Leaving Brownie, Jack turned and ran down the street, relief giving bounce to his tread. Doc would help the gal.

Maybe there is a God.

But then again, maybe he'd wait till he saw what happened with Christine before he'd completely make up his mind.

CHAPTER SEVENTEEN

Still wearing Juan Carlos's pants and white cotton shirt, Samantha watched from her bedroom doorway. Tension pinched her stomach. She clenched her hands, praying while awaiting the physician's diagnosis of Christine.

Dr. Cameron bent over the child tucked into the big four-poster bed. The glow of the three oil lamps she'd placed around the room glinted on his rumpled auburn hair and cast his black frock coat in amber light.

He manipulated Christine's limp limbs, his long fingers gently prodding for broken bones; the lamplight magnified and shadowed every gesture onto the wall behind him. In his gentle Scottish brogue, he soothed the little girl's teary protests.

Wyatt leaned over the other side of the bed, one hand fisted into a green velvet patch of the wedding ring quilt as though restraining himself from grasping his daughter to him. His haggard gaze followed the physician's every move. He hadn't left his daughter's side, except for a few minutes when Samantha had insisted he change into some of Ezra's clothes.

Under other circumstances, Wyatt would have made a comical sight, wearing Ezra's old clothes. The tan pants only came down to his shins, exposing gray woolen socks. His muscles strained against the too-small faded blue shirt. The blanket she'd wrapped around his shoulders kept slipping.

Although Wyatt hadn't voiced any discomfort, Samantha didn't like the way the skin tightened around his face from weariness, nor how his lips had remained blue tinged with cold. But she understood no amount of persuasion on her part would keep him by the fire downstairs. If it had been Daniel, she wouldn't have left his bedside either.

Wyatt had remained silent on the way home, and at the house while they had tended to Christine. Her initial relief at finding Christine alive had been supplanted with the fear of her having a serious illness. Added to those feelings was a nagging concern that Wyatt blamed her. He must. She blamed herself.

Finally, the doctor finished his examination and pulled the covers up over her still, pale form, tucking them under her chin. Sapped of her usual vitality, Wyatt's daughter lay looking little and lost in Samantha's big bed.

The doctor straightened, running his hand through his hair, causing it to stand on end. "She's a lucky lassie. Bruises, but no broken bones. I do na think there're internal injuries."

Samantha released the breath she'd been holding.

Doc Cameron lifted his hand to caution against optimism. "She's na out of the woods yet, mind. She'll probably have a nasty cold, and I'm worried about pneumonia."

Wyatt's chin whipped up. "Pneumonia!"

Pneumonia, Samantha silently echoed.

"But she's a strong lass," he said, obviously trying to reassure Wyatt. "Healthy as a horse. You've na needed my services for her since the day she was born."

Wyatt reached down to brush a stray wisp of Christine's hair off her forehead. "When will we know?"

"Should have a good idea by tomorra. I do na want her moved, and she'll need careful nursing."

Wyatt looked over at Samantha, concern in his gray eyes.

This was her chance to make it up to him—to both father and daughter—for her earlier errors. "That won't be a problem."

Dr. Cameron raised an auburn eyebrow. "I know you have your hands full, Mrs. Rodriguez."

"I'll be fine. The boys are bunking at Manuel and Maria's. Tomorrow they'll be in school. Mr. Thompson can sleep in the boys' room. I'll stay with her tonight."

Wyatt shook his head. "No."

Samantha's stomach twisted. He didn't trust her to nurse his daughter. Shame heated her cheeks.

Dr. Cameron frowned at him, his kind blue eyes turning stern. "I do na like the look of you, mon. You've done enough tonight. It won't help the lass for you to become ill too. I'm ordering you off ta bed."

Wyatt shook his head.

Cameron placed a hand on Wyatt's shoulder. "There's naught you can do right now."

Wyatt glanced down at Christine, then up at Samantha. "All right. But only if you'll wake me if I'm needed."

The doctor pulled a brown glass bottle from his bag. "If the lassie does wake and become restless, give her a teaspoon of this. I'll return in the morning."

Samantha stepped forward. "You're welcome to sleep over."

"I thank you kindly for the offer. But I'd best be getting back in case I'm summoned elsewhere."

Wyatt and Samantha accompanied the doctor downstairs and out the door. While Samantha held up an oil lamp to give him light, the physician climbed into his buggy. He snapped the reins and drove away.

Once back inside, Wyatt sagged a shoulder against the doorframe. "I don't want to burden you, Samantha."

Samantha set the lamp on the shelf of the hall tree and placed a hand on his arm. Through the worn cotton of Ezra's shirt she could feel Wyatt's muscular strength under her palm, even though she knew how exhausted he must be. Her heart went out to him. "It's not a burden. I'm grateful she's alive."

He wiped the back of one hand across his eyes. "It's been a nightmare." The dullness in his tone hinted at pure physical and emotional depletion.

Samantha bit her lip. "Wyatt, I'm so sorry. My wretched temper. If I hadn't ordered you off my ranch, why—" She stopped short, full of regret. "This was all my fault. Christine sneaking away to play with the Falabellas—"

"And here I've been blaming myself all evening." A spark kindled in his eyes. "If I'd handled the situation better with you." A corner of his mouth pulled up. "Come over hat in hand to apologize. Allowed her to continue to come here, not been away from home tonight." He shrugged. "You see how it is?"

"You must allow me to apologize. I could tell you've been angry with me."

"Angry?"

"You've barely spoken to me."

"Samantha, all I've been feeling is a bone-numbing terror. If I'd lost her." His shoulders sagged. "I still might."

"You won't!" Samantha put all the fierceness in her heart into her response.

He leaned his head back against the door frame and closed his eyes. "If only conviction like yours could make it happen."

"*We'll* make it happen."

He opened his eyes and looked down at her. "I'm glad we're on the same side this time."

"Me too," Samantha whispered, feeling as if an invisible lasso had looped around their bodies, binding them together. Was Wyatt feeling what she was? She reached out to touch his cheek. The chill of his skin shocked her into an awareness of his need for warmth and sleep. Like cold water dashing out a fire, guilt quenched her feelings. "Wyatt, you're freezing. You have to get into bed."

He straightened, his body moving stiffly. "I know. I'm going. But, Samantha…"

"Yes?"

Wyatt shook his head. "Never mind." He forced a tired smile. "Another time." He stepped away from the door.

"The boys' beds are all made up. Take your pick. Take extra blankets off the other beds. I'm sure you'll need them."

"I'll be fine. You'll call me if Christine—"

"Yes. Now get to bed. All will be well." But as she said the words, she wondered.

✳ ✳ ✳

It took everything Wyatt had left inside him to walk down the hall away from Samantha. Behind him, he could feel her standing by the front door, watching him. What was she thinking? He forced himself not to look back.

Samantha's comfort touched him deeply. She cared. That nurturing, womanly part of her that drove him crazy for the last month when she'd adopted her stray boys felt so wonderful when directed toward him and his daughter. A powerful feeling, like sharing with a wife—a helpmate…

His body ached—both from the ordeal he'd been through and from wanting Samantha. The doctor's visit left him feeling flatter than a beetle squashed under a rock. Samantha's warmth and conviction that Christine would be all right bolstered him up. But then turning his back on her had drained the rest of his meager energy until he was a mere shadow of himself.

He started up the staircase, but climbing the steps exhausted him. The farther he got from Samantha, the more he felt like his boots had turned to stone. He paused halfway up to catch his breath, no, to find his breath.

He tried to wrench his mind away from Samantha by walking into Christine's room as soundlessly as rock-hard boots would allow, not wanting to disturb his daughter. In the dim lamplight, he bent over her still form, checking for her breathing, like he had when she was a baby. During her first few months, he'd spent hours by her cradle, watching the rise and fall of her tiny chest, and talking to her about her mama.

He'd loved her with a fierce protectiveness since the day she was born, and he'd lost Alicia. But all his watchfulness had failed to keep her safe today.

He dropped into the chair by her bed. Reaching over, he brushed the hair off her face, feeling the silky strands catch on his rough fingers. He dropped the lightest of kisses on her forehead, then rested his cheek against her brow.

"Be well, my sunshine." He closed his eyes, remembering the agony he'd been through in the last hours. "Don't leave me, Christy. Your ma doesn't need you in heaven like I need you here."

His daughter slept on.

One more kiss. Then, grabbing the nearest bedpost, he pulled himself to his feet. He looked across at Samantha who'd followed him in and now leaned against the opposite bedpost. The candlelight burnished her hair to copper and shadowed her blue eyes. He fought down the impulse to go around the bed and pull her into a comforting hug. "You'll be all right staying up with her?"

She nodded, giving him a half smile. "Go get some sleep."

"Good night, then." He headed for the boys' room, needing to rest. Yet he doubted that his fears for his daughter would allow him any sleep.

* * *

Through the bedroom window, the faintest of pink and gray shadows smudged the horizon. Samantha stretched in her chair and pressed her palms into her back. In the bed to her right side, Christine stirred, muttering something unintelligible and flinging one arm outside the covers.

Samantha leaned forward and tucked Christine's arm back under the wedding ring quilt, then placed her hand on the child's forehead. Warm, but not burning hot. Only a slight fever. The child's chest rose and fell, but there wasn't any congestion or rattling to her breathing.

Samantha picked up a lamp from the table beside the bed, studying Christine's face. The pale skin of the evening before had given way to a normal rosiness. She took her hand away, releasing her breath in a sigh of relief.

Setting the lamp down, Samantha sat back in her chair. They'd need Dr. Cameron's opinion to be sure, but she thought the little girl would be all right. She closed her eyes for a moment in a silent prayer of thanksgiving.

Heavy footsteps and the squeak of the floorboards brought her out of her communication with the Almighty. She flew out of her chair, pulling open the bedroom door and beckoning Wyatt inside.

His brown, tousled hair had been ineffectively slicked back, like he'd splashed water on his face to wake up, then, ran his fingers over his head. He had more color in his skin, but the haggard look from the night before hadn't entirely left him.

"Wyatt, I think Christine's better," she whispered.

The lines on his face lifted; hope sparked in his gray eyes.

"Come see for yourself." She pulled him over to the bedside.

He took the seat next to the bed, pressing the back of his hand against Christine's cheek.

Samantha pulled over a wooden chair she'd earlier brought up from the kitchen. In a whisper, she detailed for him Christine's improvement.

He listened with his whole body, his gaze intent on his daughter. "I'll still need Doc Cameron to set my mind completely at ease."

"Of course."

"But I think you may be right."

They sat for a while in companionable silence. Slowly, the room lightened from dark to gray. The release from the tension of the last evening relaxed Samantha into an almost dreamy state. Amber fingers of new sunlight angled around the room. One drifted over the sleeping child's face, brightening her hair to a golden halo.

"My sunshine," Wyatt whispered. "If I'd lost…if…it would have taken the light from my life."

Samantha touched his shoulder in sympathy. "I know, Wyatt. But in a few days, she'll probably be up and racing around with the boys and the Falabellas. That is, if you…"

"It seems we've made a truce about the Thompson family crossing the boundaries of the Rodriguez ranch."

"We almost paid a high price for that quarrel."

"We did."

"Wyatt, I realized something last night," Samantha said in a low voice. "In my marriage…" Her voice faltered.

Christine turned over onto her side.

Wyatt placed his hand over Samantha's and squeezed. "Come on." He stood up, still holding her hand, and walked outside the room. Letting go of her hand, he pulled the door almost shut behind them, and with his hand in the small of her back, guided her over to the top step of the stairway. "Let's sit here. We won't disturb Christine with our talking, but we'll still hear her if she wakes."

Dim light from the windows in the parlor and kitchen penetrated into the hallway, but left the top of the stairway in cozy shadows.

Samantha sat down on the step, sliding close to the wall to make room for him. Wyatt settled in beside her, their shoulders touching. She resisted tucking her head against his arm. She couldn't afford to lean on him—it might become a habit. But still, she swayed closer, wanting to touch him, even in so small a way.

She glanced up at his face, then lowered her gaze, feeling almost shy. "When I lost my temper, Juan Carlos, my husband, would be so patient with me. He knew when I got angry, I sometimes said things I didn't mean. He'd allow me to calm down, not fight back. Later, when, as he'd say, my storm had passed, we'd talk."

"Your husband sounds like he was a good man."

"The best. I took so many things about him for granted—until I lost him. Then Daniel and I went to live with my father-in-law. That autocratic old man did a lot to anger me. I was forced to conform, hold in my feelings."

Wyatt reached for her hand, retaining it in his. A small smile quirked the corners of his mouth. "I can't imagine you doing that."

She grimaced. "I had no choice. No place else to go. My parents had passed away. I didn't have relatives of my own in Argentina." She hesitated. "But that's another story."

He nodded, brushing his thumb over the back of her hand. "Sometime, I'd like to hear it."

She shivered, trying to hold onto the thread of her thought. "I expected you to be like Juan Carlos." She smiled ruefully. "That somehow you'd know I didn't mean what I said. That you'd come riding over anytime and things would get back to normal. Although how you'd know to read my mind—"

"You wanted magic."

"I guess so."

This time both corners of his lips curled up, and his voice deepened. "I'll have to remember that."

Was he flirting with her? No. He couldn't be. But he hadn't released her hand. Heat crept into her cheeks. Her mouth drew up; a schoolgirl giggle almost escaped. With effort, Samantha suppressed his effect on her. She needed to finish her apology. "In the future, I will attempt to control my temper." The words sounded prim. She almost sweetened them, but stopped herself.

"Like you did with your father-in-law?"

"No, that was a furious bottling up of my anger."

He tapped a finger on her nose. "Anger isn't always bad. It's how you use your anger. I've been known to have the same problem. We're allies now. Maybe we can work together—help each other with this lamentable lapse of control." He leaned toward her, his gray eyes serious.

"Yes," she whispered. "I'd like that."

She knew she should stand up, step away, but all her attention centered on his mouth. A slow paralysis seeped into her limbs, pinning her feet to the step. Yet a desperate longing tilted her forward ever so slightly.

He brought her hand up, placing her palm on his chest, covering it with his own. She could feel the thud of his heart, strong and deep, so different from the rapid flutters of her own pulse. With his other hand, he lifted her chin. Then, with the faintest brush of his lips, he kissed her.

Her body flooded with heat, and a distant part of her mind marveled how such a small touch could send her world spinning like a globe.

Pulling back a few inches, Wyatt studied her, obviously looking for permission.

Samantha answered with her eyes. *Yes.* Her mouth, still tingling from his kiss, couldn't possibly form words.

Seemingly encouraged, he kissed her again, longer this time. His lips, cool from the morning chill, quickly warmed. He lingered, kissing the corners of her smile, then moving onto the middle, pressing his mouth to hers. His tongue gently slid between her lips.

Samantha opened to him, reveling in the touch of his tongue, the shape of his lips. Needs buried for two years, and sensations almost forgotten except in her dreams, sprouted like seedlings in the spring sunshine.

As his tongue explored her mouth, her body softened like warm honey. How could she feel so alive, yet so pliant and weak? She sagged against him. Like Sleeping Beauty, she'd been awakened by a kiss. Her heartbeat quickened. She wondered if he could hear it.

He traced a finger over her eyebrow, down her cheek, and along her jaw. Temptation trailed wherever he touched.

She shuddered as the battle raged inside her. "Wyatt…"

"Hmmm?"

His soft kisses across her chin sent a quiver throughout her whole body.

"I should be getting breakfast," she whispered, flexing her fingers on his muscled chest. "The boys will come storming through the door any minute now."

After one last brush of his lips across hers, he straightened, reluctance in his eyes. He squeezed her hand, as though hesitant to let her go. Then he stood up, pulling her with him. "You're right. I guess I wasn't thinking. With all I've been through, maybe I needed a little forgetfulness."

Sam's heart froze. Was that all it meant for him? A diversion. "Well, I hope I helped." She forced herself to give him a light answer.

"I'll be forever grateful for all you've done tonight. I'm beholden."

Beholden. Before, she would have been gratified to have Wyatt feeling he owed her favors. But now she wanted other things. What, she wasn't sure. Her thoughts and feelings were like a ball of yarn the cat had chased around and tangled up. She'd need time to sort through them. And she certainly couldn't think with the man standing right in front of her. Too distracting.

He waited for her response.

She forced herself to smile, walking a few steps down the stairs. "You told me once that people out here take care of their own. You've helped me in the past, and I'm sure there will be opportunities in the future."

He lifted one eyebrow in reply. "You can bet on that."

But as Samantha started down the remaining steps, she wondered. Dare she take that bet?

CHAPTER EIGHTEEN

Inside the barn, Jack finished currying Brownie and checked the hay level in the feed box. In the stalls on either side of him, his brother and Daniel groomed their own horses. Little Feather, who somehow always managed to know when the other boys had returned from school, helped Tim.

Jack had wiggled through school as though ants crawled in his britches, fidgeting more than Daniel at his worst. His thoughts kept wandering to the ranch, while his body sat cramped on the hard wooden desk seat. The only good part was when Miss Stanton led them in a prayer for Christine, and he'd joined in instead of shutting out the teacher's voice like he'd done in the past. He still wasn't sure about this God stuff, but maybe if the gal were all right, he'd start goin' to church with Miz Samantha.

Suddenly impatient with waiting, he tossed a balled-up rag at his brother. "Hurry on up, you slowpokes. Do I need ta light a fire under ya?"

Tim looked over at him. "What are you in such a danged hurry about? Us 'uns being there won't help the gal none."

"Want ta know if she done died on us."

Daniel dropped his comb. "Die? She isn't going to die." His eyebrows raised, and his lip quivered.

Jack rolled his eyes. "Now, don't take on, Danny boy. You know Doc Cameron will help her." He strode out of Brownie's stall, into the one of Daniel's mount. He bent over to pick up the currycomb and gave the younger boy a comforting punch in the arm. "Come on. I'll help ya. You get the feed."

Daniel swiped his hand under his nose and followed Jack's orders.

Soon they'd finished. Led by Jack, the four boys raced outside, across the yard, clattered up the steps of the porch and into the house.

Only Maria was in the kitchen, stirring a pot on the stove sending a beef stew aroma around the room. She turned when she heard them, her round, brown face breaking into a smile. She said something in Spanish. Jack didn't bother to have Daniel translate. Instead, he pushed aside the other boys and headed up the stairs to the big bedroom.

He stopped short in the doorway. Thompson sat in a hard-backed chair next to the four-poster. He'd propped open a book on the bed next to the little gal and appeared lost in its pages, his face tired even in relaxation. He looked up at Jack, one eyebrow raised.

She ain't dead. Jack relaxed his tight stomach muscles. "Please," he whispered. "How is she?"

The eyebrow lowered, and the hard panes of the man's face smoothed. He glanced down at Christine, and apparently satisfied, stood up. He stepped through the doorway and closed the door behind him. "Outside."

The boys hustled back down the stairs and through the door. Out on the porch, they lined up against the rail. Thompson towered over them, his gray gaze boring through them.

Jack squirmed, remembering they'd done wrong to Christine, but stood his ground.

Thompson ran his hand through his hair. "Doc Cameron says she needs to stay in bed for a few days, but he thinks she'll be all right. Soon, she'll be able to go home. Still might have to stay in bed, though."

Beside Jack, Daniel shifted. "So she's not gunna die?" he asked, his voice sounding small.

Thompson's faint smile crinkled the corners of his mouth, but still his eyes looked tired. "No, Daniel. Thanks to you all, she's going to be just fine."

Jack wrinkled his nose. "Whadya mean? Us 'uns done her wrong. Kept her secret."

Thompson muttered under his breath, but Jack caught the words. "Another one who blames himself." Louder he said, "I think we all can share the responsibility. I'm talking about how you all worked with me to save her." He glanced at Little Feather.

The Blackfoot shifted his eyes.

"I'm proud of you boys. You joined in the search." Thompson lifted a hand in Little Feather's direction. "Found her." He nodded at Jack. "Held the guide rope, rode for the doctor."

Warmth swelled Jack's chest and rose into his throat. He'd never made a man proud before. He wanted to wiggle away from the feeling—sort of itched his skin or somethin'—but he also wanted to sit a spell and absorb the goodness.

Thompson glanced off toward the mountains, then back at them. "In a few days, maybe even by tomorrow, Christine will be able to have company. Can I trust you boys to take it easy with her? Maybe read to her or tell her about school?"

They all, even Little Feather, nodded.

Thompson seemed satisfied. "Good, then. You boys go about your chores. I have to get back upstairs. And stay quiet, hear. Mrs. Rodriguez is sleeping. She sat up all night with Christine."

Thompson turned and went back inside. Behind him, he left silence, each boy seeming to need time to absorb the man's words.

Daniel popped away from the railing, his eyes sparkling. "I'll read to her from Mama's books, one of the Louisa May Alcott ones." His eager gaze swept the other boys, and he grinned, mischief animating his face. "I'll read *Little Men*. That book's like us—a bunch of boys living together"—he slanted a look at Jack—"getting in trouble together. She can be our Daisy, no, our Nan."

Jack rolled his eyes. Sounded like foolishness.

Dan clapped his hands. "And we can bring the Falabellas in to visit her."

Now that was a good idea. Sometimes Miz Samantha let one of the little ones into the house. Bringing in Bella would cheer the gal right up.

Solemn Little Feather surprised him by stepping forward. The boy, wrapped inside his favorite blue-and-gray-striped shirt, reached into his pocket and pulled out something closed inside his fist. He didn't show it to them. "I will share my sacred stone. Tell fire stories of my people." He put his hand back in his pocket.

The twins made eye contact. Jack expected his own skepticism to reflect in his brother's face, but instead he saw Tim's brow furrow. "When Ma was sick, she liked fer me to sing to 'er. But only when Pa wasn't around."

Daniel bounced on his toes. "You like to sing?"

"Ma taught us." Tim grinned at Daniel.

Jack turned away and walked down the steps, remembering his mother's sweet voice. She and Tim had sung together many a time. Ma used to tease Jack about handing over all his singin' ability to his brother. That's why Tim had a voice like an angel, and Jack croaked like a frog. He hadn't minded too much, until Ma took sick. She sure did love to hear Tim a singin'. Said it comforted her. Since her death, Tim hadn't sung a word.

Jack shoved his hands into his pockets and scuffed his way across the yard. He didn't have anything to offer Christine. At least when Ma took sick, he could bring her his nanny goat's milk. Said it was better than a tonic. Got so that was all she et.

If only he had his nanny goat. Could give her milk to the little gal. He just knew it would help her get better.

He kicked a rock, sending it skipping across the packed dirt and bouncing off a wooden stake of the goat pen. The two animals in the enclosure only made him feel worse. It should have Nanny inside, just like the bigger corral held his Mariposa. Tweren't right, that Widda Murphy keeping his goat. Weren't right at all.

He'd been planning to do something about his nanny goat, but had gotten caught up in the business of his new life. Guilt panged him about his neglect. She'd probably been wondering where he'd been.

The time had come to steal back his goat. Christine needed that milk, and he intended to get it for her.

✵ ✵ ✵

Wyatt's callused hands played over her body, the roughness of his skin contrasting with his gentle touch. His mouth circled kisses around her breasts. Languid warmth weighed her limbs, and she

longed for him. As if sensing her need, his hands dipped lower.
"Wyatt," she whispered. "Please."

"Please." Samantha slid from sensuous sleeping to drowsy wakefulness, the word still on her lips. She drifted, her eyelids heavy, willing herself to return to her dream—to Wyatt.

Beside her a movement jerked her to awareness. She sat up with a gasp, then remembered Christine slept beside her. The low light of the lamp Samantha had left burning for the child's sake softly illuminated her angelic features.

Good thing I didn't say anything else. For a moment, embarrassed heat flushed her. She lay back down, trying to calm herself. *I didn't do anything wrong. I'm not responsible for my dreams. And after this morning's encounter on the stairs...*

Samantha replayed her fantasy, lingering on the sensations Wyatt aroused in her. The memory lulled her back to sleepiness. But still her mind refused to allow complete repose. Something was different about this dream...

Then the knowledge came to her. She hadn't resisted Wyatt. She'd not only responded, she'd begged for him. Pleasure and embarrassment flushed her cheeks. Instinctively she knew something within her had changed. She was ready to move on from Juan Carlos.

At the thought, sadness arose, but not a painful sadness, more like a shifting of her heart. Juan Carlos would always have a special place in her heart and in her memories. As if in a vision, she could see her beloved husband. He smiled, his dark eyes full of love, one eyebrow cocked knowingly. He cupped her face with his palm, kissing her good-bye. She imagined him stepping back with a gallant bow, allowing Wyatt to come forward and take her hand. Juan Carlos would never entirely leave her, nor Daniel, but now, Samantha knew there was space in her heart and in her life for a new love.

❋ ❋ ❋

Samantha and Pamela Carter walked down the stairs and into the hallway, continuing a discussion about the Falabellas that they'd started when Christine fell asleep. They paused by the hall tree, its antlers hung with coats and scarves and Pamela's tatted brown necessary.

Pamela untied the strings of her necessary, fished around inside, and pulled out some folded money, pressing it into Samantha's hand. "I want to give you some money toward buying the foal."

Samantha shook her head. "Pamela, we should wait until the foals are born."

"No, I want to reserve one now. The others will probably be snapped up as soon as people get a look at them."

"Do you really think so?"

"Edith Grayson mentioned to me that she might want one for Ben. And I'll bet Wyatt Thompson takes one for Christine."

Both women glanced up the stairway toward the room where Christine lay recovering from her cold. Pamela had brought a basket of food. While Christine napped, the two women took the opportunity to become better acquainted. Unable to resist Pamela's warm friendliness, Samantha had found herself confiding in her new friend about the precarious state of the ranch's finances.

Samantha exhaled. "Well, selling the foals would certainly make a difference. I won't have to worry so."

"It's a pleasure to help a friend and find the perfect Christmas gift for my children at the same time."

"It will be hard keeping it a secret for so long. Let's hope your children all favor the same foal."

Pamela rolled her eyes. "Well, if they don't, Lizzy's choice wins. The other two will go along with her."

"I'm sure they'll love it."

"They'll be over the moon." Seemingly on impulse, Pamela leaned over and embraced Samantha. "I'm so glad we've become friends."

Warmth flushed Samantha's body, bringing moisture to her eyes. She'd been so ostracized by the women at the hacienda that it had been a long time since she'd had a close confidant. "I am too," she whispered, blinking back the tears and returning the hug. "I am too."

Pamela lifted a brown knitted shawl off another antler. "I'd love to stay and visit longer, but I'd best be getting on home."

With reluctance, the two women parted.

Samantha watched Pamela's dusty buggy pull away until it disappeared around a tree-shaded bend in the road. For a few minutes, she savored a feeling of contentment, reflecting on all her blessings. Her long-held dreams were finally coming true. She and Daniel had their own home. She'd gathered together her orphan boys, and they seemed to be doing well. She'd made friends. Christine would be going home tomorrow. The sale of the foals would secure the future of the ranch. And Wyatt...

A smile tugged at her mouth at the thought of him. He'd gone back to his ranch, but should be arriving here soon. In the last three days, he'd made it a point to spend the late afternoon with his daughter and had always ended up staying for supper. They hadn't continued their physical intimacy, but a connection slowly wove invisible bonds between them. Samantha tried not to think beyond that. Having unrequited deeper feelings for Wyatt could only cause her pain. But it was hard to ignore her growing attraction to him.

A buggy driving around the bend in the road interrupted her thoughts. For a minute, she wondered if Pamela had returned, but sunlight sparked off the shiny black equipage. Two people sat in the front seat. The wheels clattered across the bridge over the river, and she recognized Edith Grayson driving with her son, Ben.

How nice, Samantha thought. I've wanted more female companionship, and here I'm getting two visits in the same day.

They pulled the buggy to a stop on the hard-packed earth in front of the house. Ben, dressed in a brown suit, jumped out and secured the horses before going around to help his mother down.

Samantha walked over to the edge of the porch to greet them.

Edith Grayson straightened her feathered navy-blue bonnet, a match for her dress of soft wool challis, and took a wicker basket from the buggy. "Mrs. Rodriguez, I hope you don't mind that we've come to call."

"How nice to see you, Mrs. Grayson." She smiled at the boy. "Hello, Ben."

His sweet smile lit up his limpid brown eyes. "Hello, Mrs. Rodriguez."

"We've come to inquire about Christine." Edith held up the basket. "And our housekeeper, Mrs. Graves, made a chocolate cake."

"How kind." Samantha accepted the basket. "Ben, the boys are in the barn with the horses. Why don't you join them?"

"Yes, ma'am." He nodded, heading in the direction of the barn.

"Remember what I told you," his mother called after him. "Don't get dirty."

"It's hard for boys to keep from getting dirty on a ranch."

"Ben knows better."

"If you say so," Samantha murmured, skeptical. Not much fun for him, though. Well, maybe the boy would just sit on a hay bale and watch the others. "Won't you come in and have some tea? I'm afraid Christine's asleep, and I don't want to disturb her."

Edith hesitated. "Tea would be lovely."

Samantha led the way into the parlor, then excused herself to tell Maria to prepare for another visitor. Luckily, Samantha had baked a chocolate and cherry cake earlier.

Maria brought in a tray with the violet tea service. Samantha poured the tea and cut a slice of the torte for each of them. Tucking a silver cake fork on the plate next to the piece of cake, she then handed it to Edith.

The two women chatted about commonplaces while drinking their tea. Samantha felt more reserved with Edith Grayson than with Pamela Carter. Although she and Edith certainly had more in common—both widows with sons. However, Edith lacked Pamela's warmth. Perhaps it would develop when the two women became better acquainted. She certainly hoped so. She needed friends in this new land.

Edith set down her cake plate. "That was wonderful. I've never had anything like it."

Samantha flushed with pleasure. She prided herself on her baking. "This cake is popular in Germany. It's always been my favorite. The whipped cream and cherry preserves add an extra flavor to the chocolate."

"I'm sure Wyatt would like it. He's very partial to chocolate. Why the other night, when he dined with us, he had two servings," she said in a proprietary tone. "And that's not the first time. He just loves Mrs. Graves's chocolate cake."

"The other night?" Samantha's stomach clenched.

"Yes, the night Christine had her accident. I feel so dreadful it happened when Wyatt was visiting me. That poor child."

"A terrible ordeal for her." *Wyatt had been visiting Edith when Christine was lost.* Samantha's hands trembled, and she placed her palms on her lap to still them.

"I shudder to think of it. I almost fainted when I heard." Edith's delicate hand drifted to cover her bosom. "Why, I feel for that child almost as though she were my own."

So do I. "She's a lovable girl." *One I'd begun to imagine as mine.* Her heart cracked. She remembered Wyatt and Edith talking after church. Was he courting her?

Edith leaned forward. "I want to drop a discreet hint in your ear, dear Mrs. Rodriguez. There's been some talk in town about the amount of time Wyatt has been spending here. I have been careful to scotch any rumors of impropriety. However, you should be warned to have a care for your reputation."

Samantha was caught off guard by Edith's words; her cheeks burned with shame. "Surely everyone understands the circumstances. Christine—"

"A woman can never be too careful, my dear Samantha, may I call you that? A reputation is so easily lost."

"Yes of course, however—"

"Just be careful, my dear." Edith stood up, bringing the visit to an end.

Samantha felt like a fish swimming peacefully downstream who'd been hooked and tossed up on the shore. Her breath squeezed, and her mouth wanted to open and close in protest to Edith's allegations, only she didn't know what to say.

Still feeling unsettled, Samantha walked with Edith out to the porch. Outside, she saw Wyatt walk Bill into the yard. Her heart gave a happy bounce, before she remembered Edith's admonitions. She smoothed her black skirt, trying to compose herself.

Wyatt dismounted, looking handsome and virile. He flipped the reins to the porch rail. Wearing a crisp gray shirt and clean denim pants, he'd obviously washed up and changed from the day's labor.

He paused at the steps, touching his hat. "Mrs. Grayson. Mrs. Rodriguez." He held Samantha's gaze, a question in his eyes.

"She's fine. Sleeping."

He relaxed his shoulders and smiled.

Edith stepped forward. "I'm so glad Christine's doing well. Such a horrible occurrence—what she went through, poor child."

"Thank you." Wyatt lifted his hat and ran his fingers through his hair. "Must have given me hundreds of gray hairs."

"Nonsense," Edith trilled. "I don't see any, my dear Wyatt."

"Well, I feel years older."

"Perhaps my chocolate cake will help."

He grinned. "Chocolate cake. My favorite. Christine's too."

Samantha shifted, left out of their byplay. Was it her imagination, or did Wyatt seem happy about the beautiful widow's visit? She should have asked Pamela whether Wyatt was courting Edith—although the thought gave her a pang. Jealousy?

A wagon appeared on the road. More visitors, Samantha thought, not entirely pleased to have to undergo a third round of tea.

The wagon drew almost to the door before she recognized the woman driving. The Widow Murphy. Samantha had met her several Sundays ago.

Mrs. Murphy climbed down from the wagon and hustled over. A black straw bonnet perched atop gray hair piled into a haphazard bun. A wattle of skin drooped over the ribbons tied under her chin. The faded red apron she wore over a gray calico dress matched her ruddy complexion.

Samantha suppressed a smile. With her sharp nose and thin lips pursed into a frown, the woman looked like one of Samantha's least favorite hens when she wanted to peck at anyone audacious enough to take one of her eggs.

Samantha stepped over to welcome her. "Mrs. Murphy, I'm sure you'll be glad to hear Christine's doing better."

The woman flicked her a glance of disdain. "That's not why I'm here." She nodded at Wyatt. "Though I'm glad your daughter's on the mend."

"Thank you."

Mrs. Murphy looked back at Samantha. "I'm here because of those Cassidy twins of yours—most likely that Jack."

"Jack?"

"A thief, he is. No better than he should be." She pressed her lips together. "He and his brother should have been shipped off to that orphanage. Get them out of town. But Reverend Norton's too softhearted."

Samantha's temper simmered. "Perhaps you could explain why you're accusing *my* Jack of stealing."

"Stole my goat, he did. Right out of my yard."

"Did you see him?"

"No need to. I know him."

Samantha's anger bubbled hotter. "Perhaps the goat managed to get out on its own."

The woman drew herself up. "Mrs. Rodriguez, I insist you stop wasting my time. I've come for my goat."

"The boys are in the barn. We'll just go see about this goat business."

Samantha inclined her head to Edith and Wyatt. "If you'll excuse me." She sailed down the porch steps.

Wyatt fell into step next to her. "I'll come along."

Edith lifted a haughty eyebrow. "I shall get Ben."

Samantha could guess from the tone of Edith's voice what she was thinking. The idea of her precious son interacting with a possible *thief* was intolerable.

From the corner of her eye, she saw Wyatt stop and offer an arm to Edith.

She quickened her pace, not caring if the others followed. She used the time to try to bring her temper under control. Just three days ago, she'd promised Wyatt she'd change. Now she faced her first test. She spared a thought for the irony of the situation.

Samantha rounded the clump of bushes screening the goat pen. The boys clustered together inside the smaller enclosure. That's odd, she thought. Jack was usually the only one who played with the two goats. As soon as she thought the words, trepidation followed. There could only be one reason why all the boys were inside the small corral.

She stopped short, hesitant to face the facts. Through the rickety wooden poles threaded with wire, she could see Jack kneeling beside a brown goat, petting its back.

The others caught up with her.

"See, see." Mrs. Murphy pointed. "What did I tell you? There's my goat."

In the pen, the boys appeared to be arguing. Jack sprang up, punching Ben in the stomach. The boy doubled over, then righted himself and kicked Jack in the leg. Jack launched himself at Ben, knocking them both to the ground. They scuffled, rolling together in the dirt. The other boys cheered Jack on.

"Ben!" Edith cried.

Samantha shook off her paralysis, striding toward the pen, but Wyatt beat her to it. He flung open the gate and charged through. Reaching down, he grabbed the back of the boys' shirts, pulling them apart. "What's going on here?" He kept both boys dangling on the balls of their feet.

Edith rushed forward. "Let him go."

Wyatt released both boys.

Edith grabbed her son, clutching him to her bosom. "Ben, are you all right? What did that terrible boy do to you?" She ran her hands over his head and down his arms.

Samantha reached Jack's side and took his arm. He avoided her gaze.

Behind them, Widow Murphy's voice shrilled. "I warned you. Ruffians they are. Thieves. Should be jailed."

Samantha's temper boiled over. She whirled on the woman. "Will you be silent!"

"I will not." Mrs. Murphy bristled "There's the evidence. They're thieves."

Jack shook off Samantha's hand. "You're the thief, ya old biddy. Done stole my goat. I were just takin' her back."

Mrs. Murphy's ruddy face darkened to puce. "You hellion. How dare you call me a thief!" She thumped her scrawny chest with the palm of her hand. "Me, a God-fearing woman who took you in out of my own charity." She cast a look at Wyatt, which she probably meant to be appealing, but it made her look more than ever like a chicken. "This is how I'm repaid."

Jack balled his hands into fists. "Ya are too a thief. Took my nanny goat, which I done raised from a kid."

"I kept that goat in payment for your keep. And not just your keep. The sheets you ruined. My grandmother's serving dish that you broke. The flower beds torn up by the two of you. The fire you set to the henhouse that killed my best layer. The goat can't begin to repay me for taking you two in for a month."

"I didn't start no fire."

She bounced forward, slapping Jack's face. "And a liar to boot."

Samantha gasped. "How dare you hit him!" She pulled Jack into a protective embrace. "Touch him again and I'll slap *you*."

Wyatt stepped between Mrs. Murphy and the boy, holding up one hand to stop the widow.

Mrs. Murphy shook her finger at Samantha. "The boy's a thief and a liar. Burn your house down. Murder you all in your beds someday. Mark my words."

Jack straightened away from Samantha. "We didn't start no fire."

Widow Murphy threw a suggestive look at Wyatt. "He deserves to have someone take a hand to his backside."

Samantha iced her voice to cool her anger, drawing a defensive circle around herself and Jack. "*I'll* be the one who decides how Jack is disciplined. *No one* will touch him."

Edith, her arms still wrapped around her son, spoke up. "Well, he must be punished, Mrs. Rodriguez. Attacking my son that way. What kind of behavior is that?"

Wyatt glanced at Samantha. "Don't worry, he will be." His words sounded clipped. But worse yet was the glacial glint in his gray eyes. "In the meantime, Mrs. Grayson, I'll escort you two to your buggy. I know this has been a shock to your sensibilities. Do you need me to drive you home?"

Edith tilted her chin up, pursing her full lips. "I'd love to take you up on your offer, dear Wyatt. But I know you have enough troubles with Christine. I'm sure, for her own protection, you'll want to remove her from this house as soon as possible."

CHAPTER NINETEEN

Wyatt couldn't believe he'd actually started to trust Jack. Feeling betrayed and angry, he wanted nothing more than to escape and go somewhere he could sort out his thoughts and emotions. *Remove his daughter?* Edith's words finally penetrated his feelings. Good idea. Maybe they could find a deserted island somewhere. Live like the Swiss Family Robinson.

But he couldn't take her home today. Doc Cameron had said tomorrow at the earliest. He wouldn't go against the doctor's orders.

He glanced at Samantha, arms around Jack, like a grizzly protecting her cub. Her blue eyes sparkled with rage, and her cheeks flushed with angry color. If he took Christine home now, he'd hurt Samantha's feelings. He didn't want to examine why that was not an option, because right now he didn't want to have any feelings for her. Too many problems came attached to Samantha.

Edith stepped away from her son, examining him.

"Ben, you're all dirty." She shot a dagger glance at Jack. "You nasty boy."

"Mrs. Grayson." Wyatt's tone warned her to stop. "A boy's gonna get dirty no matter what you tell him." He leaned over Ben. With a few brushes and slaps, he cleaned the worst of the dust off the boy's suit. "There."

"Thank you, Mr. Thompson." Ben flashed his angelic smile at Wyatt.

"You're welcome." He stiffly offered his arm to Edith.

With a grateful look, she slipped one gloved hand into the crook of his arm. She placed her other hand around her son's shoulders. "Come, Ben."

They headed toward her buggy. Wyatt stayed silent, letting Edith's flow of complaints wash over him.

"It's a scandal, that's what it is. Allowing those boys to live here. Don't you agree, Mr. Thompson?"

"I certainly do." *Jack a thief.* Just when he was beginning to trust those boys, allowing them to play with his daughter, this happens. His error in judgment nagged at him. But he had yet to hear the whole story. There could be more to Jack's actions.

"I agree with Mrs. Murphy. Those boys should be sent away to the orphanage. Someone should see to it." Her upward gaze invited Wyatt to step into the role of her hero.

Yes, sent far away from his daughter. But he didn't like the idea of an orphanage for them. Maybe send them to a Midwestern farming family where they could make a fresh start. *Like he had.*

"They certainly should not be allowed to attend school. My son should be getting an education with other well-bred children. Well, not all of them out here are well bred. I have half a mind to hire a tutor from Boston. Do you think Christine would be interested in sharing lessons with Ben?"

The question jerked him out of his ruminations. "What?"

"If I hired a tutor or governess, would you want Christine to study with Ben?"

"I—"

"So much better than a rural school. I've had doubts about it from the very beginning. But my brother seemed to think Miss Stanton would do, at least for a while. But I think I really will have to put my foot down. Don't you agree?"

"Ah—"

"I thought you would. I'll write to Boston first thing."

Wyatt stopped short, turning to face her. "Mrs. Grayson, this is something I need to think about. I've been completely satisfied with Miss Stanton."

"Provincial. Why the woman's never been out of Montana in her life."

Most people in this town haven't.

"Christine needs the polish a governess will give her."

A new dilemma. He resented Edith's implication that Christine lacked polish. Christine's manners were just fine, thank you very much. Another part of him immediately worried that he wasn't doing his best by his little girl.

What would Alicia have wanted? Would she want a governess for Christine? But then again if Alicia had lived, she would have taught her daughter all she needed to know to be a lady. Not to mention that some of those highfalutin' Eastern ways were unnecessary in Montana.

Apparently not noticing his lack of enthusiasm for her idea, Edith said, "Besides, this will keep her from running wild."

Running wild? Christine?

She slanted a look at him and pursed her lips, obviously in better spirits. "You won't have to worry about her."

Could he stop worrying about her? No. But would the woman stop twisting him? First she yanked him one way and before he could think his way through his feelings, she'd spin him in another direction. He felt like a windmill. "I'll never stop worrying about her. I'll be an old man and still worry"—he stifled a groan—"only then I'll have grandchildren too."

They reached the buggy. He handed her up into the seat.

"Oh, and Mr. Thompson."

Would the woman never stop talking?

"Perhaps you'd like to come to dinner sometime this week?"

Not if he had to hear any more talk.

"I'm afraid that won't be possible. I won't be leaving my daughter anytime soon."

"I understand. Perhaps when she's better."

He gave her a noncommittal smile and touched his hat. "I'll ponder it and let you know."

As he watched her drive away, he knew he'd have to settle his windmill feelings. But first he needed to rescue Samantha from the clutches of the Widow Murphy. After that, he'd decide what to do about those boys of hers, and about his daughter.

❋ ❋ ❋

Samantha turned her back to avoid watching Wyatt and Edith walk away together. Angry fire still crackled in her chest, but underneath hurt knotted in her heart. She tried to put Wyatt from her mind.

She glanced around the goat pen. The other boys had backed to the perimeter of the rickety wood-and-wire fence—as far away from Widow Murphy as they could get. Concern about them poked through her anger. Daniel looked wide-eyed and anxious, Tim sullen, and Little Feather impassive. She'd see to their needs later. First she'd have to deal with this situation.

Her hand resting on Jack's shoulder, Samantha stared down at him. "I'd like an explanation."

Jack scuffed one booted foot in the dirt. The goat butted her head against his knee. He ran his fingers over the brown fur on her back. "Done raised her from a kid. All my own." His green eyes pleaded with her for understanding.

Compassion twined with her indignation. No matter what he'd done, she'd see he kept that goat.

Mrs. Murphy shook her head. Her wattle vibrated. "Makes no mind. I've come to take it back with me."

Jack straightened up, his skin paling. "Ya ain't takin' my nanny."

The widow shook her finger in the boy's face. "The animal belongs to me now. And if this town had a sheriff, I'd have you locked up right quick."

Samantha raised her hand in a stopping motion. "Don't be ridiculous, Mrs. Murphy. No sheriff's going to arrest a boy over a matter like this."

"A spell in jail might do that boy some good."

"I've heard enough." Samantha would have gladly thrust the widow into a jail cell, locked the door, and thrown away the key. But she needed to find a more peaceable solution. "I'll pay you for the goat."

Like a chicken eyeing a fat worm, a greedy look crossed Mrs. Murphy's face. "Five dollars."

Wyatt spoke from behind Samantha. "A bit much for one scrawny goat," he said mildly.

Samantha flashed him a *better keep out of this* look.

He ignored her, instead his gray gaze bored into the widow.

Mrs. Murphy shifted, an unbecoming flush staining her mottled cheeks. "The price of that animal don't begin to cover what those boys cost me."

Samantha pulled out some of the money Pamela had given her, slapping a few bills into the woman's hand. "There. Now I think you'd best be going."

"I'll go all right." Mrs. Murphy raised her chin; her wattle tightened. "But mark my words. Them boys are trouble." Her beady eyes darted a look at Daniel and Little Feather. "And them's not much better. And you ain't seen the last of it either."

It took every last ounce of restraint for Samantha to hold on to her temper. She balled her fists to keep from slapping the woman. Like a locomotive pulling into a station, she thought steam might be puffing out her ears. Her body trembled with the effort of fighting against the feeling. Only her promise to Wyatt put the brakes on the words that wanted to tumble from her tongue. "Please leave." She ground out the phrase.

With a sniff and a toss of her head, Mrs. Murphy scurried away.

Samantha glanced down at Jack, who'd dropped to the ground, hugging his goat to him as if he'd never let her go. He rested his cheek on the animal's head. "Nanny, oh, Nanny," he murmured into her ear.

Unexpected moisture pricked Samantha's eyes, and a flood of compassion smoothed away her anger. She blinked back the tears, sliding a glance up at Wyatt.

He was watching Jack, the look in his eyes mirroring her feelings. She softened toward him. But before she could reach out a hand to touch his arm, Wyatt turned and stalked out of the goat pen, heading to the house.

Samantha watched him go, her insides churning. Perhaps it was just as well they kept their distance from each other.

※ ※ ※

Jack hugged his nanny goat to his chest with all the joy bursting from his body. He inhaled her musky smell and rubbed his cheek across the top of her bony head.

The goat bleated, then nibbled on his sleeve.

Miz Samantha touched him on the shoulder tender-like, then turned and left him alone with Nanny and the other goats.

He plopped into a cross-legged sitting position, and pulled Nanny onto his lap. She tried to wiggle away, but he wouldn't let her go. He had to feel her realness for a while before he dared believe she was here to stay. The other goats shuffled around behind him. One nibbled on his hair, and he jerked his head away. "Ouch," he said without any heat, ignoring them.

He stroked his chin back and forth over Nanny's head. She squirmed some more, and he finally released her.

She scampered away, then stopped and looked at him as if to say, "Jack, is that really you? Are we really home?" She took two steps forward and butted his arm with her head.

"Yes, Nanny," he told her, feeling the truth in his heart. "We're home."

An unfamiliar prickle of tears confused his vision, and he blinked and looked up at the sky. "Thankee." He couldn't put more words to his feelings, but somehow, he figured that God knew anyway.

❋ ❋ ❋

The nightmare burned through Wyatt's mind. Pain from his beating rendered him paralyzed, helpless to do anything but watch the scene play out before him. The fire blazed through the night; orange flames poured from the house and licked the black sky. Gray smoke smudged the stars.

In front of the house, a ragged gang of boys circled his daughter, dancing a pagan tribute to evil. Their yells and whistles cut into his heart. He recognized the Cassidy twins among those monsters, and rage roared through him.

"*Pa!*" *Christine screamed, stretching her arms out in appeal. The wind caught her unbound hair, sending the tresses flying. Sparks flicked around her. "Pa!"*

"*Christine!*" *He yelled back, fighting to go to her. But the agony in his body held him fast. The smoke burned his lungs, setting him to coughing, and stung his eyes. Tears obscured his vision.*

The macabre dance sped up until the figures blurred.

Flames swept from the house, igniting the brittle summer grass. The fire engulfed the children, catching their clothing. They lit up like torches. Their screams pierced the night.

He groaned in anguish. "No, no. Christine, my baby."

The flames died.

His beloved daughter lay on the ground, a charred skeleton.

Sobs wrenched from his throat, waking him.

Wyatt shuddered and catapulted to a sitting position, his heart thudding so hard, he could barely breathe. Shivers rocked his body; his skin turned clammy. He leaped out of bed, needing to run to his daughter's room and clasp her to him. Then he remembered. Christine was at Samantha's house. *Safe.*

With a shudder, he sank back onto his bed and buried his face in his hands.

✸ ✸ ✸

A few days later, Jack and Tim wandered to the back of the schoolhouse, looking for Daniel. The sound of voices brought them up short.

"You're nothing but a half-breed Mexican. Think you're so smart with your midget horses."

Through the lilac bushes screening the rickety school outhouse, Jack recognized the voice of Ben Grayson. He peered through the green leaves, tiny withered blossoms showering across his face. With a rush of anger Jack realized—that Boston nose-in-the-air was pickin' on Daniel.

His twin came up behind him. Jack pulled his head out of the leaves and placed his hand on Tim's arm to stop his brother from giving away their presence.

"Think we need ta take ya down a peg," Arlie Sloan's gravelly tone threatened. "Maybe a visit in the stinkpot will do ya good."

Arlie Sloan, the school bully. Two years older than the twins and still learnin' with the little ones. Thick body and thick head. Mean to the young 'uns, but he left the twins alone. Knew better than to tangle with the two of them. Always "yes, ma'am" to the teacher, but out of her sight, Arlie could create a heap of trouble for anyone sorry enough to cross him.

Anger flared higher. He'd had enough of bullying from his pa. Never could do nothin' about that—just take the heavy fist or run away. But this was different. He wasn't goin' to let Arlie and Ben pick on the younger boy.

He backed away from the bushes, gulped in a breath of the midden-smelling air, and exchanged a glance with Tim. No need for words. His twin understood.

Tim snuck around one side of the lilacs. Jack took the other, sauntering over to where Ben and Arlie backed Daniel against the outhouse. Arlie grabbed one side of Daniel's gray jacket, twisting it in his fist, and lifting the boy to his toes.

Daniel's slanty eyebrows raised so high in fear, Jack thought they might disappear into his hair. He didn't turn his head, but his panicked blue eyes appealed to Jack for help.

That look lassoed Jack right in. "Take your hands off him," he growled.

Arlie looked over his shoulder at Jack, his narrow-set brown eyes squinting, but he didn't release his grip. "Stay out of this."

"I said, let go of him!"

Arlie laughed. "Ya goin' ta make me?"

"Yep, if I have ta."

On the boys' right, Tim edged closer.

Ben stepped between Arlie and Jack. His blue suit looked as neat as if it were Sunday morning. He stared at Jack, narrowing those calf eyes of his. "I really do think you should keep out of this, Cassidy. We're just having a little fun."

"Pick on someone who's big enough ta stand up to ya."

Ben raised an eyebrow in a way that made Jack want to rip it off his face. "What business is it of yours?"

"He's my brother." The words washed out in a gust of feeling, surprising him with their truth. Somewhere along the road, Daniel had become a brother. Not a twin like Tim, but a brother anyway.

Arlie laughed. "Then you're a half-breed Mexican too."

In a surprise move, Daniel kicked Arlie in the knee.

"Hey." The older boy let go of Daniel's shirt, dropping him, then recovered, punching him in the stomach.

When Dan doubled over, Jack sprang at Arlie's back, snaking an elbow around his neck and pressing his arm tight against the bigger boy's windpipe.

Ben yanked at Jack's arm. "Get off him."

Tim ran over, spun Ben around, and socked him in the eye.

"Ow," Ben howled, covering his eye and tottering back a step.

Daniel bent his knees and slithered out of Arlie's grasp.

The bigger boy made a grab for him at the same time Jack, in an attempt to aid Daniel's escape, pushed him from behind. Arlie tripped over Daniel's foot. He flew forward, throwing one arm at

Ben in an effort to stay upright. Both boys lost their balance and fell against the flimsy walls of the outhouse.

With snaps of splintering wood, the outhouse collapsed, Ben and Arlie sprawling on top of the remains.

Jack exchanged an amused look with Tim and draped a brotherly arm around Daniel's shoulders.

"Ugh." Ben elbowed Arlie. "Get off me."

Miss Stanton rounded the corner of the schoolhouse building. When she saw them, a look of horror crossed her face. She hitched up her green skirt and ran over. "Boys, what's happened? Are you all right?"

Ben crawled out from under Arlie. With an air of hauteur, he straightened his suit jacket, started to brush at some damp stains, then stopped, his hand hovering over his clothes. "They attacked us, Miss Stanton." He nodded at the twins and Daniel. His calf eyes looked oh-so-innocent. "Assaulted us and"—he pointed at the ruins of the outhouse—"destroyed public property."

Miss Stanton's usually kind gray eyes sharpened. The glance she threw at Jack cut. He'd never seen her look so angry.

Best face up to her. "They 'uns were pickin' on Dan, here. Tim and I just set out to stop 'em."

"I cannot believe you boys. Being mean to each other. Fighting. I will *not* tolerate such behavior. Do you hear me?"

"Yes, ma'am," they all chorused.

She crossed her arms in front of her. The movement fluttered the froth of lace she'd pinned to the neck of her dress like a butterfly. But no butterfly gentleness reflected on her face. "I expect to see all of your parents after school tomorrow. But I do not intend to see you. All five of you are suspended for the rest of the week."

Ben stepped forward. "But Miss Stanton—"

"You've heard me, Ben. Go home, all of you!"

Like putting on a new suit of clothes, Ben changed from indignant to innocent, acquiring the air of an injured puppy dog.

Jack wanted to kick his feet out from under him.

Miss Stanton's eyes lost their knife edge. But she kept her arms crossed, waiting for them to leave.

With a jerk of his head, Jack summoned Tim. The two of them walked around the bushes, heading toward the stable, saying nothing. But with the silent communication common to them, Jack sensed the worry in Tim. And underneath Jack's own feeling of frustration and injustice, fear simmered, pinching his muscles tight. Would this be the problem that finally caused Miz Samantha to wash her hands of them?

CHAPTER TWENTY

Samantha stepped out onto the porch of her house, shading her eyes with one hand. She stared past the bridge over the river, down the empty dirt road. A hawk glided overhead, drifting through the turquoise sky, then settling into a tall pine tree at the edge of the water. Everything seemed peaceable. But worry pricked at her like pins stuck into a pincushion. The boys were late getting home from school.

She could think of half a dozen reasonable explanations for their absence, but her mind refused to steady. To occupy herself, she marched into the kitchen for a bowl of peas needing to be shelled and carried it out to the porch.

Perching on the edge of the rocker, she dumped the contents of the wooden bowl into her gray apron, picked up the first pod, and peeled it open. Normally, she snuck a few peas to snack on. She loved the sweet, crunchy taste of the raw ones, but today she didn't bother.

Her thoughts drifted to Wyatt, and she wished he were here to confide in. She'd been afraid of allowing him into her life, of coming to depend on him. It wasn't that she couldn't stand on her own two feet—take care of herself and her boys—but…She remembered the comfort she took in his presence, the passion that flared between them. With his kisses, his touch, her heart had opened up to him.

She hadn't seen him for three days.

When Doc Cameron had decreed Christine fit to travel, Wyatt had thanked Samantha and taken his daughter home. Every day since, Sam had tried to keep busy, forcing herself not to stop on the porch or in the yard to scan the road for him riding to her. Now here she was, vulnerable, just like she'd feared. She needed to harden herself to him. But how? How did one heal a hurting heart? Time going by?

Savagely, Samantha ripped open a pod, releasing the crisp, green scent. A pea skittered across the porch and bounced off into the dirt.

She remembered the agony of Juan Carlos's death. It had been a sharp, stabbing grief, compounded by the death of her parents. The mourning started as she held his body in her arms and kissed him for the final time. Over the past two years, the loss had mellowed to a pain in her heart that would always be there. But how would she learn to live with the hurt of caring about a man who had turned away from her? How could she still see him and not have feelings?

Samantha finished most of the bowl before she saw the boys ride around the bend in the road, Daniel in the lead on his gray gelding. She slid back into the rocker in initial relief. But her unease didn't fade.

Fumbling the remainder of the shells open, she popped out the peas, then gathered the corners of her apron together and hurried into the kitchen. She set the bowl down on the oilcloth-covered table, then released her apron and let the pods fall into the bucket kept for waste scraps.

Hurrying back outside, she waved the boys to come over to the porch instead of riding to the barn. Close-up, she could see by the looks on their faces—Daniel's eyebrows raised in distress and the sullenness of the twins—that something had happened.

"You boys all right?"

Daniel nodded. "Yes, Mama." In a jerky motion, he slid off his gelding, looping the reins around the porch rail. Then he scrambled up the steps and flung himself at her for a long hug.

Samantha's concern increased, and she wrapped her arms around Daniel's thin shoulders. Although he'd always been an affectionate child, her son lately had been doing the ah-mama-don't-hug-me reactions of a boy growing up. She stroked his hair. "What happened?"

"Arlie and Ben picked on me." The words were muffled against her stomach.

"Picked on you?"

She glanced over at the twins, still mounted on their horses.

Both nodded agreement.

She held him back from her so she could study his face. "What did they do?"

"Called me a half-breed Mexican. Were going to throw me in the outhouse." He shivered.

Samantha closed her eyes for a second, fighting down the pain his words caused her. She pulled him closer, wishing she could shelter him from all the cruel bullies in this world. Anger ate around her pain. She wanted to find those boys and slap them silly. Couldn't they understand the hurt they'd caused? She inhaled, fighting for control. "Then what happened?"

Daniel looked at the twins; his eyebrows lifted for their help.

Jack spoke up first, his voice low and angry. "Stopped 'em."

Samantha knew she wasn't going to like what she heard. "How?"

Daniel bounced up and down, anxious to tell the rest of the story. His words tumbled out so fast, Samantha could only get an impression of the incident. But four things stood out. The school needed a new outhouse, Jack had called Daniel his brother, the twins had acted to save him, and they were all suspended.

She looked over at the twins. "Come here, you two."

Reluctantly, they dismounted, tying up their horses. They approached her, wary, as if one sharp move on her part would skitter them away.

Samantha motioned them closer. Dropping a kiss on Daniel's forehead, she set him to her side.

The twins stopped in front of her. Deep in their eyes, she saw their fear, and she smiled in reassurance. "I don't condone you two fighting. But I'm proud you stood up for Daniel. You both behaved like brothers should."

Both sets of green eyes widened in disbelief.

Jack spoke up first. "Ya ain't mad at us?"

"No." Finally, she dared to give each one the hugs she'd wanted them to have since they'd first come to her. Now she thought they were finally ready to receive them.

First Samantha enclosed shy Tim in an embrace. Then she reached out with her other arm and included Jack. The three of them paused for a moment, the boys as still as statues. But she sensed them absorbing her maternal loving like a parched desert soaked up rain.

Spontaneous tears sprang to her eyes. This was the moment she'd been waiting for—the time when they'd finally start allowing her to be their mother. Just like she had with Daniel, she placed a kiss on Jack's head, then on Tim's. "Thank you, boys, for being brothers to Daniel."

They straightened, sullen looks gone, green eyes bright and a slight flush to their freckled cheeks. As if they'd had as much mothering as they could take, they wiggled away. Not meeting her eyes, Jack sidled toward the steps. "Best put the horses up."

Call me Mama.

She grabbed the words back before she uttered them. One step at a time. She just needed to have patience.

Patting Daniel's shoulder, she scooted him toward the twins. "Go help your brothers. And hurry. Supper's almost ready."

She watched them lead the horses toward the barn, scuffling with each other, as if to shed themselves of their emotion. A tumult of feelings twisted in her stomach. While she was grateful Ben and Arlie's bullying had bonded the three boys into brothers, there were still going to be upset people to placate and an outhouse to rebuild. Another expense. She sighed in frustration. More incidents like this would jeopardize her ability to make the ranch financially solvent.

❋ ❋ ❋

"Pa." Blonde braids flying behind her, Christine barreled into the livery stable.

Wyatt halted his inspection of Bill's hoof, hastily setting it down, and stepped out of the stall.

Christine ran down the dirt aisle of the livery stable; the horses peeking over their stall doors flung up their heads. "Pa, the twins and Arlie and Ben were fighting. They wrecked the privy. Miss Stanton is sooo mad at them." She launched herself into his arms.

Not those twins again. He caught his daughter with one arm, hugging her to him, then set her down. Studying her face, he checked for any signs of her recent illness. But her cheeks glowed pink with health. He released a relieved breath. "Slowly now, tell me the whole story."

"Pa." She scrunched a face at him, huffing her shoulders in exasperation. "That *is* the whole story. They were fighting, and the privy is flat as a flapjack." Her expression turned worried. Blue eyes appealed. "What are we going to use tomorrow if we don't have an outhouse?"

"The one at the church or the one here at the livery." He tapped a finger on her nose. "But don't worry, sunshine. I'll build your school a new one tomorrow. I'm sure some of the other men will help and it will be up before your first recess."

Reassured, she smiled at him.

After the events of last week, it was a downright pleasure to make Christine smile. Her simple trust in him tickled paternal tenderness right down to his toes. He held out his hand to her. "Let's go see the damage."

As they strolled out into the sunny afternoon, Wyatt blinked and took a brief survey around. A few people strolled the dirt street of the town. Several horses were tied up at the saloon, and Cobbs' Mercantile had a one-horse surrey parked in front. But no mass stampede of indignant people headed toward the school-house. Maybe word hadn't gotten out yet.

Wyatt used the brief walk to the school to collect his thoughts. He had stayed busy in the last three days so he could keep one redheaded woman out of his mind. But no matter how hard he tried, thoughts of Samantha shadowed him. Now this new problem had brought her to the forefront of his mind. Although exasperated by the actions of her "boys," right now a secret part of him welcomed the excuse to interact with her.

As soon as he recognized the direction his thoughts were wandering, he swatted the feeling away. He didn't want to think about the beautiful widow, no matter how attracted he was to her. Samantha Rodriguez came with too many complications attached, and like a magnet collecting nails and other scraps of metal, she drew more problems to herself. He shook his head to dismiss images of her.

The porch of the school looked deserted. The children must have gone home already. He squeezed Christine's hand. "How did you hear about this?"

"Most everyone left, but I was waiting for Daniel. I wanted to tell him you said I could go see the Falabellas tomorrow."

"Is Daniel mixed up in this too?"

"Yep."

A twist of concern wound into his thoughts. If Samantha's son trailed the twins into trouble, she was going to be mighty upset. He clamped down on the protective urge that fired up. She wouldn't thank him for getting involved. She'd already made that clear.

He glanced down at Christine, skipping at his side. *He was already involved.*

They rounded the corner of the building, heading for the lilac bushes screening the outhouse, treading over a path beaten into the dirt by children's feet. He heard voices and smelled the sewage odors before he rounded the bushes.

Looking more animated than Wyatt had ever seen her, petite Miss Stanton fluttered in front of Nick Sanders, her hands gesturing in the air. There was something about the look of entreaty in her gray eyes that exposed her heartfelt yearning for the man. Nick had hitched his weight onto his back leg, as if trying to put some distance between them without actually moving away. Even his black hat tipped toward the back of his head.

As Wyatt approached, the two turned in unison. Beyond them, and apparently the reason they had gathered here, lay the jutting boards of the collapsed outhouse. The area reeked of ammonia and excrement.

Sanders, a flush underneath his tan, stepped toward them.

Wyatt almost smiled at the look of relief on the man's face. But he stilled his reaction. The teacher's infatuation for Nick Sanders was open knowledge. Given that Sanders was happily roped and tied to another woman, Miss Stanton's unrequited feelings could only cause her pain.

A tug of sympathy stopped Wyatt from walking forward. He didn't know what was worse, loving someone who'd passed, or loving someone who didn't return your affections. At least he had his memories. Miss Stanton had nothing.

Christine towed him forward a few reluctant paces. He nodded, touching a finger to his hat. "Miss Stanton. Sanders."

Sanders returned his nod. "Thompson."

Miss Stanton lost her look of vulnerability. She waved toward the collapsed remains of the outhouse, irritation edging her voice. "Mr. Thompson, you see the problem here?"

"What happened?"

"Ben and Arlie were teasing Daniel Rodriguez. The twins attacked them, pushing the boys into the outhouse."

She shook her head, a rueful twist to her lips. "We were due for a new privy anyway. The old one had almost rotted away." She wrinkled her nose. "And it desperately needed to be moved. A few weeks ago, I mentioned the topic to Mr. Cobb and Reverend Norton."

Wyatt hid a grin. No wonder the job hadn't gotten done. Neither Reverend Norton, with his flock and his religious studies, and cares-only-for-money-Cobb would put a new outhouse for the school at the top of their priority list. "Next time mention any such problem to me. I'll see the job gets done."

"Or me," Nick echoed.

"Thank you, gentlemen, I'll remember that. But in the meantime, using the livery's or the church's is going to take the children longer. I'll have to allow more time."

Christine pushed her body against Wyatt's hip. "My pa said he'd build it tomorrow and it would be done by recess," she announced, a proud lilt in her voice.

Wyatt gently tugged one of her braids. "I said if I had some help it will be done by recess."

Miss Stanton clasped her hands together. "That's wonderful. I'm sure some of the other men would be willing to help." Her gray eyes beseeched Nick Sanders.

Sanders shifted his weight back. "No problem, ma'am. Thompson and I should have it done by noon."

Pink crept into Miss Stanton's cheeks. "Oh, thank you, Nick. And you too, Mr. Thompson," she added.

Sanders jerked his head in the direction of the railroad depot. "I sent Mark and Sara for the mail. I need to round them up and head home. Thompson, can you arrange for the wood?"

"Have some leftover pieces sitting in my barn. Should be enough. I'll drive them in tomorrow."

Sanders nodded. "I'll meet you here when I drop off the children for school." He glanced toward Miss Stanton, ducked his head toward the brim of his Stetson. "I'll see you tomorrow, Miss Stanton."

The teacher smiled. A dimple showed in her right cheek. "Until tomorrow, Nick." She followed him with her gaze until he passed the bushes.

Wyatt cleared his throat. "We'd best be going too."

Miss Stanton turned to Wyatt. "Christine recited her spelling words perfectly today. She's all caught up on the work she missed."

Christine beamed.

Wyatt grinned at her and gave one of her braids another gentle pull. "She had plenty of time to study in bed."

"Christine's such a good student. She's a joy to teach."

Wyatt couldn't help the grin of fatherly pride bursting across his face. "Takes after her ma that way."

Miss Stanton arched one eyebrow. "I'm sure she takes after *both* parents."

Wyatt's neck burned. "Well, she sure has her ma's good qualities." He looked down at his daughter, who'd started to swing their linked hands. "Come on, sunshine. Let's go." He touched his hat. "Good-bye, Miss Stanton."

Christine echoed. "Bye, Miss Stanton."

"Good-bye, Christine. Mr. Thompson."

Wyatt waited until they'd walked back to the street. Then he stopped. "I think," he said, trying not to sound too eager, "we should head out and see how Mrs. Rodriguez is taking the news of the boys' fight."

✻ ✻ ✻

In front of Samantha's porch, Wyatt slowed Bill to a stop. He dismounted, taking both Bill's reins. Striding over to Christine, he lifted her from her pony. He set her on the ground, handing her the reins. "Why don't you go join the boys and play with the Falabellas while I talk to Mrs. Rodriguez."

Christine beamed. He could tell how happy having his permission to play with her precious little horses made her. "Yes, Pa."

Wyatt looped the reins of their mounts around the rail, then strode up the steps and across the porch. His heartbeat sped up with each stride. No one appeared to be outside. Should he greet her with a kiss?

Sudden doubt slowed him. What if her initial response to him was because of what they had been through with Christine? What if she'd only been feeling sorry for him? He'd better wait and see how things played out.

The door stood open. He tapped on the frame. "Samantha," he called.

Quick footsteps sounded from the kitchen.

He smiled in anticipation.

She stepped into the hall and toward the door, her gaze flying to his face. Wisps of hair curled around her heat-flushed face. Although clad in a plain black dress covered by a gray apron, her amber-and-blue beauty brightened the dim hallway. It was all he could do to keep from embracing her.

A pleased smile lit up her features. "Wyatt."

His heart kicked in response.

She smoothed her hands over her apron. "I was just getting supper."

"We won't keep you." He jerked his head in the direction of the barn. "I brought Christine to see the Falabellas."

"I'm so pleased she came with you."

"And I wanted to see how you were feeling about what happened with the twins and the school outhouse."

As if she'd stepped behind a glass window, the happiness faded from her blue eyes, leaving them distant. "If you're here to complain about the twins—"

"No, no." He held up a placating hand. "I just thought you'd like to know that Nick Sanders and I are going to rebuild the outhouse tomorrow."

For a second, her shoulders sagged, then she straightened. "Please let me know how much I owe you."

"How about dinner tomorrow night?" He made his voice light, not daring to show how important her response was.

"Wyatt, I insist on repaying you for the materials and for your labor."

Stubborn woman. "I have the lumber sitting around. The school needed a new outhouse anyway. I doubt Sanders will take money. I certainly won't."

She shook her head, a determined set to her mouth. A tendril of red hair tumbled down the side of her face. She brushed it behind her ear.

The woman was more tenacious than a mule. He'd have to find a way around her. He allowed a look of hurt to show on his face.

Immediately, as he'd known she would, she softened. "I'm sorry. I guess I was just being stubborn."

Yes, you were. But he wouldn't rub it in. "How 'bout if I have the twins and Daniel help me?"

"Good idea. A suitable punishment."

He cocked an eyebrow. "You call spending a morning working with me a punishment?"

A blush of peach tinted her cheeks, heightening the blue of her eyes. She glanced away, then back. A mischievous dimple peeked near the right corner of her mouth. "Did I say punishment? Forgive me, I misspoke. I meant a suitable *honor*."

He wanted to lean forward and kiss her dimple, then with his lips, trace the half inch of skin to her lips, until she parted her mouth to him. With difficulty, he brought himself back to the conversation. "'Honor' sounds 'bout right."

Her tone took on a worried edge. "Wyatt, the twins didn't start the fight. Arlie and Ben were teasing Daniel. Called him"—she bit her lip—"called him a half-breed Mexican and threatened to throw him in the outhouse."

Wyatt's ardor chilled; he narrowed his eyes, thinking.

Several years ago, he'd warned that bully, Arlie, away from Christine. Threatened to skin the hide off the boy if he ever teased or touched his daughter. He'd seen by the angry respect in Arlie's eyes that the threat had gone deep, that the boy had believed him.

Although Wyatt hadn't particularly warmed to Ben, the thought that he'd taken up with the likes of Arlie Sloan disconcerted him. He'd have to warn Edith. "I doubt Mrs. Grayson realizes Ben has taken to Arlie's company. I'll make a point to warn her. With her regard for Ben's associates, I'm sure she'll step right in."

Annoyance flashed across Samantha's face, heightening her color. "The way she's denounced my twins."

Wyatt raised both hands in a placating motion. "Did I say a word about Jack and Tim?"

"You didn't have to. I already know what you think of them. And I'll have you know that I'm proud"—she tilted her head at a haughty angle—"downright *proud* of them for rescuing Daniel." She crossed her arms in front of her.

His spitfire Samantha. Wyatt wanted to shake his head. Amazing how a man could be in trouble with her when he hadn't even said anything. He fought off the wish to fold her into his embrace, silence her speech with a kiss, feel her respond as the tenseness drained out of her body. He reached out his hands, cupping her elbows, urging her to unlock her arms.

The sound of running footsteps caused Wyatt to drop his hands to his sides and turn around, silently cursing the interruption.

Samantha turned, tucking wisps of hair back into her bun.

Daniel ran up to the porch. "Mama, Mariposa's foaling."

"All right, son." Samantha's voice sounded calm. "You know what to do. I'll be right there." She smiled ruefully. "I'm afraid the invite to stay to supper will have to wait, Wyatt. I don't know if we'll even have time for it tonight."

"How 'bout if you invite us to stay for Mariposa's foaling? I'll help. And I know Christine would like to see the birth."

She laughed, showing that dimple again. "Manuel's off with the hands, so I could use some help. But I think the stall's going to be mighty crowded. The boys will all want to watch too. Maybe I should sell tickets."

"I'll put some hay bales on the outside of the stall. The children can stand on them and watch. As long as they're quiet, it should be all right." He paused. "That fine with you?"

"Fine with me." She matched his tone. "You go on to the barn. I'll speak with Maria, change, and be right there."

He nodded and strode down the porch stairs. Unlooping Bill's reins, Wyatt led his horse toward the barn. They'd probably be a while, so he'd better make Bill comfortable.

He shook his head, not quite believing how anxious he was to see the foal's arrival. Still didn't see much use for the Falabellas. But, although he wouldn't admit it to anyone, they were growin' on him.

Inside the barn, he looked around. Unlike the night when he'd first brought Samantha here, the building resonated with life. The boys' horses peeked curious heads over their stalls. He noted with approval the dirt floor swept clean and the hay bales stacked neatly outside each stall, adding their fresh scent to the smell of horses.

Wyatt urged Bill into the nearest empty stall, stripping off the gelding's saddle, blanket, and bridle. He checked to see the stall held a full pail of water, then left his horse. He looked into the pony's stall to make sure Christine had taken care of her mount. Then drawn by the muted sound of children's voices, he strode to the other end of the barn.

In the second-to-last stall, the children squatted in the straw, hovering around the little gray Falabella. Jack knelt at Mariposa's head, patting her. As Wyatt entered, he looked up. Even in the dim light, Jack's green eyes appeared haunted, his skin white enough for his freckles to stand out.

For the first time, Wyatt saw Jack as a boy, young and vulnerable, not as a potential troublemaker. "You've seen foals born before haven't you, Jack?"

"Us 'uns never had us a horse. Just Pa's old mule. But I helped Nanny a time or two."

"Well, I'm sure Mariposa will be fine." He looked over at Daniel, stroking the small horse's dappled gray side. "This isn't her first one is it, Dan?"

"Her third."

"See, Jack, she's experienced. Won't be a problem."

The anxiousness eased out of Jack's face. His stiff shoulders relaxed.

Wyatt's own chest tightened. Perhaps the twins just needed some parental loving—paternal loving. He'd have to think on the matter. Later.

He crouched down next to Daniel, running his hands in assessment over Mariposa's distended belly. Under his palms, the foal heaved. If you divided a regular horse by fourths, what he was touching felt about right.

Samantha entered, clutching several old towels. She'd changed into men's clothes—white shirt with the sleeves rolled up, tucked into blue denim pants. She'd hitched up the pants with a brown leather belt with a silver buckle engraved with a galloping horse.

Seeing how those clothes molded to her body, Wyatt experienced a sensual rush and made a quick promise to himself. Sometime in the future, when they'd no longer had the chaperonage of children and horses, he'd have to see about peeling those male clothes off her very female form.

❋ ❋ ❋

Through the open window in the wall, the setting sun cast a puddle of orange light around Wyatt and Mariposa. "How is she?" Samantha kept her tone even, not wanting to betray the happiness that set her pulse to dancing at the sight of Wyatt with the pregnant Falabella. In spite of his offer, she hadn't really believed that the man who'd castigated her "midget" horses would actually help deliver Mariposa's foal.

"Feels like everything's right." He looked at her, gray gaze glinting. "I'll line up the hay bales."

"Good idea." A lock of brown hair fell across his forehead. Samantha resisted brushing it back. Instead, she glanced around. "Everyone out," she ordered quietly. "Mr. Thompson is going to put the bales around the outside of the stall so you can stand on them and watch."

All the children except Jack hustled to their feet.

Samantha touched the side of her forefinger to her mouth. "Mind you go silently."

The children tiptoed out.

Jack remained kneeling. "Can't I please stay with her, Miz Samantha? You said she was my very own horse to take care of."

Unable to resist the pleading look in his eyes, Samantha nodded. She couldn't help but be pleased at his assumption of responsibility. She stepped closer and ran her hand across Jack's unruly brown hair, something she wouldn't have dared before today. "I'm sure Mariposa will take comfort in your presence."

For her own peace of mind, Samantha needed to check on the foal. Wyatt didn't have the experience with the Falabellas that she did. She knelt down, feeling the horse's sides. "You'll be a mama again soon, my darling." She repeated the croon in Spanish.

Jack leaned closer. "She all right?"

"She's doing fine."

He exhaled in relief.

"You'll just have to be patient. Babies come at their own time. Mariposa knows what to do."

The four children climbed on the hay bales. She looked up at them hanging over the wall, crowded as close together as her garden peas in a pod. Just looking at their faces, she could tell what they were feeling: Daniel drew his eyebrows together in interest. Little Feather looked solemn, but had a spark in his brown eyes that betrayed curiosity. Tim's forehead wrinkled in concern. And Christine's blue eyes were wide with excitement.

Samantha smoothed her hands over Mariposa's sides. "Just keep talking to her, Jack, soft and gentle."

Wyatt returned, dropping into the hay next to her. "Now we wait."

Time passed. The children whispered together. The illumination from the open windows and barn doors dimmed. The horse labored. One part of Samantha's attention focused on Mariposa, but another lingered on her heightened awareness of Wyatt.

He sat only inches away. Her nose, long accustomed to the barn odors of hay and horse, filtered them away, concentrating on his musky male scent. The grayness of evening wrapped around them. She resisted the urge to lean against him.

When the shadows darkened, she looked up at the children lining the stall. "Tim, go and light two of the lanterns."

"Yes, ma'am." His head disappeared, and footsteps sounded on the hard dirt floor. Soon a far glow of yellow showed over the top of the walls.

"Miz Samantha!" Tim called, his voice sharp. "I think Pampita's foaling too."

"Jack, stay with Mariposa," she ordered in a low voice. Grabbing one of the towels, Samantha climbed to her feet. "Wouldn't you know, they'd both decide to foal at once. I just hope the other two don't follow suit." She hurried out of the stall, closely followed by Wyatt, and trotted two doors down to reach Pampita.

Inside, the little brown mare lay on her side in the straw. Samantha knelt down by her. She needed more light to see. "Tim, bring the lantern here, and take the other to Jack," she said softly.

Wyatt dropped down next to her. "She foaled before?"

"No, it's her first." Samantha ran her hands over Pampita's heaving side, softly reassuring the mare in Spanish.

Little Feather peeked around the stall door, his brown eyes wide.

Samantha waved him inside. "Come and sit by her."

The boy moved as silently as possible through the rustling straw on the floor and settled cross-legged at her head.

"Pampita has become Little Feather's shadow," Samantha explained to Wyatt. "It's comical how she follows him around."

"I've noticed," he said.

"She's going to miss him when I finally persuade him to attend school." She sent Little Feather a teasing glance.

The boy smiled back with his eyes.

Samantha shifted in the hay, making herself more comfortable. "Little Feather, have you helped birth foals before?"

The boy nodded.

"Good, then you know what to do."

The horse shuddered and moaned.

Time passed.

Voices rose in excitement from the other stall.

"Mama," Daniel called. "The baby's coming."

Torn between staying and going, Samantha looked at Wyatt.

He jerked his head toward the other stall. "Go. I'll keep an eye on Little Feather and Pampita."

She signaled her gratitude with her eyes. She briefly touched him on the shoulder, rose, and left, hastening down the aisle.

In the other stall, Jack knelt between Mariposa's hind legs, and Daniel stroked the horse's head. Two tiny hooves protruded from the birth canal.

Samantha's relief relaxed her stomach; Mariposa's delivery promised to be a normal birth, no complications.

Jack looked up at her, his eyes anxious.

"Go ahead and pull, son," she said. "Slowly. I'll help you." Samantha joined him, placing her hands over his. Together they eased the baby out, until it lay in a slick bundle on the straw.

She heard Jack's indrawn breath, and the oohs of the other three children.

Samantha handed Jack a towel. "Gently clean out the foal's nose. I'll cut the umbilical cord."

They moved through the finishing of the birth process. In a few minutes, dam and colt stood together. Jack guided the wobbly baby in under the mare's rear legs and belly, toward the mother's teats. While the foal nursed, Jack leaned back on his heels, a look of awe brightening his face.

Once again the miracle of birth swept over Samantha. She felt contentment and a connection with the Almighty. She remembered experiencing them even more intensely at Daniel's birth. She'd thought to experience that joy again, but it was not to be. An ache hollowed her womb, growing stronger to grip her heart in a painful squeeze. With a start, she realized she still wanted a baby. And not any man's baby—Wyatt's baby.

But did he want marriage and children with her?

CHAPTER TWENTY-ONE

In the lamplight, Wyatt studied the Blackfoot boy. Although Wyatt had seen Little Feather plenty when he'd visited his daughter during her illness, his mind had been preoccupied. Now he took the time to really assess the child.

The boy's long black hair was tied with a piece of leather into a horse tail. His face had rounded out, the prominent cheekbones no longer cutting through the brown skin. He still wore Wyatt's shirt. In fact, now that Wyatt recalled, he'd never seen the Indian without it. But the blue stripes had faded, and the cloth had become a bit threadbare. He'd have to see about replacing that shirt when it finally wore out.

Little Feather murmured to the Falabella in his own language. Calming words, Wyatt could tell by the cadence.

Pampita struggled to get to her feet.

Wyatt grabbed her, keeping her on her side. At least with this small one that crucial task wasn't so difficult.

A grunting heave from Pampita forced two tiny black hooves out of the vaginal opening. Wyatt waved Little Feather forward. "Go ahead."

The boy's eyes narrowed in concentration; his forehead furled. He chanted under his breath. Since Little Feather knew what he was doing, Wyatt knelt back on his heels, allowing the boy to be the sole assistant to the foal's birth.

Samantha entered the stall, the straw whispering beneath her boots. Her assessing glance took in the situation, and she touched Wyatt's shoulder, smiling her approval. Quietly she dropped down next to him.

Time passed as they watched the age-old struggle for a new life to enter the world. Although Wyatt couldn't even count how many animals he'd seen born, the wonder never left him. He saw by the rapt look on Samantha's face, that she experienced the same sense of awe.

Under the cover of the straw blanketing the floor, his hand crept toward hers, until, with a tiny electric charge, their fingers touched, entwined. He wanted her. The fecund imagery of the birth had sent primal signals coursing through him, and he could barely keep from pulling this woman into his arms. But the boy was there, and the other children filled the barn with soft laughter and cooing words of encouragement to the new mother and son. Wyatt drew in his desire and told himself there would come a day.

For the rest of the time, Wyatt alternated between observing Little Feather competently deliver the foal, and studying Samantha. The dim lantern light illuminated the panes of her face and shadowed the vivid blue of her eyes, but couldn't hide the glow of her expression. In the yellow glimmer, pride in Little Feather crossed her countenance, followed by a Madonna-like reverence for the birth process. And once or twice, Wyatt thought he caught a sideways glance at him, and a pleased expression flickering across her face.

When the delicate brown filly wobbled to her feet and Little Feather guided her to suckle, Wyatt squeezed Samantha's hand in celebration.

She pressed his fingers in return, then, releasing his hand, stood and made her way around the horses to Little Feather. She gave the boy a quick hug, as if afraid the young man wouldn't accept the embrace. But Wyatt saw the happiness in the boy's eyes, and knew Little Feather welcomed the gesture of affection.

"Well done," Samantha murmured, before bending over to fondle Pampita, crooning praises to her in Spanish.

Well done, indeed. He'd been wrong about Samantha taking in this boy. Had he been wrong about the others?

❋ ❋ ❋

Wyatt paced back and forth in front of the steps of the schoolhouse. He'd arrived early, even before Miss Stanton, and had sent the twins and Daniel around to the outhouse to stack the ruined boards. Christine had trotted along by Daniel's side, eager to supervise.

He stopped, tempted to pull his pocket watch out of the faded denim pants he wore, but resisted. Instead, he glanced around. Across the street at the mercantile, Mrs. Cobb vigorously shined the outside of the plateglass window. Even at this hour, he caught a glimpse of Henry Arden slinking through the shutter doors of the saloon on the other side of the store. Down from the schoolhouse, next to the side of the livery, Pepe perched atop a wagon of hay, forking it up through the loft window of the stables.

Wyatt had come early to catch Miss Stanton in order to fill her in on his notion to have the boys help. He knew Arlie Sloan's parents didn't care what trouble their son got into, nor about any punishment he'd receive. But Edith Grayson would be another matter. Already prejudiced against Miss Stanton, she'd be bound to blame the teacher if her son worked out his punishment. Wyatt wasn't so sure what would happen if the demand came from him. Might have to spread on a bit of charm to smooth over any rough patches.

That idea didn't sit too well with him. Nevertheless, Ben needed to be disciplined. A spot of honest labor might straighten the boy out.

Down at the end of town, he spied Nick Sanders riding his Appaloosa, Lizzy Carter perched in front of him. He turned onto the main street, accompanied by the two oldest Carter children on their ponies. Good. Wyatt would have time to run his plan by the man. Although he'd bet his ranch that Sanders would leave the sweet-talkin' of Edith to Wyatt. Until Elizabeth Hamilton happened along, Sanders had never publicly spoken more than a few words to a woman.

Amazing what love could do to a man.

His thoughts flicked to Samantha and the strong attraction pulling his emotions and body to her, regardless of what his mind had to say about the matter. Yesterday, she'd been mule stubborn about his suggestion to remain behind at her ranch and let him run the outhouse show. But he'd finally convinced her. A wave of satisfaction settled over him. He was learning to handle the lady. He knew she'd be by after school to speak to Miss Stanton and inspect his handiwork.

Nick rode up. Like Wyatt, he came dressed for messy work in faded old denim pants and a grayish flannel shirt. He touched the brown hat he wore. "Morning, Thompson."

"Sanders," Wyatt nodded a greeting. "Hello, Mark, Sara, Lizzy."

"Good morning, Mr. Thompson," the older two chorused, both sliding off their ponies.

Nick handed Lizzy down to Mark, then dismounted, untying his saddlebags. He tossed the reins over to Mark and jerked his head toward the livery. Both children started in that direction, leading the horses.

Nick hefted the bags over his shoulder. "Ready to start?"

"First I need to tell you that the Cassidy twins and Daniel will be helping us. I've already started them on the cleanup. I also want to rope Arlie and Ben in. Maybe a little hard work will make them all think twice about fighting."

"Maybe so. But Ben?"

"I'm going to speak with his mother. I'm sure I can get her to agree." *He hoped.*

Nick raised one skeptical eyebrow. "All right, then. Well, guess I'll be seein' what the boys are up to."

Wyatt laughed. "You do that. And I'll tend to Mrs. Grayson."

"Think I'd rather have my job." Nick flashed Wyatt a wry grin.

Me too, Wyatt thought. From the corner of his eye, he caught a glimpse of green through the half-open mercantile door. "Here comes Miss Stanton."

"I'll go pick out a spot for the new outhouse." Nick beat a hasty retreat.

Wyatt shrugged in sympathy. Nick didn't want to face Harriet Stanton any more than Wyatt wanted to talk to Edith.

Miss Stanton hurried over, a pile of books clutched in one arm. She stopped short in front of Wyatt, her cheeks pink, gray eyes lit with pleasure. "Mr. Thompson. I'm so glad to see you this morning. And I noticed Mr. Sanders is already here too. I certainly hope the children appreciate your efforts. I certainly do." She took a couple of quick steps in the direction Nick had gone. "And I'll have to go and tell Mr. Sanders so."

"Wait." Wyatt broke into the flow of words before she could scatter off after Nick. "The twins and Daniel are going to help us. They're already back there stacking the wood. I figured the work would be a suitable punishment for them. I'd also like to have Arlie and Ben involved."

"What a marvelous solution, Mr. Thompson." She fingered the circle of gold pinned to the neck of her dress. "They'll still have to make up any schoolwork they'd miss, plus the extra studying I'm going to assign them."

"I'll inform the other boys when they get here."

"Very well, Mr. Thompson." She turned to leave. "I'll just go check on how things are going."

With the teacher's back to him, Wyatt could safely release the smile that had threatened to leak out during their conversation. Poor Sanders. A captive for the day. Wyatt would bet money that this was going to be the fastest outhouse raisin' ever.

The Livingston buggy drove into sight; the two matched brown horses trotted with precision. Wyatt's amusement faded. He braced himself for the coming encounter with Edith. However, on closer sight, Caleb Livingston, not Edith, accompanied his nephew. Wyatt wasn't sure whether or not to feel relieved.

Livingston pulled up in front of the school. Ben, wearing his blue suit, hopped down. The banker nodded. "Good morning, Thompson."

"Livingston. I'd like a word with you."

The man hesitated, then applied the brake. Keeping a hold on the reins, he climbed down.

Dressed in an immaculate brown suit and a haughty air, the banker made Wyatt feel shabby, a familiar feeling from his childhood. He had to remind himself he was a successful rancher, and his worn apparel was practical, not a sign of poverty. But still, old shame could cling tighter to a man than a burr to woolen cloth.

"What's on your mind, Thompson?"

"I promised Miss Stanton that I'd rebuild the outhouse. The twins and Daniel Rodriguez are helping. I want Ben and Arlie to work too. Suitable punishment, wouldn't you agree?"

Livingston hesitated, apparently pondering the question. "Although Ben defended himself from an attack, he was still involved in the destruction of the facility. You're right. This will be a good object lesson for him."

"He'll need to change out of those clothes."

Livingston pursed his lips, thinking. "I'll return to the house and find something for him. If I send Ben, he'll disturb his mother. She's laid down on her bed with a headache. The situation has upset her. I think she needs a time of peace and quiet. I won't bother her about this."

"Before you go, please break the news to your nephew."

"Of course."

Better you than me, Wyatt thought. He pulled his thoughts up short.

While Livingston went over to talk to Ben, who'd been petting his uncle's horses, Wyatt contemplated his reluctance to deal with Edith. Not a good situation for a man who'd been considering taking the woman to wife.

Now he could see that with the sun of Samantha Sawyer Rodriguez blazing on his horizon, his shallow attraction to Edith had set. A feeling of relief that he hadn't started to court Edith settled in him. Even if he managed to ignore his fascination with Samantha, he was through with Edith Grayson.

❋ ❋ ❋

Ever a showman, Chico pranced as he drew near the schoolhouse, Bonita matching his pace. They pulled the buggy precisely in front of the hitching post at the edge of the steps, and Samantha halted them. The little brown stallion shook his head, jingling the harness, black mane flying as if he expected the admiration of all eyes. Unfortunately, with school still in session, no one but Samantha could see him.

Miss Stanton's voice floated through the open windows of the white frame building: "Fourscore and seven years ago, our forefathers brought forth on this continent a new nation, conceived in liberty and dedicated to the proposition that all men are created equal."

Samantha recognized the words of Lincoln's Gettysburg Address, and goose bumps shivered down her arms. Her father had been a fervent admirer of Lincoln, and had once seen the great man speak at a political rally. Many a time her father had read the famous speech to Samantha, his sonorous voice tolling out the fateful words. If her son and her twins missed this lesson by working outside, it would be a pleasure for her to help them with their homework.

As if called by her thoughts, Daniel pelted around the building. His clothes looked dipped in dust, and he had a new tear in his beige shirt. Skidding to a stop at the sight of her, he then broke into a skip step, ending with a hop to her side.

Her grasshopper. She smiled a greeting. "Hello, Daniel."

"Mama, we've finished. Come see." He bobbed up and down, face flushed, his blue eyes alight with eagerness.

Relief relaxed her. He wouldn't be so happy if Ben and Arlie had continued to be mean to him. Not that Wyatt or Nick Sanders would allow that. But still, the men couldn't be with each boy every moment.

She applied the brake and stepped down, looping the buggy reins to the hitching post. "Lead the way."

Daniel bounced beside her, spilling out the story of his day. Obviously he felt very important about having been allowed to help the men.

For a moment, sadness twisted inside Samantha. Daniel desperately needed male guidance. Unlike many men, Juan Carlos had been an active parent, spending a lot of time with his son, and having endless patience for the boy's energy—matching Daniel's high spirits with enthusiasm of his own.

She sighed, once again missing her husband and the sense of family the three of them had together. As they came around a clump of bushes, she shook her melancholy thoughts away.

Wyatt and Nick stood, both in identical poses, arms crossed over their chests, studying the results of their work. In front of them, a small sturdy building made a perfect privy, complete with the crescent moon carved into the door. Ten feet away, a raft of nailed-together planks covered the filled-in midden, where a faint odor still lingered in the air. Hammers and saws poked out of a cowhide sack near the outhouse.

Ben and Arlie sat in the shade of a cottonwood tree, looking tired, sulky, and patched with dirt, their backs against the trunk. The twins were busy scooping up wood chips and stacking the longer pieces of wood in a neat pile.

Samantha suppressed a smile. Arlie and Ben had the sullen looks worn so often by her twins, while Tim and Jack eagerly finished their cleanup job. What a change.

The men turned at her approach. The twins dropped what they were doing and rushed over. Jack reached her first. "Miz Samantha, see what we done built."

Tim pointed to the door with its moon. "Mr. Sanders did that. And I helped." His chest expanded two inches.

Daniel tugged on her arm. "I did the back part. Come see."

"All of you did a wonderful job." She included the men in her praise. "It's the best outhouse I've ever seen." She allowed Daniel to yank her along three feet to view the back of the structure. She rubbed her hand over the boy's head. "Well done, son."

Jack scuffed a clump of grass with his boot. "Think we could build us a new one at the ranch?"

Samantha couldn't help the rush of pleasure that stretched a wide smile across her face. "I think a new outhouse would be marvelous." Somehow she'd find the money.

Her eyes met Wyatt's. Amusement glinted in his gaze. He raised an eyebrow in acknowledgment of their silent communication. For a moment a connection lingered between them.

Her heartbeat quickened; she could feel her cheeks glow.

From behind them, Edith Grayson's voice cut, knife-sharp. "What is the meaning of this?" She lifted her brown silk skirt, picking her way over the dirt path to join them. The froth of lace pinned at the neck of her matching shirtwaist trembled with her indignation.

Wyatt stepped forward, his hands in a placating gesture. "Now, Edith—"

"Don't you speak to me in that patronizing manner, Wyatt Thompson. I want to know what my son is doing out here, dressed in those"—her nose pinched in distaste—"rags, instead of being in the classroom where he belongs?"

Wyatt took a visible breath. "All the boys worked with Sanders and me to build—"

"My son, a common laborer!"

"Your son, an honest worker."

Edith's bosom swelled; red flooded her cheeks. "How dare you."

"Mrs. Grayson, your brother Livingston and I agreed that the boys' rebuilding of what they'd destroyed would be a suitable punishment. That and extra studying."

"I'll certainly have to speak to my brother."

Although Samantha didn't really like Caleb Livingston, she could pity the man. She wouldn't want to be in his boots when his sister lit into him.

Throwing a venomous glance at Samantha, Edith said, "This is all your fault. If you hadn't taken in those, those scalawags..." She waved a hand toward the twins. "None of this would have happened."

Anger spiked in Samantha. "If your son hadn't been bullying my son, none of this would have happened."

"Well." Edith's mouth opened and closed like a fish's. She glared at Wyatt. "Are you going to let her speak to me that way?"

He frowned at her. "You brought that remark on yourself, Edith."

He cocked a playful eyebrow at Samantha, and gave a half grin, the one that never failed to reach her.

In spite of her anger with Edith, Samantha couldn't help but soften toward him.

As he addressed Edith again, Wyatt's expression dropped into seriousness. "I believe after what you said about Mrs. Rodriguez's twins, you should consider yourself as having gotten off lightly."

Edith's brown eyes narrowed, drawing her brows together. "I've had enough of this," she huffed. "I'm going to speak to the school board about reprimanding Miss Stanton." She threw another dart at Samantha. "And about expelling those boys of yours."

CHAPTER TWENTY-TWO

Watching the coldness in Edith's brown eyes, Wyatt wondered how he ever had found her attractive. His first instinct was to hustle the woman away before she tossed any more kindling on the fire she'd set.

Samantha clenched her fists. "How dare you."

Edith ignored her. "Come, Ben." She whirled and stalked off, her back stiff with outrage.

Samantha turned to Wyatt; her blue eyes pleaded for reassurance.

He stepped forward, taking her hand and pressing it. "I'm sorry she attacked you like that, Samantha."

Nick cleared his throat. "Now don't you worry, Miz Rodriguez. John Carter's on the school board, and he's more than a match for Miz Grayson."

Wyatt nodded. "Edith doesn't realize that I'm on the school board. If there's a meeting, we'll just explain that the boys have served their punishment. I'm sure the board will let the matter drop. Besides, we saved the rest of them from having to go to the time and trouble of puttin' up a new outhouse."

A glance at the twins' troubled faces told Wyatt they'd taken Edith's words hard. Daniel had lost his happy glow and pulled in on himself. A sudden shaft of empathy stabbed him. He remembered being a boy, standing alone, facing adults who'd belittled him. Wasn't a good feeling.

Samantha stepped in. "Well, boys. We'd best be getting home. I believe Maria has baked cookies."

The promise of the treat failed to move them.

She held out her arms. Daniel ran to her. She caught him in a maternal embrace. The twins followed more slowly. But they crowded close enough for a four-way hug, cheeks brightening with evident pleasure and embarrassment.

Wyatt's throat closed, wondering what it would have been like to have a mother's love and support, instead of the indifference from the drunken prostitute who'd birthed him, then basically let him run wild.

Samantha leaned over, resting her chin on Jack's head for a brief moment. "You've all done a good job here, boys. We'll have to start planning for a new outhouse at our ranch. Think you can do it all by yourselves?"

Wan smiles replaced their scared looks. Samantha stroked Daniel's hair, brushed the back of her hand across Tim's cheek, reached out and squeezed Jack's shoulder. "Come on."

Wyatt moved closer, wanting to share in the warmth of the circle. "You've all done good work. I'd hire you on any day."

"Oh, no you don't." He could see the effort she made to keep her voice light. "They're my hands. I couldn't do without them."

He strove to match her tone. "Maybe someday I'll hire them out from under you."

Or maybe someday we'll be a family.

❋ ❋ ❋

In the crisp June morning air, Wyatt stood with Christine's hand clutched in his. As he stared at the ruin of the school outhouse, rage rose from his chest into his throat. When Christine had insisted on a proprietary inspection of the privy they'd built yesterday, he'd never dreamed what they'd find when they'd rounded the bushes. But the odor of smoke should have warned him.

Only charred wood, black and gray ashes, and a few smoldering embers remained of the compact little building that he, Sanders, and the boys had hammered into place yesterday. Even the lilac bushes bore scorch marks and shriveled leaves, evidence of the fire.

He glared upward, trying to control his anger. Innocent puffy clouds floating in the azure sky only served to contrast with the darkened remains in front of him.

At his side, Christine burst into tears, forcing him to shelve his feelings. He squatted down, pulling her toward him. "Shush, sunshine, don't cry."

"But, Pa, it's all burnt down," she wailed.

"I know. But I'll rebuild it for you." *And catch the culprits who did it.*

She pressed her face into his shirt, sobbing, shoulders shaking.

Helplessness gripped him. His daughter didn't cry very often, but when she did, it seemed, like of Mrs. Toffels's cakes, she had layers of hurt and fear. As always, when his first solution wouldn't fix things, he flapped around with ineffectual words, feeling like a pillowcase strung out to dry on a windy day.

A gasp behind him made him glance up. Flanked by the twins and Daniel, Samantha covered her mouth with one black-gloved hand. Her distressed blue gaze flew back and forth between the ruin and Christine. "What happened? Is she hurt?"

"She's upset about the fire. I told her I'd build a new outhouse, but she won't stop crying."

"Poor child, a lot has happened in the last few weeks, and she probably has quite a bit stored up inside." Samantha stepped closer. "Let me try." She touched Christine's shoulder. "Christy, dearest, tell me what's wrong."

The words poured out, muffled against his shirt. Wyatt couldn't make out one in five. Daniel, trouble, twins, Pa, anger, privy. He couldn't string them into sentences with meaning.

Samantha seemed to have no such trouble. She nodded in understanding, and in talking back to Christine, also managed to translate for Wyatt. "You're upset that someone burned the beautiful outhouse your pa and the boys built."

Sniff.

"You're afraid the boys will be in trouble again?"

Christine nodded, her sobs starting to quiet.

Magic. How did Samantha do it? Must be one of those woman things.

"Your pa's angry and that frightens you."

Another sniff and nod.

That response caught Wyatt by surprise. How did she know he'd been enraged? He hadn't said a word. And why would that scare her? Shame followed. He wouldn't hurt a hair on his daughter's head. Didn't she know that?

Samantha rubbed the back of Christine's head. Her other hand squeezed Wyatt's shoulder. "I'll bet you don't see your pa angry very often, do you?"

A shake of her head, nose still burrowing into his chest. At least she'd stopped shaking.

"I remember when my father was angry, he'd get this look in his eyes, and his face would get all hard. That would scare me. Especially if he was upset with *me*."

That statement spurred Wyatt into talking. "I'm not upset with you, sunshine," he murmured. "Just whoever did this. It wasn't right, especially after how happy the boys were with their work. That's why I was angry." He lightened up his tone, trying to make her laugh. "I was like Warrior the bull, right before he charges. Can you see me with two horns, swishing my tail?"

That did it. She looked up. "Oh, Pa."

Christine glanced around, saw Daniel watching her, his eyebrows drawn up, concern in his blue eyes, and tucked her head back into Wyatt's shoulder.

Once again, Samantha seemed to understand. "Daniel won't be in trouble. He was home at the ranch when all this happened."

Christine tilted her head slightly, one blue eye looking up at Samantha.

"Daniel's safe, I promise."

With a sideways move of her chin, Samantha signaled to Daniel.

He shuffled closer, patting his friend on the shoulder. "We'll build you a new outhouse, Christine. Better than the ole one, right, Mr. Thompson?"

"Right, Dan."

The boy's promise did the trick. Christine pushed away from him, her face already brighter in spite of the tearstains.

How come Daniel could make his daughter the exact same promise that he had, yet it worked for the boy and not for her very own pa? he complained to himself.

But he knew the answer. There were a lot of feelings sandwiched between the two offers. Guess a girl needed to talk it out. He stored the knowledge in his brain. Something like that was good for a man to know, both in dealing with daughters, and—he glanced at Samantha from the corner of his eye—grown women.

Christine looked up at Daniel. "Can we put a moon *and* some stars on the door?"

"Yep."

Christine slid closer to Daniel. "Good." She smiled at the boy. *That's right, Dan. Promise her the moon and stars if it will make her happy. The boy was learning early.*

Samantha smiled, and met his eyes. A sense of parental connection flashed between them, then deepened into an attraction that wrapped around his rib cage and spun her to him. *One of these nights, he'd have to see about lassoing up the moon and stars for Samantha.*

Daniel grinned. This time his eyebrows winged with relief.

Another lesson, Dan. Making them happy makes a man feel as big as a mountain. He hoped the boy was payin' attention.

Christine reached over and clasped Daniel's hand. Under the boy's olive skin, red flushed his cheeks, but he didn't let go.

This time it was Wyatt who shivered, looking down a short path to the future. Sooner than he'd like, his daughter would be grown up. Some man, maybe even this one, would come a courtin', and she'd be gone, leaving her father behind.

❋ ❋ ❋

Despite the reminder of the embers smoking in front of her, Samantha glowed with a quiet sense of pleasure. Her body still resonated from the emotional connection with Wyatt. Anticipation fluttered her heartbeat and warmed her cheeks. She wanted to snuggle close to his side and feel the strength of his arm around her.

It was amazing how a strong, capable man could be reduced to jelly by female tears. She shook her head. Listening was most of the solution. You'd think eventually men would catch on to that. The bewilderment in his eyes over Christine's tears, and the helpless look on his face had appealed to all her maternal instincts. The child needed her—*he* needed her.

She enjoyed watching Wyatt go from befuddlement to gratitude as much as she received satisfaction in helping Christine sort out her feelings.

In many ways, girls were easier. They cried and talked. But boys had to hold it all in, be strong. A mother had to continually keep her instincts open, spot the needy crumbs they sparingly dropped when they were upset—or when they were up to something. Even then it often wasn't enough. A mother needed extra mind-reading skills with sons. When she got to heaven, she was going to complain to the Almighty about that deficit.

With reluctance, Samantha released her gaze from Wyatt and instead observed her son. Watching Daniel and Christine hold hands brought tears to her eyes. The two children had formed a bond that extended deeper than mere childish friendship. Daniel had been so isolated and lonely on the estancia, and she had ached with her child's pain. She glanced over at the twins, standing shoulder to shoulder, identical pleased grins on their faces. Daniel was developing a circle of companions, and Samantha was glad. *No matter what comes of it.*

"Come on. We'd better get inside." Daniel towed Christine away. The twins followed.

Wyatt cleared his throat. "Mrs. Toffels was so proud of the boys' work here yesterday that she said she was going to bake them a cake to celebrate." His gaze flicked toward the ruin.

"Although celebratin' might have to be postponed, I don't think chocolate cake should be."

"That's so kind of Mrs. Toffels."

"How 'bout I ride it over this evening?" He held her gaze, his gray eyes silvered with a deeper unspoken question.

"That sounds wonderful." She lowered her lashes to hide the spurt of joy that flared up. What if she was misreading his offer?

"Then I'll be by after supper."

"Will you bring Christine?"

He lowered his voice. "A man doesn't bring his daughter when he goes a courtin', Samantha."

"Oh." She studied the clump of grass at her feet, feeling the heat rise in her cheeks.

"Well, I never," a woman's voice huffed from behind them.

Edith Grayson. Would the woman never leave them some peace? Samantha turned slowly, hoping that the red in her cheeks could be explained by indignation over the burning of the outhouse. She smoothed the palms of her hands over her black dress to keep them from rushing to cover her face.

Edith Grayson stood with her hands on her hips, full lips pursed in obvious disgust. Her white shirtwaist dripped with lace threaded with maroon ribbon. A straw bonnet tied under her chin with matching ribbons. A maroon feather quivered against her cheek. "After the way my son slaved to build that thing, someone had the gall to burn it down?"

Wyatt rubbed his hand through his hair, his demeanor darkening. "Looks that way, Edith."

"Well, this time Ben certainly will not participate in constructing a new one."

"Won't be askin' him anyway."

Something in Wyatt's tone must have warned the woman of his mood. Edith's brown eyes softened, holding a touch of flirtation. "Now, Wyatt, you mustn't think I was belittling all your hard work. I just can't believe anyone would do such a thing."

Samantha's chest tightened with jealousy.

Wyatt looked at the destruction of his work. "Me neither."

Edith's gaze slid to Samantha, and her eyes narrowed. "Your twins did this."

"What!" Samantha clenched her jaw, fighting the impulse to claw out the woman's doe eyes. "My twins built this—with pride. They'd never burn it down."

"Where were they last night?"

"In bed where they belong."

"Did you check on them?"

Samantha gritted her teeth. "They are neither babies, nor ill." She enunciated each word. "Of course I didn't check on them."

Edith sniffed. "Then you don't know."

"I do know. I know my boys."

"You've barely had them for three months. They're probably pulling the wool over your eyes."

Wyatt stepped in. "The twins were too dang proud of themselves to pull a stunt like this, Edith. But don't worry. I'll rebuild the outhouse."

"Who's to say those incorrigible boys won't torch the place again?"

"Edith," Wyatt warned.

Samantha could tell by the tightening of his jaw that he was keeping a tight hold on his temper.

Edith lifted her chin. "Say what you'd like, Wyatt Thompson. I'm going to speak to Reverend Norton and my brother. It's time we called a town meeting to deal with this situation."

CHAPTER TWENTY-THREE

On the road leading from his ranch to Samantha's, Wyatt drove his surrey up a small hill and caught his breath at the beauty of the large crescent moon dangling just out of reach over the crest. A full moon would have been plump with luminescence. Yet the pearly surface of the sickle still cast enough light to shadow his surroundings and seemed close enough that, once he drove to the top of the hill, he'd be able to touch the bottom horn—or at least toss a rope around it.

He slackened the reins, slowing the horse, knowing that the higher he climbed, the sooner the illusion of closeness would disappear. And he wanted to preserve for a moment the fantasy that the moon was within his grasp.

The stars, by contrast, were distant pricks of diamond light, farther out than a man could dream. He sighed. Life as a rancher, or as a rancher's wife, was not moon and stars easy or romantic.

What would put stars in Samantha's eyes? Probably for him to be a father to that pack of boys of hers. A few months ago, the idea would have been unthinkable. Now he was starting to wrap his mind around the possibility. Those four had a way of getting under a man's skin. Most times that thought felt like a burr under a saddle, something to be bucked off, but other times, there was a warmth at the thought of being a pa to them, giving what he'd never gotten.

He glanced over at the chocolate cake, resting in a wicker basket on the seat next to him, remembering the times when he'd shared with Samantha the bond of parental affection about their children. Different from the tug of sexual attraction he experienced whenever he came into her presence, or the love that had been growing as he watched her rear her boys and wrest a living from a tired old ranch, until he was awed by her beautiful, feisty spirit.

Did she feel the same? She hadn't answered his comment to her about coming courtin'. What would she have said if they hadn't been interrupted by Edith? His stomach clenched with nervousness. This beginning courtin' business wasn't easy on a man. You'd think the second time around would be different, seeing as he'd had experience and all. But it wasn't. The same sweaty palms, racing heartbeat. The same wonder of what she'd look like in his bed.

Although this time it would be different. Samantha wasn't a virgin to be carefully eased into lovemaking. She'd been well loved before and wasn't a stranger to passion. Could he ignite hers enough to burn past the pain of her husband's memory? He imagined her bare of her widow's garb, with her fiery hair spread across his pillow, her breasts...

His groin tightened. Flicking the reins, he sped up the horse. Eventually the boys would have to head up to bed. Would she allow him to linger? He could hardly wait to find out.

The sooner he reached her ranch, the sooner he could see her.

As he drove downhill, the moon moved up in the sky. He'd have to bring Samantha outside to see it, give them a chance to be away from the boys. Steal a kiss or ten.

Finally the ranch was in sight, the old house a gray block against the darker shadows, yellow light beckoning from the kitchen window against a backdrop of stars sparkling in a great swath through the heavens.

He pulled up in front of the house. For a moment, Wyatt remained in the buggy, content to watch.

In a circle around the kitchen table, the four boys bent over their books. White roses nodded from a vase set in the center between two glass lamps. In the glow of lamplight, Samantha sat next to Little Feather, pointing to the book spread out in front of them, her lips moving. She must be teaching the Indian boy to read.

The lamplight burnished her hair to a copper glow. He itched to pull the pins out from the bun at the back of her head, releasing the fiery cascade, and wondered what it would feel like to run his hands down its shimmering length, feeling her naked feminine form beneath...

He shifted on the buggy seat. To calm himself before he knocked on the door, he stared at the night sky, imagining his body as cool as the distant stars. It took effort, but eventually he climbed down from the buggy and tied up. Scooping up the basket with the cake, he strode up the stairs and across the porch to the door.

He rapped four times, his heartbeat thudding to the sound of the knocking. Hearing rapid footsteps in the hall, he stepped back a pace, waiting.

Samantha opened the door, one lamp in her hand. When she saw him, her smile glowed.

An answering warmth kindled in his middle. "Good evening, Samantha."

"Good evening, Wyatt."

"As promised, I brought you the cake."

Even in the flickering light, he could see a blush spring into her cheeks. *Ah, perhaps the lady wasn't indifferent to his courtship.*

"The boys have been looking forward to it. I promised them all a piece, then it's to bed for the whole bunch."

She'd arranged to spend time alone with him. His breath shortened in anticipation.

"Please come in. The boys are just finishing their schoolwork."

"Even the extras?"

"Even the extras."

Wyatt liked to think she had hurried them on account of his visit. He followed her two steps into the darkened hall, then turned into the brighter kitchen. "Evening, boys."

"Evening, Mr. Thompson," they chorused. Even Little Feather added a low voice to the greeting.

A paternal feeling kicked up, surprising him. Later, when he was alone, he'd have to examine his reaction. He held up the basket. "Mrs. Toffels's compliments on a job well done."

Daniel's face crumpled from eagerness to woe. "It got burned down."

"That doesn't take away from the effort that went into the building of it. Life's like that. Build something, plant crops, run cattle or horse herds—storms, or varmints, or thieves come along and ruin all your hard work. Just need to pick yourself up and go on. You all are learnin' that hard lesson early."

One side of Jack's mouth pulled down. "Done learned that lesson already. Our ma's dyin' ruined everything."

Daniel's eyebrows drew together. Tim stared down at his plate.

Wyatt reached out and ruffled Jack's hair. "I know, son," he said around the sudden pain in his gut. "Loved ones dyin' does that worst of all."

Jack stared down at his book, his shoulders slumping. "Can rebuild outhouses, plant new crops," he said, his voice low. "Can't bring back them's that passed."

"That's right, boy. It's a hard fact." Wyatt didn't know what else to say. Weren't words to cover the deep, dark hell of the death of a wife or a mother. He wasn't a preacher to offer up comfort with the ease of familiarity. But he sure wished he had something more to offer the boy.

Samantha stepped into the breach. "Your ma would be proud of you boys, just like I am. I'm sure she's watching you from heaven, pleased at your willingness to work hard here at home, at school, with Mr. Thompson and Mr. Sanders."

Jack straightened his shoulders. He didn't look up, but he nodded several times, as if Samantha's words were sinking in.

Samantha reached over for the basket. "Everyone ready for chocolate cake?"

The mood in the room shifted. The boys set aside their books, and Samantha cut and dished up the cake. Wyatt pulled an empty chair to the table and sat down. Silence reigned while the boys ate with quick bites and reverent expressions on their faces. Made Wyatt think that Reverend Norton might make more of an impression on the young 'uns if he partnered up with Mrs. Toffels and served cake during the sermon.

He took a fragrant, sweet bite. Hell, might even work with him.

Daniel bounced in his chair. "Can I have another piece?"

Samantha grinned. Reaching over, she tapped him on the nose. "No."

Daniel's face fell into boyish disappointment.

"There's enough left that you can all have one tomorrow after supper."

"All right."

"Now get ready for bed, all of you. I'll be up in a minute to hear your prayers."

With visible reluctance, they scraped back their chairs.

Samantha playfully slapped Daniel's bottom with her palm. "Move along now."

Daniel skipped forward two steps.

"Say good night to Mr. Thompson."

"Good night." Not in a chorus this time, but close enough.

Jack paused. "Tell Mrs. Toffels we're much obliged for the cake."

Wyatt nodded at him. "I will."

"Yep," Daniel chimed in. "Sure was good. She can make us a cake anytime."

Samantha laughingly protested. "Daniel."

"Well, she can, Mama."

"I'm sure she knows that, son. Now scoot up to bed."

Daniel sighed and rolled his eyes, then followed the others out the door.

A clatter of footsteps on the stairs, then silence settled in. They were finally alone.

Wyatt took his last bite of cake, then scraped the side of his fork across the plate, capturing every bit of chocolate.

Samantha reached out and fingered a petal of one of the white roses in the cut-glass vase. The delicate scent drifted over. "I was so pleased when these bloomed. The bushes had looked so old and neglected, I wasn't sure they would."

"They've been around as long as I've known Ezra."

"He must have planted them for his fiancée."

"Must have."

Silence stretched out between them, awkward and anticipating. Red crept into Samantha's cheeks. She lowered her eyes.

Dark eyelashes fanned shadows across her cheeks. "I'd better see to the boys. It'll only take a few minutes. Their prayers never last long. Why don't you wait in the parlor?"

"I'll just step outside. The moon's a sight to see."

Her smile hinted of vulnerability. "I'll join you soon."

Wyatt stood up while she left the room, then strolled outside. Pacing back and forth in front of the porch, he pondered his feelings about Samantha's collection of wayward orphans.

Like the slow melting of the spring thaw, the idea seeped into his mind that he'd been mistaken about all three of the boys. He wasn't quite ready to admit he'd been wrong, but the wind was blowing him in that direction. Maybe a good home and some loving attention…

The scars in his side itched. From long habit, he rubbed his palm over them, feeling the raised welts through the cotton of his shirt. From equally long practice, he shoved aside the painful memories trying to tumble into his thoughts.

Several minutes later, Samantha stepped through the door, wrapping a knitted shawl around her shoulders. "The boys were unusually cooperative tonight—no tussling, joking, requests for water, or last-minute need to use the privy."

"Mighty smart, those boys of yours."

"They are, aren't they?"

Tired of talking about children when they could be pursuing more adult activities, Wyatt extended his arm. "Let's walk to the river."

"That would be nice."

Her voice remained calm, but her hand trembled on his arm. He wondered if she was cold or reacting to his presence.

They trod the path in silence, only the sound of the rushing river and an occasional cricket to keep them company. The nearer they came to the bridge, the more the damp scent of water increased.

They stepped onto the wood planking; it creaked under their feet. Wyatt turned her so, hip to hip, they could lean their backs against the railing.

Samantha caught sight of the glowing crescent, higher up now from when Wyatt had seen it earlier. "Such a beautiful moon." She lifted her face to the sky, absorbing the heavens through her eyes, the listening stance of her body. The faint moonlight glistened on the pale skin of her throat, long and delicate like a swan, its texture as soft as down feathers.

He wished he could reach up and twist the moon and stars from their fixed patterns, intertwining them into a necklace. The stars would be diamonds glittering around her throat, the crescent falling between the cleft in her breasts.

Wyatt reached out and cupped her neck, sliding his hand up and down the smoothness of her skin. Her pulse skittered under his touch, and her eyes widened. His thumb traced the line of her jaw.

Her lips parted. He ran the pad of his thumb lightly over them. When he reached the corner of her smile, he followed with the lightest of kisses. Her lips trembled under his. He brushed his palm down her throat, stopping when he felt the ridge of her collarbone through her high-necked gown. He didn't dare move farther.

His kiss deepened, and he slipped his tongue into her mouth. She tasted like chocolate. He ached with need.

Her fingers curled on his arm, tightening as she became more aroused.

To avoid the temptation of dropping his hand to cup her breast, he shifted his arm around her waist, pressing her toward him. The corset she wore under her dress walled him away from her softness. Damn restrictive garment. But it served a purpose, forcing him to keep a harness on his ardor. Maybe that's what corsets were made for after all.

Her head stilled to his chest. With a sigh she snuggled closer, slipping her hands inside his coat and around his waist. Body to body, man to woman. He smothered a groan, forcing himself to think of the fence that needed mending, the nails and lumber he needed to pick up to rebuild the school's outhouse—anything to calm his racing blood. Minutes passed in the struggle. Finally he was able to wrap both arms around her and rest his cheek against the top of her head.

They lingered that way for a long time. Content, peaceful, right. At one with the night, the river, the land, and each other.

❋ ❋ ❋

With her cheek against Wyatt's chest, Samantha could feel the strong thump of his heartbeat and smell the warm masculine scent of him. Enveloped by his strong arms, she felt her cares drift away like bubbles floating on the current of the river. A dreamy lassitude weighed her limbs, but at the same time filled her with a kind of strength, a renewal. Spring with its hope and promise after a bleak winter.

She moved her hands, running them up and down his sides, feeling his muscles. On his right side, her hand smoothed across ridged scar tissue.

Wyatt stiffened.

She lifted her head to look up at him. "What happened?"

He hesitated for a long moment. "I was apprenticed to a blacksmith when I was fourteen—a drunken brute of a man. One day he picked up a poker and burned me with it."

"Oh, dear Lord." Samantha lightly touched the scars, wishing she could go back in time and protect him.

"Luckily someone wandered in and saw what was happening. Stopped him, got me to the doctor."

"What happened then?"

"Ran away."

"What about your family?"

Another long pause. "My ma was dead. Never knew my pa."

"Did he die before you were born?"

"No. My ma worked in a saloon. Never even knew who my pa was. Once I was past being a little tyke, she became more interested in drinkin' than in me. I just ran wild. Got in a heap of trouble." He tapped her on the tip of her nose. "Didn't have a Samantha to rescue me."

She hugged him fiercely. "I would have wanted to."

"I know." He pinched the bridge of his nose, obviously thinking, then draped his arm back around her. "You might not feel that way when you hear the rest."

She leaned her head back on his shoulder and squeezed him tight. "Tell me."

"It's not a pretty story."

Inwardly Samantha braced for what she might hear. "I don't expect it is."

"There was a gang of boys mostly older than me. Lived in a run-down shack in a canyon outside the town of Maxwell. I ran away to join them. Some of them were just misfits, lookin' for a home. But two of them were bad to the bone. And they ended up bein' the leaders."

He paused. A cricket chirped. The water gurgled.

Samantha ran her hand over his scars.

"Things weren't bad at first. We did some petty thieving. But then they started setting fires."

Startled, Samantha looked at him. "Fires?"

"First, insignificant ones like what's happenin' here. Then they got worse. At that point, I refused to join in. But they still made me act as lookout." He ran his hand across his face.

She reached up to cover his hand with hers, holding it against his cheek. "What else happened?"

"I'll live with the guilt of this until the day I die, Samantha." He took a deep breath. "They got mad at one of the men in town— fellow owned the livery stable. Vowed to burn his house down. I refused to help. They beat me up pretty badly. Left me lyin' there. I was in a lot of pain, but I should have gone and warned the man. But I didn't."

"Wyatt, you mustn't blame yourself."

"Their daughter died, Samantha. And I could have prevented it."

The anguish in his voice twisted in her heart. "Oh, Wyatt. You were just a boy."

"I was old enough to know better."

"You didn't have a lot of choices in your life."

His tone turned bitter. "The ironic thing is that the worst time in my life led me to a better life. We were all caught. They hung the leaders. The rest went to jail. Because I was younger and hadn't participated, they sent me to a childless couple in Nebraska to work on their farm. Good people, prosperous, and related to the minister. Eventually they adopted me. Left me their farm and their business when they died. I sold up and came here to start over."

"Did they love you?"

"In their own way. They were older. Stiff and proper." He tapped her nose again. "Not like you with your boys. But they saw to it that I had a good education. I'm mighty grateful for all they gave me."

"I'm glad you had them."

"Me too." He looked up at the moon, and Samantha followed his gaze.

The moon had arched higher in the sky, riding a path of stars. A breeze sprang up, ruffling Wyatt's hair. Samantha shivered.

"It's gettin' late." Wyatt trailed his finger down her cheek, tracing the line of her jaw. "Guess my story destroyed the mood."

She turned her head and kissed his fingertip. "I'm glad you confided in me. I feel I understand you better. It explains why you objected so strongly to the twins and Little Feather."

"They stirred up memories I wanted to keep banked. And I was afraid for Christine." He grimaced. "Guess I'm a mite over-protective of her."

Samantha laughed. "Just a mite." She half turned, slipping her hand through his arm. "Come on, let's go back."

As they walked, the silence between them thickened. Glancing at Wyatt's face, she could see he'd withdrawn. She wanted to tug on his arm, pull him back to her. But she knew men had a way of going off inside themselves to think. And a woman had to let them be, no matter how much she wanted to talk.

Wyatt saw her to the door. She pushed it open and stopped. He leaned over and kissed her cheek. "Good night, Samantha."

"Good night, Wyatt." She wanted to say more, but didn't know what. So she settled on a smile that wasn't quite real. "Thank you for the cake. And for the talk…"

"I'll tell Mrs. Toffels you liked it."

He turned and walked toward the buggy.

Samantha stepped inside and shut the door. Lingering, she listened for the faint sounds of his departure. She dropped her forehead against the solid wood, feeling uneasy.

What was going on inside of Wyatt? Did it have to do with her? Was he regretting confiding in her? Regretting courting her?

※ ※ ※

Wyatt drove away from Samantha's house, every muscle of his body tense with the effort of holding onto his feelings. He looked up to his right at the crescent moon and remembered how excited he'd been, driving over. Things sure had changed.

He should have known Samantha would accept the story of his past. Hell, with her generous heart, how could she do anything but? However, what if she changed her mind about him when she got to pondering over his words? He didn't think he could handle opening his heart to another woman, only to have it broken by losing her.

His hands tightened on the reins, and he forced himself to relax. No sense letting his mind bolt away from him. If he faced things squarely, he knew Samantha's caring for him hadn't been shaken. He was the one who'd been shaken.

Confessing his past had ripped open the scars. His side burned in response, and he dropped one hand to cover the welted flesh. Yet…maybe now they'd have a chance to heal cleanly, no longer festering beneath his skin, under his thoughts.

The old wound had driven him away from the mismatched collection of orphan boys at Samantha's place. All because he couldn't face his own fear of his past—that somehow they might turn into his wicked gang members, and cause the harm to

Christine that the old gang did to that poor unfortunate girl and her family.

Deep down inside, he'd believed he deserved to be punished. Didn't he think that's what had happened when Alicia had died, making him cling that much more tightly to their daughter?

For the first time, Wyatt could feel more like a boy twisted by circumstance into terrible choices, rather than an evildoer who deserved to be punished. He released a long breath that seemed to come from his toes.

Guess maybe he'd have to get to know those boys on their own merits, without judging them from his past. They deserved that from him. *He* deserved that from himself. But would he be able to?

CHAPTER TWENTY-FOUR

Jack untied his book satchel from Brownie's saddle horn and dropped it onto the straw floor of the livery stable. He unlooped the leather thong holding his lunch bucket on the other side of the horn. Through the horse and hay odor of the stall, he caught an appreciative sniff of smoked-ham sandwich, pickles, and chocolate cake. Even after three months of fine eatin' at Miz Sam's place, he still relished the luxury of food consisting of more than gritty bread and badly cooked meat. Meals at school were something he looked forward to.

Tim reached over the stall wall and whacked Jack on the head. "Gonna tie that there pail on your nose like a feedbag."

"Hey." Jack twisted away. Any other morning, the smack and the words would lead to tussling with his twin, but Jack was too busy anticipating another day of work with Mr. Thompson and Mr. Sanders to bother retaliating against his brother.

He set the bucket carefully next to the satchel, then unbuckled Brownie's girth strap. While his hands busied themselves with attending to the horse, his mind pondered rebuilding the outhouse. He reviewed sawing and nailing planks, the piecing together of the frame. His fingers curled like he held a hammer. Somehow the feel of the smooth wooden handle in the palm of his hand had a balance and rightness he itched to experience again.

With a last affectionate pat to Brownie's side, Jack followed his brother and Daniel out of the stable. In his eagerness, Daniel swung his satchel in one hand and his pail in the other, any higher and he might dump out his lunch. But Jack knew the younger boy would settle down his fidgets right enough when they started working.

Jack did a wiggle step of his own, remembering how yesterday the two men had been patient-like with the boys—taking time to explain what they were doing. And their praise, well he'd soaked up every word. After a while, he'd been able to relax, no longer watching for the blow that might come from any little mistake he made, or for no reason whatsoever. Instead, he enjoyed his growing sense of accomplishment, something he had never really experienced before. The feeling seeped through his memory of yesterday and bubbled up in him today.

Although the morning air had a cool bite to it, it would soon be sunshiny. A good day to be outdoors instead of cooped up inside. Not that he minded his lessons so much anymore. He eyed the white schoolhouse, children heading toward it like ants to a crumb of vanilla cake. Why, he had the Gettysburg Address all in his mind—words marching in step across his brain like soldiers. Figured Miss Stanton would be right pleased with him. *Fourscore and seven years ago—*

Tim jostled his elbow. "There's Ben an Arlie."

Ben, looking like an advertisement for a haberdasher, lounged against the rail of the stairs, a scornful expression on his face. Coveralls baggy, but new enough, hair slicked down, Arlie hovered on the other side of the rail as if unsure whether to face the twins or run inside to safety.

Ben straightened and thrust out his shoulders, seeming to call attention to the contrast between his striped suit and the old clothes the boys wore. "Looks like the walking ragbags have arrived," he called out.

Daniel stop his swinging, dropping to a stiff gait. Over the top of Dan's head, Jack met Tim's eyes and shared a quick message. *Fight or ignore them?*

Tim shrugged.

No sense makin' more trouble. *Ignore them,* Jack telegraphed back with a faint shake of his head.

Tim caught it, nodded.

Jack glanced around for the reaction of the other children. Usually, they all called greetings with each other when they arrived. Even the twins and Daniel had come to be included in the early-morning ritual.

Now, Jack caught their gazes sliding away. Mark Carter's usually cheerful face seemed shuttered. Christine and Sara Carter gripped hands, distress in every line of their bodies. One of the older girls whispered to another, and both tittered with laughter.

What the heck was goin' on? Was this about the outhouse burning down?

Ben smirked. "Hey, maybe you laborers can come over to my house when you're finished here. Think I could find work for you to do."

Jack rolled his eyes but kept walking. They needed to leave their things inside, then they would be free to head around back and find Mr. Thompson. Side by side, they hurried up the steps.

When they drew even with Ben, he stepped in front of them. "Heard you two burned down Mrs. Murphy's haystack last night."

Burned? Widda Murphy's haystack? Shock shook Jack's body. His mind raced like a wild horse trying to escape a corral. But he didn't dare ask for clarification or give Ben the benefit of a response. He'd wait and ask Mr. Thompson.

Ben narrowed his brown calf eyes, until he resembled a snake. "My mother's taken care of you two," he hissed. "She's called for a meeting on Sunday after church. The whole town's going to be there. And we'll get rid of you *troublemakers* once and for all."

Jack fired up. "Doubt Miz Rodriguez gonna let that happen."

Ben leaned forward until they almost touched noses. "My mama is going to speak with the Cobbs and with Mack Taylor."

"So."

"My uncle's the banker in this town, numskull. The man with the money. If my uncle won't loan your mama money, and the Cobbs don't let her shop at their store, and Mr. Taylor refused to sell her hay or grain, how are you all going to fare?"

"So what? Us 'uns will manage." He'd see to it if he had to plant a whole farm to feed them.

Ben straightened, a triumphant smile squeezing his face. His sneer included Daniel. "She'll lose her ranch, that's what. Then all of you will be gone. Run out of town to beg and cause trouble somewhere else."

Jack's stomach lurched; he needed to get away from Ben. Looking over at his brother, he jerked his head toward the back of the school. He grabbed Daniel's arm, pulling him with them down the steps. Still carrying his satchel and lunch pail, Jack strolled as if he didn't have a care in the world. He refused to let Ben see how upset he was.

When they'd rounded the corner of the building, Daniel stopped short. "Could they do that to my mama?"

"Don't know."

"We gonna lose the ranch?"

Don't know that either, but Daniel's eyebrows had winged upward again. "Na," Jack said, lying to give the younger boy some comfort. But the word came out sounding flat rather than bouncy with encouragement. "Come on. Us 'uns got a privy to build."

More anxious than he cared to admit, Jack picked up their pace until they almost ran around the bushes.

Mr. Thompson and Mr. Sanders stood before a pile of new lumber, talking in low tones, their faces serious. They looked up. The seriousness didn't leave their faces, only seemed to deepen.

Jack slowed his momentum; dread made his boots heavy.

Mr. Thompson nodded. "Morning, boys."

Daniel scuttled forward. "Morning, Mr. Thompson, Mr. Sanders."

Jack and Tim remained silent. Something wasn't right. A familiar feeling crept through him, probably through Tim too. When they'd felt it before, they'd learned to walk soft and be ready to run.

Jack's body tensed.

Mr. Thompson glanced at him, gray eyes sharper than nails. "You boys know anything 'bout the fire at Mrs. Murphy's?"

Jack met his brother's gaze and saw the old familiar sullen look slide over his twin's face. He knew his own features must be reflecting back a similar picture. He didn't really want to look that way, but his body hardened to stone, a granite mask like the ghost face nature had carved into Haunted Mountain. But he had to say somethin'. "Us 'uns just heard. Ben tole us."

The men exchanged glances.

Mr. Thompson ran his fingers through his hair. "Tell me straight. You boys have anything to do with that fire?"

Hurt pierced the rock surrounding Jack's heart, a pain deeper than the slashes caused by the Widda Murphy's haranguing, Mrs. Grayson's threats, and Ben's taunts. Thompson's disbelief cut to the core.

He couldn't even speak. The silence stretched.

"I'm waiting for your answer," came Thompson's clipped demand.

But Jack's throat froze tighter than Osomaemie Crik in winter.

Tim spoke up, saving Jack from having to reply. "Us 'uns didn't have nothing ta do with it."

"Where were you two last night?"

Daniel bobbed up and down. "They were asleep in our room." His voice rose. "You saw us, Mr. Thompson. My ma tucked us up."

Nick Sanders cocked an eyebrow at Thompson, a brief twinkle lurking in his eyes.

Thompson shifted. "But I didn't check on you all night. But maybe Mrs. Rodriguez looked in on you."

A flash of anger melted Jack's paralysis. The man didn't believe them. Hurt, shame, betrayal all balled up in a need to run. "Come on." He turned tail on the two men, dragging Dan with him.

He whipped around the school, heading for the livery stable, Daniel gabbling behind. Tim followed, silent and understanding. Jack didn't bother to stop and explain. He needed to get out of there, away from people who looked down their noses at him and Tim.

Inside the livery, it didn't take more than a moment to saddle up Brownie and tie on the satchel and lunch pail. The other two followed suit. They led the horses outside and mounted.

Out of the corner of his eye, Jack could see Thompson heading for them. Jack pretended not to see the man. Instead, he set his heels into Brownie's sides, urging the horse to a canter. He was through with people who didn't believe him—through with this whole dang town. He weren't never comin' back. Not if Thompson crawled and pleaded.

They left behind the last of the buildings, heading out to the ranch. While one part of him wanted to go to Miz Sam for comfort, Ben had also threatened her. If she kept on the twins, took their side, she might lose the ranch. And he knew how much the ranch meant to her. Heard it in the tone she used in talking about the future. Watched the look of pride that would light up her face brighter than a sunrise when she looked around her land.

Miz Sam had been good to them—better than anyone since their ma. And to be honest, maybe better than his ma. The traitorous thought made him squirm in the saddle. But that was the truth. Miz Sam stood up to people. Probably would even have faced down his ole man. He could just see her takin' a skillet to the side of his pa's head. He doubted she'd back down from warrin' with the townsfolk, and she'd lose the ranch for sure.

He couldn't let that happen.

Little Feather had lived in a cave when his family had died off. Said it kept him snug and dry, with plenty of water nearby. He remembered the Indian's description of the long series of tunnels that started near Thunder Gulch. Jack had even told about the caverns in school one day, Sharin' Day, they called it. Miss Stanton had been mighty interested in his description, mentioned wanting to see them for herself. If Little Feather had survived in a cave, living off the land, Jack and Tim could do it too.

A pang of doubt seized him. Little Feather had been mighty scrawny when he first came to live with them.

Jack pushed the doubt away. He was sure Miz Sam wouldn't begrudge them some supplies, blankets, and knives. He'd miss Brownie and Mariposa somethin' fierce, though. Reaching down, he stroked his mount's neck. Too bad he couldn't take the horses.

But if he did, he'd be strung up for a horse thief sooner than you could say Jack Cassidy.

He couldn't even let himself think how he'd miss Miz Sam.

But it was for her own good.

✸ ✸ ✸

Standing in the middle of the street, Wyatt stared at the retreating backs of the boys riding their horses out of town, and debated about rushing to the livery stable to saddle up Bill and go after them. He didn't feel good about how Jack had just taken off, and sensed how hurt the boy had been by Wyatt's distrust. But if Wyatt couldn't give Jack his complete trust, what good would it do to ride on after them? Might make things worse.

Still feeling torn, Wyatt turned back toward the school. He'd promised Christine he'd rebuild the outhouse. And he had some powerful thinking to do. He strode along so deep in thought he barely registered Reverend Norton waving at him. Only when the minister motioned so strongly that his white hair flew up to match his fluttering arms did Wyatt stop.

"Good morning, Reverend Norton."

"Good morning, Mr. Thompson." The minister's forehead puckered. "Have you heard about the town meeting?"

"Meeting?"

"Mr. Livingston and Mrs. Grayson have insisted everyone meet to discuss the burning of the school privy and Mrs. Murphy's haystack."

A stone settled in Wyatt's gut. "They're blamin' the Cassidy twins?"

The minister nodded, blue eyes distressed. "Perhaps I made an error in judgment when I didn't send the twins away."

"No." The word slipped out before Wyatt could think. "I didn't agree with you at the time, but the boys have done well with Mrs. Rodriguez."

"I thought so too. But now…"

"Reverend, we've never been a town takin' to stringing up criminals without a trial. If those boys were adults, they'd get a fair hearing. And in a real trial, I doubt there'd be enough evidence to lock them away."

The minister stroked his beard. "You are right. Tempers are running a bit high, but I'm sure calmer heads will prevail."

"We'll just have to see to it."

"I've asked John Carter to run the meeting. He's just the man we need—calm, rational, and well respected. I'm sure he won't let things get out of hand."

"Good choice." Relief settled Wyatt's stomach. Carter should handle things just fine. Now, if Wyatt could keep his hotheaded Samantha from firing up against everyone…He ran his fingers through his hair. That might be the hardest part.

Reverend Norton shifted his weight forward. "So I can count on you to be there? Sunday after the service?"

"Wild horses couldn't drag me away," he said with a wry grimace. "Now, if you'll excuse me, Reverend, I have another outhouse to build."

"Certainly, certainly. Good day, Mr. Thompson."

"Good day."

The minister hurried off to round up more of his sheep for the Sunday meeting.

Deep in thought, Wyatt strolled toward the school. Although he wasn't entirely sure the twins were in the clear, his gut told him they'd told the truth. And he trusted his gut. He had learned what happened when he went against his instincts.

But if the twins weren't setting the fires, who was?

❋ ❋ ❋

Run away!

Samantha stared down at the slate left on the kitchen table and tried to will her racing thoughts to slow long enough for her to absorb the words. In Jack's scrawl, the chalk letters spelled a message that weakened her knees and thumped her heart in slow beats of dread.

She touched the cool black slate, rubbing out the tail of a J. Then she forced a slow breath into her restricted ribs, the rose scent from the flower-filled vase on the table cloying amidst the sharpness of her fear. She reread the message:

Dear Miz Sam,

Tim an Little Feather and me dun gone away. Mrs. Grayson's right angry. We don't wan to cause no more troble. If we don leave we might make ya lose the ranch. We took the clothes ya gave us and some food and some suplys. Don't you worry nun, Little Feather knows a place were we'll be saf. Tel Dan goodby. Much ablyjed for al ya dun.

Jack

A clatter of running footsteps thumped up the stairs, across the porch, and into the kitchen. Daniel skidded to a halt in front of her, his thin chest heaving under his blue-striped cotton shirt.

"Tim an Jack an Little Feather are hiding from me, Mama. I've looked all around and can't find them."

"They've run away." Her calm voice belied the shaking of her hands.

Daniel's blue eyes widened, and his eyebrows lifted.

To avoid the puzzlement and hurt dawning in her son's gaze and reflecting in her heart, she looked down at the slate, then read the message out loud.

Storm clouds gathered on Daniel's face. He stomped his foot, unaccustomed rage narrowing his eyes. "That Ben," he growled. "I could light into him myself."

Samantha restrained a gasp. Her son looked and sounded so much like his grandfather. For a few seconds the thought so unnerved her that she didn't notice what he'd said. "What do you mean, 'Ben'?"

He looked down, fidgeting his shoulders. "Tole us his mama had called a town meeting. They're gunna make us lose the ranch if the twins didn't leave town."

Samantha reached out and cupped Daniel's chin, lifting his face to her. "What do you mean?"

"Ben said if you kept Jack and Tim living here, his uncle wouldn't give you money, and you wouldn't be able to buy anything at the Cobbs'."

Samantha released an angry breath.

"Could they do that, Mama?"

"They could try, I suppose."

"What if we run out of money?"

"Then I'll just have to sell your grandmama's emerald earrings." She hoped that would be enough. She forced a smile to reassure him. "But just because Ben's mama wants something, doesn't mean it will happen."

But even as she said the words, they echoed back to her, vibrating in her head. She placed her hands to her temples and squeezed her forehead until it wrinkled. She didn't know which problem to think through first. Chewing the inside of her lip, she came to a quick decision. Even if she lost the ranch, she'd not lose her three other boys. She'd keep them with her no matter what.

She dropped her hands. "But why did the twins run away? I'd think they'd fight rather than run."

He dropped his gaze, kicking a chair leg with one scuffed boot. "Mr. Thompson asked if they'd burnt down Widow Murphy's haystack."

Like colored glass in a kaleidoscope, Samantha's world turned. One minute one pattern, then with a quick shift of the wrist, another, then seconds later, another. "Did Widow Murphy's haystack burn down too?"

"Yep, last night."

"And Mr. Thompson blamed the twins?"

As if remembering, Daniel's head swiveled back and forth in a slow *No*.

"What then?"

"He asked them if they knew anything about it." Daniel rocked forward, his next words rushing. "At first Jack had this hurt look, then quick as a wink, his face went to lookin' like he did when he first lived with us."

Samantha understood. Sullenness over the hurt. Her heart ached for them. "Then what happened?"

"Jack grabbed my arm and pulled me away. We took off running to the stable and saddled up the horses and rode home. When we got here, Jack said we needed to stay away from you until we'd calmed down a bit, or you'd know for sure something was up. He tole me to go stay with Maria at her house."

"They must have waited until I was working in the garden, then snuck into the house, packed up, and left."

Daniel's face twisted. "Why didn't they take me?"

"Oh, Daniel." Samantha put the slate on the table and hugged him. "I'm sure they wanted you with them, but no one in town is mad at you and wants you to leave. Just them. They might have even thought I wouldn't come after them. I don't think they completely trust in my love. But they know I'd track you down."

"We'll go find them, won't we, Mama?"

She squeezed him again. "Of course. Right away. You run and saddle up the horses. I'll change clothes."

Relieved, he skipped out of the house.

Through the window, Samantha watched him run toward the barn. She was fairly sure the boys would head for the caves where Little Feather had lived. The Indian knew the caves well, so they should be all right.

An idea came to her, and she dropped into a chair to think it through. Maybe she shouldn't go after the boys until after the town meeting. Telling people they'd run away rather than jeopardize her ranch should garner them some sympathy—perhaps sway people over to her side. And if worse came to worst, and anyone forcibly tried to take the twins away from her, they wouldn't know where to find them. And she could truthfully say she didn't know either.

An image of Wyatt came into her mind. The look in his eyes as he'd stared down at her last night. The brush of his hand against her skin. His kisses that fulfilled an empty place inside her, at the same time leaving her wanting more.

Will Wyatt stand by my side? Help me in this fight? She'd thought from the way he'd been behaving toward the boys that he'd accepted the twins and Little Feather—indicated a willingness to make them part of his life. But he still had doubts about her boys. That thought speared a shaft of pain through her heart. He hadn't completely accepted her because he hadn't completely accepted them. Would he give up courting her?

Samantha stiffened her shoulders. She wouldn't sacrifice the boys for Wyatt's love. Then she softened, biting her lip. To be fair, he hadn't asked her. If they discovered the real fire-setting culprit, then things might change for the better. The townsfolk would drop their angry accusations. The boys could return home. She wouldn't lose her ranch. Wyatt would court her.

But those thoughts didn't bring the satisfaction they should. The truth was, she wanted all those things to happen without Wyatt discovering who the real arsonist was. She wished for everyone to believe in the goodness of Jack and Tim, because she did.

She firmed her mouth. *I'll do whatever it takes to save my boys. Wyatt or no Wyatt.*

CHAPTER TWENTY-FIVE

The church overflowed with people, many, like Henry Arden, not often seen darkening the doors of the hallowed building. A few folks, such as the Carters and the Sanders, had greeted her before the service and acted their normal friendly selves. But the majority of the people had avoided eye contact or kept throwing curious stares at Samantha during the service.

Pink roses stuffed the green glass vase on the altar. The summer dresses of flower-sprigged cottons and the flowers in the bonnets of the women lent the room a festive air, at odds with the oppressive atmosphere settling like fog before a storm. Even singing joyful hymns had not lifted the restive feeling of the congregation.

After the service, Reverend Norton dismissed the children. Daniel gave Samantha a quick hug, then scampered past the Carters and across the aisle to join Christine. As the two children met, Wyatt sent Samantha a bolstering grin. Feeling trembly anticipation, she could only manage a half smile in response.

The parents who'd brought their children to church shooed them outside. As Christine left with Daniel, she flipped Samantha a small wave and a bigger grin. Ben appeared to argue with his mother, then gave in. He stood up, tugging on his blue suit, then sauntered down the aisle, avoiding looking at Samantha as he passed.

The Carters shepherded their three children outside, leaving Samantha alone in the pew.

The quietness of the empty space next to Samantha was worse than having to keep a sharp eye on the behavior of a wiggly Daniel and reluctant set of twins. She missed those mischief makers. An ever-present worry about the well-being of the twins and Little Feather distracted her for a moment. She trusted the boys enough to let them camp out in the caves for a few days, but that didn't mean she liked it. Tension squeezed a vise around her temples until each one of the hairpins, jabbed into the braided coil of her hair, stabbed into her skull.

As if trying to settle her restless spirit, Samantha smoothed her black silk dress, then pinched a bunch of fabric by her knee, rolling it between her thumb and forefinger.

Nick and Elizabeth Sanders joined Samantha in the pew. Elizabeth reached over and briefly squeezed her hand.

The Carters returned from escorting their children outside. Pamela slid into the empty seat next to Samantha and gave her an encouraging smile. John Carter paused by her, about to speak. Then with a sigh, he brushed back his thinning rusty hair, and walked up the aisle to shake hands with Reverend Norton. The two stood quietly talking for a moment. Although she strained, Samantha couldn't hear what they said. Then the minister took a seat in the front row next to his wife.

John Carter stepped up to the pulpit and cleared his throat. The buzz of conversation that had started at the close of the service died down.

John placed both hands on the pulpit and leaned forward. "We have gathered together to discuss the recent fires plaguing our town. There have been three fires—two involving Mrs. Murphy's haystack and the school privy. We—"

Mrs. Murphy bobbed up. "We ain't here for no discussion." Her cheeks mottled. "We want them Cassidy boys shipped out of town on the next train."

John's calm voice chilled. "Anyone who interrupts me again will be asked to leave the meeting." His hard gaze bored into Widow Murphy.

She flushed, shaking her head; her wattle slid from side to side.

John narrowed his eyes.

With a shrug, she plopped down in her pew.

Inwardly Samantha applauded. John Carter had always acted so mild mannered and kind, but when he chose, he had a glare that could stop a raging bull in its tracks.

He used it now, sending his gaze over the whole room. "This is not a hanging jury. If anyone has evidence against the twins, instead of illogical emotions, they may speak up at this time."

Edith stood. Dressed in rich plum silk, she radiated elegance. "Jack Cassidy assaulted my son."

John raised one eyebrow. "Perhaps I should have been more specific. If anyone has evidence about the *fires*, they should reveal it now."

Edith lifted her chin. "Those twins burned down the outhouse because they were punished by having to build it after they'd destroyed the first one."

"Do you have evidence to this accusation, Mrs. Grayson? This is merely speculation."

"Well," she harrumphed, then tossed her head and sat down.

Widow Murphy bobbed up again. "They burned down the haystack when they was living with me. Last week, Jack stole my goat. I confronted Mrs. Rodriguez about it. She paid up, but Jack took revenge by burning down my new haystack."

John sighed. "But do you have evidence they did this? Did you or anyone else see them? Did they admit it?"

"Of course they wouldn't admit it. Lied through their teeth. But I know."

Samantha couldn't keep still any longer. She rose to her feet. "When they lived with you, did they do other damage to your possessions, Mrs. Murphy?"

"Yes, those hellions did." The woman readied to launch into a litany.

Samantha forestalled her with a raised hand. "When they did something else wrong, like breaking your grandmother's serving platter, did they admit it?"

The widow wrinkled her forehead, appearing to think. "Yes."

"Was the fire the only thing they denied?"

The woman pursed her lips.

John leaned forward over the pulpit. "Please answer, Mrs. Murphy."

"Well, I reckon so."

Samantha couldn't help her triumphant smile. "That's been my experience too. Each time they've gotten into mischief, they've been truthful with me, even when they feared the consequences. Therefore we need to believe the twins when they deny setting the fires. Because they didn't."

Across the aisle, Wyatt met her eyes. He winked and nodded. Warmth flooded her.

His bulbous nose even redder from apparent anger, Mr. Cobb bellowed out. "They're just pulling the wool over your eyes."

Samantha iced her voice. "I think I'm quite capable of telling when one of my children is lying to me." She looked around the room. "I'm sure the other mothers here would agree that they can tell with their children too."

A few female heads nodded. Good, Samantha thought. Maybe they believe me.

Edith Grayson lifted her chin, but didn't rise. "My Ben doesn't lie. Therefore I have no need of such ability."

I'll bet he doesn't. Sam bit her lip to keep the words bottled up.

Widow Murphy waved a hand, indicating the whole room. "These mothers have raised their children from babies. Of course they know them well. You've had those hellions only a few months."

Samantha fired up. "They're not hellions."

Cobb yelled out, "You're just too softhearted."

Reverend Norton rose from the first pew. "Now remember, Mrs. Rodriguez is to be commended for doing her Christian duty by the twins. I think her maternal feelings for Jack and Tim do her justice."

In the silence that settled after the minister's words, Wyatt unfolded his body from the pew. He stood for a few seconds, looking stern and handsome. "I'd be the first to admit that I was against Mrs. Rodriguez adopting Jack and Tim. I did my best to dissuade her." He shared a remembering glance with Samantha.

Her heart swelled with pride, and she allowed herself to sit down.

"I've come to know the boys, and I believe they are good at heart—just have some rough edges. With more time and love, even those will wear away."

Samantha bowed her head in relief. Wyatt cared about her boys. Now, if only she could keep the twins...

Cobb raised a fist. "You're just partial 'cause you're courtin' the lady."

"I'm partial to the lady, yes." Wyatt raised his voice over the murmur of the crowd. "But I've also recently spent more time with Jack and Tim than anyone else here. Therefore, I'm in more of a position to judge."

Edith Grayson's cheeks paled. She cast a look of dislike at Samantha.

Wyatt lowered his voice. "In fact those boys helped me find my daughter when she had her accident. Without them, I might have lost her."

John leaned over the podium. "I'm glad to hear a good account of the twins. Can anyone else—?"

Miss Stanton waved her hand. She'd braided her light brown hair into a dignified bun, but a few tendrils escaped to frame her pretty face. "The boys have been good students and well behaved in class. I must admit they surprised me, but they've worked hard to try and catch up with their classmates."

Samantha sent Miss Stanton a grateful smile.

The teacher nodded to her; her gray eyes looked worried.

Nick Sanders stood, a slight flush to his cheeks. "The boys did a good job on building the outhouse. They worked hard and were willin' to learn. Very pleased with the outcome, they were. I don't believe Jack or Tim would have set fire to it." He nodded decisively before sitting down.

Widow Murphy shrilled, "We're here about the fires, not to hear about this other nonsense. I want Mrs. Rodriguez to repay me for the loss of my haystack, and I want those twins sent away."

"Hear, hear," Cobb grumbled.

Several other heads nodded, including his wife's. The bird on Hortense Cobb's bonnet bobbed forward. "Next be burning us all in our beds."

"No." Samantha protested, her stomach feeling as if it contained a pincushion.

Caleb Livingston rose, looking cool and aristocratic. "Perhaps we need to go about this in a more democratic fashion. I suggest we vote on whether or not to send the twins to an orphanage."

"No." Samantha shot to her feet. "They're my boys." She threw the words at the banker. "You will *not* take them from me!"

"You have not formally adopted them, Mrs. Rodriguez."

"But I love them."

"Such sentiments do you credit." His brown eyes warmed to her. "However, tragedy happens. There will be other children who are orphaned and in need of the loving home you can provide. Children who won't be so disruptive to the community."

Samantha gritted her teeth. "Children are not interchangeable, Mr. Livingston."

"I'm not suggesting that they are, Mrs. Rodriguez." He turned toward John. "Carter, I call for a vote. And"—he glanced around—"because I believe Mrs. Rodriguez should feel this is fair, I suggest we allow the women to vote as well."

John let out a sigh and gave Samantha a long, questioning look.

In her mind she frantically counted the people she knew were on her side. Maybe there'd be enough. She nodded her acquiescence, and started to pray.

Pamela reached over and took Samantha's right hand. Samantha squeezed, grateful for her support.

"All in favor of Jack and Tim Cassidy being allowed to continue to live with Mrs. Rodriguez raise your hand."

With a rapidly beating heart, Samantha lifted her left arm high and firm. Other hands fluttered up. Wyatt and Mrs. Toffels, the Carters and the Sanderses, Miss Stanton, Reverend and Mrs.

Norton, and some people she didn't know but would be eternally grateful toward.

But was it enough? It didn't look like half the room, but maybe some others would abstain.

"The count is thirteen for the Cassidy twins remaining here. Now all those opposed."

Some hands shot up, while others rose more reluctantly. But Samantha could see without counting—she'd lost the boys.

Her heart contracted into a tight little ball, throbbing with pain. Tears sprang to her eyes, but tilting her chin, she refused to allow them to fall.

John's voice seemed heavy with sorrow. "The count is twenty-five against." He looked directly at Samantha, blue eyes sympathetic. "Mrs. Rodriguez, I'm sorry."

She shook her head at him, but didn't dare voice her realization that it wasn't his fault. But in spite of all her control, one tear spilled down her cheek.

Wyatt stood up. "If the boys must be sent away, I'm against sending them to an orphanage. I know several respectable farming families in the Midwest. I'll write and inquire if they'll take them."

John nodded. "That sounds suitable. I'm in agreement."

Widow Murphy jumped up. "And in the meantime, are we to be burned in our beds?" She shrilled, "Send the boys to the orphanage. If Mr. Thompson finds someone to take them, fine. But the town has voted. They leave."

The room buzzed. Reverend Norton tottered to his feet, seeming older than he'd been an hour before. "I'll be by to pick up the twins tomorrow morning, Mrs. Rodriguez."

Samantha willed her voice to clear, pitching her tone so the whole room could hear. "You can't, Reverend Norton. They heard threats that the bank, the mercantile, and the livery would withhold their services from me, thus threatening the prosperity of the ranch. Fearing that I would lose the property if they stayed, the twins and Little Feather ran away Friday afternoon. They left a note and took supplies." Her voice wavered. "I don't know where they are."

✳ ✳ ✳

Voices all at once. Dabbing at her eyes, Samantha stood and let the wave of sound break over her. Most of the people had risen to their feet, some gesticulating wildly.

Amid the noise, Mark Carter slipped in and made his way to his mother's pew. He reached over and touched her on her sleeve.

Pamela turned her head. "Mark, you're supposed to be outside." Then catching sight of his troubled expression, she said, "What is it?"

Mark looked back and forth from his mother to Samantha. "Daniel told us about the twins and Little Feather running away. Ben remembered Jack talking about the caves Little Feather lived in, and Ben and Arlie set out to look for them."

Samantha leaned toward Mark. "Oh, dear. His mother won't be pleased. I understand there are several different cave systems around here. Does he know that?"

"Don't know. But Daniel and Christine rode off together on her pony. Dan said to tell you they were going to warn the boys." Mark's usually mischievous features screwed up in distaste. "Ben fancies himself a sheriff. He's got his rifle with him."

Samantha gasped. "Oh no." Fear jolted through her; she wildly looked around for Wyatt.

Her outburst caught the attention of several people around her, including Wyatt. Bringing his conversation with Mr. Cobb to a close, he strode over to them. Anger glinted in his gray eyes, but changed to concern when he reached Samantha.

Pamela stepped into the aisle so Samantha could follow and speak to Wyatt.

He touched her shoulder in a silent gesture of sympathy.

Samantha beckoned him closer and when he'd leaned down, she whispered, "Ben and Arlie have gone to look for the boys. Ben has a gun. Daniel and Christine rode off to warn them."

His silver gaze sharpened. "Do you know where?"

"I just know they're in a cave near Thunder Gulch. Do you know where that is?"

"I do." His voice sounded grim. "That area's more riddled with holes than Swiss cheese." He glanced around. "We're going to have to speak up. Mrs. Grayson needs to know, also Arlie's parents. I'll organize some search teams."

He squeezed her shoulder, then headed over to John Carter and spent a moment in low-voiced conversation with him. John fisted his hand and banged on the pulpit. The room hushed. "Thompson, here, has something to say."

He stepped down, allowing Wyatt to take his place. "Apparently the boys have taken refuge in one of the caverns near Thunder Gulch."

Voices buzzed in curiosity, and he sliced the air with his hand. "That's not all." He looked at Edith. "Ben and Arlie took it into their heads to play sheriff and went after them."

"Oh, dear God." Edith swayed against her brother. "My baby. Caleb, you must go after him at once."

"Your *baby's* carrying a gun," Samantha snapped.

Edith appeared shocked. "Are you going to let her speak to me that way?" she said to her brother.

Caleb Livingston ignored her.

Wyatt held up one hand for silence. "There's more. My daughter and Daniel rode to warn the boys about Ben and Arlie. Now we have seven children going into caves. Since Ben, Christine, and Daniel aren't familiar with those caverns, they could find themselves in danger." He glanced at the Sloans, sitting in the last pew. "Arlie ever do any exploring there?"

Charlie Sloan nodded slowly, as if having to ponder each word. He stroked his scraggly brown beard. "Took him myself once, went to that there crystal one with the river running through it."

Wyatt swung his gaze back to Samantha. "Sound like the place Little Feather described?"

Samantha shook her head. "He mentioned cone-shaped columns and small pools of water."

Henry Arden, sitting small and shriveled in his pew at the back of the room, spoke up. "Then there's that one south a bit." His voice quavered. "The one used by the rustlers thirty years ago. Played there myself as a boy."

Wyatt looked down at Edith, who dabbed at her eyes with a lace handkerchief. "We'd better form three search parties, one for each cave. Arden, you lead a group to the rustlers' cave."

The little man blinked, then sat up straighter.

"Sloan, you and Livingston and some of the other men check out the crystal one. Sanders, Carter, come with me."

Samantha stepped forward. "I'm going too."

"Oh, no you're not, Samantha. It's too difficult."

"Yes, I am. They are my sons. If you don't take me, I'll just follow."

Wyatt obviously knew when to accept defeat. "All right. Stay close to me though."

She nodded.

Wyatt gazed around the room. "Gentlemen, I suggest you go and get changed. Bring some blankets and plenty of lanterns and rope. Let's meet at the Rodriguez ranch."

The people scattered.

Pamela Carter touched Samantha's arm. "If you don't mind, Beth and I will go home with you." Her brown eyes radiated concern. "We'll have food and coffee ready at the house. And if any of the children come back, we'll send word."

"Good idea." Wyatt strode back to the group clustered around Samantha. He searched her face, relieved to see gratitude replace the anger in her eyes. Not caring what the others thought, he took her hand and held it tight, striving to give her reassurance. "If we hurry, we might catch up with our two."

Samantha looked down, smoothing her black skirt with her other hand. "I'll need to change. A dress isn't the best apparel to wear crawling around caves."

"Fine. Need to pick up rope and lanterns from your place anyway."

Pamela looked over at her husband. "Let's first catch up with the Cobbs. If we can persuade them to open up the mercantile, we can get some extra food and coffee. I'm sure Samantha isn't prepared to have most of the town descend on her home."

"Thank you." Wyatt answered for Samantha as if knowing she'd fire up with false pride. He placed his hand on the small of her back, steering her toward the door. "Best be going. Longer we wait, the more chances those children have to get themselves into trouble."

* * *

Wyatt slowed Bill to a halt, pointing to a narrow crack leading into the mountainside. Driving the buggy behind him, Samantha reined in Chico and Mariposa. The four unlit lanterns piled on a stack of blankets in the seat next to her clanked together. John Carter and Nick Sanders stopped on her other side.

She shaded her eyes against the afternoon sunlight, trying to make out the details of this part of the mountain. Several pine trees shadowed the slash into the earth, and some bushes fringed both sides. If Samantha had been by herself, she'd never even have noticed anything out of the ordinary.

Wyatt slid off his horse, tying the reins to a bush. "This is the entrance closest to the house." He strode over to Samantha, motioning to her to hand him a lantern. "Don't see Christine's pony. They might have gone in another way."

With a surge of fear, Samantha tightened her gloved hands on the reins. She could tell Wyatt was staying calm for her sake. What if the children were wandering lost in these twisted tunnels? What if they were hurt? What if the searchers couldn't find them? She shook her head, forcing herself to stop the litany of her fears.

John urged his black stallion closer. "There's another opening farther down. As I remember, it's bigger than this one. Hand over a lantern and some blankets, and Nick and I will head over there."

Wyatt nodded. He walked around the buggy, pulled out a second lantern and two blankets, and gave them to the two men.

Nick touched his hat to Samantha. "Good luck with your search, Miz Rodriguez."

"Thank you, Nick. You men take care of yourselves."

He flashed her his sweet smile. "Did some climbing in these here caves as a boy, with my pa. We'll be just fine."

They kneed their horses forward and soon disappeared around a bend in the trail that circled the base of the mountain.

Wyatt reached out his hand, palm up.

Samantha placed her hand in his and stepped down from the buggy. Just the act of touching him gave her courage. This was the first time the two of them had been alone today, and she had to resist throwing herself into his arms for an encouraging hug.

Seeming to sense her need, he pulled her toward him in a tight embrace. "We'll find them, Samantha. I promise."

She rested her head on his shoulder for a few precious seconds, storing up the feeling of his strength for the search ahead. Then, taking a deep breath, she stepped back. "Let's find them before anyone gets hurt."

CHAPTER TWENTY-SIX

The narrow entrance to the cave was just Samantha's height. Wyatt ducked in first. She followed, the rope Wyatt had coiled around her waist bulky and heavy. In the light of the lantern she held, Samantha could see they walked through a stone corridor, but Wyatt's broad back blocked her view of what lay ahead. The farther in they traveled, the more the air cooled and moistened, a not unpleasant contrast to the sunny outdoors.

The ceiling lowered, forcing Wyatt to walk with a low stoop, and even Samantha had to keep her chin tucked to her chest. Her heartbeat thudded to the sound of their boots ringing against the stone floor, and her breath wheezed in and out. She made herself take deep inhalations, and to distract herself, started to recall folktales of trolls, dwarves, and other mythical beings who lived under the earth.

They rounded a bend, and Wyatt straightened, taking several slow steps into a cavern before stopping. Samantha paused at his side, wrinkling her nose at the acrid smell. She caught a glimpse of some odd rock formations, then something fluttered low across the room, darting close before winging upward. Samantha gasped and ducked, almost dropping her lantern.

Wyatt chuckled. "Just a bat. Harmless."

"A bat."

"Yep. Hundreds of them in this cave." He lifted the lantern.

On the ceiling she could see tiny brown bundles bunched together. She hunched her shoulders and squinted up, fearful the bats might move. She crouched a bit, ready to dive behind the nearest boulder if one so much as twitched.

"I should bring you and the children over at sunset one evening. The way those critters stream out of the cave is a sight to see."

Samantha shuddered. "I think it's one I can live without."

Wyatt grinned down at her. "Trust me. It's interesting." He studied the floor, the smile slipping from his face. "Bat droppings. That's what causes the smell. But they're only in this one. I don't see any footprints. None of the children have been this way."

Samantha sucked in her breath in disappointment. The powdery gray floor looked undisturbed. "Should we go back—try another way?"

"No." He pointed toward two openings. "We'll go through." He started toward the one on the left. "If I remember right, there's a series of small rooms, then an underground pool room. But"— he grimaced—"from then on it will get harder."

Samantha clenched her jaw. No matter how difficult, nothing would keep her from finding her boys.

※ ※ ※

In the darkness of the cave, Jack lay on his grass pallet staring at the ceiling. The light from the single candle flickered on crystals embedded in the roof of the large cavern, each one sparkling like the diamond ring he'd seen Ben's mother wearing.

Over on the right, several massive columns guarded the exit leading to the underground river. And on the left, two upside-down cones almost touched noses with triangles of stone beneath them. The steady drip of water splashing into a tiny shallow pool at the back of the room soothed him enough to make him sleepy. Jack's excitement during their initial running away had faded. Now boredom set in.

Tim and Little Feather sprawled out on their makeshift beds. In the flickering light, they both seemed deep in thought. Were they missing home as much as he was?

Jack let his fingers wander over the stone floor next to his pallet. He captured a pebble, tossing it in the direction of the water, and heard it thunk off a wall. He'd never counted on gettin' attached to Miz Samantha, to the little horses, to his new brothers. Never counted on having a place he'd call home, ever again.

Crossing his arms over his chest, he dug his fingers into his muscles. Somehow love and belonging had crept under his skin, become part of him. The loss burned behind his eyes. Never again would he let himself grow attached to anyone or anyplace. Just him and his twin. He'd better get used to it. Although maybe, just maybe, he could say a prayer. *"Please, God, somehow make everything work out right."*

The scrape of footsteps and the glow of lantern light near the entrance to the room alerted him. His drowsiness vanished. He jumped up, the other boys following. Had they been caught already?

Hand in hand, Daniel and Christine crept into the room. Daniel held a lantern high. In the dim light, Jack could see the boy's raised eyebrows relax when he caught sight of them. He skipped into the room, jerking Christine behind him. "We found you. Mama's been so worried. Why didn't you take me with you?"

Jack couldn't help but smile at Daniel and Christine, even though he'd have to send them away right quick. He held up his hand to halt Dan's flow of questions. "What cha doing here?"

Christine slid forward. "We came to warn you."

"Warn us?"

Daniel wiggled. "Yah, Ben and Arlie are playing sheriff. They figured out you'd be holing up here in these caves and set out to find you."

Jack met Tim's eyes, and his brother nodded in agreement. No matter what, they didn't want those two bullies to be the ones who found them. "Thanks for the warning." He looked at Little Feather, standing silent, one hand clutching the hem of his blue-striped shirt, and said, "We ain't done much exploring, 'cept around this here cave. Ya know the way in deeper. Can ya find a place where us 'uns won't be found?"

The Blackfoot boy nodded, brown eyes solemn. He squatted, picked up the matchbox, and lit the lantern.

Tim knelt down and rolled up the blanket he'd draped over a pallet of leaves.

Jack laid a hand on Daniel's shoulder and squeezed. "Much obliged for the warnin'. Now you two lite on out of here. If you stay, won't be nothing to keep your pa from coming after us."

Christine tilted her chin. "My pa will come anyway. He wouldn't leave you alone here." She glanced around, blue eyes huge, and shivered.

Daniel squeezed her hand. "I like it here," he said to her. "You'll get used to it, I'm sure. I want to go with them. You coming along or going back?"

Alarm shot through Jack. "Wait a doggon minute. You two ain't coming along."

Daniel's eyebrows drew together in a stubborn look. "My mama wanted to find you right away, but then she thought we should wait until after the town meeting. She wanted to be able to say that she didn't know where you all were. She was mighty upset that you all ran away."

Christine released Daniel's hand, propping her hands on her hips. "Are we going to stand around all day and argue, or are we going to find a hiding spot away from those bad boys?"

Jack growled in frustration. "Come on, then. But once we find a hidey-hole, you can't stay. Deal?"

Daniel's grin showed all his teeth. "Deal."

Rolling his eyes, Jack tucked up his supplies in his blanket. Deep down inside, he knew they were only headin' into trouble.

❄ ❄ ❄

Samantha's hands and knees ached from crawling on the stone walkway. As her knee landed on yet another pebble, she bit off an unladylike exclamation. She didn't dare let Wyatt know how sore she was. After all, she was the one who had insisted she accompany him.

Black shadows closed in around her. Flickers from the light of the lantern she shoved in front of her exposed copper and green tints in the rock of the tunnel, with an occasional vein of blue or purple. A pleasing palette, if she hadn't been too miserable to admire the formations.

The small corridor widened into an alcove. Wyatt paused, sitting back on his haunches, his head bent at an awkward angle. "Let's take a breather." He scooted around until he could place his back against the wall, legs stretched out. Patting the floor next to him, he said, "Come here."

"Gladly." Samantha snuggled next to him, trying not to let him hear her ragged breathing.

He rested an arm across her shoulders, pulling her close. "This tunnel goes on for about another twenty, thirty yards. Twists around some. Then it opens up into a big wet room. Water seeps everywhere, and there's a waterfall in the corner. We'll hear it soon. Have to be real careful. The floor's slick."

"All right."

"From there, two other tunnels eventually lead to other exits. Unfortunately, either one involves a lot more crawling."

"Remember, I've been worshiping in a Catholic church for many years." She kept her tone light. "I've hardened my knees from kneeling on the stone floors. I'm probably better off than you."

Wyatt shook his head. "I should have thought to bring rags to wrap around our knees for protection."

"It isn't like this is a pleasure jaunt, Wyatt. We were in a hurry. I'll be fine."

He grinned at her. "Not sure I will be, though. By the time we're through, I'll be walking like an ol' grandpa. But maybe I can head off old age." He unlooped the blanket from over his head and fished around in his coat pocket, pulling out a knife.

First Wyatt cut four long strips from the blanket. Then untucking his shirt, he sawed eight long ribbons of cotton from the bottom. "Here." He handed her two blanket pieces and four of the rags. "Bind these around your knees."

Samantha rolled her denim pant leg up beyond her knee. She heard Wyatt make a sound deep in his throat.

He took back the blanket strips from her. "Allow me," he said, his voice husky. Sliding his hand up her leg, he traced one finger around her kneecap.

She trembled at the feel of his callused hand on her bare skin.

Seeing her reaction, a wicked grin curled up the corners of his mouth, and he tickled her calf. Leaning down, he kissed the top of her knee. "This is a promise for the future. When this is over, I want to become very familiar with these knees."

The phrase "weak-kneed" took on new meaning for Samantha. His touch tingled through her body, causing her breasts to ache and sending moisture to warm her most private area. If it weren't for their quest for the children…

Seeming to follow her train of thought, Wyatt became serious and wrapped first one knee, then the other.

She restrained a sigh.

As he unrolled her pant legs down to her boots, he gazed deeply in her eyes—spinning the contact between them into a web of longing. In the dim light, his eyes glinted mirror silver, reiterating his words.

When this is over…

CHAPTER TWENTY-SEVEN

The tunnel narrowed, and Jack had a choice between a duck waddle and a baby's crawl. He settled for being a duck, knowing he'd soon have to change when his leg muscles wore out. The waddle made it easier to carry the candle and balance the rolled-up blanket. The rest of his gear he'd stuffed into his satchel, which he'd draped behind him. It bounced against his back with every movement.

Carrying the lantern, Little Feather led, followed by Tim, then Dan, then Christine. Christine crawled in front of Jack, her skirt tucked up, booted feet scuffing along the stone.

The passageway was barely wider than his shoulders, with a wavy ceiling that sometimes curved down as low as two feet above his head. Jack wondered how snug the tunnel might become. Visions of sticking tighter than a cork in a bottle, unable to go forward or back, slowed his pace. With a swallow, he pushed the fear aside, trusting Little Feather to see them through. The Indian boy never said much, but, the rare times he'd chosen to be the leader of the bunch, he'd displayed a quiet competence that was all the more reassuring for being silent.

Still, maybe this warn't such a good idea. Jack felt as if they'd been snaking through this shaft forever. Much more of this and he'd start to feel the walls closing in on him. Only the distant sound of falling water encouraged him to go on. The soles of Christine's feet disappeared out of sight around a bend.

A shot rang out, muffled and echoing.

Jack jumped in reaction, bashing his head on the low ceiling.

Christine screamed, and Tim yelped.

Jack's heart thumped so hard he thought it might bang out of his chest and against the wall. *What the hell?*

Waddling forward as fast as he could, he found himself in a huge chamber, the vaulted ceiling not visible in the lamplight. A quick glance showed the other children standing, not appearing wounded. Water dripped everywhere, running down the walls and across the floor. A narrow waterfall splashed between two dark holes. Other passages out of the cavern?

He slowly stood up, careful to shield the candle. Then he lifted it high, adding to the light of Little Feather's lantern.

Ben huddled in the driest corner of the room, a rifle held in from of him. Jack wanted to jump in front of the others, spreading wide his arms in protection. Instead he raised the candle. "What in tarnation do ya think ya are doin'? Aim to kill us now?"

Ben lowered the rifle. "Thought you might be a grizzly."

A grizzly. Jack wished he had something to throw at the other boy. "Ya sure are an idjit, Ben Grayson. Ain't no grizzles gunna be prowling these here caves. Can't likely fit in the first place."

Jack strode over and yanked the rifle out of Ben's hands. He wasn't going to allow that bully to cause any more trouble. Then Jack took a closer look at the boy. Ben's shirt collar twisted around his neck, rips and wet splotches on his suit. Could that be tearstains on his cheeks?

The children circled him.

Jack calmed himself. "What the heck are you doing here? I thought you was all set ta play sheriff."

"I've broken my leg. Arlie went for help, but he took the candle. I've been alone in the dark here for ages."

"Well, you ain't no more," Jack said matter-of-factly, a plan forming in his mind.

Ben's calf eyes narrowed. "Don't just stand there, do something," he ordered.

Jack turned to the rest. "Someone here still hasn't learned his manners. Come on, everybody, we're leaving."

' Christine looked like she would object, and he sent her a "be quiet" stare, jerking his head back toward the opening.

Ben jerked upright, then winced. "Noooo."

Little Feather ducked into the tunnel. Daniel followed him.

Ben held out his hand, calf eyes pleading. "Wait, please."

Pretending to ignore the injured boy, Jack squatted down at the entrance and crawled in a few feet, motioning Little Feather and Daniel near. The younger boy had those eyebrows up again, a sure sign of his agitation. "Dan, you and Little Feather go back through the tunnel. Then you ride into town for Doc Cameron," he whispered.

Daniel nodded, his brow relaxing.

Jack leaned close to Little Feather. "You git to the house an git help. Keep an eye on Danny." He lightened his voice. "Don't let him go crawling off on any side ways."

Daniel cuffed Jack's shoulder. "There are no side ways."

"I know." Jack gave him a gentle shove. "Come on, git."

Ben's pleas grew louder.

Backing out into the cavern, Jack stood up.

Christine edged closer to Ben, looking like she might burst into tears any minute.

"Here." Jack untangled his blanket, dropping some food and clothes on the stone floor. "Put this around him. But be careful of that leg."

Christine scuttled closer, kneeling down to tenderly cover Ben. The boy appeared grateful for the attention, for the first time losing his I'm-better-than-you air.

Jack held up a chunk of cheese. "You hungry?"

"A bit." Ben's words seemed reluctant.

Jack tossed the cheese over.

Ben caught it with both hands, and nibbled like a mouse.

Christine sat cross-legged next to Ben, patting his shoulder.

Tim unfolded his bedroll. "Here, Christine." He walked over and handed her the blanket. "Better sit on this. If you catch cold, your pa'll skin us 'uns alive."

Now that Ben acted more cooperative, Jack was ready to move to the next stage of his plan. "Well, now that you're warm and fed, us 'uns will move on with our explorin'."

Panic squished Ben's face 'til he looked about two years old. "No, don't leave me."

Jack could almost pity him, but he didn't let that feeling show in his voice. "Us 'uns are the bad twins, remember." He ground out the words. "The ones who set fires. The ones who your ma is so dang hot on shipping out of town." He strode closer until he towered over Ben. "If'n they catches Tim and I here, they'll probably blame us 'uns for that there broken leg of yours. So us 'uns'd better be off."

"No, no. They won't blame you for my leg. It was Arlie's fault. He pushed me, and I slipped and fell."

"Yah, but all ya have ta do is point the blame at us 'uns, and everyone will believe ya. After all, they already think us 'uns set those damn fires. Us 'uns need to git."

"But you didn't," Ben blurted. "Arlie was the one who burned Widow Murphy's haystacks each time. But we both set the one that burned down the outhouse." He hung his head. "We wanted you twins to be blamed."

Jack wanted to grab Ben around his neck and throttle him. "You, you…" He couldn't even find the words to throw at the other boy. "Why?"

Ben stayed silent a long time, gaze fastened on the ground. "I didn't like you, and I thought it would be fun." His tone turned defensive. "It was just an outhouse, not a building. Nothing important."

Tim stepped over to join Jack, his body shaking. "Fun." Outrage made his quiet twin speak up. "Did ya ever stop to think about livin' in an orphanage? Would ya like ta go ta one? That's what ya would have done ta us 'uns."

This time Ben remained silent.

Tim turned away in disgust. "Us 'uns should go away and leave ya. If'n it was us 'uns hurt here, that's what ya would do."

Jack nodded. "Yah, and laugh while ya were goin'."

Christine stirred. "But we're not going to leave?" She clutched her fingers together. Blue eyes appealed to them.

"Christy gal, us 'uns ain't like him." A surge of emotion welled up in him. What it was he couldn't quite tell. Something good though. He placed his hand on Tim's shoulder, and the two exchanged a look. "Us 'uns are stayin'."

❋ ❋ ❋

Wyatt could hear the waterfall and feel the dampness on his face several paces before he came to the final obstacle between them and the cavern around the corner. A row of slender columns about as thin around as his fist barred their paths. Between the two in the middle, enough space gapped for them to squeeze through. Luckily the ceiling rose enough so they could stand up. Or at least Samantha could. Wyatt still had to hunch.

He sucked in his breath, jamming through, the fit so tight it threatened to rip the buttons off his coat. Once on the other side, he extended a hand to Samantha. She gave him her lantern, which he took and set on the ground.

She placed her hand in his, sending him a confident smile that shafted straight to his heart. Even in her discomfort and worry for the children, she glowed with a beauty and determination that was so special.

He pressed her hand. "This'll be a story to tell our grandchildren. How we searched through the labyrinth to rescue their parents."

"I'm sure with time, the telling will grow." She fingered one of the columns. "We'll say these were so close together we left skin behind on them."

He grinned, leaning his head through the gap to kiss her. "Only if we were bare skinned in the first place."

She laughed against his lips.

Reluctantly he pulled away. "We're a mite busy now, but in the future we can crawl around this place buck naked. Doubt we'd get far, though."

"Wyatt, how you talk." To hide her blush, Samantha tapped him on the chin. "Doesn't sound comfortable."

"I'll bring blankets."

Over the clatter of the waterfall, they heard a voice call out.

Samantha's eyes widened. "The children." She eased herself through the crack far more nimbly than he had. They grabbed for the lanterns and hurried down the tunnel. Overhead, the top of the corridor wall was open to the cavern on the other side. The children's voices drifted over, muffled by the waterfall, but still audible.

Wyatt could make out Jack's tones, and Ben's too. Ben's words floated over the wall. "Arlie was the one who burned Widow Murphy's haystacks both times. But we both set the ones that burned down the outhouse."

Behind him, Samantha gasped. She opened her mouth to speak, but he held up his hand to stop her. He placed a finger across his lips and assumed a listening attitude, striving to get a grip on his temper.

Samantha slipped her hand in his.

As the conversation played through, anger and relief warred within his chest. Christine was safe, and the twins hadn't set the fires. Yet the anger in his stomach threatened to boil over. He wanted to charge into the cavern and confront Ben about all the anguish he'd caused Samantha and the twins. But he held himself back. It sounded like Jack had things well in hand.

❄ ❄ ❄

Wyatt stooped through the narrow opening, and, reaching back through the hole, helped Samantha through. Standing, she shook her legs out, relieved to stretch.

The children were about twenty yards away. Ben slumped against the front wall of the cavern facing them, Christine sitting next to him. The twins, standing in front of Ben, turned at Wyatt and Samantha's approach. Jack held a rifle in one hand. Their green eyes lit up when they saw Samantha; ecstatic grins stretched across their faces.

Samantha couldn't help the smile that burst from her heart to her lips.

"Pa." Christine perked up, scrambling to her feet, preparing to run to her father.

"Don't move, Christine," Wyatt said sharply, holding up a hand to stop her. "I don't want you to slip and fall, sunshine. We'll come to you."

With a sudden click of fear, Samantha realized Daniel and Little Feather weren't there.

Wyatt tucked his hand under Samantha's elbow, guiding her across the slick floor. When they reached the children, he released her, hugging his daughter.

Samantha glanced around, her eyes searching the dark hollows and crevices. "Where are Daniel and Little Feather?"

Jack pointed to Ben. "He done broke his leg. Daniel and Little Feather went to get help."

Her concern must have shone on her face, for Jack shuffled closer to her.

The boy placed his hand on her arm. "They'll be all right, Mama Samantha. The way back is easy."

Mama Samantha.

Jack had called her mama. Firecrackers of joy burst inside her chest. Releasing Wyatt's hand, she gave Jack a fierce hug, then smoothed back his unruly hair and dropped a kiss on his forehead. "I'm so glad you children are all right."

Tim slid forward, and she repeated the process with him. Then she slipped one arm back around Jack, pulling both twins tight to her sides.

Jack glanced up at her, his face glowing with an inner joy. "Ben tole us he and Arlie burned down the outhouse."

She playfully tapped his chin. "We heard."

Wyatt crouched down by Ben. "Where does it hurt?"

Ben pointed to a spot several inches above his right ankle.

"We have to splint this before we get you out of here." Wyatt stood. His gaze roved around the cavern and over the small pile of supplies. Forehead puckering, he tightened his jaw. "Don't see anything we can use."

Samantha released the twins, waving toward Ben. "How are we going to get him out? Is there an easier way?"

Wyatt ran one hand over the top of his head. He indicated the other dark hole on the opposite side of the cave. "That way's cramped, isn't it, boys?"

They nodded.

"Any obstacles blocking the path?"

"No."

Wyatt rubbed his forehead. "I'm not going to be able to carry him. We'll have to rig up a sling, or a travois or something, and I'll have to pull it." He slid a sidelong glance at Ben and lowered his voice. "Hate to think about what that kind of jolting will do to him."

Samantha snapped to a decision. "The twins can go get Chico. We'll put Ben on a blanket, and the horse can pull him out."

Wyatt nodded. "Might work—if we can get Chico in here."

"We can," Samantha said with a confident nod. "While the boys are at it, they can find some straight sticks to use as splints."

Jack shifted his shoulder back, standing straighter. "Be back in no time."

Pleased at the boy's assumption of responsibility, Samantha rubbed her hand down Jack's arm. Her thoughts flitted down the corridor they'd crawled through to get here, and through the other imaginary tunnels. She chewed on her lower lip before turning to Wyatt. "Should they go out the way they came and run for the horses, or retrace our path?"

"Their way. There's no offshoots to other caves, so we don't have to worry about them getting lost." He dropped a hand on Jack's shoulder and squeezed, then proceeded to describe where to find the horses.

Christine dropped into a cross-legged position next to Ben, her hand patting his thigh.

As angry as Samantha felt with Ben, she couldn't turn away from a hurt child. The sight of his woebegone face did a lot to reconcile her toward him. Perhaps he'd been adequately punished. Christine seemed to think so, and her little-girl compassion shamed Samantha for her own lack and tugged her toward the boy. She should take a closer look at Ben's injury.

Wyatt finished up his instructions. "Hurry, but be careful."

Jack flashed him an impudent smile.

Samantha touched Jack's arm. "Go with God, son." She patted Tim's cheek. "You too."

Tim flushed, ducking his head.

Jack nodded, seemed about to say something, then turned, grabbing a lantern, and ducked into the tunnel, Tim on his heels.

Plucking a knife from his pocket, Wyatt said, "While we're waiting, I think I have to sacrifice the rest of your blanket, Samantha."

"Go ahead."

Wyatt cut the blanket into strips. "Need some of these to cushion the splints. And"—he cocked an inquiring eye at Christine—"the children probably need their knees padded. What do you say, sunshine? Your knees hurtin'?"

"Yes, Pa."

He pulled off his jacket, handed it to Samantha, and unbuttoned his white shirt.

"What are you doing?" stammered Samantha.

"Tear the shirt into strips. We'll need plenty to tie the splint in place. Not to mention the padding. The shirt's already ruined."

Heat rose in Samantha's cheeks. As he undid each button, a corresponding warmth tingled in her breast.

Wyatt shrugged himself out of the garment and handed it to her. The lantern glow flickered over his torso, highlighting and shadowing his muscles. Samantha knew she should modestly look away, but like metal drawn to a magnet, her gaze pulled to him. Her hands took on a life of their own and wanted to follow, touching, exploring…

Seeming unaware of her reaction, Wyatt slipped his jacket back on, erasing the view of his body from her sight, but not from her mind. The memory of his broad shoulders, the downy black hair on his chest, and his well-defined arm muscles, made her ache inside with need—the reality better than the dreams that had shadowed her nights since she'd first met him.

A whimper from Ben wrenched Samantha's thoughts back to their situation, and she chided herself for allowing them to stray in the first place. What kind of woman was she to be dreaming such thoughts when a child was in pain? But a more tolerant voice reminded her that it was only natural that seeing the half-naked body of the man she loved would distract her.

Soon. Soon they'd emerge from the nightmare of the last few days. But first they had a lot of wrongs to right.

CHAPTER TWENTY-EIGHT

Jack's happy feelings floated like foam frothing on a river. He shoved the lantern a few feet in front of him. The base scraped across the surface, the light catching the wavy copper, green, and brown lines weaving through the rock. He crawled toward the lamp, then propelled it forward again. Behind him, he heard Tim's harsh breathing and the thud and rasp of his hands and knees as he followed.

The insides of his stomach seemed so light, even the bruising of his hands and knees on the uneven floor couldn't stop the unfamiliar emotion. He wished he could halt and savor the experience like he had that first peppermint candy stick Miz Samantha...his mama—he couldn't help but smile to himself at calling her that—had given them the first day of school.

His bubbliness on the inside contrasted with the weight of duty riding him like a saddle. But the sense of responsibility brought its own share of goodness.

Thompson trusted Jack and Tim to do the job right. Just the thought made him want to straighten, but if he did, he'd bump his head on the sharp stone jutting down from the ceiling in the middle of his path.

He maneuvered around the pointy part, mentally measuring the distance between the tip and the sides of the tunnel. Chico should still be able to fit; it would be tight though. But Jack would bet anything the vain little stallion would be only too glad to be the hero of the rescue.

Tim spoke up, his voice echoing through the darkness. "Almost there. I remember this here pointy stone. Bashed my head on it."

Jack winced in sympathy. "Next time through here, us 'uns will warn the others. Don't want Mama"—he rolled the word around on his tongue, making the syllables last—"Samantha bumping her head."

"Yep. Don't want nothin' to hurt our Mama Samantha."

Just the manner his twin echoed Jack's way with that special word squeezed some wetness into his eyes. Tim had suffered even more than he had when their ma died, a piece of his twin curling up inside in a ball of pain that even Jack couldn't reach. Maybe now that part of his brother would unwind, be more like the boy he'd been. No—Jack blinked back the moisture, amending his thought—be better than the boy he'd been.

A few more push crawls brought him in range of the pear-shaped opening of their living cave. He scampered through and straightened. With a rickety gait, he picked his way around the remains of their bed pallets, his twin close on his heels, and ducked out the exit.

Jack bounced a few steps down the slope of the mountain. Then he set the lantern at his feet, stood, and stretched. Tim almost collided with him, then scrambled the rest of the way to the flatter ground.

Taking a second to breathe in the pine-scented night air, Jack admired the faraway white stars winking at him in the blackness of the sky, while the fat three-quarter moon beamed down approval. He tilted his head to listen to the hoot of an owl. Being under the mountain for several days sure made a boy appreciate the outdoor life.

Jack grabbed for the handle of the lantern, and loped down the slope. "Come on," he called to Tim, snagging Tim's arm as he passed. "Us 'uns got a job ta do."

Half stumbling, half running, the twins fumbled their way across the valley toward where Wyatt had left the horses. They had to watch for an occasional bush eager to reach out whippy branches to catch them up, but for the most part the way was free. Cattle had grazed here recently, otherwise the grass would have been knee-high.

In spite of the seriousness of their errand, Jack reveled in the feeling of freedom. He leaped over a low bush, throwing his arms up—soaring like an earthbound bird and causing the lantern to sway.

Tim laughed, hopping like a grasshopper over a clump of flowers. Together they skidded around a root of the mountain jutting into the valley, and pulled up short before the horses.

Startled, Bill jerked his head up and backed up to the end of the reins tied to a bush. Chico snorted a greeting, and Mariposa stretched out her nose, looking for a treat.

Jack placed the lantern on a flat rock. "You take Bill." He ambled over to the Falabellas. He rubbed Chico's nose. "Us 'uns got an adventure in store for you, boy." Hugging Mariposa around the neck, he said, "I've missed ya, little lady. Ya miss me?" He untied the reins, walking with them toward the buggy seat.

Voices echoed through the darkness, causing Jack to spin around and squint down the valley. Lantern light bobbed, outlining shadowy forms. "Over here," he called, waving his arms.

Help had arrived.

For the first time in hours, Jack relaxed. Doc Cameron would see to making things right with Ben.

Livingston, Cobb, and Arlie Sloan's father appeared, wreathed in lamplight. Jack opened his mouth to greet them, but suddenly all the men seemed to move at once. The banker and Sloan each seized one of Tim's arms. Cobb pounced on Jack, thumping his chest with the palm of his hand, pushing him against the buggy. The air whooshed from Jack's lungs.

"Caught you red-handed, you little thief," Cobb hissed, spraying Jack with onion breath. His red nose twitched. "Stealing the horses. Gunna string you both up for this one."

"No." Jack wiggled, trying to escape.

"That's enough, Cobb." Livingston's voice sounded knife-sharp. "We'll decide the penalties for these two ruffians later. For right now, I want to know about my nephew." He looked down his nose at the twins. "Do you know where he is?"

Jack stared back defiantly. "He's in the caves. Done broke his leg. Us 'uns are bringing the horses to help."

Tim made a jerky motion toward the buggy. Livingston had a firm grip on his shirt collar.

What? Jack wanted to ask. And then he understood. His twin was signaling him to steal off with the buggy. He nodded his agreement.

Tim stopped the jerking, hanging almost limp in Livingston's grasp.

He was a right smart brother, was Tim.

Cobb shook Jack. "Little liar. No horse is going to get through that cave system. Now tell the truth."

Desperation edged Jack's voice. "I am tellin' the truth. Mr. Thompson and Miz Rodriguez is with him. They sent us to git the horses and bring some splints too."

Cobb's squinty eyes narrowed further. "Splints?"

"Tole ya, Ben broke his leg."

"Where?" Cobb jerked his head toward the cave entrance. "There?"

"No." Jack pointed up the valley. "Through the other one."

Cobb's hold on Jack loosened. The merchant stepped away from the buggy, holding Jack's elbow with his hand. He looked at Livingston. "What are we going to do now?"

Jack jerked his arm from the man's grasp, leaped into the buggy, and snapped the reins. The little horses took off at a gallop.

"Hey." Cobb sprang after him, tripped on a clump of grass, and sprawled to the ground. That slowed him enough for the buggy to pull away.

As Jack gained distance from them, he could hear the men's shouts. They'd follow, dragging Tim along. But at least Jack would get Chico to Wyatt like he'd promised. And there were enough trees by the entrance. He could grab some sticks. If he had time...

❋ ❋ ❋

Wyatt squatted next to Ben, carefully cutting open the pants of the boy's suit, and examining his leg. At least the bone wasn't sticking out. But the boy's face showed signs of strain—paper-pale cheeks, smudged and tearstained, and a hollow look in his big brown eyes. They'd tucked a faded Indian blanket around him, but occasionally he shivered.

The sensation of being underground pressed on Wyatt, and he had to restrain from pacing the cavern. The dark silence, broken only by the splash of the waterfall in the corner, weighed heavy and oppressive. Wyatt longed to be outside—to turn his face to the sky.

Samantha sat on a blanket next to Ben, Christine snuggled on her lap. The strain of the past few days reflected in her tired eyes, shadowed by tiny lines he could have sworn hadn't been there before. When this was over, he planned to chase her care-worn look away—if she'd let him.

Christine kept one hand on Ben's uninjured leg, occasionally patting the boy with an expression of sympathy in her big blue eyes. Quite a little Florence Nightingale, his daughter. Perhaps he shouldn't have worried about the influence of Samantha's boys on her. Maybe he should have trusted Christine's innate goodness of character.

He shook his head. He hadn't been wrong to be protective. That was a father's job. But he'd been more than protective, he'd been prejudiced. That had been wrong. All from a shameful secret.

He'd revealed his past to Samantha and had experienced a sense of relief. But he had known he loved her and had believed that no matter how she reacted to the information, she wouldn't reveal it to anyone else. This was different.

He made up his mind. The time had come to expose his past, to use it to save another young boy from following in the evil footsteps of Wyatt's childhood gang. Maybe if Ben heard about that young girl's death because of a fire set by Wyatt's gang, he'd reform. Wyatt knew he was risking having the information become gossip or being used against him in some way. But he was no longer that lonely wayward boy. He'd built himself a good life—a life of prosperity.

He glanced at Samantha, cuddling Christine. He had a daughter he adored and had found a second chance at love. His past no longer mattered.

Wyatt took a deep breath and leaned forward. "Ben, I want to tell you a story."

❈ ❈ ❈

Samantha leaned back against the hard rock of the cave wall, listening to Wyatt repeat the tale he'd told to her a few days earlier. This time, his words flowed, no long pauses, no fighting against revealing a shame he'd kept hidden for so long. The story echoed around the cavern, accompanied only by the fall of the water. Even Christine sat silently on Samantha's lap.

Ben looked enthralled, seeming to almost forget his pain. He listened with a deep absorption that Samantha had never seen in the boy before. Maybe Wyatt was getting through to him. But even if Wyatt's revelations of his past failed to make an impact on Ben's future behavior, it was making an impact on her.

A glow of pride warmed Samantha's heart. She knew how difficult this must be for Wyatt—to humble himself, to share a part of his past that might change the high regard in which the townsfolk of Sweetwater Springs held him.

While he talked, his features—high cheekbones, aquiline nose, cool gray eyes—seemed to soften, as if he were removing each brick in the wall he'd built around himself.

As Wyatt became more vulnerable, Samantha's own barriers to loving and being loved by this man melted like ice in the spring sunshine. She now understood: Wyatt was nothing like Don Ricardo. Wyatt's controlling attitudes and behavior really stemmed from his attempts to protect himself and his daughter.

She thought of the way he'd taken charge of the search parties. Decisive. Thorough. A good man to have on your side. And in spite of his doubts about Samantha's assumption of the ranch and adoption of the boys, he'd acted in a supportive manner toward her.

They'd exchanged kisses and confidences. What would be the next step? Would Wyatt be willing to take on the raising of those very boys who'd been the cause of so much disagreement?

A scrape of hooves against stone and the sound of a boy's voice broke through Samantha's ruminations.

The twins.

Patting Christine's back, she encouraged the child to jump up, then rose to her feet, shaking her legs out to stretch them.

Wyatt strode over to the entrance, leaned over, and extended a hand to help Jack crawl out. The boy grimaced at Wyatt, reached back, and guided Chico into the room. The long buggy reins trailed behind the little stallion. Jack yanked on them and a bundle of tree branches tied to the ends of the reins slid into the cavern.

Wyatt grabbed them. "Good boy."

Samantha gave Jack a quick hug. "Where's Tim?" She stroked Chico's head while awaiting the answer.

Jack slapped his fists against his hips, his green eyes sparking emerald with anger. "Livingston, Cobb, and Sloan done caught us 'uns. Said us 'uns were stealin' the horses. Cobb said us 'uns would hang for sure. Livingston put him off, though. I got away, but they still have Tim."

"Well." Samantha expelled her outrage in a sharp breath. "We'll just have to see about that."

Wyatt reached over and squeezed Jack's shoulder. "There will be no hanging done, Jack. I promise you, soon as we get Ben out of here, we'll set things right. But now I need your help to rig up a harness and a sling while I work on Ben's leg."

Jack nodded, some of the fire fading from his eyes, and he bent to his task.

Samantha helped Wyatt with Ben, but while her hands stayed gentle on the boy's leg, her thoughts whirled, sharp and dangerous.

CHAPTER TWENTY-NINE

Jack wiggled forward on his hands and knees, thankful for the strips of blanket padding them. He hadn't spared himself on the last trip in. Back in the cavern, he'd been careful to hide from Thompson and Mama Samantha how bruised and bloody he was. They all had more to worry about than some cut and scratches.

He pushed his lantern forward. Behind him he could hear Christine breathing hard and Mama Samantha coaxing Chico. The Falabella towed Ben, who lay on a blanket litter attached to the harness, his suit jacket tied under his head to protect it from bumping too hard through the dark tunnel.

Thompson crawled after Ben, making sure the rickety travois didn't hit the walls. The injured boy moaned at each jolt, and Jack could even find it in his heart to feel sorry for the poor cuss. For all Ben's better-than-you ways, he'd sure come to a bad end. Jack reckoned the other boy wouldn't be in much of a position to plague the twins or Dan ever again.

Jack set his hand on a pebble and winced. He bounced up and hit his head on the jaggedy rock in the roof. He bit his tongue, and suppressing a string of cuss words, rocked back on his haunches, gripping the rock. "Christine, Mama Samantha, watch out for this here monster. Likes to thump ya on the head. Done got me twice."

"Thank you, Jack," Samantha said. "I'll be careful." She raised her voice. "Wyatt, did you hear? Watch out for this sharp stone sticking down in the middle of the tunnel."

Thompson's voice echoed up. "I hear."

Jack leaned past Christine, flipping Mama Samantha an encouraging smile. "Our living cave is just ahead. Pass through that and we'll be outside."

"Thank God for that." She lifted her chin. "Lead on, son."

Son. The warmth of that word made up for the last three days of cave living—days and nights of feeling like ice had settled in his innards.

It didn't take long to reach their camp in the living cave. Jack wound around the remaining pallets to reach the other side. On the verge of slipping through the exit, he paused, thinking better about stepping through the opening. "Don't reckon I should go out there. Those men'll probably nab me first and talk later."

Mama Samantha bristled like an angry porcupine. "They do and they'll deal with me."

Thompson touched her shoulder, then ran his hand down the back of her head like he was smoothing down her spiky quills. "I'll go first."

Mama Samantha's mouth tightened.

Thompson quirked an eyebrow at her.

She half smiled at him and relaxed. "Good idea."

With a wink, Thompson slid one leg through the opening, and ducking back, slithered the rest of his body through.

Mama Samantha clicked her tongue at Chico, her hand on the horse's neck. She squeezed out and turned back for the stud. Chico tossed his head as if primping for a grand entrance, then, leaning into the harness, the little stallion followed her outside.

Jack grabbed the ends of the blanket and lifted, trying to spare Ben as much of the bumping as possible. The boy lay limp, his eyes closed. Perhaps he'd fainted. Just as well. This next part would be the worst.

But then a spark of worry ignited. What if Ben stayed unconscious for a long while? What if no one believed Jack's word about Ben's confession?

❋ ❋ ❋

Samantha emerged from the cavern into a crowd of men and horses illuminated by the warm glow of lanterns. Out of the blackness of the cave, the night glowed with brightness; stars dotted across the sky. She took a deep breath of the pine-scented air, and urged Chico forward. Searching the small crowd for Tim, she saw him held firmly by Mr. Sloan.

Her anger flared. Only the need to guide Chico restrained her from running over and tearing her boy away from the man.

At the sight of the litter, the men surged toward them. Dr. Cameron beat everyone to Ben's side. "Back off, men. Give me some light."

They raised every lantern. Caleb Livingston dropped down on his knees by Ben's side. "Is he still alive?" he asked in a hushed voice.

A rise of sympathy penetrated Samantha's anger.

Dr. Cameron touched the side of Ben's neck, feeling for his pulse. "Yes, he's alive, all right." He eyed the boy's leg, roughly splinted. Crouching, he examined the injury. Then, rising, he looked at Caleb Livingston. "He's unconscious. Better let the laddie be 'til we get him home." He motioned to Mr. Cobb. "Untie the blanket, Frank. Easier to have two men carry a litter until we can get him to a wagon and into town. I'll take care of the leg there."

He glanced over at Wyatt and Samantha. "Daniel and Little Feather are at your house."

Samantha's little niggling worry about the two boys' safety subsided. "Thank you, Doctor."

Caleb Livingston smoothed back the hair from Ben's forehead. Getting to his feet, he turned toward Samantha.

Wyatt stepped forward and draped his arm across her shoulder. She could feel the protectiveness in his stiff frame, and she leaned against him. Jack came to stand beside her. She pulled the boy into a loose embrace in front of her.

Mr. Livingston narrowed his eyes. "Your twins did this. We caught them trying to steal the horses." He pointed one accusing finger at Jack. "That one got away. After my nephew is seen to, I'm going to make it my business to see them shipped out of town."

Samantha tightened her arms around Jack. Her anger flared hot, but her words came out winter cold. "I think not. Ben admitted to setting the fires. He and Arlie Sloan. It's *your* nephew, Mr. Livingston, not my twins, who needs to take responsibility for the damage."

Wyatt spoke up, his voice hard. "Arlie pushed Ben. That's why he broke his leg. Mrs. Rodriguez and I *sent* the twins for the horses."

Arlie stood half behind his father, clearly wanting to hide. Mr. Sloan released Tim, turned around. "This true, boy?"

"Ain't dun nothin', Pa." His tone sounded sullen and not very believable.

"You're lyin'." He cuffed Arlie.

The boy flung his arms up and cringed. "Just wait until we get home, boy." The man seized Arlie and dragged him off.

Tim sprang away, running around the men surrounding the litter, straight to Samantha and Jack. She gathered him to her, hugging both of them.

They're mine now. No one will take them away.

Wyatt ignored the Sloans, focusing on the banker. "The boys, all the children, helped in the rescue effort. You owe them a debt of gratitude, Livingston."

Mr. Livingston's handsome face slackened with shock. He moved his mouth before he forced out the words. "Ben? Set the fires? Let the twins be blamed?"

"Yes," Samantha said, almost feeling sorry for him.

Livingston cleared his throat. "Please accept my apologies on behalf of my nephew." He paused. "You must also accept my apologies for my own behavior as well." He swallowed. "I was wrong to accuse the twins based on my own opinion—without proof."

Although the words sounded stilted, Samantha could sense his sincerity. "I accept your apology, Mr. Livingston."

The banker assumed a businesslike manner. "I was inflexible in refusing an extension on your loan for the ranch. I'm sure we'll be able to work out acceptable terms."

She nodded.

Dr. Cameron picked up his bag. "Enough talking for right now. I want to get Ben back to town before he regains consciousness." He winked at Samantha. "Maybe in the next few days, I can speak to you about buying two of your wee Falabellas. My wife fancies having a buggy like yours."

Samantha grinned at him. "I'd be delighted, Doctor."

She leaned against Wyatt, watching the rest of the men surround the litter carried by Livingston and Cobb. One of the men gathered the horses and led them away. When they rounded a bend, she released a prayer of happiness. She hadn't lost her ranch, or—she hugged the boys one final time—her twins.

❋ ❋ ❋

That evening, Samantha sat in her parlor, surrounded by celebrating friends and neighbors. She held a cup and saucer in her hand, sipping fragrant Earl Grey tea and eating the sugar cookies the women kept pressing on her. Elizabeth and Pamela refused to allow her to do anything but relax and enjoy herself. Instead, Maria and Mrs. Toffels had taken over the kitchen, while Elizabeth, Pamela, and Miss Stanton saw to the serving. Although Samantha's knees sported bruises, and her palms were crisscrossed with scrapes, she floated on a bubble of happiness, barely aware of her aching body.

She allowed the conversation to flow over her, watching with appreciation how every man found time to apologize to the twins. The women had all been generous with hugs for the children, and Samantha had never seen such wonder and joy as her twins showed on their freckled faces.

Even her solemn Little Feather radiated contentment, allowing himself to be drawn into descriptions of the cave systems with men he formerly would have fled from on sight. And Daniel bounced about the room, his high spirits revived by excitement. Often Christine trailed him, sometimes coming over to Samantha or her father for a reassuring hug, before running off to play.

Wyatt stood surrounded by several men, repeating once again the story of their trek. She even caught a phrase or two of praise for her Falabellas. Now that was a wonder. Even the comical sight of him wearing a too-small tan shirt of Ezra's couldn't hide the qualities of command and strength Samantha had come to admire in him.

Wyatt glanced over at her. The proprietary look in his gray eyes shivered her to her toes. For the whole evening, they'd exchanged looks, never losing their connecting thread, no matter how many people separated them. While glad to be merry-making with the people who'd come to be her friends, she could hardly wait until the company left, they'd tucked the children in bed, and she and Wyatt could finally be alone. Her heart quickened at the thought.

Reverend Norton tottered over to Wyatt and whispered something in his ear. Wyatt nodded. Raising his hand, he said. "Quiet everyone. Reverend Norton wants to say his piece."

An amused smile softened the minister's austere face. "I believe thanks are in order to the Lord for the safe deliverance of our children and the end to the strife permeating our community. Let us pray."

Samantha bowed her head, her heart so full of thankfulness she needed to pass some of the joyful emotions on to the Almighty. After all, a heart could only hold so much. Surely, it had already expanded to fill her entire chest. She peeped at Wyatt from under her eyelashes, had a feeling she might need some extra thankful space in her heart very, very soon.

CHAPTER THIRTY

Late that night, Wyatt strolled hand in hand with Samantha down the path to the river. The three-quarter moon provided enough light for them to see without using lanterns. The stars dotted the sky like bright freckles in a friendly face. He relished the feel of Samantha's hand in his. Peacefulness settled between them, edged with a passion held in check by only a loose rein.

A cool breeze had Samantha pulling her jacket tighter with her other hand. She still wore her men's garments, not having had time to change clothes. The festive gathering of the townsfolk had lingered late into the night. To an impatient Wyatt, it took forever to tell their story again and again and eat all the food pressed upon them by Pamela Carter and Elizabeth Sanders.

Once that they were alone, he chivied Samantha out the door so they could enjoy the freedom of the night. When they reached the bridge, by unspoken consent, they paused.

Samantha turned slightly away from him, looking up at the sky.

Wyatt remembered the necklace he'd imagined for her. Keeping a hold of her hand, he reached out, tracing one finger down the line of her throat, under her collar, and stopping at the hollow of her neck. "If I designed a necklace for you, Samantha... little diamonds for stars and a pearl-encrusted crescent moon... would you wear it?"

The glimmer of the moon's light reflected in her eyes. She lifted a finger and touched his lips. "Yes."

He kissed her fingertips, then tangled his fingers in hers. "Can you forgive me, Samantha, for my harsh opinions about your boys…your Falabellas…your keeping the ranch?"

Her countenance glowed brighter than the moon. "Yes, Wyatt, I already have. You expressed some harsh opinions, but in spite of them, you were always a good neighbor."

"I've wanted to be more than a good neighbor." *I love you.* The words trembled on his lips, ones he hadn't uttered since he'd buried his heart with Alicia. His heart, once more whole and bursting with love, beat in cadence to the rushing river. A breeze feathered across his cheek like a caress.

Alicia's spirit giving them her blessing?

He'd like to think so—that she approved of his choice of wife and mother for their daughter. At that thought, the gentle gust vanished, leaving the night to the lovers. With an ebullient lightness in his heart, Wyatt released the words. "I love you, Samantha."

She melted against him, circling his waist with her arms. "I love you too, Wyatt."

Leaning over, he kissed her, light and soft, with a promise of more to come. "Will you marry me, Samantha? Be a mother to Christine? Allow me to be a father to your boys?"

Amusement danced in her blue eyes and curled the corners of her lips. "And my Falabellas?"

"I know they're part of the package." He dropped his tone to mock seriousness. "I'm sure we'll find some use for them."

"In that case, Wyatt Thompson, I'll marry you."

He moved his hands to cradle her cheeks, trying to convey his joy and love through his palms. Finally, he bent his head to place on her lips a kiss of promise for all the years to come.

About the Author

USA Today bestseller Debra Holland is a psychotherapist, corporate crisis counselor, and martial arts instructor, as well as an acclaimed author. It wasn't until she finished many years of grad school that she began her writing career in earnest. In addition to her historical westerns, Holland is also the author of the self-help book *The Essential Guide to Grief and Grieving* and two books of fantasy romance, *Sower of Dreams* and *Reaper of Dreams*. She lives in Southern California, where she was born and raised.

Don't miss *Wild Montana Sky*!

Seeking a fresh start in Montana, a Boston belle confronts the challenges of ranch life and must choose between an offer of stability and the cowboy who loves her.

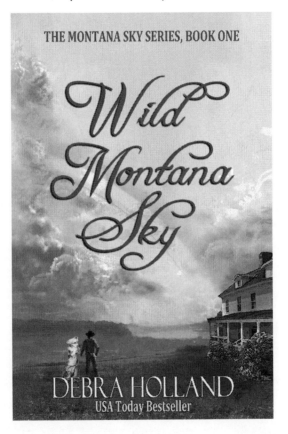

THE MONTANA SKY SERIES, BOOK ONE

Wild Montana Sky

DEBRA HOLLAND
USA Today Bestseller

"A wonderful story. If you loved *Little House on the Prairie* and the Wagons West series, as well as early Linda Lael Miller and Susan Wiggs, you'll enjoy *Wild Montana Sky*."
– Bestselling author Colleen Gleason